Watcher

Julia Guroff

This book is dedicated to my father, who has been supportive of all my endeavors in life, but especially of my surprise writing career. I have loved having him read my books, and provide feedback speculating about what "the author" is doing with the story. Thanks, Dad.

Contents

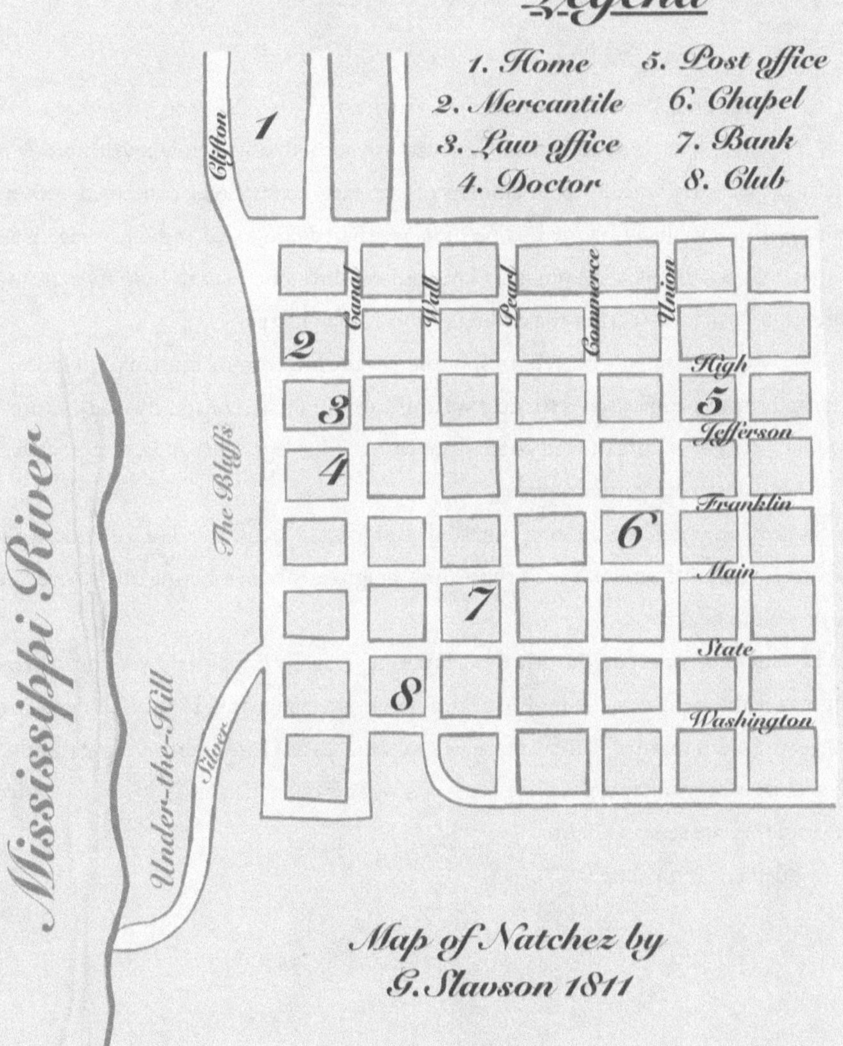
Legend
1. Home   5. Post office
2. Mercantile   6. Chapel
3. Law office   7. Bank
4. Doctor   8. Club
Mississippi River
Under-the-Hill
The Bluffs
Clifton
Canal
Wall
Pearl
Commerce
Union
High
Jefferson
Franklin
Main
State
Washington
River
1
2
3
4
5
6
7
8
Map of Natchez by
G. Slavson 1811

Preface

We are one. We, the Guardians, the watchers of souls. We merge together between lives, having little sense of identity or individuality while awaiting our next lifetime. We carry with us the memories of our past incarnations, contained within the souls of those we had Guarded. The souls we shared and loved and encouraged, as we watched over our beloved humans. The souls we brought back to hold forever, to live forever, to love forever, after the ending of the human lifespan.

We ever increase in number, corresponding to the burgeoning human population. As the quantity of people grows, so must we multiply our ranks, constantly ready to provide a soul to each new human who comes into being. Our legion expands, matter attracted exponentially to our gathering mass.

Some of our members are new, untested. But most, like me, have Guarded many times before. We savor the memories of those lives, poignantly remembering our beloved ones, as we wait to begin again.

The summons can come at any time, randomly, eagerly anticipated yet unpredictable. It is at the moment that the individual human brain, achieving the growth necessary to trigger the mechanism which can attract a soul, reaches out to the surrounding multitude. One of us is drawn forth, the Guardian who will devote a lifetime of love and service to the soul they are sent to Guard.

Suddenly, it is my time.

Chapter 1

Happiness

August 25, 1810
Ellis Cliffs Plantation, Mississippi Territory
Ayola's

My beloved will be born tonight. Here in this rustic cabin, well behind the main house, her mother attended only by the other enslaved women of the household. The wind whistles through cracks in the rough-hewn walls, causing the single candle to flicker. The feeble light wavers as the tiny flame leaps and bends, the illumination briefly reflected in the dark eyes of the laboring woman, before she seals her lids as another contraction seizes hold of her. She is silent despite her pain.

I sense the child, unusually alert for one not yet even in the world, pulling me to her. My matter is attracted, almost magnetically, to the mind of the unborn girl, as her soul blooms into existence along with my presence. It has been only moments since I was pulled from the surrounding mass of waiting Guardians, singled out by the newly formed subconscious of the baby, drawn to her, to be hers. To be her Guardian. I will Guard her, as one with her soul, living her life together with her, watching, whispering.

And loving. As I arrive I already love the child, as fiercely as one being can love another.

The child is very small, I sense, coming sooner into the world than the mother had expected. A premature birth, explaining the abrupt nature of my summons. With most births, the Guardian is drawn to the infant a few days before childbirth, the brain having developed sufficiently to trigger the process which ensnares the Guardian and the attendant soul. With this child, the birth appears to be imminent.

As I acclimate to this new existence, I begin to take in my surroundings. The other Guardians focus on their own Guarded, of course, but I am able to absorb their knowledge, and begin to understand the circumstances into which my beloved will be born.

The joy of the birth, of the new life beginning, of a new existence for me, is immediately tempered with sorrow. The mother of my beloved has lived a life of hardship and despair. Torn from her home at a young age, sold to uncaring masters, forced to harsh manual labor, her body exploited for both her master's financial gains and physical lusts.

The result is the child, my beloved, the reason for my existence in this world. Her mother has not been excused from her heavy duties despite her pregnancy, which has triggered the early labor.

The child, though, is very healthy, despite the coming early birth. The mother's Guardian senses this as well, and whispers comforting words to the woman, attempting to convey a sense that all will be well, that the baby will survive the birth and thrive as a strong and flourishing child.

The mother's contractions reach a climax, and she is encouraged by her companions to push now, to help the baby come into the world. I watch in wonder, witnessing the miracle of childbirth anew. Although the circumstances of every birth are different, ultimately every birth is the same. The mother toils, the Guardians encourage, the child finally emerges.

This birth, however, I realize with shock at the moment the new life begins, is not the same. This child is different from any I have known before. A dazzling light radiates from her aura, startling every Guardian nearby, as she opens her eyes immediately following birth and gazes directly at me.

She is a Seer.

Hester

The poor dear clenches her lips together, refusing to make a sound during her labor pains. I know Dalila fears to attract the attention of the family in the big house.

She is such a scrawny little thing, it is probably best that the babe is coming too early. Especially knowing the Master is the father. He is such a large fellow that if his child had a chance to grow all the way to term, it could kill Dalila to birth it. Even with the babe being small, it is a struggle.

Always, it is a struggle, for all of us. Knowing the coming baby, who we will helplessly love, will be another slave. Knowing we might not be able to keep it for long, that we cannot protect it from a life of hardship and grief.

Still, there is always the joy. I've helped so many of us bring forth babies into the world. And no matter how hard the labor or the life, there is always a happiness that comes when the mother sees her babe for the first time.

And so it is for Dalila. When the tiny slip of a girl finally comes out, I wrap her up in the cloth I have set aside for her, something the Missus gave me to use just for the newborns. Softer and warmer than the cloth we make our garments from. It is her way of trying to show that she is not entirely heartless.

The baby doesn't cry at all, even though she has been brought into this shocking new world in the middle of the warm and humid night. She stares around herself, squinting even though the light from the candle is just as dim as it can be.

The new mother is worried because her daughter is not crying. It is the crying that tells us the child has survived. I quickly hand the baby over, so she will know that her child lives. As soon as she has the baby in her arms, her lovely face splits into a happy smile, through the tears left behind from the birth. Dalila is dark, dark like midnight, dark like only those who came here on the boats can be. Her tears reflect the candlelight against her ebony cheeks.

She brings the tiny baby up to her lips, kissing her forehead. "My sweet Ayola," she calls her.

"What was that?" I ask her. "Ayola? Is that her name? What does it mean?"

"Yes," she murmurs in the soft accent of her native tongue. "Ayola. It means happiness. Because she is my happiness."

Chapter 2

Extraordinary

Marguerite Ellis

The sun has risen over the cliffs standing behind the house. On the veranda, I take my morning tea, while the sun shines down from behind, lighting the waters of the Mississippi River. The opposite bank of the river, where the Louisiana territory begins, is more visible than usual this morning, as the early mist has already cleared and I can see the trees rising above the sparkling water. It is a beautiful morning.

I sigh and take another sip. Another beautiful morning, to be spent here, supervising the plantation while my husband travels on business. As usual.

Hester comes from the house, crossing the patio to my table, to refresh my cup. "Good morning, Missus." I set down my delicate china cup to allow her to pour more tea into it.

"Good morning, Hester. How fare the field hands today?"

She moves the sugar bowl closer, to be within my reach. "Very fine, Missus. Most of them have been in the field since dawn. One, though, cannot work today."

"Who?" I ask, using the polished silver spoon to stir the sugar into my tea.

"Dalila, Missus. She had her baby overnight."

I call to mind the face of Dalila. She is a slight, unmarried young woman, very dark-skinned, who was purchased by my husband some two years ago to work the fields. I have considered moving her into the household, as she seems very delicate for field work, but I fear she may catch the eye of my husband. He is not so advanced in age that I do not see him sometimes looking at the women. I try not to spend time thinking about what else he might be doing with them.

Despite that, I need to deal with Dalila. I believe I will need to move her now that she has an infant. At least for a while. I will simply have to monitor whether she is attracting too much attention.

Obviously she has caught the eye of some man.

I return my attention to Hester, standing quietly by my side, still holding the tea pot. "Oh? How is the child?"

"It is a little girl, Missus, very tiny, but seems to be healthy."

I nod. Later I will add the child to the roster of plantation slaves. "How is Dalila?"

"She is very tired, Missus, but she got through her labor all right."

"Very well. She may rest today. I will go to visit her and the child this afternoon to make sure they are well."

"Thank you, Missus."

Dalila

My little baby sleeps near me, the tiniest little thing I have ever seen. It is hard to believe she is healthy, since she is so very small, but Hester told me that there is nothing to worry about. She can open her eyes and look at me, she can feed at my breast, she can mess her napkin and move her limbs. She has not cried, but she makes tiny cooing sounds, softer than a mourning dove. Everything seems fine, even though she is so small I can scarcely feel her weight as I clasp her to me.

Hester and the other women had to leave me here in the cabin alone with her at dawn, to go attend to their own duties. Hester assured me that the Missus would allow me to rest for the day. She told me not to worry about emptying the chamber pot when I use it, she will take care of it for me later. It is painful to use, more clots of blood coming out and the urine burning my sore skin, but it is a relief to know I do not need to clean the pot myself right now.

Ayola and I have drifted in and out of sleep, between sessions of feeding her. It feels so right to have her latching on to my breast.

Now that the sun has risen properly, and the light is coming in through the small window, I can inspect her more closely. Her skin is much lighter than mine, as I had expected considering that Master got her on me.

I suppose they'll call her a mulatto, but it won't make any difference. She'll still be a slave. Master often made me spend time alone with him after he brought me here, whenever he was home from his travels. But after I started to show, he seemed to lose interest and left me alone. I have been very relieved for the last few months not to have to hold myself still any more while he does his business. I am sure he knows the baby is his, but he obviously doesn't care. She will just be another one of us.

I only hope I can keep her. I have seen too many women lose their children, heard too many horrible stories about babies or mothers being sold apart from each other. I have only known her for a few hours, but already I know I could not bear to lose her. Already she owns my whole heart.

I stroke her fuzzy head. I wonder whether her hair will be tightly curled and black like mine, or straight and brown like Master's.

She opens her eyelids, feeling my touch on her hair, and gazes into my eyes. She is the most beautiful sight I have ever seen. I wish my mother was here to see her. But of course my mother is far away, back at home, where I will never set foot again.

Only this baby has been able to lessen the grief I have been feeling for all of these years since I was stolen from my home. She is my happiness. My Ayola.

Ayola's

It is extraordinary. Ayola peers around herself, inspecting her surroundings, including me in her encompassing gaze. I am as real to her as anything else she can see. The sensation of having the eyes of my beloved rest upon me is unlike anything I have ever known.

"My darling, my beloved, we are together, I will share your life with you. I will do everything within my power to serve you in any way I can. We can enjoy this life, beloved, find the beauty within it."

The newborn has no concept of the difficulties which face her. Her mother, of course, is fully aware. As she feeds the newborn from her body, and tends to the needs of the infant, she glows with a love tinged with fear. She knows how bleak are her circumstances, how powerless she is to determine her own fate. She is aware that she is at the mercy of the whims of other humans, those who consider themselves her owners. She knows how fleeting this moment of joy with her infant might be.

Still, she genuinely feels the happiness for which she named the child.

As do I. My joy is extreme. I must be cautious, though. Understanding the fraught situation in which my beloved finds herself, I wish only to assist her, to increase her safety and well-being. And it seems to me that in order to do so, I must help her to hide her nature from those around her. As a Seer, she is exceptional, and it will be very difficult to avoid drawing attention to her remarkable qualities. Other humans cannot see their Guardians, cannot hear their whispered words. But she can. If others take note that she is unusual, even as a baby, it could be unsafe for her. A strange slave, a slave who makes others uneasy, could be at higher risk of sale, injury or death.

Of course, she is far too young to understand any of this, and her reactions cannot be trained until she has grown. I cannot advise her not to look at me, not to speak to me. She cannot possibly understand until she is older.

All I can do is try to create in myself the qualities which would assist with this process. I make the decision to leave my form nebulous, so as to not draw her eye overly much to my location. Most Guardians form an image, crafting their matter into a material manifestation which typically appears to be a human form. Although humans cannot see their Guardians, it helps to form an emotional attachment for the Guardian to resemble their own beloved. As the Guardian of a Seer, who actually can see me, my first instinct would be to immediately craft such a form, making it as detailed and tangible as possible, to ease her ability to communicate with me.

However, I sense that to do so might put her at risk. If I caused her to stare too obviously at me, others would notice. I must avoid this. Therefore, I not only refrain from creating an image, but I deliberately suppress any visible manifestation. I know that she perceives me as an unformed mass, a cloud of matter floating in the air. Even this I try to minimize. Her eyes will seek me, but they will find very little to rest upon. Perhaps she will detect a slight residual mist nearby when she looks in my direction. I do this to protect her.

However, I will whisper to her, words of encouragement and learning, of love and joy. Always, I will whisper. I will keep my voice soft, soothing, quiet, again to avoid creating a noticeable reaction by her. I will craft my voice to be similar to that of her mother, soft and low, with a lovely African accent. This should be useful to her without attracting unwanted attention. And, unlike in all the times I have Guarded before, it is delightful to know that she will hear my words, and know my love.

We will be one.

Hester

After I have served the Missus and set the kitchen back in order, I have a few minutes to dash back to the slave cabins and check on Dalila. I cross the large vegetable garden and duck through the rows of trees hiding the cabins from the big house. They don't want us too close, don't want to see us unless we are serving them.

She is in the first cabin, closest to the house, the one where the unmarried women sleep. The rough logs form a square structure, the door hung loosely in the frame, the wood floor elevated only slightly from the dirt. I step up and push into the door.

Dalila is on her low cot to the left of the door. The rough blanket covers them both, but I can see that the baby is still in the softer cloth I had wrapped her in after she was born. The other cots are crowded into the small space, empty now while the others are all working in the field or in the big house.

She and the babe are sleeping, and appear to be well. I go to check the chamber pot, and take it outside to slop into the cesspit. I inspect the contents before I toss it out. I told her not to empty the pot, both so she would not have to exert herself, but also so I can check to see if there are large clots or too much blood. No, this appears normal. I know the Missus relies on me to tend to the others, and this is one of my duties. I must help during and after the births.

When I return, Dalila opens her eyes. The babe is still sleeping.

"How're you feeling?" I ask her, straightening her blanket.

"Sore, and tired, but good. Do I need to get to work?"

"No, Missus said you can rest today. She will come by this afternoon."

Her eyes widen. She is afraid of the Missus. She has never spoken to her. As the wife of the Master, Dalila feels the Missus must be a fearsome creature. I suspect she also worries that the Missus will be angry with her for getting a baby from the Master.

"Don't worry, honey, she just wants to check on you and the baby."

Dalila's forehead wrinkles. To ease her worry, I pull some brown bread wrapped in a napkin out of my apron pocket. "Here, you need to eat, so that you can feed the baby. Is she nursing well?"

She takes the bread gratefully and tears off a bite with her teeth. "Yes, she has been eating off and on all morning."

I lean over, and move aside the blanket just a little so I can see the child's sweet, tiny face. She looks so peaceful and innocent. She has no idea what is waiting for her in life. But we do.

"She's a little angel," I tell Dalila, patting the baby's sweet shoulder before heading back to work.

Chapter 3

Maid

Marguerite Ellis

After luncheon is cleared away from the table in the parlor overlooking the veranda, I tell my daughters that they should come with me to the slave cabins. "Nancy, Margaret, get your shawls. We must check on the new mother and baby."

Margaret rises to comply, but Nancy lingers behind and sighs melodramatically. "Must we come, Mama? We don't have anything to do with that."

I give her a sharp glance. "Yes, you must come. You both must learn how to run an estate, and this is part of it. You'll be married before long. I want you to be capable of managing things for your husbands."

Nancy looks at Margaret and grins. "I think Margaret is much closer to needing to know that."

Margaret smacks her lightly with her fan. "Hush now! You don't know what you're talking about." She quickly leaves the room, crossing through the entrance hall, to go upstairs for her shawl. Nancy follows behind, chattering away.

"Oh yes I do," I hear her say. "Didn't I just see you with Mr. Elliot last week? And then yesterday Mr. Simson was coming around to call on you?"

They burst into peals of laughter as they reach the top of the stairs.

Nancy is right. Margaret is nearly nineteen years old, and a number of young gentlemen have come courting. She is a lovely, delicate, and sweet-tempered girl. We should be able to find a good match for her soon.

Nancy is a different matter. She is so outspoken, so gregarious. It is unseemly for a young lady, but nothing I do seems to quell her nature. She can be relied on to blurt out the most uncomfortable truths at the worst possible times. She has some time to mature, though, before we must seriously seek a match for her. She has not reached her fourteenth birthday, not ready yet for courting. Quite.

As the girls return, their brother Richard comes pounding down the stairs, robust and tall for his age, trailing his hand along the curving chestnut banister. I can see that Nancy would rather run amuck with him, like she is another ten-year-old boy, rather than tend to womanly duties with her mother and sister. She is brought under control with a slight shake of my head. She gazes longingly after her brother, his manservant following frantically behind him.

"Richard," I call to him before he can escape the house. He skids to a stop and looks at me, clearly unhappy to be apprehended. "Have you finished your studies?"

He seems relieved to be able to tell me, "Yes, Mama, Mr. Pryor said we are done for today."

"Very well, go on." I will check with the tutor later to make sure my son is making good progress. Richard rushes out the doors to the veranda, clearly intent on playing near the river. I know his manservant will attend him.

As the girls walk with me towards the cabin area, I consider the situation. I feel that I should move Dalila into the household while her baby is young and nursing, but what would be her position? Sewing, perhaps? I do not know how good a seamstress she might be, as she has been a field hand since arriving here.

Margaret clasps her shawl closer to herself, although the day feels warm. I consider what Nancy said, about the beaux who have been calling on my eldest. Margaret is grown now, perhaps it is time for her to have a lady's maid. She will need more help with her dressing and other personal requirements as she approaches the time to be married.

It seems I have solved my problem. Also, if Dalila is in the company of his daughter, I do not believe my husband's eye will rove in that direction.

I nod to myself with satisfaction. Another household puzzle solved, another duty fulfilled.

Margaret

It makes me anxious to approach the slave cabins, but Mama is as serene and commanding as ever, her slender form held perfectly straight as she leads us across the garden. Two of the slaves are kneeling there, tending the vegetables.

She pushes open the door, and waits for us to enter the dim, dirty place before her. I want to hesitate, but she looks at me sternly, so I brace myself and go in.

I hear Nancy suck in a breath and hold her hand to her mouth. It is dreadfully smelly, the air very close with only one tiny window in the wall, the small room crowded with cots and rough blankets and belongings. Only one bed is occupied. This must be the new mother.

Mama crosses to her, while the girl opens her eyes with a start. She struggles to sit up. Nancy and I hang back by the door. There isn't really any room for us to get closer anyway, this cabin is so small and cramped.

Mama stands over the girl on her cot. "Good afternoon, Dalila, is it?"

The girl's eyes are huge in her dark face. "Yes, Ma'am," she says softly. I don't think she's any older than me.

Mama peers down at the baby lying in a blanket on the cot. I've never seen such a tiny baby.

"Is your daughter doing well?" Mama asks.

"Yes, Ma'am." I think the girl is terrified of Mama. I can't really blame her. Sometimes I think I am, too. There is something very intimidating about my mother's soft-spoken voice, combined with the steel of her gray eyes.

"Let me see her," Mama says. The girl lifts the baby up in her blanket and offers her to Mama, looking like she is afraid to give her up.

Mama takes the little bundle and moves aside the blanket. The baby must be awake now, as her little hand comes out of the blanket and waves around.

"Girls, come and see the child," she tells us. Nancy and I exchange a glance and move a little closer. Mama holds the baby up so we can see her tiny face. She is lighter than her mother, and her eyes are open, gazing up at Mama. Mama pokes her finger into the baby's little fist, and I see her smiling when she feels the baby grab onto her.

The girl on the bed is sitting tensely, watching this.

Mama takes her finger back out of the baby's hand, folds the blanket over her and hands her again to the anxious new mother. The girl takes the child with obvious relief and holds her closely, still staring up at Mama.

"Well, Dalila, how are you feeling? Was the birth very hard?"

"No, Ma'am, it was not too hard. I am feeling fine." Now that she has said more than two words, I can hear the soft accent in her voice. She must have come from far away, probably on one of the boats across the Atlantic.

"Good." Mama glances over at me, a strangely speculative expression on her face, then back over at Dalila. "You will need a few days to recover, and to tend the child. I will not expect you to return to your work for a week."

Dalila's mouth falls open, then I see her eyes rimmed with tears. "Thank you, Ma'am, thank you so much."

Mama goes on, "You have been working in the fields?"

"Yes, Ma'am."

"And you are unmarried?"

She looks down. "Yes, Ma'am."

Nancy's head quirks sideways, and she looks at me and whispers, "How'd she get a baby if she isn't married?"

I shush her.

Mama views Nancy sternly, then returns her attention towards Dalila.

"Do you have any skills other than working in the fields? Have you worked as a house servant?"

"No, Ma'am."

Mama sighs. "Well, be that as it may, I have decided to move you into the household for now. You will find it easier to tend to your baby than you would working in the fields."

Dalila's eyes grow even huger, almost comically so, and I can't tell whether it is because she is scared or grateful.

"Yes, Ma'am. Thank you Ma'am." Her forehead is wrinkled with anxiety.

"You can wait on my eldest daughter, Miss Margaret."

Pardon me?

I look at Mama, alarmed. I didn't know she was planning to do this. I am too surprised to know how to react. "Mama," I begin, but she silences me with a glance.

"Margaret, Dalila will be moving into the house next week. Hester can make a place for her and the baby to sleep in the corridor beside your door."

Her tone brooks no disagreement. When Mama has made a decision, God himself could not dissuade her, so I do not even try.

She reaches out one more time to pat the little bundle in Dalila's arms. "We will let you rest now, Dalila. I will talk to Hester about making the arrangements to move you up into the house. She will help you learn everything you need to do."

Dalila nods her head vigorously. I think she is too overwhelmed to speak, even to say "Yes, Ma'am."

Just then, the baby makes the first little noise I have heard from her, just a tiny hoot, soft like a distant owl. It makes us all smile, breaking the tension.

As we are walking outside into the sunshine, I glance back at Dalila, still sitting motionless on her cot, clutching the baby.

Well, apparently I have a maid now.

Chapter 4

Natchez

September 1, 1810
Natchez, Mississippi Territory
Gregor

The waters of the Mississippi River slip by, scarcely a foot below where I sit on the deck of the boxlike flatboat, surrounded by piles of lumber on one side, and smelly chicken coops on the other. This floating box is certainly not one of the most elegant means of travel.

But, it is a means. To travel. And that seems to be all I want to do any more. I have felt nothing but restlessness for years now, unable to settle in any one place.

I had hoped, when I first came to the new country, that I would find enough adventure and delight to fill my long days, and that I would be content.

Perhaps it is not to be. Contentment, I have learned, is difficult to achieve and transitory at best.

Wolk whispers, "*You will find contentment again, dearest.*"

I glance sideways at my Guardian. He has slipped back into his wolf form today, his standard default when I have not asked for another persona. His name means "wolf" in my native language, after all. "Such an optimist," I think silently to him.

His wolfish face grins. "*Always.*"

The sun is sinking on the right side of the boat. I wonder where I will be tonight when it is dark. I look up at the oarsmen on the roof of the central structure of the boat, straining to control the enormous steering oar jutting out over the stern to land in the water behind us. "Where do we stop next?" I call up to them.

"Natchez," one of them replies, continuing to wrestle with his end of the giant oar, steering the flatboat safely around sandbars and other hazards in the river.

I nod.

Wolk regards me. I shrug. Sounds like as good a place as any to spend the night.

When we approach the dock, before I hop off, I peel away some of the bills from the wad in my pocket. I know I already paid my passage, but these oarsmen worked hard today, and I hardly have need for all the money in my possession. They might have families, and they can put it to better use than I. Handing the bank notes to the shipmaster, I murmur, "For the crew," then jump across to the dock before I must listen to their effusive thanks.

He does not let me depart in silence though. He calls out, "Watch out for the Kentucky Tavern, it is a damned rascally place."

Oh is it?

Sounds perfect.

Wolk rolls his eyes, a peculiar sight in his wolf form.

I walk away from the river, trying to get my bearings. The port is bustling, the flatboat I was on joining many others being serviced by dockworkers. Some of the boats are tied to rough docks, others are pulled up directly onto the muddy shoreline. There seem to be one or two narrow dirt roads along the flat area near the shore, and a variety of buildings erected in a haphazard way, some sturdily made with planks, others appearing to be no more than shacks made of spare wood loosely hammered together. Up on a bluff over the port I see the edges of a town which seems respectable. Closer to the water, the area looks less so. I see what seem like assorted taverns and brothels, still quiet in the late afternoon, but I imagine things will pick up after the sun goes down and the workers are finished for the day.

"Where is the Kentucky Tavern?" I ask a passing dock worker, hoisting a heavy box on his back. He raises his eyebrows, chuckles, and points his chin behind him.

I head in that direction, Wolk trotting silently beside me along the muddy path.

Sometimes I wonder what everyone else would think if they could see him. The dock worker raised his eyebrows at my question about the tavern. Imagine if he could see my Guardian. I know it's a good thing nobody can see him but me. Other people pay no attention to the fact that a shining wolf accompanies me everywhere I go.

In fact, he often assures me that even the other Guardians pay no attention to us. Long ago our friend, the only other Seer I have ever met, taught him how to cast a glamour over both of us. I've always known that a Seer would attract the attention of every Guardian nearby, and Wolk and I both assumed it was just how life had to be. But our friend's

Guardian had learned otherwise, and soon Wolk was able to keep us incognito. So, I can walk among the humans and their Guardians, none of them the wiser about what I am.

Which suits me perfectly.

Stephen

Normally Thomas and I stay up on the hill, in Natchez proper, even after I close the doors of my medical practice in the evening. We usually dine at the American Eagle Tavern, the club where the gentlemen like to gather before returning home to their families. I often take turns helping to manage operations and events there. I see this as one of the ways to increase my standing in our society.

Tonight, though, Thomas tells me he's of a mind to go down the bluff to Natchez Under-The-Hill. He is apparently in the mood for something a little rougher.

I had no meetings planned at the club, so I'm willing to accommodate him. I think he's feeling lonely. He'll certainly be able to find companionship down below.

We take the steep and narrow footpath down towards the docks, avoiding the ruts worn by hooves and carts in the packed earth of Silver Street. "Well," I ask, "where to now? You're in charge."

He looks up and down the rows of ramshackle buildings, the lamps starting to glow through the windows, the ladies starting to peek out into the street to see if customers are approaching.

"Oh, let's start at the Kentucky. A hand of cards and some whiskey sounds about right."

I nod, my fingers laced behind my back as I follow him back towards the tavern at the base of Silver Street. I don't think I should play many hands, since I need to be careful with my funds. I'm trying to build up a reserve, for my practice and eventually for when I find a bride. But I'll be glad for a glass of whiskey after seeing patients all day.

When we enter, we see a game of poker already ongoing, a fellow I don't recognize at the table with two acquaintances who work at the docks. I check the pile of chips in front of each, just to see how goes the game. I hear Thomas emit a low whistle, and know he has done the same. The stranger is clearly winning.

As we pass by to order our whiskey at the bar, John sees us and calls out, "Hey, Stephen! Thomas! Come and join us! Save us from this fellow tanning our hides!"

Thomas laughs, ready to join in. Fine. I'll come along, only a hand or two. We bring our drinks and sit down at the table. Thomas reaches his hand out to shake the stranger's. "How'd you do? I'm Thomas Butler. This is my friend Doctor Stephen Duncan. Pleased to meet you."

The stranger shakes our hands. "Gregor Slavson," he says. He's a thin fellow with sharp, angular features, and seems to be in his early twenties, about our age. He has dark eyes and thick dark hair, and apparently hasn't shaved for a few days. His clothes are fine but worn.

"Care to deal us in?" asks Thomas.

"Of course," Gregor says, cutting the cards. He has an accent I can't quite place. European of some kind.

Gregor's

As always, I give Gregor all the information at my disposal. I explain to him who the newcomers are. *"Both gentlemen arrived here in Natchez about two years ago, to make their fortunes. Doctor Duncan has used his experience as a physician's apprentice in Philadelphia to open a medical practice in Natchez. Mr. Butler is a lawyer with political aspirations. They share lodgings in Natchez on the hill."*

He does not need to nod or acknowledge my words. We have been doing this for many, many years. Our communication is instinctual, thorough, both comfortable and intense.

As the two new men join the game, I continue to relay the information about the cards to my beloved. I have switched my appearance, no longer appearing as my usual wolf. I currently look like a man, walking around the table to peer at the hand of cards held by each player. I do not need to do this to see the cards, of course. But it helps orient Gregor to see which player I am observing when I tell him what is held within their hands.

He is careful not to win every hand, just frequently enough that his winnings accumulate over the course of the evening. He does not truly need the money he is winning, but I am pleased he is feeling entertained by this activity. The last few years have been hard ones, my dearest one feeling the weight of his lifespan pressing upon him. He has been dissatisfied and restless. We have journeyed throughout the land, never settling long in one place. He has funds in banks all over the country, and accesses them as needed. Life for him has been a long game, seeking new experiences, trying to alleviate the restlessness he often feels with his situation.

I do everything I can to assist him. If he wishes to cheat at cards, I am delighted to help him do it.

Chapter 5

Companion

Gregor

I make sure to be generous with the money I have won from them, paying for all their drinks, recommending whatever food or other hospitality the tavern might offer.

The two laborers have retired for the night, but the gentlemen seem content to remain a while longer. Finally, though, the doctor makes his excuses, explaining that he needs to sleep since he must tend to his patients early in the morning.

"Are you coming, Thomas?" he asks his companion.

"Thomas is considering whether he might remain in Natchez Under-the-Hill to seek female companionship," Wolk helpfully informs me.

"Say, Thomas," I ask him, "where would be a good place for me to stay tonight? Someplace where I can have a bath, maybe find some other comforts?"

As I knew he would, Thomas turns to his friend. "You head on home, Stephen, I'll help our new friend get settled. I'll be along later."

"Stephen believes he will not see Thomas again before the morning, as usually occurs when Thomas stays behind in this area."

"Thank you, Thomas," I tell him, then turn to Stephen. "It was a great pleasure to meet you. I hope to see you again very soon."

"Are you staying in town long?" he asks me.

"I just might do that. I haven't even climbed the hill to get into Natchez proper. I'll have to do so tomorrow. Perhaps I will see you there."

"Very good," he says. "Have a pleasant night." He glances at his friend with a raised eyebrow, then departs.

"Well," Thomas says, smiling and clapping me on the back, "I know just the place for you to get a bath and bed. And 'other comforts' as you put it."

"Lead on," I tell him, looking forward to lying my head someplace other than the ground. It has been a few nights of staring at the sky overhead from whatever bed of leaves I can find.

"*That's your own doing,*" Wolk reminds me. "*You could always have found lodgings, you just couldn't be bothered.*" He's not wrong.

When we get to the brothel, the ladies clearly are very familiar with my new acquaintance. They cluster around us in the parlor, smiling and petting. An older woman, presumably the Madam, approaches us. "Who is your friend, Thomas?" she asks with a mercenary smile.

"This here is Gregor, new in town, and looking for a place to stay."

"Welcome, Mister Gregor," the woman says, her rouged cheeks lifted in a steady smile. "What is your pleasure tonight?"

"Thank you." I tell her what I want directly, "I would like a private room to stay the night, and to have water fetched for a bath."

"And a companion?" she asks. "You can select any of my ladies here." They strike poses meant to be appealing.

"Yes, a companion as well. I will leave the selection in your capable hands." I reach into my pocket to the pile of coins I acquired in the poker game. I am pleased to find a use for them. I hand far more to the Madam than I am sure she is accustomed to receiving. Her eyes widen.

Although it seems somewhat tedious to conduct this transaction, I know I will not sleep unless I experience sexual release. Sleep has come less and less easily to me over the years, and I have found that the only way to ensure I can rest is to utilize such services. And of course, the experience itself is always welcome. Wolk smiles knowingly at me. Then, knowing my preferences, he quickly transforms back into a wolf. It seems to me more natural just to have an animal nearby when I am enjoying the services of a lady, rather than having him appear as a human.

"Rosy!" she commands. "Take Mister Gregor to the best room. I will send up the water for his bath shortly." A plump girl with wavy brown hair, wearing a corset which accentuates her bosom, approaches with a smile.

Thomas grins as I allow the girl to lead me towards the stairs. "Enjoy!"

"Thank you, Thomas, perhaps I will see you in the morning."

"Oh, I think you may," he says, looking around at the remaining selection of women. "I think you just may."

Rosy

At least he is young, and even good-looking. He is not the tallest man I have seen, but seems strong and fit. Still better, he wants a bath, which means he won't be smelly. This beats what I get most nights.

At the end of the hallway upstairs, I take him by the hand. "Right this way, Mister Gregor," I tell him, batting my eyelashes as I have been taught.

He chuckles and glances down at the faded runner covering the wood planks of the floor, then follows me into the room. It is the largest chamber, more luxurious than any of the others. We don't use this room every night. Madam Beverly saves it for the biggest spenders. He must have handed her a lot of money.

I close the door behind us, then turn to him and place my hands on his arms. "Let me help you off with this coat, sugar," I tell him. He shrugs it off his shoulders and allows me to draw it from his arms. I lay it across the armchair in the corner.

There is a knock on the door, and already the servants are here with buckets of hot water. I know it will take them several trips to fill the bath, because it is such a large metal tub, much fancier than the wooden barrel we girls use downstairs. A couple of the other girls have even been added to the water crew, dumping their water as they meet my eyes with expressions of humor and envy.

He watches as they pour their buckets into the tub, then go out to retrieve more. He leans over and peers into it. "This is a nice big tub," he comments. His way of pronouncing his words is different from anything I have heard before. He must be from far away.

"Yessir, it is our finest."

He glances over at me. His dark, deep-set eyes are gentle, but somehow also seem fierce. "I believe there will be room enough for two in there."

It makes me laugh. "Oh, no sir, I can help scrub your back though."

He glances down again. "We can make it work. You can sit on my lap." He looks at me with a crooked grin.

I feel my face reflect my surprise.

Now he's the one laughing.

Gregor

It is charming, how a lady of the evening can seem young and inexperienced. How can it possibly surprise her to be asked to share a bath? Although, I must always keep in mind how young these people really are. I wonder how long she has been doing this.

"She has been working at this brothel for four years, since she was fourteen years old," Wolk clarifies for me. *"She began working in the kitchen for the first two years, before being transferred to her current position."*

As always, it is convenient to have a Guardian who constantly knows the thoughts of everyone around us.

I know we will have to wait a while for the staff to finish bringing the bathwater.

"Please," I invite, "sit with me." I take a seat on the settee at the foot of the bed, and pat the cushion next to me. I want to make her comfortable before we proceed. And, it is always interesting to hear about somebody's life. Despite how many life stories I have heard, I am always eager to hear more.

She places herself close to me, and at once begins to move her hands across my chest, clearly thinking that I wish to begin our physical interaction immediately. I draw her hand into mine, linking our fingers together and resting them quietly between us. A flash of confusion enters her eyes.

"So," I ask her, making conversation. "Is your name really Rosy?"

Her mouth quirks. "Well, it's short for Rosalind."

"Rosalind," I repeat. "What a lovely name."

She looks at me with her simple brown eyes. "Thank you," she says, wondering what I really want.

I don't keep her in suspense. "Let's just have a chat, while we're waiting for the bath to be filled. The night is still young, and I am in no hurry."

She visibly relaxes.

"She is relieved that you appear to intend to keep her for the whole evening. In this way she will not be called upon to service another customer."

I clarify, trying to keep her relaxed, "I plan to keep you all to myself tonight."

She smiles.

Gregor's

My beloved has long since given up on finding a love of his own. Human lives are so brief, and he has mourned enough that he never wishes to subject himself again to the grief of loss. Although hiring prostitutes is far less satisfying than his early loves, it fulfills his physical needs. This, then, is his custom.

Still, though, he cannot help but see each woman as a complete human being, worthy of his attention and care. He knows these women are treated ill by many of their customers, and are almost valueless within society. The bargain he has made with himself, the justification for his support of such a distasteful and exploitative system, is that he strives to ensure the time they spend together is actually enjoyable for both parties.

He questions her in a leisurely way about her background, her family, the sad story which has led her to this place, this occupation. It is always a sad story.

When he decides it is time to move on from talking, I take my wolf form across the room and lay my head down on my paws, closing my eyes to appear asleep. Of course he knows this doesn't make any difference. It is not like these are real eyes I actually am using to see. Regardless of what I am doing with my manifestation, I see and hear and feel and know everything he is doing. But this is how he prefers it.

After the bath has been filled, he gently helps remove her clothing, then his own. Much to her astonishment, he does find a way to share the bath, leaning back and looping his own legs outside the tub to make room for her on top of him. It is not a terribly comfortable position for him, but he disregards the discomfort, knowing no lasting damage can be done. She expects to wash him, but does not expect him to do the same for her. Every action he takes is gentle, and slow enough for her to adjust to what is happening.

It is only after quite a bit of time has passed that he begins interacting with her sexually. He guides her out of the tub, to sit upon a wooden chair he has drawn over to the side. He spreads her thighs, looking into her eyes to reassure her that he will care for her. While he remains in the tub, he lowers his head, and begins by tracing a line of kisses up her inner thigh. She draws in a sharp breath, flinging her head back against the chair.

Soon she is panting, moaning, tangling her hands in his hair. He is pleased with her responsiveness, planning to move on only after she has been thoroughly aroused and satisfied.

"*Just a little more to her left,*" I can't stop myself from advising him.

"Back to sleep, Hound," he silently instructs me, amused. "I know what I'm doing."

I remain quiet for the rest of the evening.

Chapter 6

Introduction

Ellis Cliffs
Dalila

My week of resting has passed both slower and faster than I could have imagined. I have never had so many days where nothing was expected of me. But at the same time I have never been busier. The sweet duty of caring for my darling baby occupies every waking minute of my time. If I am not feeding her or cleaning her, I am gazing at her, marveling at her adorable little self.

She has already grown, I can tell. She seems to have a good appetite, and my milk appears to be plentiful.

This will be our last night in the cabin with the other women. Tomorrow we will be moving to the big house, where I will learn my new duties as the maid to Miss Margaret. Hester has assured me that I will do fine, but I am terrified I will make unforgivable mistakes. I have no idea how these people live in their fancy home, or how I should behave while I am there. Just be agreeable, Hester told me, and do whatever you are told. You will do just fine.

I hope she is right. And I hope that this is truly what will be best for little Ayola. I know it will be easier to have her in the house with me, where I can perform my duties while I carry her at my breast wrapped up with a sash, the way the women in my village did, long ago. If I had to go back to work in the fields right now I don't know how I could keep her clean and fed properly. I'm grateful to the Missus for arranging this.

The bitter resentment I have always felt since the day I found myself seized by the hands of kidnappers remains, of course. This is not the life I wanted, not the life I would ever have chosen, and certainly not the life I wish for my child. Every day it is galling to have to submit to these people, submit or suffer, submit or die. But I have new reason to do it now. It is the only way to protect my sweet baby, the innocent little girl who I would not have if I were still across the ocean, back at home. I will resign myself to this fate, for her sake.

I hope Miss Margaret is pleased with me. I did not think she seemed happy to hear her mother tell me that this will be my new position. I will strive to give her satisfaction, in the hopes that Ayola and I will be secure in our new circumstances. Working as a lady's maid should be easier, and safer, than working in the fields. And I hope her father can see fit to leave me alone now that I have his baby.

I must keep that a secret, of course. Miss Margaret must never learn that Ayola is her half sister. I do not know what would happen if she discovered the truth, but I am sure it would not be good.

Ayola's

Despite my determination to keep my appearance nebulous, my beloved never fails to seek me out. Only a week old, and already her perception of the world around her grows firmer, her eyes seeing more every day.

Although, so far her world has been limited to this cabin, where her mother has been allowed to rest since the birth. Tomorrow she will find more to catch her gaze, as her mother moves into the house with the Ellis family, to begin her new duties.

Ayola has finished another meal, and her mother has propped the baby up on her shoulder, firmly patting her back. I move behind so my dearest one can gaze upon me, as she seems always to wish to keep me in view. I continue to refrain from forming any specific appearance, determined to help her avoid drawing attention to herself. But even as I am, this flimsy wisp of matter, she already loves to see me. She stares at me over her mother's shoulder, her eyes wide, her head bobbing as she tries to hold it up with the undeveloped muscles in her tiny neck.

"My darling, here I am, here for you, as I will always be."

Margaret

Hester has arranged a sleeping mat on the floor in the vestibule right outside my chamber door, for the new girl and her baby to use. Mama has instructed me about what to expect. I have never had my own maid before, and I understand now that I did not pay sufficient attention to the duties performed by Mama's maid. I have realized this week how much there is to learn about the roles of the servants in a household. And the roles of the mistress in supervising them. Mama is right. I am eighteen years old now, marriageable age, and soon I will have the responsibility of managing a household.

I don't have the faintest idea how that will come about, though. I know Mama has her eye on various young gentlemen in the county, but none of the ones I have met are very appealing. They all behave in a manner too arrogant, or too immature, or sometimes both. None of them seem interested in hearing what I have to say unless it is some form of flattery to them. I suppose eventually Mama will recommend one of them to Papa, and he will make the final choice. I only hope it is a husband I can like, and that whoever it is will treat me well.

It is out of my hands. It occurs to me that most things are out of the hands of the people whose lives are affected. Women must do as their fathers or husbands instruct. Slaves obviously must do as their masters instruct. Hardly anyone gets to do as they please. Only the men, really. I wonder if sometimes even they feel they are not fully in charge of their own destinies.

I shake my head. Why am I thinking of such things? I believe Mama would scold me for being fanciful. I must attend to my responsibilities this morning.

Hester is bringing Dalila up from the slave cabin.

Hester

Dalila has wrapped up her few sparse belongings, tied together with a rough string, and I carry the small bundle for her while she carries the baby. She has shown me the clever way that she uses her blanket as a type of sling, to hold the baby securely to her breast while she walks. She told me this is the way the women of her village did it, and I have to agree that it is better than the way most women carry their babies on their backs. I will have to remember this and teach it to the other mothers.

I have tried to explain to her in the evenings over the past week what will be expected of her in the house, but I know she will not really understand until she can see it with her own eyes.

When we enter the back door into the kitchen building, her eyes grow wide as she stares around herself in amazement. It is only the kitchen, the area with a large fireplace containing a spit and cooking pot, the cast iron stove, the surfaces for chopping food, the buckets of water drawn from the well. Still, I am sure it is the grandest room she has ever been in.

"Well, honey," I tell her, "get used to it. This is the kitchen, I expect you'll be spending much of your time in here, when you aren't attending Miss Margaret. Now come along."

I take her into the big house, along the gallery leading into the entrance hall. I point everything out to her as we cross the house, the dining room, parlor, living room, library, and the Master's study. I don't expect her to remember it all at once, but I am sure in a day or two she will have it straight. We approach the grand staircase at the other end of the gallery.

Before we climb the stairs, I pause and look back at Dalila. As I feared, she seems entirely overwhelmed. She nervously pats the back of her baby, who is snuggled into her sling, her little eyes peeping out over the blanket, watching the tour along with her mother. I smile down at her. "Look," I tell Dalila, "she is awake. I think she's enjoying seeing this house more than you are."

Dalila focuses on her babe for a moment, and as I had hoped this is enough to quell the panic I had sensed growing in her. I pat her arm. "It will be fine, child, you will grow used to this house very quickly." She takes a deep breath, and nods. "Let's go on up," I tell her.

Miss Margaret is waiting for Dalila in her chamber. Before we go in, I show Dalila the sleeping place I have made for her to use at night. "You will be close enough here to wait on Miss Margaret if she needs anything in the night."

She looks at the sleeping mat, concealing any emotions she may be having behind a carefully expressionless face. I wonder what she is thinking, but I feel it best not to ask.

"All right, come along."

I knock on Miss Margaret's door, and open it when she calls, "Enter." She is sitting at her writing desk, but rises when we get inside. Dalila casts her eyes to the floor, not brave enough to greet her new mistress.

Miss Margaret, who has always been the kindest of the Ellis children, seems to understand. "Welcome, Dalila," she tells her softly. I do believe the Missus has been giving her instructions. "I hope you will be happy here."

"Yes, Miss," Dalila replies, as I have taught her.

"Miss Margaret," I say, "would you like to go on down to luncheon, and I can show Dalila around, so she can learn about what she will be doing?"

"Yes, that sounds fine," she says, and I sense both girls are very relieved to have their introduction concluded.

I'm glad of it. I'll have an hour or so to show Dalila where Miss Margaret keeps her things, and teach her a little about how to attend her while she dresses, and otherwise make herself useful. I am as interested in the success of this arrangement as any of them. I do want the best for Dalila, and her sweet little baby.

Chapter 7

Incognito

Natchez

September 2, 1810

Gregor

The soft light of early dawn filtering through the window awakens me. I feel the warmth of the luxurious feather bed, and of the young woman softly breathing at my side. I can hardly believe how refreshed I feel after sleeping for - what, it must have been several hours?

"Good morning, beloved. You were asleep for over five hours. This is quite an accomplishment."

Indeed. I don't remember the last time I slept for so long. I feel wide awake, but so comfortable, and I do not wish to disturb Rosalind. I kept her up extremely late, engaging in very vigorous activity for a great long time. I think I showed her several things she had never before imagined, even working in her profession. I am grateful to her, for the use of her body which allowed me to wear myself out enough to finally sleep. She deserves her rest.

Wolk can keep me company while I lie quietly, waiting for her to rise.

I ask him to give me a description of the town up on the hill over the port where I spent the night.

"Natchez is a growing town, with a population of about fifteen hundred persons. Surrounding the area are numerous farms and plantations, where cotton is the primary crop. The town above the hill is more respectable than this row of businesses where you spent your evening. There are a number of shops and other business establishments, many residences, and some boarding houses and taverns. Your friend Doctor Duncan maintains an office

where he sees medical patients in one of the storefronts. Mr. Butler practices law at another office nearby."

"Where do Thomas and Stephen live?" I silently inquire.

"They share rooms above the medical practice. A hired servant cleans for them weekly, and they take their meals elsewhere, often at a private gentlemen's club they both like to frequent. Stephen helps to manage the club, and often conducts business there for a social group called the Natchez Dancing Assemblies."

I am enjoying listening to this description while loafing in this soft bed, a beautiful woman at my side. My current level of comfort stands in sharp contrast to the last few weeks, maybe even months, of roaming aimlessly throughout the land, spending nights under trees or in fields, scarcely eating, hardly ever sleeping. It seems like I had forgotten how nice a simple luxury like a bed can feel. Not to mention a warm bath, and the body of a woman.

"Will you remain in Natchez for a time, beloved?"

"Perhaps. We shall see what we can find up in the town."

"You might return to this establishment upon occasion as well, to enjoy the comforts here."

I gently play with the long brown hair spreading out from Rosalind's pillow, careful not to disturb her. I curl a lock around my finger. "Yes, I might."

Amazing how one pleasurable night can change one's perspective.

Wolk nods, still in his wolf form, patiently lying on the ground. I close my eyes, content to wait until a later hour before rising.

Rosy

The sun streaming in through the window plays with my closed eyelids, bringing me awake. I open my eyes, realize I am not in my usual cot, and lift my head from the pillow to try to see where I am.

"Good morning, Rosalind," I hear a man's voice say softly from behind me. I swing my head around and see Gregor lying there next to me, grinning in a very self-satisfied way.

As well he might. The things he showed me last night were very instructive. I may have learned more in a few hours than I have in the past two years. The most important thing I learned, I believe, was how good those things can feel. My work has been tolerable, but never before so pleasurable. I feel that my eyes have been opened.

"Good morning," I smile at him. I start to snuggle down against him, but then I suddenly remember my place. Madam will not be pleased about my lying in bed half the day. The sun is already high in the sky.

"Relax," he tells me, pulling me down against his bare chest, thin yet muscular. "Don't worry about your Madam. I'll pay for another day of your time if she insists."

I settle down, happy to remain hidden here with Gregor for as long as he wants.

Rosy's

My beloved relaxes again in the arms of her customer. It was deeply gratifying to observe her enjoying the physical intimacy of the previous night, so different from the usual brief and impersonal transactions conducted by most of her customers. This man, despite his youth, seems to have a wealth of knowledge about sexual activities, far more than any of the men Rosy has previously serviced.

She glows with a happiness I have scarcely ever before observed in her.

This customer, Gregor, is unusual, in a way I cannot quite define. His Guardian for some reason maintains the physical manifestation of a wolf, which in itself is strange. I have almost never seen a Guardian manifest an image other than that of a human. Even more oddly, the consciousness of both man and Guardian seem strangely cloudy and inaccessible. Normally I can know the thoughts of all humans and Guardians in my vicinity, and cannot understand why this is somehow blocked in this pair.

It is unimportant. What matters is that my beloved has had a pleasurable evening, and is currently feeling very content with this man. I hope this happiness follows her even after the man has departed. If she can maintain a bit of this joy, it would be a delight for us both.

Gregor's

I am pleased my beloved is feeling content in his current circumstances. Perhaps the restlessness which has driven his constant travels for the past few months will subside for a time, allowing him to find a place to feel settled.

He and the woman renew their intimacy of the previous evening, but in a slower, far more gentle way. The night before was almost frenzied, so eager was my beloved to exhaust himself, while being attentive to the pleasure of his companion. This morning he has achieved the rest he needed, and is content with an unhurried and tender bout of lovemaking.

I feel the puzzlement of her Guardian, the probing attempt to penetrate my thoughts, or those of my Seer. Of course this is unsuccessful. I learned long, long ago how to mask our presence, disguise from all around us who he truly is. The Guardian quickly abandons the effort, as they always do, returning to whispering encouragement and love to the woman. A Guardian is primarily interested only in their own Guarded, not in unraveling random mysteries which present themselves.

This has always worked to our advantage. Gregor decided a long time ago that remaining incognito is his highest priority. He can move through human society, the wealth he has accumulated over the long years of his life smoothing his path, without attracting too much attention. Once he sees that others are starting to ask questions about who he really is, or when he begins to feel restless again, he moves on.

His apparent youth helps him with his endeavor to seem unthreatening. It is not unusual for a young man, especially one of means, to travel and explore extensively before settling down. This in itself does not attract too much attention. Of course, the other humans are all deceived in this.

My beloved is not a young man, not by centuries. When he was actually young, we did not realize how being a Seer would affect his lifespan. We began to notice other indications of his unusual attributes, though. He never experienced illness. Any injuries, even if they were severe, healed very quickly. He had other qualities which were exceptional as well, such as eyesight unimpeded by darkness. He found himself increasingly less in need of sleep, even of food. He still enjoys food and sleep, but can go without for long periods of time.

However, it was only after he was some decades into his life that the strangest aspect of his existence became clear. He began to recognize that the aging process was somehow passing him by. His peers grew more feeble, the visible signs of old age increasing along with diminishing vitality. But not for Gregor.

I have never understood the mechanism by which this is so. He can sense me, when no other humans can sense their Guardians. There must be something about his composition which both gives him the ability to see the matter of which his Guardian is made, and also has kept him healthy and long-lived.

When we met the only other Seer we have known, more than a century after Gregor's birth, and he explained that he was even older than Gregor is now, we realized that this must be the way of things for Seers. He mentored Gregor for some years, and his Guardian taught me how to disguise our presence so other Guardians and humans do not notice Gregor's extraordinary nature. That Seer had learned from hard experience that it is best to remain hidden from the world. Gregor has taken this advice to heart, and his priority is always to conduct himself in such a way that he feels no threat to his identity or his well-being.

Sometimes this is a terrible burden, and he finds himself going through periods of restlessness or depression. Occasionally, though, like this morning, he is able to find a renewed delight in life. Despite everything, he is after all still human.

He is enjoying this humanity together with the young woman. My wolf form remains unobtrusively to the side of the room, where Gregor is less likely to be distracted by my presence. She is enthusiastically practicing some of the techniques he introduced to her last night. He is glad to enjoy the benefits of his instruction.

After, they cleanse themselves in the now cooled water remaining in the large metal tub, and dress to face the day.

Chapter 8

Exploring

Stephen

I hear Thomas come in at dawn. Shaking my head, I lift my pocket watch from the table next to my bed, and squint at the hour in the early morning light. Well, it was almost time for me to rise anyway. I sit up and stretch as he enters our room.

I watch as he sits on his bed and reaches down to pull off his boots.

"Did you sleep?" I ask him. I know he has to be at work later today at his law practice across the street from my medical office.

"Only a little," he says. "I was... busy." He struggles to yank his boot off. If we had a manservant it would make it easier, but we live more frugally than that.

I shake my head again. "Apparently. Did you see that other fellow?"

He drops the first boot on the floor. "Gregor? No, he went upstairs with Rosy. Do you remember her?"

I nod. I have become acquainted with Rosy as well. I might be less inclined to spend my money at gambling and whoring than Thomas is, but I am not immune to the occasional urge.

He goes on, finally managing to get off his second boot, "She took him up to the best room. I've never even been in there. Apparently he had a wad of money to spend. Including the money he won off us, of course. I've never seen Madam Beverly so excited to accommodate a customer."

He takes off his coat and waistcoat as well, and lays down against his pillow in his shirtsleeves and breeches. "Anyway, they were still up there when I left. I wonder if we'll see him today?"

I am moving around the room, starting to prepare myself for my day. "Maybe. He said he planned to come up here, didn't he?" I'm fairly neutral about this prospect. I have other things to consider. My medical practice, my finances, my plans for the future. Thomas is much more engaged with what is happening in the current moment. I am always thinking ahead.

As I leave the room to go downstairs and arrange the office for my day, I can already hear Thomas softly snoring.

Gregor

After a leisurely breakfast served in my room, which I insist Rosalind share, I prepare to take my leave. I embrace her, giving her a gentle kiss. "Thank you, Rosalind, for a very enjoyable evening."

She lowers her eyes, then boldly smiles up at me. "Thank you as well, Mister Gregor. It was enjoyable for me too."

I grin. I made sure it was. "I'm glad."

She leads me back down the stairs, where I can settle up with the Madam. Again I pay more than expected.

"Before I go, Madam Beverly, I would like some advice." If I am going to stay in town, I probably shouldn't be found loitering overnight in the shrubbery. I'll have to get something that seems respectable.

She smiles at me after tucking away the banknotes. "Of course, sir, I would be delighted to help you in any way I can."

"Excellent. I plan to go up to the town on the hill. I have never been there. Do you know of any inns or boarding houses which may have rooms available? I believe I would like to remain in Natchez for a while. Although I admired your room here very much, I think I should find a longer term arrangement."

She smiles and bats her eyelashes at me. I refrain from sighing. "Of course, Mister Gregor, although you are always very welcome to return here."

She offers a handful of suggestions, of places where I might find rooms to let. I suppose they are all places where her own acquaintances run the business, and wonder idly if she has a financial arrangement for referral fees. "Don't bother," I quickly think to Wolk, "I don't really need to know the details." It doesn't matter.

When I take my leave, it is already noon. I find the path leading up the hill, and climb to the upper level of the town. It is a fine place, which appears to be growing and thriving. Some of the streets are even paved.

I stroll about the area in an unhurried manner, hands in my pockets, exploring the town. I always like to see new places. I look with interest at houses, enjoy the view along the bluff, peer into shop windows in the business district. What appears to be an old military fort on the bluff is probably the original foundation of the community. The civilian town is laid out in a regular grid pattern, and most of the wooden buildings seem no more than a couple of decades old. I find only one building made of brick, none of the stone or marble in more established communities. The town has a fresh, new air, very different from older cities in the northeast, or in Europe. This town was clearly founded fairly recently. It is doing well for a new community, with a thriving population and business enterprises, clearly all sustained by the river traffic.

Wolk pads alongside me, offering insights about the people I see moving about the town. As the afternoon wanes, I find what must be the medical practice of my friend from last night, Doctor Duncan, with a sign over the door displaying his name. However, he is not in today, as the door is locked and the shades in the windows are drawn. I am about to pass by when I see a paper posted on the door, and approach close enough to see it is a notice that Doctor Duncan has been called out of town until tomorrow morning. Wolk tells me that my other new friend, Thomas, is working in his law office nearby, but I choose not to disturb him with a visit.

I am pleased to find the town has a bank, the Bank of Mississippi, as is shown on the sign above the door. I will have to make arrangements to have funds transferred here. I will surely have moved on from Natchez by the time the funds arrive, but I like to spread my capital out between various regions. I move around so much, it is worthwhile to have convenient access to money when I need it.

I note the location of a post office as well, from which I can post instructions for this transaction. It is in a room inside the King's Tavern on the outskirts of town, near a road which appears to lead north out of the area. I speculate that the postmen must arrive on this road with mail from the north. Wolk nods confirmation.

After I have taken in what appear to be all the sights, I settle on one of the boarding houses which Beverly had recommended, and enter the front door. The matron greets me, and offers me the only private room available. I am glad to take it, and I pay in advance for a week.

She asks if she can have a servant carry my luggage in for me, and seems surprised when I tell her that there is no need, I have no luggage. I never carry luggage with me. Why would I wish to be so burdened? I am always able to find whatever I need as I move through life.

I suppose I should at least make an attempt to obtain another suit of clothing, if I will be staying here for a week. The garments I am in are quite travel-worn.

I climb the stairs with the matron to inspect the room, then she leaves me there to "settle in". I gaze around. It is small but serviceable, with a narrow bed, a chamber pot in the commode, a small table with a straight chair.

I suppose I must be planning to stay in this town, now that I find myself with a list of chores already in place. Tomorrow I will visit the bank, the post office, the tailor.

In the meantime, it is suppertime. I let Wolk guide me to the gentlemen's club that my friends mentioned last night, the American Eagle Tavern in the town's one brick building. I will have some food, possibly introduce myself to some of the local gentlemen. How odd to be so much in the mood for company. It's been a while since I wanted much interaction.

Wolk clearly approves of my seeking out companionship. I suppose being my only friend must be quite a burden. The wolf snorts out a laugh, but otherwise keeps his opinions to himself.

Thomas

When I get back from my office after working for several hours on my current project, churning out legal research and documents, I find a note that Stephen left on the front door of his medical office. It tells any patients scheduled for the next day that he has been summoned to the Ellis Cliffs plantation to treat an injury, and will be back by mid-morning tomorrow. It's far enough away that it makes perfect sense that he will stay the night down there.

I head alone to the club for my evening meal, and sit in my accustomed spot, a low stuffed armchair at a table along the back wall. The place fills with the usual crowd of gentlemen, landowners and bankers and merchants from town, here to enjoy a meal, or at least brandy and cigars, before heading home.

I order food for one, then while I wait for it to arrive I lean back in the chair and watch the entrance to see who else might be arriving. Almost immediately, the door opens and I see it is Gregor, who so cheerfully relieved me of my money last night at poker. I beckon him over, inviting him to join me at my table. It will be nice to have a friend to share a meal even though Stephen is not here.

Gregor quickly makes his way through the room to join me. "Have a seat," I invite, gesturing to Stephen's usual spot.

"Thank you," he says, peering around the room, "how nice to see you again. I appreciated your recommendation for lodgings last night. I passed a very enjoyable evening."

I grin at him. "I imagine you did. Rosy is quite the girl."

He returns my smile, but it does not seem quite genuine. "Indeed."

"So," I ask, "are you going to stay down there again tonight?"

"No, I have taken a room in town. I believe I will remain in Natchez for a week or so."

"Is that so? What do you want to do while you're here?"

"I have not yet decided. I will need to visit the bank tomorrow to make arrangements for funds."

"Well, I can help you with that," I tell him.

"Oh?"

"Yep." I gesture across the room. "That there is Stephen's uncle. He's one of the bank's founders."

"Oh! Well that is helpful."

"Come on over, I'll introduce you."

I lead him over to Stephen's uncle, who is enjoying a cigar with another couple of the men in town. "Gregor Slavson, this is Samuel Postlethwaite. He is a bank founder, and our mutual friend's uncle."

Samuel stands up, clenching his cigar in his teeth, and reaches his hand out to shake Gregor's. "How do you do?"

Now that we're over here, I wonder if it would have been better to just let Gregor go into the bank tomorrow, rather than disturb the banker at his club, but here we are. I need to work on the impulsivity issue Stephen keeps nagging me about. He always tells me I seem far too reckless to be an attorney. I tell him it is the recklessness which will take me far. You can't progress without risk, I tell him, but he will insist on always being cautious.

Gregor pauses a moment, glances at me, looks down with the faintest smile, then says to Samuel, "I am very pleased to meet you, sir. I will be visiting the bank tomorrow to arrange to transfer some funds from New York. I should let you get back to your brandy."

"Very well, very well," Samuel says, sitting back down and gesticulating with his cigar gripped between two fingers. "Ask for me when you arrive, I will see to you myself."

Chapter 9

Injury

Ellis Cliffs
Margaret

Mama has told me not to be too impatient with my new maid, and lord help me I am trying. I'm accustomed to dressing myself. Having to wait for someone, who obviously hasn't the foggiest idea what to do, to bring me my garments and help me on with my corset seems like far more trouble than it is worth. Mama says that eventually she will get better at it, but in the meantime it seems like a real trial.

I can't say I don't like Dalila, though. It takes some getting used to, seeing her dark face here in my room with me, but her voice is lovely, whenever I can get her to say anything. She has told me she was born in some village in Africa that I have never heard of, and her accent is beautiful. Very soft and soothing.

And her newborn baby is the sweetest little thing. I have never heard her cry, which I think is a blessing, since they sleep right outside my door and I wouldn't want to be kept awake. Despite being so young and tiny, she is very alert. If she isn't asleep or eating, she is staring around herself all the time, looking for all the world like she knows exactly what is going on around her.

Dalila is trying to arrange my hair for supper, standing behind me and brushing it out. Hester has demonstrated this more than once, but she still struggles with it. I don't think she has ever had to brush hair before, not even her own since her hair is so different, those tight spongy curls. I hear little Ayola making her tiny cooing noises from the sling where she spends her days fastened to her mother's chest, and feel Dalila bump her against me.

"Dalila," I say.

"Yes, Miss?" She immediately stops what she is doing and waits to see what I want.

"I think it might help you if you didn't have your baby there getting in your way."

"Oh, Miss Margaret, she is not in my way at all."

"Still, why don't you let me hold her while you are doing my hair. I think it will help."

"Miss Margaret, she is fine where she is. I can keep on going. You don't need to trouble yourself."

I turn around to look at her. "I know you can keep going, Dalila. But, really, I'd just like to hold her. I haven't had the chance yet. Would it be all right with you?"

I see shock on her face. She can't speak for a moment. I don't know if she is afraid to hand over her baby, or surprised that I asked permission to hold her. But she lays down the hairbrush, unfastens her sling and passes the baby over to me. I give her a smile of thanks.

I lay the little creature down on my lap, her head close to my knees, cradled in the white cotton fabric of my skirt. She stares up at me, her little eyes wide, her mouth open, her tiny fists and feet waving excitedly in the air.

I think I might just lose my heart to this little girl, dark-skinned or not, slave or not.

"What a beautiful baby she is, Dalila."

In the looking glass I see her smile behind me, as she lifts the hairbrush and tries again with my hair.

Marguerite

It is nearly time to get ready for supper, and my son still hasn't come inside to clean up and dress. I turn to the servant behind me to tell him to go find Richard and tell him it is time to come inside. But before I get a chance to say anything, one of the newer boys from the garden comes running into the room.

"Missus! Missus!" he says, clearly greatly disturbed by something. He would not normally dare to come inside and speak to me.

"What is it?" I ask him. I try to remember his name. Isaiah, maybe? Yes, I believe so.

"Master Richard, Missus, he fell out of his tree, he hurt his leg! Samson told me to come and get you!"

I jolt to my feet. "Show me where," I tell him and rush after him out the door. I see the overseer standing near the porch, and tell him, "Mr. Brandeis! Richard has been hurt. Come with me!"

Our group doesn't have far to travel. Richard has taken to climbing a tree on the edge of the garden, a huge old oak which was left standing closer to the river when the land was cleared to build the house. He has started to build a platform up in its branches, with the help of his manservant Samson. He has clearly fallen from the platform, a distance of six or eight feet.

He is lying on the ground, grimacing in pain, clutching his leg. Samson stands over him, frantic, not knowing how to help.

I feel the deep calm that comes to me in the midst of trouble. I always experience the opposite of panic during times which cause most others to lose all control. I drop to the ground next to Richard, careless of how this will dirty my gown.

"Shh, shh, honey, I'm here," I tell him, laying my hand gently on his head. He opens his teary eyes and looks at me, his face contorted with pain. I caress his cheek. "It's all right, darling, you are going to be fine. We will help you."

I see him gain some control over himself. He starts to sit up, but I stop him. "Wait, don't move yet. Show me where it hurts."

He moves his hands from his upper leg, and I see with dismay that the bone is clearly broken, the leg bending at an unnatural angle above the knee. I can't let him see how alarmed I am.

"All right, dear, we will get you fixed right up." I glance around me for the resources at hand. "Mr. Brandeis, may I please have your belt? Samson, you too." The overseer takes his leather belt out of his pants loops, and Samson hands me the rope holding up his breeches. He has to clutch them with one hand to keep them from slipping down his legs. "Isaiah," I tell the boy, "go over there and fetch me three straight sticks, as long as your arm and about as wide as your thumb. Quickly now."

It only takes a few moments. I take the sticks and belts, and carefully secure them to Richard's leg, soothing him as he whimpers. I do not try to straighten his leg, I only want to hold it in place while we move him.

"Samson, Mr. Brandeis, let's move him into the house. Carefully, now, don't jostle his leg at all."

We get him settled onto the sofa in the living room. I tell a kitchen girl to bring him a cool drink, and a damp cloth to wipe his face. I turn to Mr. Brandeis. "Take the carriage into town, quickly now, and fetch a doctor here."

He nods and speeds back out of the house.

I know it will be some time before he returns. I think of what else I can do to make Richard comfortable while we wait.

Margaret

I am just as surprised as can be when we hear the commotion downstairs, and rush out of my room to see Richard being carried in by the servants. Nancy is already running down the stairs. Dalila follows me quickly, and watches from the side of the room as we all try to situate Richard and make him comfortable while waiting for the doctor. We know it will be hours before Mr. Brandeis can get all the way to Natchez and back.

After a few minutes of hustle and bustle I find myself standing a few feet from the sofa, trying to think of some other comfort for my poor brother, when I am surprised by a gentle touch upon my shoulder. I turn to see Dalila standing there, Ayola wide awake in her sling.

"Pardon me, Miss Margaret, but I know a remedy for pain that I learned in my village." Her dark eyes are filled with concern.

"Oh? What is it?" This is the most forward I have ever seen her.

"It is willow bark tea, Miss. It helps a great deal with pain. There are willow trees growing along the riverbank. I can make some tea for him that will help. May I do it?"

I look over at my mother, to see that she has been watching and following this conversation. She nods and gestures for Dalila to proceed. The girl rushes out through the patio doors to the veranda, the quickest route to the trees growing near the river.

Before too long, she returns from the door to the kitchen building, the cook in her wake, carrying a cup of hot tea. She brings the cup to my mother. "Here is the tea, Missus, I hope it can help."

My sister and I help lift Richard a little so that he can drink it, then I resume reading the book to him while Nancy plies him with sweets to help him forget his pain.

In another half an hour, we can all see him relaxing, and can tell that the willow bark tea has brought him some relief.

Stephen

My last patient of the day left some time ago, and I am making notes about everything I have done today. When I was apprenticed to Doctor Rush in Philadelphia, he taught me to always keep charts for each patient, so that I will remember next time what I had done for them. I am always very fastidious in maintaining this practice.

I am just finishing, and wondering if Thomas will be ready to join me at the club for supper. I hear the door open, and look up to see a man standing there, removing his hat.

"Can I help you?" I ask.

"You the doctor?"

"I am. Are you the patient?"

"No. It is a boy, he has broken his leg. Mrs. Ellis sent me to fetch you."

"Mrs. Ellis?"

"His mother. The Mistress of Ellis Cliffs plantation. I am the overseer there."

"Oh, I see. Of course, give me a moment to fetch my bag."

I ask him for any details he knows of the injury, and he tells me enough to know to add a few extra supplies to my bag. Very soon we are in his carriage speeding down the road south to Ellis Cliffs.

I am acquainted with the boy's father, Abraham Ellis. He often frequents the club in Natchez. He is quite prominent in the community, the owner of extensive holdings in the area. I look forward to being of service to his family, possibly to becoming better acquainted with his circle. When I came to Natchez it was with the view to make my fortune, which is always made more likely by having the proper connections.

The overseer drives the horses along the rutted dirt road as fast as he dares, but the plantation is some fifteen miles south of Natchez, and it is already nearly dark by the time we arrive. By his estimation, it has been some three or four hours since the injury occurred.

He pulls the carriage to a stop right in front of the main entrance, handing the reins to a waiting slave to tend the horses. He quickly escorts me into the house. We are greeted by the family gathered around the injured boy, who is lying on a sofa in the living room off the front foyer. I glance around and do not see Mr. Ellis, which I had expected as I have not seen him at the club for some weeks. I assume he is traveling.

Mrs. Ellis rises from her son's side to greet me. "Welcome, Doctor. I am Mrs. Ellis. Thank you for coming."

"At your service, Mrs. Ellis. I am Doctor Stephen Duncan," I tell her, briefly bowing my head. "How is the boy doing?"

"I believe his upper leg is broken. His sisters are keeping him as comfortable as they can. One of our slaves offered to make him some willow bark tea, which seems to have relieved his pain to some extent." She glances over at him. "Please, come this way."

I follow her to the sofa where the boy lies, with two young ladies tending to him. One of the young ladies has sweetmeats on a plate in her lap which she has presumably been offering him, and the other sets aside a book she must have been reading aloud.

"Richard," his mother tells the boy. "This is Doctor Duncan. He is going to take care of you."

The young lady with the sweets steps aside, but her older sister remains close by her brother's side. She is a lovely young woman, but I focus instead on the boy.

I open my bag and begin the examination.

Marguerite

The doctor is young, but he seems competent. He carefully examines Richard's leg, asks a number of questions about what has happened, then tells Richard that he must straighten the leg before setting it in place with splints. "It will hurt, son," he tells him seriously, "I won't lie to you. You'll have to be brave."

Richard nods, his face pale. The doctor has the overseer and Samson hold Richard in place, and Margaret and I both hold his hands.

The procedure to straighten the leg is an ordeal none of us would want to repeat, but thankfully it is over soon. By the time the doctor has wrapped up his leg and Samson carries Richard up to bed, we are all exhausted.

I follow behind Samson to get Richard settled for the night, and tell the manservant to bring his sleeping mat over to the foot of Richard's bed so that he will be available to give him any assistance he needs. I am quite sure it will be a difficult night. "You may have my maid fetch me if I am needed," I tell Samson.

When I get back downstairs, Margaret and Nancy are talking to Doctor Duncan in the living room. They have offered him refreshments, as is proper, and seem to be having a lively conversation. It is far too late to have Mr. Brandeis drive him back to Natchez, so he will have to spend the night.

"Thank you, Doctor Duncan," I tell him, "Richard seems settled down for the night. It is very late, may I offer you a guest room tonight?"

"Yes, that would be very kind. I would like to be able to check on Richard in the morning before I return to town," he says.

I turn to Hester, who has been supervising the servants throughout this difficult evening. She anticipates my question, saying, "The blue guest room has been prepared for the doctor, Missus."

"Very well."

Now that the hubbub has died down, I am able to consider the situation. Margaret and the doctor seem to be enjoying their conversation quite a bit. The young gentlemen callers she has entertained have evidently not been able to excite her interest to this extent. I regard the doctor speculatively.

"Doctor Duncan," I ask, "will Mrs. Duncan be worried when you do not arrive home tonight?"

He gazes at me, clearly knowing exactly what I am really asking. "I am unmarried, Madam, there will be no cause for anybody to worry."

I smile and nod. I will arrange it so that the couple can continue getting to know each other, without the presence of her mother which I know can be daunting for any new relationship. Hester will serve as chaperone. "That is good to know. Margaret, I am quite fatigued after this trying evening. I will retire for the night. Please see to our guest. When you are finished with your refreshments and conversation, Doctor Duncan, Hester here can show you to your room, and get you anything you might need."

"Thank you," he says with a knowing smile, again giving the impression that he knows exactly what I am about. "I will see you in the morning, Mrs. Ellis."

Chapter 10

Smitten

September 3, 1810
Margaret

I could scarcely sleep last night. Not only for worrying over my brother, who I heard being cared for by Samson and Mama during the night.

But also because of this little flutter in my heart that I get when I think about the handsome young doctor who tended him. Doctor Stephen Duncan. After the worst was over, and he had managed to straighten Richard's leg and bind it up, I had the chance to have a conversation with Doctor Duncan.

I spent the rest of the evening admiring him. Everything about him seems admirable. His dark hair, his fine, even features, his deep-set eyes, his straight teeth. He cuts an elegant figure, tall and lean. His voice is pleasant, with the tones of his native Pennsylvania.

We lingered late into the night, talking in the living room, long after Mama and then Nancy retired, and I sent Dalila upstairs to bed down with her baby. Hester settled in a chair near the door with some mending, to wait until we were done, so it was all perfectly proper.

I have never had a man listen to me like this before, question me about my interests, seem to genuinely care about my responses. Even though my life is quite dull, he acted like he found me fascinating. We even talked about some of the novels I have read, although as a gentleman he prefers more substantial books.

He is far more interesting than me, and I was very pleased to learn about his background. He is only four years older than me, and he has already made a name for himself in the world. He got a medical degree from a college in Pennsylvania, and trained as an apprentice doctor. He already has his own medical practice in Natchez, where he tells me that most of the locals come to him for treatment when needed. He impressed me greatly last night with his knowledge, and how well he cared for my little brother.

I rise early, with the dawn scarcely breaking, but Dalila is already prepared to help me get dressed. She brushes out my hair, Ayola back in her sling. I stare dreamily into the looking glass, seeing only Doctor Duncan's face. I suddenly realize that Dalila is smiling, and I meet her eyes in the mirror.

"What is it?" I ask her.

"I'm sorry, Miss, it is nothing." She tries to straighten her face.

I turn around and face her. "No, really, what is it?"

"Well, forgive me, Miss Margaret, but you seem very distracted." She gets a mischievous glint in her eye. "And I believe I know why." The smile is back.

I break out laughing. It's just like how Nancy teases me. "Very well, you might be right. I think I know why too."

She joins me in laughing. I feel a bond growing with her, and find myself glad that my mother decided to place her here.

"I'll make sure to get your hair right this morning, Miss Margaret," she says, briskly returning to her task. "You'll want to look extra pretty at breakfast!"

Stephen

I heard the family up with the boy during the night two or three times, and each time I rose to check to see if my help was needed. They were merely trying to arrange him to make him more comfortable, nothing requiring medical attention. I have assured them that after a few days have passed, he should start to feel better. Since the skin was not broken in the fall, I do not believe there is concern of a fever setting in, so he will just need to endure the discomfort until the bone starts to mend itself. I am quite certain that I set it straight, so as long as they keep the splints in place, it will heal straight and not impede his walking once he has recovered.

Another member of the family occupied my thoughts during the night as well. The eldest daughter, Margaret, is a charming creature. She is soft-spoken, very demure, yet animated when drawn out in conversation. Her eyes are the softest color of blue, and her hair a pale brown. Together with her ivory skin, and a faint pink blush to her cheeks, she gives the impression of a painting done all in pastels. She is a very soothing presence.

It is clear to me that her mother considers me a suitable prospect. I have not been able to fathom before now how best to encounter the sorts of young ladies who I might consider courting. Since my arrival in Natchez, my time has been occupied either with patients, or other gentlemen in the club, or with the ladies Under-the-Hill who are obviously not suitable candidates for courtship. But young Richard's fall might be propitious for me in more ways than one.

At the breakfast table, I am able to further engage the mother and sisters in conversation. A tray is brought to Richard's room, as he will be unable to traverse the stairs for some time.

The light of the morning does nothing to diminish Margaret's charms. On the contrary, in the daylight her beauty seems to glow even more vibrantly than it did by the light of the candelabra last night.

I believe I just might be smitten. And judging by her attentiveness, both last night and this morning, I dare to hope that she may feel the same.

Marguerite

The Lord seems to have miraculously transformed bad fortune into good. Richard's injury appears to be on the mend thanks to Doctor Duncan's services, and I begin to hope that a resolution to Margaret's position might be on the horizon as well.

I see how they look at each other this morning, after their long interlude of conversation last night. I am pleased that Dalila finally seems to be getting the knack of attending Margaret, as her hair and clothing are quite in order today. Of all mornings, this is the right one for her to appear at her best.

The doctor says nothing about it, of course, not to me. He focuses on his patient. "After breakfast, Mrs. Ellis, I would like to examine Richard one more time. Then I must ask to trouble you for your overseer's time again this morning to convey me back into town."

"Of course, Doctor, you are most welcome to use our carriage. I cannot express to you our appreciation for your diligent care of our Richard."

"I will come back in a few days to check on him again, but I can bring my own horse, so it won't be such trouble for you."

"Yes, please do. I will feel so relieved to have you keeping track of his progress. Thank you."

And of course, I know Margaret will be excited to see him again. My husband is expected back in the next day or two as well, and I look forward to telling him about all of these developments. Finding a match for our eldest has been an important priority for the last year, and now that I feel progress is being made, I hope Mr. Ellis will be very pleased.

Chapter 11

Gossip

Natchez

Gregor

I arrive at the bank shortly after the doors open in the morning. As he had suggested, I ask for Mr. Postlethwaite, and am soon ushered into his private office.

"Mr. Slavson," he heartily greets me, shaking my hand. "I am glad to have a better chance to talk than we had at the club."

"He is eager to hear more about the transfer of funds from New York which you mentioned last night. He hopes this means there will be a significant financial transaction to boost the bank's liquidity. This institution is quite new and he wishes to increase its reserves."

Always useful, that Wolk.

"I am glad to talk to you as well, Mr. Postlethwaite. Thank you for seeing me."

"So," he goes on, "apparently you know my nephew?"

"Yes, but only recently. I met Stephen when I arrived in town two days ago. He and his friend were quite hospitable."

"Glad to hear it, glad to hear it. Will you be in Natchez long?"

"I do not know yet. I have no set plans, but I would like to transfer some funds here to be available for anything I might need. Even if I have left town by the time the money arrives, I would be comforted to know that it will be available in this region of the country."

"Of course, I will be happy to help you."

He draws a pad of paper to himself, ready to prepare the transaction, and begins asking me the necessary questions. His eyes widen when I tell him the name of the institution in New York City from which the transfer will be made, and the name of my agent who can be contacted with any questions. Both are well known. When he asks how much

I would like to have transferred, I double the amount I had been considering, based on Wolk's description of Samuel's motivations. This should keep me on his good side.

After I affix my signature to some documents he has prepared, he says, "My boy, I am delighted to take care of all the particulars for you."

"Would you like me to send a letter to my agent?"

"Only if you wish to, but I assure you that we can manage the transaction quite efficiently without. I have all the information I need. The funds should be here within two or three months, hopefully less."

I nod. "Excellent. Thank you very much for your assistance."

"Of course, my boy, of course. I hope to see you again at the club. Next time, please come and join me for supper."

Yes, the higher transaction amount was the right decision.

Stephen

When the Ellis Cliffs overseer drops me back off at my office in Natchez, there is a small crowd waiting outside the door. I had several appointments scheduled for earlier in the morning, and most of the patients have been waiting there in the hopes that I would soon return. I apologize for my lateness, and begin work immediately.

I am ravenous by the time I have finished my work for the day, having had no chance to take a break or have a bite since breakfast early this morning in the Ellis dining room.

I have not seen Thomas since early yesterday morning, and find myself in the unusual position of having to seek him out to ask him if he is ready to go to the club for supper. I climb the stairs around the back of the building to briefly check our rooms, and when I find them vacant I assume he must still be working.

I cross the street to enter his office, and find him hard at work. Sometimes it is difficult for me to come to terms with the fact that my happy-go-lucky best friend is also somehow a diligent attorney. He looks up from the stack of tomes spread before him on his desk. He has not yet even lit any candles, so apparently engrossed is he in the work, and I wonder how he can see to read in the fading light coming in through the window.

"Thomas, it is too late to be working. Are you done? I'm ready to drop dead of starvation."

He whistles and pushes back from his desk. Standing and stretching his back, he says, "Thank you for coming to my rescue. I was trapped down that cavern of law books and I don't think I ever would have made my way out!"

I laugh and pat him on the back. "Come on, let's get supper."

Walking up the street to the club, I am pleased to see our new friend Gregor coming out the door of a boarding house just as we pass by. "Gregor!" Thomas enthuses. "Are you dining again at the club?"

"Yes, and I had hoped to join you again."

I look back and forth between them. "I am gone for one night and apparently already you are the best of friends."

They both laugh. Gregor says, grinning, "I was a poor substitute for you, Stephen. I found the sad Mr. Butler sitting all alone, and had to join him because he looked so pitiful and lonely."

"Hey!" Thomas protests.

Laughing boisterously, we all enter the doors to the club together.

Gregor's

How delightful! It has been quite some time since I last heard my beloved laugh with friends. They appear to all the world to be nothing more than three young fellows enjoying an evening together. It is refreshing for Gregor to feel included in this group.

When they enter the establishment, their number soon grows, because they are immediately beckoned over by Stephen's uncle, Mr. Postlethwaite. "Uncle Samuel," Stephen begins, "I would like to introduce...."

Samuel laughs. "No need, my boy, no need. Gregor and I are already old friends, are we not?"

Gregor smiles and glances down at me, in my usual wolf form, then back up to his friend. "I met your uncle here last night, and he helped me today with some business at the bank."

Stephen shakes his head. "My goodness, you have all been busy without me, haven't you?"

"Speaking of which," Thomas says, as Samuel gestures for the three newcomers to take seats at his table, "what have you been up to? Your note said you had to go to the Ellis Cliffs plantation? What happened?"

Stephen says, "The son of Abraham Ellis fell out of a tree and broke his leg, and Mrs. Ellis sent for a doctor."

Samuel leans in, interestedly. This is riveting news, something to be savored in such a small community. The men would never acknowledge that they are gossiping just as the women do. No, they would insist, they are bringing each other up to speed on current events. Men must know such important news. Gregor, though, smiles as he recognizes this for the tittle-tattle that it is. Most humans share the desire to talk about their fellows.

The men are interrupted briefly by a server who approaches to offer food and drinks, then return to their conversation. They listen attentively as Stephen describes the journey to the southerly plantation, his treatment of the boy, and his conversation with the family.

Thomas raises an eyebrow when Stephen seems to gloss over the information about the family. "Wait a moment," he says, pointing at his friend. "What is that expression on your face? What aren't you telling us?"

Gregor watches, amused, as Stephen's face actually seems to grow flushed.

"Come on, now, nephew, out with it!" insists Samuel.

"Well," Stephen admits, "I confess I did find myself greatly enjoying the conversation I had with Miss Margaret Ellis." Samuel's eyes light up. Here is a topic to keep them busy for the rest of the evening.

Gregor

They are all so young. Even Samuel, who Stephen and Thomas view as their elder, is only in his mid-thirties. They animatedly discuss the opportunities Stephen might have to court the young lady. They see so many possibilities in the future. It is charming but poignant to behold. Their lives will pass by in a flash, marriage and children followed oh so quickly by the grave.

But it is a privilege to be included in this intimate discussion, to watch their schemes unfold. I can't help but be caught up in their enthusiasm. I even find myself offering a few suggestions about how best to court a lady.

Such things are in my past, abandoned long ago. Once I, too, cared about courtship and love and planning for the future. It led to more grief than I would have thought any one person could bear. Human lives are so short, it brings only sorrow to become entangled too deeply.

But, this I will allow myself, this blossoming friendship with these youngsters. I can be entertained by watching them make their plans.

Wolk watches from the floor at my feet, not needing to comment on my thoughts. He shared my grief, he understands my motivations.

Samuel wants Stephen to make tangible plans. "If you are going to pursue Miss Ellis," he advises, "you must do so quickly. I understand she is already eighteen years old, her parents must be making plans for her. You will have to get the better of any other gentlemen."

Stephen nods gravely.

"When do you think you can see her again?" Thomas asks.

"I told Mrs. Ellis that I would come back in a few days to check on Richard."

Samuel smiles, and lifts his glass to Stephen. "Perfect. Tomorrow?"

"No, I only left there this morning," he replies. "Perhaps in another two or three days."

"Will the Ellis overseer return to fetch you?" Samuel inquires.

"I will ride my horse. I would not wish to further inconvenience the overseer. I'm sure he has better things to do than cart me around."

"Too bad you don't have a buggy," Thomas inserts. "It would be wise to bring a friend to keep an eye on you."

Stephen laughs. "Do you want to go?"

"Regrettably, no, I can't take the time from work."

I impulsively offer my services. "I would be pleased to accompany you, Stephen, as your second."

He stares at me, an expression of confusion on his face. "My second?"

"For your duel, of course. The pursuit of love is a battle, you must follow the rules of engagement!"

I mean it as a joke, but it falls strangely flat. Wolk fills the awkward silence which follows my statement by explaining, *"Stephen's father was killed in a duel when he was quite young. I am afraid the gentlemen are not amused by your jest."*

Oh. Dear. Well, I can't very well apologize for my gaffe, since there is no legitimate way for me to know this information. Happily, Samuel fills the silence, by offering his own buggy for the journey.

"You must allow me to assist in your endeavor, nephew, you shall borrow my buggy for the trip. You can show young Gregor here the sights along the way."

I am grateful to Samuel for covering my mistake.

Wolk adds, *"It is a good thing, my dearest, for you to make the occasional error. Perfection would only draw suspicion."*

I silently laugh at him, and think, "Only you could find a way to make my mistakes a virtue as well!" His shining wolf form huffs.

Chapter 12

Stripes

September 4, 1810
Ellis Cliffs
Abraham

As the driver steers the horses around the final bend in the road leading up to the house at the foot of the cliffs, I am surprised to see that Mr. Brandeis is laying stripes across the shoulders of a slave bound to the whipping post. Although of course it is the overseer's prerogative to discipline any of the hands, it is not a frequent occurrence, at least on my plantation. I am even more surprised when we draw close enough that I can see the unfortunate is Samson, my son's manservant.

It is unusual enough that I have the driver pause here rather than going on to the stables. The crowd of field hands, gathered around watching in stony silence, parts to make room for the buggy. Brandeis stops what he is doing, coiling the whip in his hand, and looks up at me, somewhat breathless. Whipping can be hard work.

"Welcome home, Mr. Ellis," he greets me.

Samson looks back over his bloodied shoulders, his hands still lifted over his head in the shackles fixed to the top of the post. I am sure he and I are both wondering how many more stripes he has coming to him.

"What is happening here, Brandeis?" I inquire, skipping any pleasantries.

"Samson allowed your son to fall and suffer an injury."

"What?"

I am ready to leap from the buggy and race to the house, the slave forgotten, but Brandeis immediately assures me, "Richard is fine. His leg was broken in a fall from the treehouse, but Mrs. Ellis summoned a doctor who was able to straighten the leg and wrap it. The doctor says he will fully recover."

I nod, my heart racing from the shock of hearing this news, but relieved to hear Richard is all right. I am sixty years old, and didn't sire my only son until I was fifty. I will never have another heir.

"And this?" I ask, indicating the whipped slave.

"He needs to learn to better attend his master. He let the injury happen, and caused me to have to waste the better part of two days driving the doctor back and forth from Natchez."

"Very well, carry on," I tell him. I'm not going to question his decisions as the overseer. Before I turn back to the driver and tell him to drive on, I see Samson shut his eyes and brace himself. I hear the lash fall as the carriage moves towards the barn.

Marguerite

I hear the buggy's wheels crunching against the gravel drive as it enters the carriage house, and quickly move out to the front porch to greet my husband. He approaches, and my smile falters when I see that his expression is grim.

"Welcome home," I tell him, reaching out for both of his hands.

He automatically kisses me on both cheeks, then asks, "How is Richard?"

"He will be fine, my dear." I wonder how he knows already.

"I came across Mr. Brandeis disciplining Samson. He told me what happened."

I seal my lips in distaste. I do not approve of the decision to whip Samson. It may interfere with his ability to assist Richard for a few days. But I have no say in such matters.

"Come up and see Richard," I invite him. "He will be glad to have his father home."

I lead him up the stairs, after the servants relieve him of his hat and coat. As we are approaching the door of Richard's chamber, Margaret comes out of hers. "Father!" she smiles sweetly at him. "Welcome home!"

"Thank you," he says, then his eyes move to the figure of her new maid standing behind her in the doorway. Dalila lowers her eyes, clutching her baby in the sling she keeps her in.

Abraham seems surprised by the fact that his daughter now has a maid, but he does not mention it. "Come and see Richard, Father, he is already doing much better," Margaret tells him. We all walk across the hall and enter Richard's room together.

Dalila's

My beloved falters in the doorway as she sees that the Master who impregnated her has returned. She has dreaded seeing him again. After he briefly glares in her direction, he is diverted by his family leading him on to the room of his son.

Dalila returns to the room, shaken.

She had been clinging to the smallest hope that Abraham would have forgotten all about her, and would be utterly indifferent to her presence. Clearly, she can see, this is not the case. He remembers her, and wonders what she is doing inside the house. He had taken advantage of her easily in the past, drawing her from the fields where she worked. Inside the house this would be more difficult, but her presence will be a constant provocation.

Furthermore, obviously, he notices the child. Another bastard, he thinks, unconcerned. But it is the presence of my beloved which perturbs him, and draws his thoughts in a direction he feels he must suppress in the presence of his wife and eldest daughter.

I worry not only for my dearest, but for her daughter, the Seer. The child is precious, and there is a risk involved in exposing her to a man who has lustfully victimized her mother. The safety of the child would be of no concern to the man were he to find an opportunity to accost Dalila.

I must set my own worries aside and attempt to comfort my beloved.

"My darling, you see, the man moves on from you, and we can hope that he will leave you alone. You are fortunate to have your marvelous child, and your new position will benefit you both. And I will share it all with you, of course, my beloved."

Hester

I see what she is doing. Dalila is hanging back in Miss Margaret's rooms whenever she can, trying to avoid the Master. And I certainly can't blame her. I see what he is doing as well. He follows her with his eyes whenever she is in the family areas, while she waits on Miss Margaret. She cannot escape her responsibility to attend her mistress, as her duties extend beyond simply dressing her in the mornings. She must be available at meals, or when Miss Margaret is doing needlework, or any number of other times. The Master watches her constantly, apparently thinking that nobody notices, but I do, and I believe the Missus does too. He obviously cares nothing for the child he got on her, but it looks like he still lusts after Dalila.

It is disgusting. And there is nothing at all that any of us can do about it. Our helplessness was demonstrated anew when poor Samson was whipped by the overseer for the crime of allowing Master Richard to be hurt. Every person on this plantation knows how willful Richard can be, including Mr. Brandeis. There is nothing Samson could have done to prevent the accident, and in fact it is only due to his diligence that Richard hasn't managed to kill himself with some recklessness long before now.

After Samson was let down off the pole, the men lifted him into his cabin, where we women helped his tearful wife rub salve into his wounds, and try to ease his pain. In the morning I begged Missus to excuse him for the day, suggesting that Richard could be properly tended by some other slave since he could not leave his room anyway. She relented, and I believe she had already planned for this. She knows what a whipping can do. I have seen the disapproval on her face whenever it happens.

Richard has the household in an uproar, though, even confined to his room. He was peevish when told his manservant was feeling poorly and could not be with him today. He adores Samson, and despite everything, Samson is very fond of the boy as well, admiring his high spirits and inquisitive nature. Nobody wishes to tell Richard the reason that Samson is indisposed today. I don't know whether he will ever know.

In the meantime the servants are kept busy throughout the day running up and down the stairs, bringing him treats or trinkets or whatever might catch his fancy. His sisters contribute to the effort, spending time with him and trying to keep him amused. With Dalila's clever willow bark tea, his pain is kept at a low enough level that he finds the energy to be demanding, and demanding he is. He is running us all ragged.

We all hope for his speedy recovery, the family and slaves alike.

Chapter 13

Pleasure

Natchez

Gregor

After the very enjoyable meal and conversation at the club, I spent the night in my small chamber, pacing. I could not sleep, of course, and had nothing to do to fill the hours until dawn. I used to be able to sleep as a child, but once I was grown it stopped being so necessary. It occurs only infrequently now, but if I let it go for too long, more than a week or two, I grow exhausted and desperate for rest.

I often enjoy spending my nights wandering in the moonlight, but I could not very well be seen roaming the streets of Natchez all night like some sort of ghoul. So I just stayed in my room. I was not particularly interested in Wolk's offers to entertain me yet again with tales of his past lives. I walked back and forth, the three steps it took to traverse the space, peering out the window into the street with each turn, never seeing anything of interest to observe. It seemed a very long night.

Today I intend to spend my time more fruitfully, obtaining some supplies to prevent a recurrence. I visit various shopkeepers in the area, purchasing books, candles, writing materials, even maps of the area. I must have something to keep myself occupied if I am going to be remaining in this area for any length of time. Which begins to appear more likely.

As the day wanes, I find myself feeling restless again. But I do not intend to succumb to the urge to move on from this place. I feel committed to remaining at least for a few days, to accompany Stephen on his journey to the plantation, and to track the transfer of bank funds which Samuel has started. The idea of another meal at the club does not appeal, and instead my thoughts return to how I spent my first evening in the area.

I soon find myself walking towards the path to Natchez Under-the-Hill. I happen to pass Thomas coming out of his law practice while I am still in the main town, and I murmur to him that I have plans for the evening. I ask him to make my excuses to Stephen. Thomas grins at me and watches as I begin to descend the steep path down the bluff.

When I enter the door of the brothel, it is still early enough that most of the ladies are in the parlor awaiting the arrival of any customers. They lounge upon the couches and chairs, scandalously clad only in undergarments, or even less.

"Mister Gregor, welcome back!" Madam Beverly enthuses the moment I arrive. I force a smile to my face. The women begin to cluster around me, quite a bit more enthusiastically than I would have expected.

"Rosalind has shared with them the tales of your prowess, my dear. I am afraid that you have already developed a reputation with the ladies."

I do not roll my eyes, but Wolk sees me visualize it, and he laughs.

"May I offer you a new companion for the evening?" Beverly asks.

I see Rosalind towards the back of the group, her round shoulders exposed over her corset, her plump face blushing charmingly. And shockingly considering her occupation. Again it strikes me that these people are all so young.

Normally I would be delighted to sample a different lady, usually wishing for as much diversion as possible. But tonight I am strangely in the mood for something that feels familiar. "If Rosy is available, I would be pleased to have her company again."

Beverly's eyes gleam, and I don't even need Wolk to translate. I know she sees profit in a customer who develops an attachment to one of her ladies. I don't care.

The smile that comes to Rosalind's face seems genuine, not the practiced expression of her profession. I suddenly am very glad to be here.

Rosy

I find myself strangely nervous to be summoned again by Gregor to his room. I have spent a great part of the past two days thinking of him, even daydreaming when I should have been attending to my other customers. The other girls were amazed and entertained when I described the things he did, and how he made me feel. I can sense their jealous gazes on my back as we walk up the stairs.

When I close the door behind us, he draws me into his arms and gives me a gentle kiss. "It is good to see you again, Rosalind," he tells me. It gives me a little shiver to hear him use my full name. It seems so elegant in his mysterious accent. Nobody ever calls me anything but Rosy.

"Thank you for having me again, Mister Gregor," I tell him. I hesitate a moment, then find myself wanting to simply be honest with him. "I have been thinking about you every moment for the last two days."

His eyes seem to light up with delight. "Will you show me what you have been thinking?" I feel my cheeks flame, but I want so much to please him.

It wasn't the conversations we had that I was dreaming about, although that part was very sweet. It was the other things he showed me. Especially the things he did with his mouth, and how he explained the best way to use mine. I know many men like me to use my mouth on them, but Gregor took the time to describe exactly the way to move, how to place my hands, the rhythm to use. Other men have always seemed very abrupt, but Gregor apparently had infinite patience with me. I have been longing to try again. I did attempt to recreate it with a couple of other customers, but they were done so quickly that it did not seem at all the same.

I lower myself to my knees before him, maintaining eye contact the entire time. When I reach to unfasten his breeches, he inhales shakily, and I am flooded with joy to know I am having an effect on him. But he gently moves my hand, and says, "Do you remember what we did first?"

"Oh, well, yes, but we don't have the bath tonight." He had declined having another bath prepared, which does not surprise me, since he does not seem to me to be the type to engage in unnecessary luxuries. Two baths in one week would be excessive.

He shakes his head, seeming amused, and lifts me back up to my feet. "There is always a way. This is part of the pleasure." He looks down into my eyes, and waits for me to nod my head, before he begins to undress me again. I am shivering with anticipation. After he has removed my garments, he allows me to remove his.

When we are both unclothed, he utilizes the washbasin and towels which we find in the room, again cleansing both of us in a movingly tender and intimate way. After he has finished with me, he places the washcloth in my hand, and guides my movements as I rub the soapy water across his body. I do not avert my eyes, but rather find myself boldly staring, enjoying the sight of his lean and muscular form. He seems amused, but also I can see quite plainly that he is very aroused.

After I finally wring the washcloth and place it across the rim of the basin, he caresses my cheek with the tips of his fingers, then brushes my hair back from my face. "Now, Rosalind, where were you when I interrupted you?"

I return to my place on the floor before him, and hear his ragged breathing as I show him that I remember what I have learned.

Chapter 14

Astonishment

September 6, 1810
Ellis Cliffs
Gregor

I sit on the bench next to Stephen as he drives Samuel's buggy south, the reins held loosely in his hands. He provides an interesting narration of the sights along the dirt road, facts about the river and plantations and residents.

But my mind is diverted, listening to him with only a part of my consciousness. The other half is remembering how sweetly Rosalind recreated my lessons the other night, asking for more instruction when she felt she needed it, and finally driving me to a level of excitement so intense that, again, I was able to slumber for several hours afterwards. Sleeping twice in one week is quite unusual, and obviously Wolk takes notice. I can tell he views Rosalind quite favorably, as the tonic which has given me relief. I agree.

It is a long drive, but somehow it seems to pass in a moment, listening to my new friend while reflecting on my new lover. For Rosalind seems more than a prostitute somehow, even after such a short acquaintance. I smile when I think of her joy when I assured her that I would return soon. There is no harm in indulging this desire, this simple pastime. I am in no danger of falling into the trap which in the past led to grief. Wolk remains resolutely silent on the topic.

Before I know it, the horses are pulling the buggy along a gracious drive leading to a manor beautifully situated between the river and the nearby cliffs. A slave comes over to take the reins and lead the horses away, while another leads us up the steps to the front entrance.

We are welcomed by a genteel woman who is obviously the mistress of the house. Her white gown is elegant, and her hair is arranged in a meticulous bun upon her head, secured by a lace cloth. "Good morning, Mrs. Ellis," Stephen greets her. "May I introduce my friend Gregor Slavson, who is visiting the area and accompanied me on my drive today."

"It is good to see you, Doctor, Mr. Slavson. You are both very welcome. Please come in."

"How is my patient?" Stephen asks, as we cross the entrance hall. He is answered not by Mrs. Ellis, but by an older man who comes striding towards us from another room.

"He is very well," he says, reaching out and firmly shaking Stephen's hand. "I hear that is thanks to you. Welcome, Doctor Duncan."

Stephen smiles. "Thank you, sir. Abraham Ellis, may I introduce my friend Gregor Slavson?"

"How do you do, Mr. Slavson?" Abraham asks, then returns his attention to Stephen, to discuss the condition of his son.

Mrs. Ellis turns to me. "Mr. Slavson, would you like to wait in the parlor while the doctor examines my son?"

"Of course, thank you." I allow her to lead me to a small sitting room, where she asks me to take a seat. She directs a servant to bring refreshments.

"Will you excuse me, Mr. Slavson? I would like to join my husband and the doctor while they examine Richard."

"Certainly, please. I will be most content right here."

"I will send my daughters down to keep you company, and we should all join you shortly."

I smile and nod. Excellent. I will be able to evaluate the object of Stephen's affection for myself, and offer him my insights as I am sure he will insist on our drive back to town.

Soon, I am sipping sweet tea, with a tray of biscuits close at hand. Southern hospitality is certainly on display in this home, I think, and Wolk wolfishly grins at me from his position by my feet.

In another moment, two young ladies enter the parlor, obviously the sisters. The elder approaches, saying, "Greetings, Mr. Slavson, my mother asked us to keep you company while Doctor Duncan examines my brother." I smile and nod. "I am Margaret Ellis," she goes on, "and this is my sister Nancy."

"I am very pleased to meet you, ladies" I say, continuing with the pleasantries necessary in modern human society. I try to subtly inspect Margaret, to assist in my later discussion with Stephen. She is beautiful in a pale, quiet sort of way, her coloring somehow muted, but with a lovely blush adorning her high cheekbones. I can understand the appeal that she holds for my friend.

I glance around, and see a maidservant quietly enter the parlor behind the young ladies, moving to stand unobtrusively with her head bowed along the side of the room, obviously waiting to see if her services might be needed for anything. I note that she carries an infant with her in a sling across her chest.

I begin turning to the young ladies to try to make further conversation with them, but suddenly realize that Wolk is reacting with astonishment to something. He seems remarkably disconcerted, so much so that his wolf form actually wavers. I have never seen him in such a state. Well, only once before, but -

"Gregor!" It is a sign of his agitation that he addresses me by my actual name, rather than one of his usual flowery endearments. *"The child!"* I gawk at Wolk, then turn to stare at the infant carried by the servant. It begins to dawn on me that the baby seems unusually radiant, something I have not seen for many, many years, just as Wolk goes on. *"The child is another Seer!"*

Margaret

I pause in my attempt to converse with the stranger, because he suddenly begins behaving in such a peculiar manner. His eyes grow wide, he looks at the floor, then lifts his face and stares at Dalila's baby in the strangest way. It is like he is completely shocked to see a slave being allowed to carry her child while she works. I hope he is not offended.

Nancy notices too, and loudly whispers, "It's like he's never even seen a baby before!"

I have to shush her. I don't want him to take offense at that too.

When he doesn't stop staring at Ayola, I offer, "Please excuse my maid, sir, it is easiest for her to keep her newborn with her, and it doesn't interfere with her duties at all."

Dalila seems terribly uncomfortable to be the object of attention, and stares at the floor, patting the baby in her sling.

He makes an obvious effort to bring himself under control. Frankly, if he is offended by Dalila keeping her baby with her, I am offended by him. She is my slave, I can allow this if I want.

But he assures me, his voice initially coming out in a strange croak, "Of course," he pauses to clear his throat, "yes, it seems quite fine for the mother to keep her baby with her." He looks over at me, his eyes still seeming somewhat wild. "It is just," he pauses again, then finishes somewhat lamely, "I am only admiring the sling she is using. It is a clever technique."

Well, yes it is, but honestly, what a fuss over nothing. This Mr. Slavson is an odd fellow. He has a strange accent, maybe they have different customs in whatever place he is from.

Ayola's

I am growing accustomed to the reaction of other Guardians to the wondrous presence of my beloved. A Seer is a remarkable being, and will always attract the attention of our kind. The new fellow's Guardian, who has taken a very unusual wolf form, seems particularly impacted by the realization of what she is.

Even the man seems startled when he looks at Ayola. I wonder what it is that he is seeing which seems to surprise him so, but find it impossible to know his thoughts. How odd. Normally human thoughts are easily available to all Guardians nearby. I turn my attention to his Guardian's thoughts, and realize that they are equally hidden.

I have never seen anything like this. I try to disregard this unusual development, but I cannot help but sense that it could somehow impact my beloved. I do not know how, but I feel I must carefully observe this man and his Guardian while they are in her company.

I do not know what might develop, or what any of this might mean.

Stephen

"I am very pleased with Richard's progress," I tell his parents. "The swelling is minimal, much less than I would normally expect. The splints appear to be properly holding the leg in place. Everything indicates that he will heal completely. I expect him to be up and running around again in a few months, possibly even sooner."

His father clasps my hand and shakes it vigorously. "Thank you doctor. That is such a relief to hear."

The boy, observing this exchange, impatiently chimes in with, "Well, what about now? I'm bored to tears sitting here in my room. Can't I at least come downstairs?"

His mother smiles at him fondly, then turns to me to hear my answer.

"Well, Richard, you cannot put any weight on your leg for at least a couple of weeks, or it won't heal properly," I caution him. "No walking at all, do you understand? Not even across the room. And you need to keep the foot elevated as much as you can, so it doesn't start swelling. Later, after a couple of weeks go by, I can provide you with some crutches to use while walking, but for now you must stay lying down. Do you hear me?"

"Yes," he replies sullenly, crossing his arms.

"However," I go on, and chuckle to see his face light up with hope, "if we can have you carried everywhere, I see no reason you cannot move about the house."

He whoops with delight. "Samson can just carry me, can't you Samson!"

His manservant, who has been standing silently to the side during my examination, answers, "Yes, Master Richard, of course."

"Let's go!" Richard cries out enthusiastically.

"Wait just a minute, there," Mrs. Ellis intervenes with obvious amusement. "Let me go downstairs first and arrange a place for you."

Richard huffs and leans back against his pillow, tragically, as though waiting another five minutes is the most extreme hardship of his life. His father and I look at each other, grinning at the impatience of youth.

Marguerite

I quickly descend the stairs to the living room. The parlor, where our other guest is waiting with my daughters, I consider, will not be large enough for our increased numbers. The living room will do. I enter that room, beckoning two servants over. I instruct them to arrange blankets and cushions upon the largest sofa, so Richard can recline with his foot elevated as the doctor instructed.

Then I enter the parlor, to tell my daughters the good news. "The doctor says Richard is healing well, and he will allow him to be carried downstairs to visit."

Nancy claps with delight, and Margaret exclaims, "Oh, how wonderful!" I know the girls have been as busy as the servants tending to Richard, and they have all been eager for him to be allowed to leave the sickroom.

"Samson will be carrying him downstairs in a moment, and I have arranged a place for him in the living room. May I suggest we all make our way in there?"

Margaret invites Mr. Slavson to follow her, and he rises silently to comply. He seems slightly overwhelmed by all the activity he has found in this home, and I wonder if it has been long since he left his family, or if he has siblings. I suppose that having a number of young family members around must seem like an awful bustle if one is accustomed to being alone.

Chapter 15

Examination

Stephen

I supervise the slave as he lifts Richard, making sure he is heedful that the broken leg is not jolted in any way. He is large and strong, easily able to carry the child. He is also exceedingly gentle and careful with his young master, although I see him wincing as he lifts the boy. I wonder if he has suffered some injury.

As Abraham and I follow after, I quietly offer, "As long as I am here, I would be happy to look after any other persons who might be in need of medical assistance. Either free or slave."

Abraham says, "That is very decent of you, thank you. I will have to ask my wife if she knows of anyone needing attention. I only returned a day or two ago from a business trip, so I wouldn't know."

We arrive in the living room, where the ladies are arrayed around the couch which has been prepared for Richard. Like some kind of pampered prince, he is conveyed to the sofa, and settled in with a great deal of adjustment of pillows and blankets. He lies back with a huge grin, obviously thrilled to be back in company, even if it is just his family.

Mostly family, because of course Gregor and I are here as well. I glance at Gregor and am surprised to see him looking somewhat ... uneasy? I cannot tell. He has always seemed perfectly calm when I have seen him before, when we were playing poker, or laughing at the club, or even when he was approaching the brothel. For some reason now he seems somehow unsettled. Can it be the presence of the injured child?

But I soon lose interest in whatever my new friend is bothered by, as Margaret approaches and thanks me for tending to her brother so well. I am lost again in her pale blue eyes, precisely the color of a cloudless sky overhead at dawn before the sun has crested over the horizon.

Gregor

I am relieved by the commotion caused by the arrival of the injured boy, because while the family fusses and clusters around him, I am briefly forgotten and can try to calm myself. My mind is in a tumultuous uproar. How can I have encountered another Seer? Since such a great length of time has passed since I parted company with my friend, I determined long ago that he and I were the only such creatures in existence.

When Wolk calms himself down enough, I am able to get some more details. This Seer is a newborn girl, another surprise to me, as I had always assumed any Seer would be male, like myself and my old friend. But apparently we can be either gender.

Wolk gives me some additional details. She was born early, he tells me, and was especially small, but quite healthy. This seems unsurprising, since I remember both my friend and I, when comparing notes, realized that neither of us had ever experienced illness of any kind, and enjoyed remarkably robust good health. So presumably this tiny infant, although many babies born so small can not survive, will enjoy similar good health.

At various times in my past I have worked as a medic, including with pregnant women and newborn babies, so I have knowledge of the reproductive process. From what I can see without conducting an examination, the mother is healthy and already recovered from the childbirth which Wolk tells me took place about two weeks ago.

The child, curled inside the protective sling worn by her mother, appears to be about the size of a small newborn, but Wolk says she has grown substantially since her birth. Her mother has apparently arranged her deliberately to have the upper part of her face uncovered and facing the room, as I see her eyes peeking up and examining her surroundings. Wolk tells me that her mother believes this is the best way to keep the baby quiet and content as she performs her duties. Indeed, the child is clearly deeply engaged in looking about herself, an expression of intelligence and understanding in her large round eyes.

The most amazing thing to me about her appearance is the sheen that I see glowing off of her skin, exactly the way I perceived my friend long ago. I have never seen this in any other human. It is just like the shining aura which surrounds Wolk regardless of what he is doing with his appearance. He might be a wolf of any color, or a man, or a woman, or any of the many other forms I have seen, but in every case there is a luminescence that radiates from him.

He and I have often discussed this, and I believe that whatever he is made out of is somehow inside of me as well, which is the reason I can see him. And the reason that the other Seer I knew had the same unearthly glow.

In the dark I can even perceive it, dimly, radiating from my own skin. If I hold my hand before my eyes on a moonless dark night, it is almost as though another faint moon is shining upon it. It is not as strong as the light I see from Wolk or this little Seer. Only Seers can perceive this glow, either in their Guardian or in other Seers, Wolk has opined. It is one of the aspects of my identity that he habitually keeps hidden, as he shields our thoughts from the other Guardians.

As I stare at the baby, who is facing to the side due to the placement of her mother lingering behind Margaret, I revel in seeing this light glittering from her face.

The mother turns, lifting a pillow to place it under Richard's leg at the direction of Mrs. Ellis, and the child is now facing towards me.

Her eyes, so huge in her tiny face, immediately meet mine. I know they are drawn to the same luminescence that she can perceive in me. I wonder to what extent her perception of the glow is dampened by Wolk's shield, which was designed only to deter other Guardians. It is clear she sees something different about me. We stare at each other, this newborn infant and I, and I feel something passing between us. An awareness, a camaraderie, even a love. It is the same feeling I experienced in the presence of my old Seer friend. She has not even been in this world for a month, and already she senses that I am like her. She can feel the same appeal.

"What is her name?" I silently ask Wolk, staring transfixed into the captivating little eyes.

"*Ayola.*"

Stephen

My admiration of Margaret seems boundless, nearly involuntary. When I left her home the last time, I wondered whether I should pursue her, but I am utterly committed now. It is not even within my control any longer. The strategy session I shared with my uncle and friends, jovially discussing methods and reasons and timing, is nothing to me now. I will not rest until I have achieved her hand.

Never before have I felt this way. I have had my dalliances, of course, with the ladies Under-the-Hill, and even have had my share of flirtations with more respectable young ladies during events sponsored by the Natchez Dancing Assemblies, but this is entirely different. I want her. I need her. I have no idea how somebody I had never met a few days ago has become the most important thing in my life, but somehow she has.

I see her parents watching us, and suspect I know what they are thinking, but I can't stop staring at Margaret, trying to draw her out, hanging on her every word.

I'm half-tempted to tell them my services for Richard are free of charge, because the little tyke has done the most important favor of my life by breaking his leg and getting me here. I look down, amused at myself. Don't be ridiculous. I'm very pleased to be able to bill for my time, this will be a great boon to my financial future. Especially if that future will include Margaret.

I'm glad her parents seem quite pleased with the situation. And that she does as well. She gazes at me, her pale eyes filled with what might be admiration, I flatter myself. I think this could actually happen.

Mrs. Ellis comes back to the room, after having departed a few minutes ago to take care of something. When she sits back down, she addresses me. "Doctor Duncan, my husband mentioned that you offered to see to anybody on the plantation who might have need of your attention. Although I wouldn't want to bother you overmuch, there are a few people who could benefit from your expertise. Are you truly willing?"

Oh! "Yes, certainly Ma'am, I would be very happy to help."

"In that case, if you will follow me, I will take you to my husband's private study, which seems like it should be an adequate place for you to work. There are only a few people to see, just some of the servants. The rest of the family is quite well."

"Of course." A servant brings me my bag, which has been in the entrance hall since I finished examining Richard earlier. Mrs. Ellis leads me to the study at the back of the house, across from the grand staircase. I see there is a desk, some chairs, and a sofa upon which a patient could recline for examination. "This will do nicely," I tell her. "Please send them in."

The first patients are unsurprising - the people I had already noticed. Richard's manservant enters first, ushered in by Mrs. Ellis, who has a strangely firm set to her jaw. I understand why after she closes the door behind her and he removes his shirt to show his flayed back. Mrs. Ellis must not approve of whipping. I inspect his back, and see that somebody has tended it with salve and strips of cloth. It is healing about as well as can be expected. "This looks all right, Samson, whoever nursed you did a good job. The scabs might stiffen and itch as they are healing, but I don't see any infection forming, so you should be fine." Some of the stripes are across old scars, so I know he is already aware of the process.

He nods, looking at me like he is suppressing indignation, but says nothing except, "Yes, sir." I refrain from suggesting that he avoid whatever misbehavior caused this in the first place. It is not my place to question the discipline of other households.

The next person who Mrs. Ellis brings in is Margaret's maidservant with her little baby. I tell her to sit on the couch, and I take a chair I have drawn up next to it. "When was your baby born?"

"Almost two weeks ago, sir," she answers in a gentle, softly accented voice.

"Are you feeling well?"

"Yes, sir."

"Are you still bleeding?"

"Only a little bit, sir," she asks, looking away from me, probably embarrassed to answer such personal questions.

"Do you have any symptoms you need to ask me about?"

"No, sir." In that case I will not subject her to the embarrassment of a physical examination. She seems fine.

"Very well, let me examine your baby, just to make sure everything is all right."

She draws the infant out of the sling she has contrived, and lays her on the sofa next to where she is sitting. I lean over to inspect the child. She is wearing nothing but a little napkin to catch any messes; presumably staying close to her mother's chest keeps her warm enough. She is very small, but quite alert. She stares up at me, her little lips pursed, waving her tiny arms around. "Was the birth early?"

"Yes, sir."

I nod. "Is she eating regularly?"

A smile flashes across her face. "All the time, sir."

I see the benefit of the sling. Keeping a premature infant close enough to stay warm and nurse constantly can only help with growth. "Has she grown since she was born?"

"Yes, sir."

After inspecting her limbs and reflexes, tracking her eyesight and hearing, listening to her breathing, I pronounce the infant to be in good health. I watch as the mother picks her up and re-fastens her in the sling around her shoulders. I tell her, "You are doing a very good job as a mother. Your child is quite healthy."

She smiles softly. "Thank you, sir."

I add, impulsively, "Margaret is lucky to have you as her maid. You obviously know how to care for others."

Her face splits into a true grin. "Thank you, sir," she repeats.

I have a few other patients, who have suffered typical injuries working as field hands, which can be a grueling and even dangerous job. One older slave has a chronic cough. I do what I can for them.

It is growing late in the afternoon before everything has finished and we are getting ready to depart. Gregor and I have shared luncheon with the family. He has been very quiet all day, and I can only hope that he paid enough attention to Margaret while I was busy to be able to offer his opinion about my chances.

The family bids us farewell, Margaret has the grace to seem sad at my departure, and Abraham assures me that he will call on me when next he is in town, and will take me to supper at the club. The buggy is brought back around from the carriage house, the horses tended and ready.

Then we are on our way.

Dalila

After the gentlemen leave, Miss Margaret and I return to her room to rest before supper. I help her out of her corset so she can relax for a time. She seems flushed, and I know she is still thinking about Doctor Duncan.

I have been waiting to tell her what he said. "Miss Margaret?" I ask after I have finished tending her, and before I leave the room to let her rest.

"Yes, Dalila?"

"Your Doctor Duncan said something to me about you."

Her strange pale eyes grow wide. "What did he say?" she whispers.

"He told me I am doing a good job taking care of my baby, and he is glad that you have me to take care of you too."

"He said that?" she gasps.

"He did. He is the one who mentioned you. He is thinking about you too. I can tell he cares for you, Miss Margaret."

When I leave the room, her face is full of all of her dreams and hopes, and I hear her give a happy little sigh.

Just then Ayola coos out a soft sigh too, and I smile at her and settle down to feed her, now when I have a chance before I have to help with supper.

Chapter 16

Coincidence

Natchez
Gregor

"*Stephen is going to want to hear details about any interaction you had with Margaret. You must focus, beloved, we will have all night to talk about the new Seer.*"

I sigh. "I know," I think to him. Wolk knows the direction my thoughts have taken. All of my plans have instantly changed. There is no longer any question of my leaving this area. I must take care to nourish my friendships with Stephen and the others, now more than ever. If I am to establish myself in this community, I must behave normally, not raise any suspicion. Concealing my true nature, my new purpose, becomes more important than it has ever been.

Stephen doesn't even wait until he has guided the horses around the bend out of view of the house. "Well?"

I force myself to set aside my obsessive thoughts about the little Seer. I have plenty of time later to obsess some more.

I grin over at him. "You have my permission to pursue the young lady," I jest.

He barks out a laugh. "Tell me what you thought of her."

"She is obviously lovely, but I don't believe you need me to point that out to you. I suspect you may have already noticed."

He shakes his head, grinning.

I try to be more serious. "I find her to be very refined, and her conversation seems intelligent. She appears to have a very gentle nature. She is loving and patient with her troublesome little brother. She will be a good wife."

He nods enthusiastically. "What about when I was out of the room, seeing patients? What did she say? Did she seem to miss me?"

I laugh. "Yes, she positively languished whenever you were out of her sight!"

Gregor's

My beloved participates in this conversation with evidently deep interest all the way back into town. He is actually interested, of course, and normally would be thoroughly absorbed in what is an enjoyable topic.

However, he is entirely shaken by what we saw at Ellis Cliffs. As am I. To have the two Seers together in one room was overwhelming. I had truly not expected Gregor to ever again encounter another one such as he. After centuries of roaming the world, to have only met one other Seer, I had come to agree with him that there simply were not any more.

But now, there is a new Seer in the world. The fact that she and my beloved arrived in the same area within days of each other seems an extraordinary coincidence. There is truly no such thing as fate. Nothing is predestined. Humans forge their own path in life, accompanied by their Guardians, without direction from any higher power.

But Gregor now sees fate as having led him to this place to fulfill a great purpose. As he was once mentored by an older Seer, so he intends to assist this newborn. He will remain in the area, see to her well-being, find ways to watch over her as she grows.

He knows he has much to plan, much to discuss with me. We are both aware that everything has changed. I will help him, as always, to do whatever he chooses. But this is a choice I would make as well. I agree with him that it is imperative to make whatever modifications to his lifestyle might be necessary to find a way to be a part of this child's life.

Thomas

When Stephen and Gregor return from their trip to Ellis Cliffs, it is nearly time to go to the club for supper. I see them pass by the window of my office on their way to the stables to return Samuel's buggy.

I lock the door behind me, then walk over to meet them at the stables.

"Welcome home, gentlemen," I greet them. "How was your day?"

Stephen grins and waggles his eyebrows up and down. Gregor laughs and tells me, "Doctor Duncan has successfully treated every malady at Ellis Cliffs, including the pining heart of one particular young lady."

"Oh really?" I ask interestedly. I can tell that it must have gone well, by all the grinning I am seeing from both of them. "I want to hear all about it over drinks!"

After Stephen hands over the reins to a groom, we turn back in the direction of the club, but somewhat to my surprise Gregor leaves us rather than entering. "You will have to excuse me, I am fatigued after our long day. And I had been up quite late last night."

Stephen looks at him, somewhat perplexed. "Aren't you hungry?"

"No, the Ellis luncheon included very generous portions."

"Oh, come with us," I plead. "I can't rely on Stephen to truthfully relate his interaction with Margaret Ellis today. He will exaggerate. Or leave things out."

But he shakes his head. "I apologize, but I really must retire for the evening. I will come by your office tomorrow, Thomas, while Stephen is too busy to come and listen, and we can compare notes to see if his account of the events matches mine." He smiles conspiratorially.

Stephen laughs and raises his right hand. "I promise to tell the truth, the whole truth, and nothing but the truth, counselor," he tells me teasingly.

Gregor claps Stephen on the back, then turns and walks towards his boarding house. Stephen shrugs and leads the way into the door of the club.

Samuel

I have been waiting for them to return, and am pleased to see Stephen and Thomas enter right as I am being served my supper. I do not see Gregor with them, which is a disappointment since I wanted to offer him an update on his bank transfer. I dispatched a messenger to New York soon after I spoke with him the other day, wanting the transaction to take place with even more alacrity than would be possible using the usual post. I instructed the messenger to change horses as needed along the route up the Natchez Trace path northward, to rest no more than absolutely necessary, and to transfer to one of my other messengers in Nashville. With a relay of messengers and horses, if the weather remains fine, and they encounter minimal trouble on the road, it is possible that Gregor's funds will arrive within a month and a half. The amount Gregor requested is not insignificant, and I want to make certain that he is pleased with the bank's services.

Founding this bank is the most important thing I have ever done, and I am committed to ensuring its success.

The boys join me at my table and quickly order their meals. "No Gregor tonight?" I ask Stephen. "Did you wear him out with your conversation?"

My nephew chuckles. "Apparently. I admit that I did make him talk about Margaret all the way back from Ellis Cliffs."

"And?"

He looks at me not with the grin I would have expected, but with a quite serious expression. "I want to marry her, Uncle."

Thomas goggles at his friend. Apparently this is the first he has heard of Stephen's decision.

I exclaim, "Oh! I see! That developed far more quickly than I would have expected."

"Well," Thomas asks reasonably, "does she feel the same?"

"I don't know, but I think so. I wish Gregor was here, he could provide more details since he actually spent more time with her than I did."

"How on earth did that develop?" I burst out. "Nephew, have a drink. Then you must explain everything to us."

Chapter 17

Steamboats

Gregor

I absolutely could not bear to spend another moment discussing the lovely Margaret with Doctor Duncan. Yes, of course this is the most important moment of his life, the day he set his sights upon the woman he plans to marry. And yes, I am very pleased for him. It is a good match, and both parties appear quite entranced with each other.

But watching one short-lived mortal make plans to unite with another short-lived mortal seems insignificant compared to my discovery of today.

I glance at Wolk, expecting him to chastise me for my uncharitable thoughts, but he simply regards me. I suspect that he agrees.

I'm sure I will feel guilty later about leaving Stephen alone to explain his blossoming love to Thomas and, I imagine, his uncle as well. But for now, I must allow myself to focus entirely on the reason for the cataclysmic shift in my reality which I experienced today.

Ayola.

It is overwhelming. I scarcely know how to begin.

I look at the shining wolf, not lying quiescent at my feet, but rather standing in the center of my small room, and decide that I do not want to discuss this with a wolf. "Man," I say to him.

He immediately transforms his appearance, the wolf melting away and being replaced with the figure of a man, the fellow who I have always felt most comfortable talking to when weighty matters are at hand. He appears to be an older man, far older than I will evidently ever appear, with silver at his temples, and creases on his forehead. He wears the old-fashioned garb of long ago, the simple peasant clothing I saw in my youth, a coarse tunic and hose, loose-fitting leather shoes, his head covered with a simple linen coif. I am comfortable with this man. I never knew my father, and Wolk long ago created this fatherly image to use when he knows I need guidance. He helps me concentrate and learn. And to cheat at poker, as we did the other night.

Wolk smiles, pleased that I can bring some slight levity to our momentous situation.

I collapse onto the wooden chair before the small desk. "I have to stay," I begin.

He nods, and seats himself upon the bed. I long ago became used to the fact that he can appear to do this, but the bed pays no mind. The mattress and covers remain stationary, unaffected by the apparent weight of the man upon them. "*Yes,*" he replies.

I realize my long period of roaming has ended. I will not go anywhere as long as Ayola is here in this area of the world.

I glance around the small boarding house room. "This will not do."

"*No. If you are to be useful to the child, you would be well-advised to become a more permanent member of this community, rather than a passing traveler.*"

"Well, let's make a plan, then. I'll have to find an occupation of some kind. And an actual residence."

"*What sort of occupation would you prefer?*"

I do not know. It has been years since I practiced any kind of profession. I have been a wanderer for a long time.

"*Possibly something similar to one of your new acquaintances? A doctor, perhaps? You have more medical experience than Stephen. Perhaps you could ask to join his practice?*"

"No, it would be peculiar to wait a week, watch him tend patients at Ellis Cliffs, then suddenly announce that, by the way, I am a doctor too."

"*True. Banking then? Law?*"

"No. The same problem would occur."

"*Merchant? Planter?*"

"It would take too long to establish myself. I have no land or goods. I wish to have a position as quickly as I can."

"*You do not mind manual labor. Perhaps you could apply at the docks?*"

"No, I've already become known here as a gentleman. That won't do either."

It seems too overwhelming, too much of a project to try to structure an entire life all at once. If my actual goal is the well-being of the child, maybe it would be better to simply approach it directly. I wonder if there is any feasible way to keep her with me. I feel my face wrinkle in distaste when I realize that there is a way.

"*Yes,*" Wolk comments. "*You could ask Abraham to sell her to you. Presumably you would want her to be able to stay with her mother, so you would have to buy Dalila also.*"

Ugh. I refuse to own slaves. The whole system is repulsive. But it is true, this would be one solution. "I would have to leave, though, immediately. I could not settle down in this area with the former maid of Margaret Ellis. It would seem very strange to everyone. Stephen would be annoyed with me for disappointing his intended. Besides, I don't have a home here, or anywhere else for that matter. Well, not nearby, where I could feasibly travel to with a newborn baby. I can't very well take her right now and then have no place for her, have no arrangements made for her well-being. Besides, I don't think disrupting her entire existence on a whim would be good for her."

"She does appear to be safe where she is, at the current time. Her mother is no longer working in the fields as she was before the birth."

I grimace again. I didn't know that. But it is true that Ayola seems safe enough inside the Ellis home, with her mother being allowed to keep the baby with her at all times in a sling.

"I guess I should leave her where she is for now. As long as she is safe and healthy at the Ellis plantation, I shouldn't try to swoop in and steal her away. I can just watch, and wait, and not take any action unless I need to. If any situation develops which seems unsafe for her, I can try to ... buy ... her then." I can barely make myself say the word out loud. The idea is revolting, but I will have to leave that open as a future possibility.

"In that case, you are back to the original problem of how to establish yourself in this community."

Yes. And I still have no idea how. What to do with myself in Natchez? We lapse into silence. I cast my mind around, picturing the town and surrounding area, trying to imagine where to fit myself into this society.

"Perhaps there is some way for you to enhance the area. Is there something that Natchez lacks, which you have observed elsewhere?"

Many things. For instance, transportation is limited, with traffic on the Mississippi River being essentially one-way only. The flatboat I rode into town is typical of the method used by most visitors arriving from the north. But there is almost no way to convey such a vessel back upriver. The current is too strong. In fact, the shipmaster was telling me on our journey that the boat I rode on was doomed, like most of the other flatboats, to simply be dismantled and sold for parts once it reached its destination in New Orleans. This is one of the reasons I will have to wait for weeks if not months for the funds to arrive from New York to Samuel's bank.

If only the new type of steamboat I saw demonstrated by a friend of mine three years ago in New York was available here.

I stop in my tracks. I had not even noticed that I had risen and was restlessly pacing again.

Steamboats.

My friend Robert Fulton had created new technology which allowed a boat to be propelled by steam. The ingenious design used burning coal to boil water, and the resulting steam then caused pistons to rotate a paddlewheel. When he demonstrated the newly built boat on the North River between New York City and Albany, his critics were silenced as it became clear that his boat was far faster and more powerful than those powered by sails or oars.

I believe the steamboat would be able to fight the current of the Mississippi River, and allow northward river traffic.

My mind spirals with the possibilities. Commerce and trade would be transformed. Passenger travel would become more popular. The cotton grown on the southern plantations could be easily transported to the other territories, not only in this region but more widely. Getting goods to northern and Atlantic ports would facilitate international trade.

I have quietly sponsored some of Robert's earlier experiments, investing in the intriguing ideas he presented. I am always searching for investments, not just for financial gain, but also for development, for progress.

I believe it is time for me to approach Robert again, propose that he consider turning his attention southward.

I drop back down to the chair at the writing desk, sweep off the books with my arm, and dip a pen into the inkwell. It is time to write letters.

Gregor's

Gregor lights one of the candles he purchased during his recent shopping expedition, not because he cannot function in the dark without it, but because it makes it somewhat easier to see the page, and the golden glow feels familiar. Much like food and sleep, the light of a candle is an optional comfort, which he utilizes because he enjoys it.

My beloved has found an ideal solution. As a gentleman newly arrived to this area, it will be welcome news to the town to hear that he intends to settle here and invest in improvements to benefit the business conducted at the docks. Many other men have done much the same, come to Natchez and determined how best to generate additional commerce in the new community. The river traffic is crucial to the area economy, and the promise of an easier method of transportation will be of deep interest to the local populace.

Gregor will be able to be productive and engaged, and will be seen as a valued member of the society. This will facilitate his actual purpose, which is to be nearby and watch over Ayola as she develops. He will ingratiate himself with the gentry, socialize with the proper families, find excuses to visit her home as frequently as possible. He will focus on her, and her needs, and will ensure that she thrives as she grows up.

I am struck with wonder and not a little amusement when I realize that he intends, essentially, to become her Guardian.

Chapter 18

Purpose

September 7, 1810
Gregor

As the dawn light begins filtering in through the window, I finish with my correspondence. I have a small stack of letters to take to the post office. I have written to Robert Fulton, describing the situation with the river in this area, suggesting that it would be profitable to establish a steamship route down the Mississippi River to New Orleans and then back north, and offering financial backing for the endeavor. Another letter instructs my agent in New York to provide the necessary assistance to Mr. Fulton should he request it, and furthermore to arrange additional funds to be transferred to the Bank of Mississippi, on top of the transfer request already made. I have even prepared letters to some additional acquaintances in the New York region, hoping to generate increased interest in commerce with the south.

I lean back after completing the last letter, and think about what my next step should be. Wolk waits quietly, having reverted to his wolf form while I completed my task.

It is too early for the post office to be open. I am brimming with energy after my night of writing, fully rested after having slept twice in the past week. I decide to return to Natchez Under-the-Hill, this time not to patronize any businesses, but simply to inspect the dock, and view the river.

Rosy

I rise with the dawn, alone in my accustomed cot, in the crowded room used by any ladies who have not spent the night with a customer. I know I am not entitled to have any expectations of a customer, yet I have been disappointed when Gregor did not return each of the last few nights. The last time he left me in the morning, he kissed me so tenderly and promised to return soon. I suppose it was too much to hope that meant he would be back in just a couple of days.

I have been warned by Madam, and by some of the more experienced ladies, not to grow attached to any of the customers. It will always lead to heartache, they told me, those men will never truly want you. They only want your body, and only for a little while, they admonished me.

But Gregor seems quite different. He is so gentle, even when greatly excited, and always pays attention to how I am feeling. The way he speaks, the way he listens to what I say, the way he makes me feel cared for, all draw me in. I fear that I have ignored all the warnings I have received, and feel myself already forming an attachment. And I dare to hope he feels the same thing. He has come to me twice already, even choosing me himself when he could have had anybody else.

I wonder when I will next see him again.

I rise from my cot, quietly moving from the room so I don't wake up the other ladies. After using and cleaning the chamber pot, I make my way to the parlor. Nobody else is awake yet.

I am gazing dreamily out the window, wondering when I will see Gregor again, when I gasp. There he is. Walking along the river, staring out at the water from the dock. He has apparently already passed by our building, and is walking in the opposite direction. What is he doing? Apparently just taking an early morning stroll?

I rush to the room where we prepare ourselves for our customers, and check the mirror to make sure I am presentable. I run a hairbrush through my brown hair, so long that it brushes against the small of my back. I inspect my brown eyes to make sure there is no morning crust, pinch my round cheeks to bring a blush.

In a few minutes, I am back in the parlor, ready to receive him. I check out the window again to see whether he is approaching, and my heart falls. I see that he has already passed by the building again, and is heading towards the path back up to Natchez.

Without coming to see me.

I feel tears spring to my eyes, and I angrily wipe them away. This is my fault for not listening to the advice I was given. I must remember my place. Gentlemen like Gregor are not truly interested in me, no matter how much they might like to use my body. I am not worthy of such a man.

Gregor's

He is filled with the most intense sense of purpose I have felt from him in decades. Possibly in his entire life. His mind swirls with thoughts and plans, idea mounting upon idea to form a complex strategy. People he must speak with, actions he must take, items he must acquire. I note and catalog it all. One of the functions I fulfill for him is memory.

He relies on my ability to relate to him any detail regarding experiences he has had or plans he has made. The entire being of a Guardian exists to enhance the growth of the human soul, to then forevermore retain the soul, full of all the memories of the human's life. In a sense we are built out of memories. We forever remember everything, every moment, every experience and thought our beloved humans have ever had. In my unique situation, in which the life of my Seer continues indefinitely, I accrue his memories over the years, decades, centuries. It is an extraordinary privilege to Guard a life which shows no signs of ending. I hope to never collect his soul and move on. My bond with him is extreme, far more intense and indelible than any other Guardian can know.

I marvel at his focus. For years he has drifted, aimlessly, feeling like a bit of flotsam floating above the waters of the human race. Now, he intends to dive deeply into the waters, with a very specific aim.

He will be a resource to Ayola. He does not know what this will require, or what form his participation will take. But he wishes to thoroughly prepare for every eventuality. He will bring all resources to bear upon his effort. His vast hidden wealth, collected over centuries and invested globally, will be used to support this goal. He will be a powerful ally to the young Seer.

He has not yet begun to make plans about her position in society. He knows that she and her mother are both enslaved, and therefore her social status is both objectionable and risky. However, his observations at the Ellis plantation convinced him that she is currently in a position which will best promote her well-being. Her mother is engaged in duties within the home, is allowed to constantly remain with her daughter in order to care for her, and is clearly a loving and diligent parent. The family appears supportive and reasonably kind. If he were to obtain information leading him to believe that this placement is risky to her, he would make a plan to change the situation. However, for now he believes she is in the best place for her current age and circumstances. This gives him some time to execute his plans for the steamboat project, which is the societal cover he will use to explain his presence in the community. None of the other humans will know of his true purpose.

After his inspection of the river along the dock, as he returns to the hillside path to the main town, I sense Rosalind's disappointment as she observes him pass by the brothel without stopping. I do not mention it to Gregor, as he is intensely concentrating on his unfolding scheme. All thoughts of dalliances with prostitutes have left his mind. It will not assist his mindset to be cautioned that a young lady is feeling sad due to his absence. It has happened countless times throughout his life, and in the grand scheme of things is unimportant.

When he returns to the main town, he first visits the post office to send off his letters. He knows it will be at least some weeks before he can expect any replies. In the meantime he intends to cement his relationships in the town, begin the search for a more respectable residence than a boarding house, and start to learn from the locals about river navigation. He has heard that the Mississippi River is difficult to traverse, and wishes to have all available details when he is able to discuss it further with Mr. Fulton.

Leaving the post office, he peers up and down the street. There is no question of him simply relaxing. He is far too energized. "What are Stephen and Thomas doing?" he thinks to me.

"They have both begun their days of work. Stephen is preparing to meet his first patient. Thomas is at his desk but has not yet begun the task he intends to fill his day."

He nods and briskly strides to the law office of his friend.

Thomas

I'm dawdling over my books, not really awake enough yet to concentrate on legal research. Once I get going on such a task, there is no stopping me, but I often find it hard to start. So when I hear the office door open I am not unhappy for the distraction.

Gregor comes in. "Good morning, Thomas. I hope I am not disturbing your work?"

"Not at all, Gregor, I'm very pleased to see you!"

"I promised to come by to give you a full report, and Stephen is already seeing patients. Is now a good time?"

"There could not be better. Sit down!"

He sits across the desk from me, with a crooked smile and a twinkle in his eye. He seems very excited to talk about Stephen's young lady.

"Well, Thomas, what do you want to know?"

"Everything, obviously. He actually told his uncle last night, perfectly seriously, that he wants to marry Margaret Ellis. So I want to know it all. I'm sure as an impartial observer your information will be more accurate than his."

He chuckles. "I doubt it. We thoroughly discussed every possible aspect of their encounter on our ride home, and I think he sees everything much as I did. But I will try my best to describe the visit. First, Margaret Ellis is quite attractive. She is delicate and pale, with clear blue eyes that followed him everywhere he went. She is clearly as smitten as he is."

I smirk. "Leave it to Stephen to settle on a delicate beauty!"

He goes on, "There is more to her than that. She seems intelligent, and is very kind and helpful in tending to her injured brother. I think she will be a good partner for him." He pauses, looks to the side, then says, "The only impediment to their relationship I can see at this point is the distance from here to Ellis Cliffs. It takes an hour or two just to get there, and the roads are no doubt not always in fine condition. I doubt that Miss Ellis would frequently have the opportunity to come north into town for a visit. It will always have to be Stephen riding down to her."

I shrug. An hour isn't too much of a distance, although it is true that Stephen will no doubt always be the party who must take the time to travel to her if he wishes to court her. He won't often have hours of spare time to spend on traveling.

Gregor says, "It might be better to take a boat to visit her. Her family's home is right on the river. The journey there would be much smoother than by horse."

"Well," I explain, figuring since he is new to the area, he must not really understand the way the river flows. "It would certainly be easy to go downstream for a visit, but it isn't possible to get back upstream. The river flows very strongly, so rowing a boat upriver is almost impossible. They have to be pushed along with long poles, or sometimes dragged by ropes that men hold from shore. It's really more effort than it's worth. You'll hardly ever see a boat headed north."

"You know," he says, strangely enthusiastic, "I saw a boat a few years ago that I'll bet could do it. It's a steamboat that was demonstrated on a river in New York."

"A steamboat?"

"Yes, they've invented a way to power a boat with steam. It's very impressive. I'll bet it would be strong enough to go north against the river's current here."

I can't picture it, so he asks for a pen and paper, and he draws a little diagram to show how the steam engine on the boat works to make the paddlewheels push the boat along. "It's far more powerful than rowing or sails," he tells me. "I'm sure it would work."

"Well, that is interesting. I wonder if we'll ever see any of those boats down here? I doubt it - Mississippi is a long way from New York."

He just grins.

Gregor's

My beloved has begun very deliberately sowing the seeds of interest in his steamboat project. As he has with Thomas, he will introduce the topic into conversation whenever possible. He knows from long experience that the best way to gain acceptance of a new idea within a community is to contrive a way for the topic to be discussed with regularity. The more it is brought to mind, the more people will want to discuss it. He will have Natchez clamoring for steamboats before too long.

Chapter 19

Productive

September 8, 1810
Stephen

Margaret has been on my mind all day. Those gentle blue eyes gaze at me no matter where I am actually looking. Examining a patient? Blue eyes. Writing notes on a chart? Blue eyes. Trying to walk without tripping over my own feet? Blue eyes. How have I become so thoroughly distracted?

I'm relieved when the day ends and it's time to meet at the club for supper. Thomas is already there when I arrive, and Gregor is just walking up to the door. We shake hands, then go inside to find Thomas and my uncle Samuel sitting together again.

"Welcome, lads," Samuel says, "good evening!" Sometimes I wonder whether his wife ever gets tired of him lingering here having supper almost every night. Shouldn't he be at home with his family occasionally? When Margaret is my wife, I won't neglect her like this. I feel a smile coming to my lips at my presumption. I should not count my chickens before they hatch.

Gregor chuckles, and I look over at him curiously. Did I miss something that somebody said? He just shakes his head.

We quickly start discussing the most important topic, of course, my pursuit of Margaret Ellis. Since Gregor has not been here for the past couple of nights, apparently being too fatigued to join us, he did not participate in our conversation. Samuel wishes to hear his insights about Miss Ellis as well as discuss some financial matters with him.

While Samuel is talking to Gregor about a banking transaction, Thomas leans over and asks me, "When will you be going back to Ellis Cliffs?"

"Another couple of days. I shouldn't act too eager. It will seem natural to go to check on my patient's progress every few days, but more could be awkward. Would you like to come with me next time, see the young lady for yourself?"

"I absolutely would," he says enthusiastically, then chuckles softly. "Gregor had the crazy idea that it would be nice to take a boat south to Ellis Cliffs, and I had to explain to him that the boats don't make the return trip north."

Gregor obviously overhears this conversation, for he breaks off what he is saying to Samuel. "Yes, Thomas explained about the river current to me. But I was telling him I've seen a boat which could go upriver against the current."

Samuel laughs. "Don't tell tall tales, my boy!"

"No, really," Gregor insists. "A few years ago I saw a steamboat demonstrated on a river in New York. It is powerful enough that it could easily navigate the Mississippi, going both south and then back north. It is quite fast, too."

I shake my head doubtfully, but Thomas chimes in. "Gregor was telling me about this the other day. He even drew me a picture of how it works, with a steam engine turning wheels covered with paddles to drive the boat." He pats the pockets of his coat and brings forth a paper with a diagram on it, and hands it to Samuel to inspect. He goes on, "I think it could be true, this kind of engine might be able to push a boat north against the current. But there's not much chance of getting a steamboat down here all the way from New York."

Samuel passes the diagram to me to examine. I try to understand what it is showing.

"Well," Gregor says, "I do know the inventor of the boat. I believe he might be interested in a venture to bring a steamboat here."

Samuel's brow furrows thoughtfully. "You really believe the boat could actually go against the current on our river?"

Gregor nods firmly. "I am absolutely certain of it."

Samuel leans back in his armchair, crosses his arms over his chest, and tilts his head to the side. "I do believe that would be a very fine development. Imagine how much easier it would be for our planters to ship their cotton if they could send it north on the river."

I laugh. "You're just thinking about how much money would come rolling into your bank if that could happen."

He raises his eyebrows and smiles at me. "Yes, indeed, nephew, that is exactly what I am thinking about. Yes, indeed."

Gregor's

His plan is already unfolding. He disingenuously asks, "Really? Do you think a steamboat could make much money for the planters here?"

"Oh, yes," Samuel says, pleased to have the "younger" man turn to him for wisdom and guidance, when of course it is Gregor who is directing the course of this conversation. My beloved knows how to subtly use every tool at his disposal, including flattery, to achieve his ends. Samuel goes on explaining, but of course Gregor already knows almost everything about the topic, having spent the entire day directing me to eavesdrop on all the townsfolk and relay every piece of information about river navigation and transportation alternatives that I learn.

"Since the flatboats can't go back upstream," Samuel tells Gregor, who directs an earnest gaze upon the banker, "they are usually sold for lumber either here or when they get to New Orleans. Then the boat workers have to travel overland to get back up to their home ports."

"That sounds terribly inconvenient for the workers," Gregor observes.

"Oh, you don't know the half of it!" Samuel enthuses. "Those Kaintucks usually stop off in town here first, causing all sorts of mischief Under-the-Hill. Then when they are walking up the Trace half of them turn bandit and rob any honest folk trying to travel on the road."

"The Trace?" Gregor inquires, continuing to unobtrusively lead the conversation.

"The Natchez Trace," Thomas interjects. "It's the trail to Nashville. It's really the only way to get back north from here. It starts right in Natchez, on the other side of town. Goes about four hundred miles over the worst terrain you can imagine. They call it the Devil's Backbone. You have to go through swamps, hills, rocks, mosquitoes, rattlers, brush, forest. Half the time it is so hot that people simply faint along the path. It's a dreadful road. Even going as fast as you can, it takes at least three weeks to get all the way up to Nashville."

Stephen adds, "President Jefferson sent some troops to try to clear it out, though, so I've heard the Kaintucks say that it is easier going now than it used to be. And I know the mail is able to get through to Nashville in closer to two weeks, changing horses along the way."

"Well," Samuel says, "even if the road itself is better, there are so many rascals out there ready to rob and pillage travelers that it is still a dreadful thing."

Gregor, eyes wide with apparent alarm, says, "I hadn't realized when I took passage on a flatboat to get here, it would be so much trouble getting back. Looks like I'm stuck here unless I want to suffer through the Devil's Backbone and risk getting robbed."

Samuel offers a smile. "Just stay here in Natchez, son, it is a fine place to settle, and with the funds you are having transferred you'll be able to set yourself up here in no time."

Gregor nods. "I might just do that." He pauses significantly, swallowing some whiskey, then adds, "It is a shame about the river, though. I would like to see those steamboats get established here, and spare travelers having to walk a dangerous road back north."

"But my boy," Samuel says, "didn't you just say you know the fellow who built that steamboat? Why don't you send him a letter, see if he'd like to consider bringing one of those boats here to Natchez? I'm sure if he could get a route established down here on the Mississippi, he'd end a wealthy man."

Gregor grins. "That, my friend, is an excellent idea. I think I should send that letter!"

"In the meantime," Stephen says, still squinting at Gregor's engine diagram, "I can't make heads or tails out of this picture you drew, Gregor. How does this thing work?"

Gregor leans in, enthusiastically pointing out the mechanics of the steam engine to his three companions.

"This is unfolding just as you planned, my dear."

"I know," he thinks silently to me, terribly pleased.

He is glad to know his scheme is going so well, but I can also see how much he is enjoying having a sense of purpose, regardless of the underlying cause. Yes, his goal is to be established in the community in such a way that his stewardship over Ayola will be both effective and unnoticed. However, even without that impetus, I know his energetic enactment of the steamboat project is good for him. He needed to find a reason for his life to be so prolonged, a way to feel useful, something productive to fill his endless days.

This is perfect.

Chapter 20

Visitors

September 10, 1810
Ellis Cliffs
Abraham

Marguerite has invited me to take tea with her on the veranda, which has always been her morning custom. I do not always join her, but this morning I would like to hear her report on the workings of the estate in my absence. We have not had the opportunity to do this since I arrived home. Richard's injury and the visits from the doctor and others have occupied much of my time.

The servants set tea and other refreshments on the table, then wait at a respectful distance. The morning is pleasant, the air already warm and dense with humidity. The insects buzz in the trees. The sky is a striking blue color, but the temperature has not yet climbed high enough to be uncomfortable. It will be a hot day again.

The Mississippi streams by, the water glistening in the sun. The ubiquitous Spanish moss droops from the trees along the river, and where the tendrils have grown long enough to dip into the water they are pulled south, making the strong southerly current clearly visible. I watch a flatboat glide past on its way to New Orleans, the oarsmen on the top fighting the lengthy oar, steering the boat away from the shallower waters and the sandbanks which can make navigation treacherous.

The summer is waning, and soon it will be time for the cotton to be gathered. I plan to discuss with Marguerite whether there have been any changes to the numbers of slaves available for the harvesting. I need to plan for any necessary modifications in assignments, to make sure we have sufficient field hands for the task. I know that she has moved at least one hand into the house to work as Margaret's maid. I want to make sure we aren't short in the fields.

"It will be harvest time soon," I tell her, once she has prepared our cups of tea.

She nods.

"I noticed you have moved one of the field hands into the house. I have to make sure we aren't short for the harvest."

"She just had a baby," Marguerite says, gazing at me from over the rim of her teacup. "She needed time to recover. And besides, Margaret needs a personal maid now that she is grown."

"Hm," I grunt. I don't approve of the new placement of the slave, but I certainly cannot explain why to my wife. She has placed temptation closer to me, right under my nose, but less attainable than in the fields where my family never goes. My wife no longer is interested in servicing my needs. I must take my comfort where I can find it, and having Dalila available in the fields made this easy enough, before she became too thick to be of further interest. I have noticed that now she is regaining her proper shape, although it is hard to see too clearly with that baby she insists on wearing slung across her chest. I would like to get a better look, but it will be difficult in the house with my wife and children constantly around.

Before I can inquire further about whether she has left sufficient field hands in place for the crop, Marguerite asks, "How familiar are you with Doctor Duncan?"

"I've seen him at the club in town a number of times. I believe he helps manage their operations sometimes. He seems respectable. Why?"

"Surely you noticed how Margaret was watching him?"

"What do you mean?"

"Oh, honestly, Abraham," she huffs. "Obviously your daughter has taken a fancy to Doctor Duncan. She has had a number of gentleman callers over the last few months, and none of them seem to have interested her as much as he does. I want to know more about him, so we can be ready to make a decision if he requests her hand."

I set my cup down, and watch as she refills it. "Her hand? Isn't that getting a little ahead of ourselves? They only met a few days ago."

She shakes her head briskly. "These things can progress quickly. And I believe that the regard is not only on Margaret's side. He seems to be interested as well."

Women! Is this the only thing they ever think about? I will leave such considerations to them. I need to focus on the coming harvest. I'll go seek out my overseer, he'll probably have better information anyway.

I stand. "Good morning, Marguerite. I should be back for lunch."

Margaret

It's been over a week since Richard's fall from the tree, and his quick recovery is definitely a mixed blessing for all of us. Of course, the family and servants are all delighted that he is getting along so well. We have all heard stories of people who end up getting a fever and dying after breaking a bone. Richard is apparently going to be just fine. He is definitely feeling better too. Dalila's special tea has become less needed every day, as his pain is subsiding while the bone mends within the splints provided by Doctor Duncan.

This is all wonderful news. The problem is that he is feeling so well it is becoming a real chore to keep him from jumping up and trying to walk around. We have reminded him over and over again that Doctor Duncan was very clear that he must not walk, even a tiny distance, for at least two weeks.

So, Richard being the most energetic and adventurous boy ever, he is insisting on being carried about all over the house by his manservant, trying to find something interesting to see or do from his enforced prone position.

We are currently sitting out on the veranda overlooking the river, Richard propped up on a chaise, Nancy and I trying to keep him still and stop him from running down to the water. It is a hot day, but Richard refused to remain indoors, so Samson has carried him out here. As a diversion we have recruited the garden slaves to bring up flat rocks from the shore, which we are trying to stack in towers along the paving stones. Richard has decided that Nancy, Samson and I must have a competition to see who can build the highest stack without the stones toppling over. We are all crouched on the ground before Richard's chaise, which has been drawn into the shade of a nearby tree, piling stones and teasing each other. He is laughing at our efforts, and we are all engrossed in our task, when the doorman approaches.

"Miss Margaret, Master Richard, Doctor Duncan has arrived to check on his patient." My mother must still be upstairs resting, as she often does in the afternoons, because the doorman would normally bring this information to her rather than me.

I stop what I am doing, my fingers poised to add another stone to my stack, which is currently the tallest of the three. I suddenly tremble, causing my stack to fall. Nancy laughs.

I quickly rise to my feet, smoothing my skirt. "Please show Doctor Duncan this way, it will be easier than moving Richard back inside."

I glance over at Dalila, and she quickly approaches, gives me an appraising look to make sure that my hair and clothing are in place, makes one or two minor adjustments, then nods and steps back. Little Ayola is awake, in her sling like always, but staring around herself, apparently enjoying the view of the sunshine, trees and water.

I check behind me, and see Nancy still sprawled on the ground next to Richard's chaise. "Nancy! Up!" She is nearly a young lady, but has not yet started to develop any sense of decorum. She looks up from the rocks she is still stacking, sighs, and rises from the ground to stand beside me.

The doorman arrives with Doctor Duncan. I feel my heart hammering and my cheeks blazing as my eyes fall upon him, looking as tall and fine as before, and I realize that he is staring straight back at me.

Nancy

My sister scolds me into standing up with her, but then she doesn't even have the presence of mind to greet our guests. She only has eyes for Doctor Duncan, staring at him, practically drooling. She obviously hasn't even noticed that two other gentlemen are with him. And she thinks I'm the one who doesn't know how to act like a lady.

So, I step forward, leaving her there with her eyes bugging out, and greet the visitors just like Mama would. "Welcome, gentlemen, to Ellis Cliffs. We are very pleased to see you here. Thank you for returning, Doctor Duncan." The men all smile and nod.

This shakes Margaret into action. I think I shamed her, having her baby sister take on the hostess role. She comes back to life and greets the gentlemen as well.

Doctor Duncan says, "I am happy to be back. My friend Mr. Slavson you know from our last visit, but may I also introduce another friend of mine, Mr. Thomas Butler."

We offer seats on the patio to the gentlemen, and Margaret sends to the kitchen for cool drinks and refreshments, while Doctor Duncan draws a chair over to the chaise where Richard is lying. While he spends time examining Richard's leg, Margaret talks to the other men.

The servants come with beverages and sweets, and serve everybody. Mr. Slavson takes a drink but he is still being very odd, not saying a word, and I can tell that he is staring at Dalila and her baby again. But as soon as I think that, he looks away.

Mr. Butler is laughing and talking to Margaret about boats or something. He has the most interesting face, with sleepy eyes but a happy expression, and this contradiction in his features makes me want to keep looking at him. I see him glancing my way as well.

Chapter 21

Stroll

Gregor

It is astonishing what a delight it is to be in the little Seer's presence. The radiance of her being is like a salve to my soul, bringing a sense of healing to a wound I hadn't realized was there. It is as though I had not even noticed that I felt a terrible loneliness, and being with her suddenly relieves the feeling. It is very strange, and very welcome. I savor every moment she is nearby.

I am calmer than I was at our first meeting, now that the shock has worn off. So I am better able to analyze her situation. She has grown even more, and although still less than a month old, she is remarkably alert. Her eyes seek me out quickly, and she stares in my direction. I wonder what she is seeing and feeling. I know that Wolk hides us, but clearly she senses more than the other humans around us do.

"Her brain is obviously undeveloped at this young age, so her thoughts are not yet fully organized. Her eyes are drawn to you by the same glow you sense in her, even though it is concealed from her Guardian by the glamour I have cast over you. Her Guardian is perplexed by your presence, and cannot fathom why the little Seer is so taken by you. I do not know how long my concealment of our thoughts can endure with this pair."

"Try to keep it up for as long as you can, Wolk," I think to him. "I believe it would be best for Ayola for me to remain as anonymous as possible until she is older."

"I will redouble my efforts," he assures me.

I glance at the shining wolf sitting attentively at my feet. I wonder what form Ayola's Guardian has taken.

"Her Guardian has thought along the same line as you, that anonymity would be the best way to protect the new Seer. The Guardian has chosen to remain formless, in an effort to

avoid having Ayola staring too obviously in that direction. The child can see only a slight shining mist."

I am glad to know her Guardian is already trying to find ways to protect her. Her position is inherently risky, her safety only possible as long as the Ellis family chooses to indulge her mother's protection. I am very pleased that Dalila has been assigned to be Margaret's maid, especially if Margaret and Stephen are going to be eventually married. Dalila would presumably accompany her mistress to whatever home they choose, and I feel this would enhance Ayola's safety going forward.

"Who is her father?" I silently ask Wolk.

"Abraham Ellis."

This is unpleasant but also unsurprising. One of the horrifying aspects of the slavery which has been established in this land is the liberty owners feel to sexually abuse their slaves. The serfdom into which I was born had some similar aspects to the modern day system of slavery, but the serfs were generally treated like human beings, not like beasts or chattel. Many of today's owners indulge their lusts freely, without regard to the feelings of their victims, and as is obviously the case here, pay no heed to the offspring of such liaisons. Except to note that a new slave must be added to the roster.

I will monitor the situation as closely as I can, and if I get wind that there is any danger to the child, I am not above offering to purchase Dalila and her infant myself. It would be awkward and raise eyebrows, and would probably necessitate moving to a different area to avoid gossip. I would prefer to let things unfold as they are now, with the steamboat project already underway. If my plan works, I will be seen as a prosperous investor and member of the community, and it will be some years before I will need to make further arrangements for Ayola.

Stephen

"I am pleased with how your leg is progressing, Richard. You aren't trying to get up and walk at all, are you?"

His middle sister, obviously eavesdropping on my examination of her brother, lets out an abrupt laugh. I look over at her. "Oh? Is there an issue?"

Richard crossly commands, "Be still, Nancy!"

But she pays him no mind, and tells me, "We have had to practically tie him down to keep him from trying to walk."

I do not let a smile come to my face. I had surmised as much. "Richard," I say, trying to sound serious and stern, "you must be patient for another few days. It is really very important that you don't put any weight on the leg, because we do not want the bone to slip out of place while it is mending. If it did, you might end up walking with a limp, and I am sure you don't want that."

"Richard, you must listen to Doctor Duncan," I hear his mother admonish him, and look up to see her coming onto the veranda from the house. "I must apologize for not being available to receive you earlier, gentlemen. Welcome to our home."

I stand and make a brief bow, then introduce her to Thomas. We are soon joined by Abraham as well, who has apparently been surveying the fields with his overseer.

I explain to Richard's parents that my examination of his leg shows his progress is satisfactory. I tell them quietly that I actually have brought crutches with me to leave here, and although Richard should not use them yet, I believe in another three or four days he can be allowed to try them, still avoiding placing weight on his leg. But with the crutches he should feel a better freedom to move about. I suspect that the entire house will be pleased by this development.

Now that my medical duties have been discharged, I feel at liberty to join Margaret who has been speaking with my friends. As I sit nearby, I see her appealing blush grow deeper, while she meets my eyes then looks demurely away. The pale blue eyes which have been haunting me are even more beautiful in reality than in my dreams.

The afternoon is very pleasant, and when Abraham offers to bring us on a brief tour of his grounds, including a walk along the river, we are all pleased to accept. Margaret and Nancy both accompany us, so our afternoon stroll is taken in very charming company.

Gregor, who has seemed oddly distracted, at once becomes engaged when we approach the shoreline, questioning Abraham about the riverboat traffic which passes the plantation, and asking his opinion about whether he would find a benefit to having access to a steamboat for shipping his cotton. Once he explains the concept, Abraham seems quite interested.

In the meantime, Margaret and I are simply enjoying each other's company. She has taken my arm as we stroll about the grounds, and we are mostly silent as the others discuss shipping and other plantation business. Every moment I spend with her cements in my mind my desire to have her.

As Margaret and I are absorbed in each other's company, and Gregor and Abraham animatedly pursue their conversation about shipping, Thomas and Margaret's little sister are left to pursue their own discussion. He is a good sport, seeming quite happy to entertain the little girl while the adults are occupied.

I begin to plan my courtship. Gregor is right, the distance does present an impediment, but I am committed. I am pleased that for at least the next few weeks, my ongoing care of Richard will give me the excuse to come to Ellis Cliffs two or three times a week. By then I will have made my intentions clear, and my visits will be acceptable without the pretense of medical necessity.

Too soon, it is time to take our leave. We regretfully decline the invitation to stay for supper, as Thomas has a meeting scheduled this evening at the club, to discuss a position in the militia which has become available to him.

I kiss the hand of the lovely Margaret, trying to imbue my action with enough feeling that she cannot mistake my purpose. Her blush grows, yet she does not drop her eyes. She smiles, gives me a brief nod, and my heart leaps to believe this is her answer. Soon, I resolve, I will find the opportunity to draw her aside and speak to her in a more private manner of my intentions.

A stableman pulls Samuel's buggy around, leading the horses by the reins as he walks in front. The Ellis family gathers to say their farewells, Richard held gently in the arms of his manservant. Gregor quite cheerfully clambers back onto the little luggage bench at the back of the buggy, which he had offered to take in relinquishing the spot on the bench in front to Thomas for our journey. At least he won't have to hold the crutches I brought for Richard on the way back up.

As we round the bend, Thomas is waving goodbye to the family.

"Well," he immediately starts once we are out of sight, "you have certainly selected the perfect prospect for a wife, Stephen. She is wonderful. I wish you all the best."

I encourage my friends to discuss this in more detail, eager to hear every perception, every suggestion to advance my cause.

Gregor chuckles from his perch on the rumble seat, "Stephen, I believe your cause is already won. Every member of the Ellis family seems half in love with you already. Your only danger is in waiting too long to propose."

Thomas laughs and agrees. "They are a very pleasant family. Margaret's little sister is quite a lovely young lady as well."

I glance sideways at him. "She is a child, Thomas. Hold your horses."

He shrugs, unconcerned. "Nancy told me she is nearly fourteen years old. That is not so very young. In a couple of years, she will be fully as beautiful as her older sister, don't you think?"

Gregor laughs from behind us.

We continue to chat amiably all the way home.

Chapter 22

Awaken

September 18, 1810

Natchez

Gregor's

It has been nearly two weeks of non-stop activity on the part of my beloved. His days are filled with tours of Natchez, becoming acquainted with all of the shopkeepers and property owners, charming the ladies and impressing the gentlemen. He regularly visits the docks, to observe the river traffic and talk with the shipmasters about their opinions regarding navigation on the Mississippi River. He dines at the American Eagle club every evening, almost always joined by his friends Thomas and Stephen, and frequently Samuel.

He has accompanied Stephen twice more to Ellis Cliffs, and delights in the presence of little Ayola who stares transfixed at him whenever he is nearby. Her Guardian continues to wonder at the unusual obfuscation which interferes with any attempt to understand the thoughts of Gregor or myself, but begins to grow accustomed to our presence and less concerned about the sense of mystery created by my glamour.

Throughout all of his activities, Gregor inserts the concept of steamboats into his conversations with other people at every opening. The community indulges his desire to constantly discuss the issue of shipping, both intrigued by his interesting personality and mysterious accent, and gratified by his substantial expenditures wherever he goes. His generosity with money has caused him to request a line of credit from the bank pending the completion of the funds transfer, which Samuel was more than delighted to supply.

At night, he reads books, reviews any navigational charts he has been able to obtain from boat captains, creates maps of the ports along the river. He has discovered a publication called The Navigator which details the waterways in the region, and often studies it carefully. He has me constantly on the lookout for any thoughts that the humans in the area have about shipping, navigation, or travel.

He knows that he has at least another month to wait before his funds arrive, and probably longer until he receives a reply from Robert Fulton regarding the possibility of bringing a steamboat to this area.

He has decided to reside in the boarding house for an indefinite time, having determined that there are a number of other gentlemen or travelers who do this. It is not considered terribly unusual by this community to stay in such a place rather than obtaining a more permanent residence. Remaining here for at least a while longer will not raise unwanted attention. He knows that eventually he will have to move to a more respectable home.

For now, he is perfectly content with the lodgings. He has never slept in the narrow bed, does not even consider whether it would be comfortable. In fact, it is as though he has entirely forgotten the concept of sleep.

His body has not, though. Even though such rest is not as necessary as it is for other humans, he cannot go entirely without sleep for this long without suffering consequences.

It is late. Supper was hours ago, and his friends have long since retired. He stares blearily at the map he is perusing, and discovers that it shakes slightly with a tremor in his hand. He feverishly stares around the room, abruptly feeling claustrophobic and unsettled.

He suddenly realizes what is causing his problem. He feels burdened by the weight of his terrible fatigue. "How long has it been since I slept?" he wonders.

"It has been two weeks, my dearest. Too long."

He sighs and nods, defeated. He crosses from the desk to the small bed, pushes aside the books and papers he has stacked upon it, and lies down, closing his eyes.

It does not work. Even as exhausted as he is, sleep eludes him. He restlessly turns over on the narrow bed. He remembers the last time he slept, the method he used to achieve it. Rosalind comes into his mind for the first time in many days. He is shocked to realize that even though he had been so taken with her before he met Ayola, he has given her no thought at all. The memory of his time with Rosalind is titillating, and he finds himself growing aroused.

He sits back up. "What is she doing?" he asks.

"Rosalind has finished with her work for the night, and is sleeping on her cot in a room with a few other ladies."

"Hmph." He lies down again, but knows it is futile. After a few minutes he pulls a random book off the floor next to the bed and holds it up, but is too tired to focus on the words. He drops the book and covers his face with his hands. He considers masturbation, but knows that it will be insufficient to bring him relief and rest.

"My darling, although Rosalind is sleeping, Madam Beverly is awake and some other ladies are still available for the evening."

"What time is it?"

"Nearly midnight."

He looks around the darkened room, then suddenly sits back up and starts putting on his shoes. He cannot bear the idea of another sleepless night of pacing, unable to either read or sleep. "I wish Rosy was available," he grumbles.

"Although she is sleeping, my dear, I suspect that Madam Beverly would be perfectly willing to rouse her for your benefit."

"It would be rude to disturb her."

"Frankly, beloved, she believes you have already been rude to her."

"What?"

I have not shared with him the longing of Rosalind, because I did not wish to disrupt his plans, but I sense this is the right time. *"She has been very disappointed not to spend time with you after your last night together. She has even seen you through the window, passing by the brothel as you approach the docks and speak with shipmasters, and feels quite neglected when you do not visit. You had promised to return to her very soon. It has been two weeks."*

He is staggered. "Oh," he breathes, stalled for a moment in his preparations to leave his room.

He recovers quickly, retrieves his coat, and puts it on as he runs down the stairs and towards the path leading to Natchez Under-the-Hill.

In a few minutes he is being greeted by Madam Beverly. "Welcome back, Mister Gregor, we had begun to fear you were never going to return," she smiles at him.

"Is it too late to order a bath and a room?" he asks.

"Not at all. The best room is still available this evening, and the staff could have water boiling for a bath in a few minutes. We are most happy to oblige." She glances at the few women still lounging in the parlor, waiting for any late-night customers who might come trailing in after visiting the taverns and gambling halls. She beckons them forward. They begin to approach sensually, but Gregor stops them. "I would like to have Rosy for the night, if you please."

Beverly dons an expression of deep regret, and tells him, "I am grieved to tell you, but Rosy has already retired for the evening. Any of these other ladies would be delighted to serve you."

"I prefer Rosy," he says, uncharacteristically heedless of how this statement will be received by the women he is rejecting. He is determined to make amends to Rosalind for having ignored her for two weeks. "I will pay double."

Her eyes widen. "Of course, I will go rouse her at once."

"I would like to do it."

She begins to disagree, as the customers are never allowed in the back room, but he goes on, "Please, I insist. I promise that I will not disturb any of the other ladies."

She is loath to disappoint such a big spender, so she defers to his request. "Very well. Please follow me, very quietly."

Rosy

The hands which rouse me are unusually gentle. Normally in the morning we are just awakened by an unceremonious shake. I open my eyes, assuming it is time to get up, but am confused when I see it is still dark. Is something wrong?

I swivel my head around, both sleepy and alarmed, and I hear a soft "Shhhhh."

When I focus on the source, I am utterly shocked to find Gregor kneeling here next to my cot, Madam Beverly silhouetted in the doorway behind him. The other girls are still sleeping all around me.

"Please, Rosalind," he softly whispers, clearly making every effort not to wake anyone else, "would you be willing to come upstairs with me?" I can't make out his face in the dark, but his manner is so gentle, softly caressing my cheek as he speaks.

I realize I am only wearing the plain nightgown I sleep in, not my usual costume that I don to appeal to the customers. I'm sure my hair is in a complete tangle. I am not presentable at all. "But I'm not dressed," I whisper.

I hear a very low chuckle. "I prefer you this way. Please."

He holds my hand in one of his, and with the other he reaches behind my back to help me to my feet. Madam Beverly steps back from the door to let us through, then closes it quietly behind her. Nobody else even knew Gregor was in the room.

I meet her eyes, wondering what is happening, and she remains silent but nods. I know that she has agreed to this.

I need to use the chamber pot. As we move past the antechamber where we dress, I indicate the door with my hand and start to ask, "May I…"

"Of course, please," he says. "I will wait here. Please don't bother with dressing." He smiles warmly at me, like he knows exactly what I was thinking.

I feel myself blushing and step through the door.

Rosy's

She has longed for him, alternating between anger at his neglect, and self-loathing for what she assumes are her deficiencies leading to the loss of his desire.

Finding him crouching at her bedside in the middle of the night is both bewildering and exhilarating. She ducks into the little chamber to use the pot and swish water in her mouth, then quickly rejoins him in the hall. Without speaking, he takes her hand and leads her to the stairs.

Madam Beverly tells him, as they pass, "The hot water will be up shortly."

He nods, leading my beloved to the room they have enjoyed before.

I continue to be perplexed by the unusual opacity of his thoughts, along with those of his Guardian. It is unsettling not to know the plans of a man interacting with my beloved. He does not appear likely to harm her, but I would prefer to be able to anticipate his movements, adjust my whispers to her accordingly.

Once they are inside, before he commences any physical interactions, he simply stands before her and states, "I owe you an apology, Rosalind. I told you that I would come to visit you again soon, but I have stayed away too long. I am sorry for disappointing you."

She considers objecting to his statement, claiming that of course she is not disappointed, that he is perfectly free to come and go as he pleases, but she does not. There is something so sincere in his tone. She believes he truly comprehends how she has been feeling. She does not wish to belittle his understanding of her sentiments. She simply nods, staring at him with wide eyes.

He apparently wishes to clarify. "Can you forgive me, Rosalind?" he asks.

"Yes, Gregor, of course," she murmurs. A smile brightens his face, and gladdens her heart.

He begins to reach for her, but she is embarrassed over her appearance, in the nightgown she would normally never allow a man to observe, her hair in a loose nighttime braid. She feels disheveled and unprepared for company. The gown provides far more coverage than her usual costume, but in it she feels more authentically herself, rather than armed for the role she plays for the customers. It feels more intrusive, more personal, for him to see her in this way. She nervously runs her hands over her hair. "I must look a fright," she says, lowering her eyes.

He smiles at her. "I like this so much more than your other costume, Rosalind. You look like a genuine woman, a warm and loving creature, not someone being paid to act a role. I would love to see you as a woman who wants to be with me, just as she is."

She does not truly understand what he means, but she is happy to be with him, and tries not to be embarrassed over her attire.

He laughs softly. "You know, Rosalind, if you are embarrassed about what you are wearing, I can quickly solve that for you. We'll have this nightgown off in no time, and you will only be wearing your glorious skin. Will that make you feel better?"

She giggles back at him, and relaxes into the experience.

Gregor leads her to the settee to relax while they wait for the water to be fetched for the bath. She leans against him, enjoying the familiar experience, and the unhurried manner in which he conducts himself. It is so different from all the other men, who usually rush to complete the sexual act then go on their way. With this man, it seems that he wants to enjoy her company, not merely her body.

"I saw you from the window a few times," she boldly tells him, sensing that he would find it acceptable for her to make conversation. "I was afraid you were going to get on a boat and go south, but instead you just walked around or talked. What were you doing?"

"That's exactly what I was doing. Walking around and talking. I have an idea for a new kind of boat that might be brought to Natchez, and I am trying to learn everything I can about the boats which dock here." He seems amused by the turn this conversation has taken. It continues to slightly frustrate me to not be able to penetrate the meaning behind his statements.

"What new kind of boat?" she inquires.

He chuckles. "I have done nothing but talk about boats for two weeks. May I tell you later? I would rather concentrate on you."

She blushes, and nods. In silence, he begins to undo her braid, and spends the minutes until the bath is prepared simply brushing and caressing her hair. She feels it as an intensely intimate and arousing experience.

"My darling, enjoy the attention this man is paying to you, revel in the delights you know he will bring to you tonight. I will enjoy it all with you, my dear, this will be an evening of pleasure and joy."

Gregor

I don't know how I let two entire weeks go by without remembering the luscious Rosalind.

I feel Wolk's amusement. He knows exactly how it happened, and truly I do too. I was so obsessed with my project, I simply forgot about her. But being here again, enjoying her sweet presence and placid nature, I am resolved to visit more regularly. I should not allow myself to be so distracted with my work that I grow exhausted. Being overly fatigued might interfere with my plans, cause me to make mistakes. I cannot allow that to happen, and visiting Rosalind is the preventative. This is simply another important piece of business I must attend to.

Wolk actually snorts out a brief guffaw.

All right, fine. It is not just business, it is admittedly pleasure.

Once the bath is prepared, Rosalind delights me by assuming control. She is the one who undresses us, guides me to the large metal tub, tenderly washes my body, then allows me to wash hers.

Next she recreates the scene from our first night in reverse, instructing me to sit upon the chair next to the tub while she remains within and demonstrates the techniques she has learned so well.

Hours pass as we drive each other into a veritable frenzy, and eventually collapse together, exhausted, into the feather bed. She has again brought me the sweet bliss of rest. I needed this, so much more than I had realized. I needed her.

Chapter 23

Engagement

October 4, 1810
Ellis Cliffs
Margaret

I knew when to expect Stephen's arrival this time. When he last visited, he was focused on helping Richard move about with his crutches, allowing him to start trying to rest just the smallest amount of weight upon his foot when he stands. We will all be forever grateful to the doctor for tending Richard so diligently. It is clear that he will heal completely and have no permanent impairment to the injured leg. He will continue to grow as strong and fine as he was before the accident.

Stephen and I have not had the chance to speak privately before now, with the family always being nearby. But he told me last time, drawing me aside to speak quietly out of the hearing of the others, that on his next visit he wishes to speak to me alone. He told me the planned time of his next trip to Ellis Cliffs, so I have been eagerly waiting for him since an unnecessarily early hour of the morning.

My heart is thundering in my chest as I see him arrive in his buggy, this time accompanied by his friend Mr. Butler. I know Nancy will be pleased by that. She seems to have taken a liking to Thomas Butler.

I have discussed with Mama what Stephen told me, about wanting to speak with me alone. She nodded wisely and said, "Leave it to me."

So, after we have greeted the gentlemen and brought them through the entrance hall into the parlor, I am not surprised when Mama contrives a way for us to speak privately.

"Nancy," she tells my sister, "perhaps you can show Mr. Butler some of your drawings." She turns to Mr. Butler, and goes on, "My daughter is becoming quite an accomplished artist, and has made several sketches of the trees along the river. I believe you will find them to be admirable."

As they turn their attention to the sketches, Mama mentions, as though just remembering, "Oh, that reminds me. Margaret, do you remember while Nancy was sketching, we were trying to discover a good place to build a dock for the boats which Mr. Slavson speaks of? We had hoped to show him on his next visit, but since he has not come today, perhaps you can take Doctor Duncan down to the river and ask his opinion about the best location." Stephen immediately stands and reaches down to help me rise as well. Mama goes on, "I'm afraid, Doctor Duncan, that Mr. Ellis is occupied at the moment with his overseer, but after you view the river location I am sure he would like to hear your thoughts about a suitable place for a dock."

Bless her heart, my Mama knows exactly what she is doing.

Stephen offers me his arm, and we cross to the doors open to the veranda. The warm breeze is coming in, blowing the curtains, offering little relief from the heat. It is a very bright day, and Dalila quickly fetches my parasol for me to use to shield my face from the sun. Stephen offers to hold the parasol for me in his other hand.

"You may wait here, Dalila," I tell her.

I am both eager and terrified to hear what Stephen wants to tell me while we are alone. He is silent as we step off the patio and approach the river, but once we are at the shore, gazing out over the swiftly flowing water, he turns to me, and takes my hand in his. He still considerately holds the parasol with his other hand, to keep the sun from my eyes.

"Margaret," he says, gazing at me, "I hope you have noticed how I feel about you."

I feel a blush climbing up my throat.

"We have not known each other for very long," he goes on, and I am surprised to hear a slight tremor in his voice. Can this accomplished and confident man actually be feeling nervous to talk to me? "But since we have met, every time I see you I admire you more and more. Not only your beauty, but your thoughtfulness, your kindness, your whole demeanor."

Can a blush grow so hot that it actually causes a person's cheeks to burst into flames? It feels likely. Although, I am lucky to be in the company of a doctor in case it happens. This silly thought lifts my lips in an amused smile, and I am relieved to see that rather than being taken aback by my apparent attack of humor, he seems encouraged.

His words grow more rushed, seeming less like a rehearsed speech and more like a spontaneous outpouring of what is contained within his heart. "I think of you every moment, Margaret. When I go back to Natchez all I can do is long to come back here, to see you again. I can hardly sleep at night for imagining your face, and when I do sleep all I do is dream of you."

I feel my mouth fall open in amazement, for he is describing exactly the way I have been feeling. He stops talking, suddenly seeming tongue-tied and more nervous than ever.

I am moved more than I can ever express. "I feel exactly the same way, Stephen." He closes his eyes for a moment, as though savoring the sound of his name on my lips. "I dream of you every night, and think of you every day."

Joy floods his face. "I was afraid I was imagining it," he whispers hoarsely. "Can it be? Do you really want me too?"

Emotion seizes control of my voice, and all I can do is nod fervently.

"You have made me happier than I have ever been," he says, and I hear all the emotion in his voice as well. "I love you, Margaret, I think I have loved you since the first moment I saw you, reading a book to Richard."

I feel tears spring into my eyes, and I whisper the truth that only my own heart has heard until now. "I love you too."

His face transforms into an expression of firm resolve. He drops to his knee before me, the parasol abandoned on the ground, and clasps both of my hands in his. "Then, Margaret Ellis, will you have me? Would you agree to marry me, and be my wife? I will promise to spend every moment of the rest of my life loving you."

I can scarcely speak, but I manage the most important word I have ever uttered. "Yes."

Marguerite

While Nancy and Mr. Butler are occupied with her drawings, which he peruses with apparent interest and delight, I am keeping my eye on the scene down by the river. They have conveniently paused right in a spot where there is a break in the foliage and I can see them through the parlor window.

My heart surges as I see him drop to one knee before her, take her hand, and ask the question I know it must be. When she agrees, they both seem filled with joy.

It has only been a few weeks since they met, but that does not make their feelings any less real. They have clearly been enamored with each other during their entire acquaintance. A speedy engagement will seem less scandalous as long as we allow a decent length of time to pass before the actual marriage.

My mind is already swirling with plans as I see him rise and take her arm again. I watch them stroll together along the river with all apparent happiness, until they have passed beyond my sight.

I am sure that even Mr. Ellis will be happy with the new arrangement, when Doctor Duncan comes to ask his permission and make the engagement official.

This is a very good match, made in obvious love, and will be quite suitable for everyone. The question of where the new couple will reside shall be resolved in time. My mother's heart is content.

Natchez
Samuel Postlethwaite

I have not been to the club for supper in some days, well over a week. I wished to do my duty to my wife. She was safely delivered of our son William last week, to join his sister, my darling little Matilda Rose. I feel that I have allowed a respectable enough passage of time before returning to my habitual meetings at the club. My position with the bank requires me to spend time with the other gentlemen of the community, and dining at the club is the best way to accomplish this.

Furthermore, I wished to return in the hopes of hearing from my nephew whether today's mission, for which he again borrowed my buggy, was successful.

I arrive early enough that my nephew and his friends have not yet arrived. However, Gregor comes in soon after me, and joins me at my table.

"Good evening, Samuel," he greets me in his unusual accent, which I have grown accustomed to hearing in the month or two since he arrived in Natchez. "I have not seen you in a few days. I hope all is well at home?"

"Indeed it is, my boy, indeed it is. I have a fine new son, William."

He smiles and reaches over to shake my hand. "Congratulations. This is wonderful news."

I thank him, then add, "Once my nephew arrives, I hope to hear more good news. I believe he had made specific plans for his trip to Ellis Cliffs today."

Gregor grins. "I know. No-one of Stephen's acquaintance could possibly avoid hearing about it constantly for the past week."

I laugh. "I have rarely seen a man so enthused as Stephen has been over the lovely Miss Ellis. Let us hope that his planned proposal went as he hoped."

Speak of the devil, the man himself enters, with his friend Thomas. I can see at once the answer to my question. Stephen's face is split into a grin so wide that I can scarcely imagine how it fits onto his head.

He can't even wait to sit down before crowing, "She said yes!"

"Congratulations!" Gregor and I exclaim at the exact same instant, leading to hearty laughter by all.

Soon Stephen is providing all of the details of his romantic proposal to the young lady, their mutual professions of love, his later conversation with her parents. Far more information than is truly seemly to share between gentlemen, but it is hard to disapprove of my nephew's exuberance. Young love is a charming thing to behold. Thomas is mostly smiling in silence, presumably having been treated to this narrative already on the drive home from Ellis Cliffs.

"When will the wedding take place?" I ask Stephen.

"Her mother wishes to wait until sometime next year. She seems to think that decorum requires a lengthy engagement, considering how quickly the proposal took place."

Thomas guffaws. "What, you mean a month after meeting is considered a fast proposal?"

Stephen protests. "It's been more than a month!"

Scoffing, Thomas teases, "Barely!"

Just then, another gentleman approaches and interrupts our conversation. Militia Inspector Moore sits with us for a few minutes to speak to Thomas about a matter with the militia. It soon becomes clear that he is planning to recommend Thomas to the governor to lead a new cavalry regiment. Apparently Thomas has been considering how best to eventually move into politics, and feels a military commission would be a beneficial step.

After the discussion is completed, Gregor raises his glass, and says, "Gentlemen, I believe we must have a toast. Congratulations are in order for all of you. In one moment it seems we have a son, a spouse, and a soldier. Huzzah!"

"Hear, hear!" I exclaim, lifting my glass and taking a hearty gulp. "Now, if only we can acquire your steamboat, there must be superlative congratulations all around."

Gregor grins. "It will happen quite soon, I feel certain."

Chapter 24

Mail

October 19, 1810
Gregor

I am just leaving the boarding house in the early morning, intent on walking to the King's Tavern to visit the post office and see if any mail has come for me, when a young messenger rushes up to me. "Mr. Slavson," the boy says breathlessly, "Mr. Postlethwaite sent me to tell you that he would like to see you at the bank at your earliest convenience."

Ah! This can only mean one thing. My funds must have arrived at the bank. "Thank you," I tell the lad, and follow him through the streets of Natchez, crossing the short distance to the bank on Main Street.

When I enter, Samuel sees me from his private office and beckons me over. With a smile, he says, "I am very pleased to tell you that your funds transfer has been completed!"

"What excellent news, Samuel, and very impressive timing. It has not even been two months. I appreciate the alacrity with which your bank was able to handle this."

There are some additional transactions to conduct, involving the arrangement of accounts, and the payment of the line of credit I have been drawing against since I arrived. I am left with substantial funds, nearly ten thousand dollars, enough to serve my current purposes.

After we have concluded our business, he asks me, "So how is the steamboat project coming along? Have you ever heard back from your friend in New York?"

"Not yet, but I expect a reply any day now. In fact, I was just on my way over to the post office to check for letters when your messenger arrived. Once I hear back, I am hoping to be able to get to work on coordinating with my friend. Also, by the way, I wrote to my agent and asked for additional funds to be transmitted, which I expect to be arriving soon as well. If things unfold as I expect with the boats, I will need more than what you have obtained for me."

His face glows with a mercenary delight. "Pleased to be of service, my boy, very pleased indeed."

"You are clearly succeeding in cementing your friendship with Samuel, beloved," Wolk wryly comments as I leave the bank.

"It must be due to my charming personality," I silently reply. "It can't have anything to do with the money, can it?"

The wolf yips out a laugh. I have to avoid laughing myself, lest passersby think I have lost my wits to be laughing at nothing in the middle of town.

My next stop is the post office, and although I have been checking daily for replies to my letters, I have not really expected any quite yet. However, I am excited to find that Robert Fulton has indeed responded to my letter. I tear it open and read it where I am, standing heedlessly on the street.

In five minutes I am back in Samuel's office.

Samuel Postlethwaite

As the boy leaves the bank, I shake my head in wonder. He really is a perplexing fellow. He is quite young, no older than my nephew certainly, yet he manages his substantial wealth with a nonchalance I rarely see. I have tried to question him about his background, about the source of all this money he has access to, but have not managed to learn anything very tangible. He seems quite good at deflecting questions. I get the impression that he comes from some sort of minor European nobility, but the details are very vague. He apparently lost his parents at a young age, but has an inheritance which sustains his quirky lifestyle.

Most of the people I know who have access to this kind of money would enjoy more lavish living. At least would insist on more luxurious living quarters. But Gregor still lives in that modest boarding house, for God's sake. He could easily rent or buy any decent house in town, now that he appears to have decided to settle here. But he seems content to live a plain life, even as he generously spends money at all the merchants' shops in Natchez. Including mine, the general store I founded when I first arrived in town a few years ago. I am obligated to spend more and more time at the bank lately, and have had to hire help for the mercantile. There isn't enough time to spread around between the two enterprises.

The bank keeps me busy enough, and with more customers like Gregor infusing capital, it is beginning to thrive. Still, his unusual spending and living situation are perplexing.

Well, as long as he lets me manage his funds for him, I suppose it is not for me to question his unusual life choices.

"Samuel?"

I look up from Gregor's papers, which I am gazing at unseeing while I allow my mind to speculate about his background, and find him standing before me again.

"My boy! I had thought you already left. Did we forget something?"

He has an excited grin on his face, and he is grasping a sheet of paper in his hand. "No, this is something new. There was a letter for me at the post office, from Robert Fulton. He agrees with the idea to bring a steamboat to Mississippi, and plans to start work on it immediately!"

"That is tremendous news! What does he say? When does it start? What can I do to help?" He stands still in front of my desk, and I belatedly invite him, "Please, sit down."

He settles again into the chair across the desk, and begins to fill in the details. "Mr. Fulton tells me that this was an idea he had already considered, and had even sent an expedition down the Mississippi River last year in a flatboat to explore and evaluate the possibility of navigating a steamboat along the entire river route."

"Is that so?"

"Yes. In fact, he says that the explorer stopped here in Natchez. His name was Nicholas Roosevelt, he traveled together with his wife. Do you happen to remember hearing about this?"

This is astonishing news. "Remember hearing about it? Why, my boy, I greeted Mr. Roosevelt myself! He came into town for supplies, and I met with him when he came to the bank to exchange some notes. We had just opened the bank last year, you know, he was one of our first customers. What a small world! I had no idea he was exploring for the inventor of the steamboat. He only told me that he had been hired to map and evaluate the river."

"What a coincidence that is," Gregor says, clearly amazed.

"Now that I think of it, I remember they had some trouble with their boat while it was docked here. The river level got so low for some reason that their flatboat was damaged by the mast of a sunken ship below where they were docked. They had to acquire a rowboat here to go the rest of the way to New Orleans."

Gregor's eyes are wide, so interested is he in this news. "Indeed?" he exclaims, then tells me, "Well, Mr. Fulton says that when the Roosevelts returned to New York, Nicholas supplied him with a detailed report on his findings about the river. This convinced him that navigation would be possible. Robert has already decided to begin building the steamboat he plans to make the voyage."

"It is already being built?"

"Not quite. Robert has been seeking investors. He has one, Robert Livingston, but he will require additional funding. I had told him in my letter that I would be pleased to sponsor his project, so he has already contacted my agent in New York. Plans are underway to begin construction in Pittsburgh soon. It might have already begun, since this letter was sent a few weeks ago."

"They'll build the steamboat in Pittsburgh?"

"Yes, and from there it will travel down the Ohio River to meet up with the Mississippi. Robert is optimistic that by the end of next year, we will see a steamboat in Natchez!"

The weight of the moment descends upon me, a sense of destiny. This enterprise could transform our region. We are isolated, rich with farmland and cotton, but poor with the ability to transport it. Here I sit, in the midst of a plan that can change everything.

"This could change everything for Natchez," Gregor says seriously, clearly thinking along exactly the same lines as myself. "For the entire region. Once shipping up the Mississippi River is possible, cotton production will be even more profitable than it is now."

"I know, my boy, believe me, I know." I grin at him. "I don't know what made you decide to stop off here in Natchez, but I am surely glad you did. I believe this just might be the thing that really puts us on the map."

He nods happily.

"Well, in the meantime, Gregor, what else can I help you with? What do you think you will need to do now?"

"I believe I should open an office here in town. I will need someplace better than my room at the boarding house to collect the papers and maps and things that I have been preparing. Over time perhaps it can become a sort of depot to help arrange for shipping and transport, but for now I just need a simple place to work. Do you have any suggestions for where I can find a location?"

"Yes, my boy, I do indeed."

We get to work.

Chapter 25

Property

November 26, 1810
Ellis Cliffs
Abraham

It is hellishly aggravating. I could simply return to the fields to pull one of the female hands away to service my needs again, but I don't feel the urge while I am outside, during the day, working with my overseer. I am older now, I do not feel aroused as frequently as I did when I was a younger man.

But here in the house, it seems every time I look up, there is my daughter's maid lingering about, and it reminds me, provokes me. I've had many slave women, of course, but there is something about Dalila that particularly fans my flames. I don't know what it is. Her figure is nubile, of course, and has returned to its prior slender state, now that the little bastard is a few months old. Something about Dalila's indigo dark skin, or her gentle gracefulness, or her clear dread of me, is enormously enticing. It makes me feel like a young man again.

But I am stymied by the constant presence of my family. Every time I see the slave, of course she is with her mistress, my daughter. My wife and other children seem to be constantly in every room of the house. I am entitled to use my property however I please, but I know Marguerite would not approve, and I do not want to face her pursed lips and stern frown.

I feel somewhat preposterous to be fantasizing like I did when I was a youth. It is distracting, preventing me from focusing on business.

I push aside my books of account. It is late, already after midnight, and I am sure everyone else in the household has long since retired. The candles are burning low in my private study where I spend my evenings. I can't concentrate.

This is ridiculous. She is my slave, this is my house. How can I be so timid, to allow the fear of annoying my wife to prevent me from taking what is mine?

I leave the study, prepared to retire for the night. But after I climb the stairs in the darkened house, only a few candles left burning by the servants to light my way, I pass Margaret's room.

Dalila is there in the alcove, on her sleeping mat near Margaret's door. The baby is sleeping on the floor next to her, in a little cradle made of a box I suppose someone has helped her to contrive to prevent the child from rolling off in the night. It is dark, so dark I can barely make her out, her skin blending into the night. But I see the glint of her open eyes, the dim candlelight penetrating the darkness just enough to reflect there as she waits in silence, watching warily as I pass by.

It is those watchful eyes that are my undoing. I must have her.

I step over to stand at the side of her sleeping mat. "Get up," I command in a whisper. The fear that springs into her eyes arouses me even further. She reaches to lift her baby, but I tell her, "Leave the child."

She silently obeys, rising to her feet, her face lowered so far that I cannot see her eyes any more. "Follow me," I tell her.

I lead her back down the stairs to my study. It is private here, far enough away from the family sleeping upstairs that no sound will disturb the silence. It is nobody else's business what I do, what I must do.

As I close the door behind her and grasp her shoulders to force her to face me, the tears silently beginning to flow down her expressionless face only serve to excite me more.

Dalila

I have only the power to prevent myself from crying out. So I endure in silence, holding myself still, making no sound. I cannot stop the tears. I cannot keep him away from my body. But at least I can refuse to let my voice be heard in response to what he does to me.

When he's done, he lifts himself off of me, and brusquely says, "Go." He doesn't even look at me. I prefer it that way.

I try to rearrange my skirt as I slip quietly back out of his study. I have to stop by the chamber pot we slaves are allowed to use in the closet where cleaning supplies are kept. I need to try to clean up, wipe away the mess he left behind. I don't want to climb the stairs, lay down next to my baby, feeling him still leaking out of me.

I know it was too much to hope it wouldn't happen again. He has been staring at me ever since he found me here in the house. I should try to feel lucky that I have had a few months of peace. I must try to suppress this rage, this despair.

I wipe away the last of the tears as I climb the stairs and lay down again on my mat. Ayola is awake, but not crying. She never cries. But I can tell she has been waiting for me. She is lying on her stomach, and when she sees me arrive she pushes up with her arms, raising her head and shoulders above her blanket, and offers me a smile. She's grown big enough that she can roll over now, lift herself up, grab hold of things. She is my light, my love, my life. I would give up and let the despair take me if it wasn't for her.

I pick her up, since she's already awake, and cuddle her to me. She lays her head down on my chest, and I feel her little hand reach out for mine. She holds one of my fingers in her fist. I feel the peace that comes from holding my baby flow through me. I can ignore what the Master does to me, endure anything, as long as I can keep her with me.

Margaret

When Dalila comes in to tend me, holding Ayola in her arms rather than the sling she used to carry her in, she seems unusually subdued. She lays the baby down on the floor, where she can roll around and kick her legs, then comes over to start arranging my hair.

I look up at her reflection in the mirror. Her eyes are rimmed with red. "Are you quite well, Dalila?" I ask her.

"Yes, Miss Margaret, I am fine," she says very softly, then doesn't say anything else. I suppose whatever it is, it's none of my business if she doesn't want to talk about it. Ayola is obviously fine, so apparently there isn't anything that need concern me.

Ayola starts babbling out a little stream of sound, in her tiny voice. "She is trying to learn how to speak," I say, hoping to distract Dalila from whatever is on her mind.

It seems to work. Dalila doesn't quite smile, but she replies. "Yes, she truly is. I keep hearing things that sound like words, but she's only three months old. She can't talk yet. She's just practicing."

Ayola babbles some more, then reaches down and discovers her foot, and shoves it into her mouth. She talks to us some more around her toes, and there is no way for even Dalila to avoid laughing.

There, that's better now.

Marguerite

The plans for the wedding are proceeding. We have determined to wait until next September for the nuptials, giving about a year from the proposal, which seems a proper length of time. Stephen comes to visit Margaret at least once a week. Whenever they are together, they have to be prodded to stop mooning at each other and help plan for the future. I declare, those young people would spend the entire next year gazing romantically into each others' eyes if I let them, and never accomplish a single practical thing.

Abraham has determined to make a wedding gift to them of the land and house at Homochitto, a property much closer to Natchez. They can establish their own home and plantation there. Whenever Stephen visits, after I manage to pry Margaret off of his arm, Abraham spends time with him in his study, and around the grounds, advising him about how he should manage his own plantation after the wedding. I am relieved that Abraham appears to be keeping his increasingly erratic temper under control as he interacts with our future son-in-law.

Stephen checks Richard's gait every time he visits, but the broken leg has long mended, and my son seems more rambunctious than ever, driving his tutor and manservant to distraction with his wild ways. I sometimes feel it is more difficult to manage him as a healthy young man than it was while he was an invalid.

There is so much to consider, to arrange, to plan. I find myself increasingly fatigued as I attempt to undertake the project of planning Margaret's wedding and future home. Margaret and Nancy help as much as they can, but they need so much guidance from me still. My days are so full I can scarce keep my eyes open after supper, before I must retire for the evening. I often even have need of rest during the afternoons. I must be getting old. I am glad that I will see my eldest daughter settled soon.

Chapter 26

Connection

November 30, 1810
Gregor

My regular correspondence with Robert about the progress of our project fills me with optimism, but also dread. I begin to realize I will have to go to Pittsburgh to oversee some of the operations. The delay in corresponding by post is lengthening the time which will be required to complete the project. I am heavily invested in the building of the steamboat, and it would seem peculiar indeed for me to be so disinterested that I could never be bothered to lay my eyes on the production of the ship.

I have never before been so reluctant to travel. But the very impetus which caused me to become involved with this project, is the same thing that holds me back from fully participating.

Ayola.

I cannot bring myself to abandon the little Seer by leaving this area for the months which would be required to travel to Pittsburgh to view the boat's construction. I have vowed to be her protector, to watch over her. How could I do that from a thousand miles away?

I continue to be fairly confident that her current position is safe. Her mother's status as a house servant provides her with some security and stability. I also know she is unlikely to fall victim to any illnesses which might visit the household, assuming that she is as healthy as I have always been. Wolk believes it is so.

But there is no way to predict the future. I cannot know if some dire circumstances would arise in my absence. It is unthinkable to be unavailable in the case of some catastrophe.

I am stymied. It is almost a relief that the year is far enough into the colder season that leaving any time soon would be impractical. It gives me an excuse to continue dallying while I try to decide what to do.

Today I am accompanying Stephen back to Ellis Cliffs for his weekly visit to the family of his fiancée. Thomas is with us as well. Once my funds were fully transferred to Samuel's bank, I was able to purchase a more suitable carriage for travel, so all three of us are now able to sit in comfort for our excursion. I admit I don't miss perching on the rumble seat at the back of Samuel's buggy. Holding the reins during the journey is vastly preferable.

All three of us have reasons to eagerly anticipate the visit. Stephen, of course, is so overcome with love for his Margaret that he can think or speak of little else. It is deeply pleasurable to watch their love, pure and new and young. Humans have always coupled, have always found mates, but rarely do the emotions involved burn as brightly as theirs. Even Wolk marvels at the intensity of their love. Margaret is truly a lovely young woman, perceptive and kind and thoughtful, and Stephen is lucky to have found her.

Thomas is infatuated with her spirited little sister. Stephen thinks little of this, because Nancy is not old enough yet for true courting, or to be considered as a possible bride. However, I see the situation for what it is. Nancy might be not quite fourteen years old, but Wolk tells me she feels the same way about Thomas. They are each quite determined to pursue each other, even though they are both aware their wait must be longer before they can become engaged. Furthermore, fourteen years old was not too young to be married in the era I was born. My first wife and I were barely older than that. But in the current society Thomas will just have to be patient.

And I, of course, savor every moment I can spend with the little Seer. As she grows, she appears ever more wondrous to me. Her development seems somewhat accelerated, her abilities coming to her a bit faster than most infants. She is just over three months old now, and despite her premature birth, is advanced in her skills. She rolls over easily, reaches for objects, is beginning to try to communicate verbally. Nothing the other humans really notice as being unusual.

They do notice, however, that she never cries, is incredibly alert and engaged with her surroundings, and watches everything around her with a knowing expression of deep interest. They find it endearing, enjoying having such a happy infant in the house for the first time since Richard was young. Even the Ellis family admires the baby of Margaret's maid, playing with her and sometimes even holding her quite naturally, as though she is a member of the family.

None of them except Abraham and Dalila know that she actually is a member of the family, the half-sibling to the Ellis children. Marguerite suspects but does not allow herself to spend time speculating. Wolk has told me that Dalila wants very much to keep the knowledge hidden, fearing Ayola would be unwelcome if the truth were known.

In the meantime, it is soothing to see that Ayola is in a situation where she is being cared for and loved. Her father disregards her, but everyone else in the house, whether family or servant, is fond of her and watches out for her well-being.

The thing I can see, which none of the other humans will ever behold, is her radiance. Her eyes seek mine at every opportunity, and I have become the frequent recipient of her charming baby smiles. I watch her from across the room, not wishing to be too obvious in my admiration of her sweetness. Her creamy brown skin, her caramel colored eyes, her growing curls, an adorable little dimple in her cheek. And of course the shining aura surrounding her. I adore it all. Even as an infant, she is entrancing.

I know I will never have a child of my own, but I suspect that the love I feel for the little Seer must be as strong as that of any parent.

Dalila

The gentlemen are visiting with the ladies in the living room, not the smaller parlor since there are more seats here for the whole group. I am standing at the back, behind Miss Margaret, alert as always lest she might need anything.

Margaret glows happily as she gazes at Doctor Duncan. I am glad for her in her love, despite what her father has been doing to me at night after everyone else is asleep. I am relieved he has not come to join the group yet today, so he isn't here to stare at me and make me dread what is coming to me later. I push down that thought. I try to separate those times from everything else, treat it as though it is only a bad dream, to be forgotten in the light of day.

I am holding Ayola, who has grown enough that she is squirming around, rather than contentedly snuggling against me as she used to do. She reaches for the floor, but it wouldn't be seemly to set her down in this company, so I just shift her over to my other side and keep holding her.

But she is dissatisfied with this. It is funny how sometimes she seems like she is another adult, the way she looks at me with such knowing eyes. She starts loudly babbling, as though she is scolding me for not letting her down to play. "Ma ma ma ma ma!" she exclaims. I am torn between laughter and fear. I do not want her antics to cause me to have to start leaving her alone while I am working. I try to shush her.

Margaret turns around with a laugh, hearing Ayola's little speech. "I declare, it sounds like the baby would like to join the conversation!" I start to apologize, but Margaret stops me. "Why don't you lay her here on the floor, Dalila, I know she likes rolling around. You wouldn't mind, Stephen, would you?"

"Of course not," he smiles at her. Although I know if she asked him if he wouldn't mind jumping off the roof or being buggy-whipped he would say the same. I am certain there isn't anything he wouldn't agree to for her.

I am nervous to do this, afraid that not everyone would agree, but when I glance over at the Missus, she smiles and nods. "Go ahead, Dalila, you can let Ayola play on the floor. She's never any trouble."

So that is how she ends up laying on the ornamental rug in the middle of the group, and entertaining all the white folks. Even the gentlemen seem amused, laughing while she waves her arms at them and babbles some more, then starts gobbling on her own foot. Richard plunks himself down on the floor next to her, and starts playing peek-a-boo, obviously relieved to have something better to do than listen to the adults chatting. After a while everyone returns to their conversation, and Ayola seems happy. So I just leave her where she is and stay back behind Miss Margaret, watching as my baby starts rolling herself over.

Gregor

It could not have worked out better. Usually I find my visits somewhat frustrating, because I have to make sure not to spend the entire day obviously staring at the baby. I think having a grown man spending too much time ogling an infant would seem disturbing to some. So, having it arranged that the primary entertainment of the visit is to have the entire group gathered around while Ayola cavorts on the floor is perfect.

I see her gaze around the group, trying to locate me, and quickly her eyes meet mine, as they always do. She has learned how to roll over, and is becoming more proficient at it. Once the conversation resumes, and Richard manages to slip outside to find some other amusement, I am the only person paying true attention to the baby, except for her mother, of course. And soon enough, I realize what she is doing. She is pumping her arms and legs to make herself roll over, then once she gets her bearings she rolls over again.

She is coming to me.

"Yes, my darling, Ayola wishes to be near you. She is trying to reach you."

My heart soars, to see this tiny infant, barely old enough to control her movements, making a deliberate effort to reach me. I can't go and help her, it would seem strange to the others, but I watch intently as she makes her way across the floor.

Margaret is also watching her again, and laughs as she sees the little display. "Look at that!" she says. "She is rolling over just like a log in the river!" There is a general outburst of amusement at the baby's entertaining antics.

Sooner than I would have expected, she is about to roll right onto the feet of the side table next to my chair. Alarmed that it might hurt her, I impulsively reach down to prevent her from colliding with a hard object. As she rolls from her stomach to her back one more time, I nudge her aside, using my hand to shield the side of her head from hitting the wooden table leg.

As I make contact, as we touch for the first time, I am instantly flooded with a tremendous warmth and joy, my entire body flushing with the connection. It takes my breath away. I haven't felt this since the last time my old Seer friend, Yosh, gave me a final embrace as we said farewell. It was ever this way with him, this sublime sensation. Like the warm sun on a cold day, like a delicious meal while starving, like cool water after walking in the heat, like sexual release after a long deprivation. It brings a sense of completeness, of relief, of fulfillment. There is nothing else that can truly compare. I doubt that normal humans have ever felt anything like this.

It only lasts a moment, because Dalila quickly rushes over and picks her up. "Excuse me sir," she apologizes, as though Ayola's intrusion was somehow unwelcome. I can only nod to her. There is nothing I can say to express how welcome it actually was.

But, as soon as she lifts Ayola away, the baby lets out a whimper, clearly not wanting to be parted from me.

Margaret looks over at Dalila, surprised. "Well, it looks like she's had enough excitement for one day. Why don't you go ahead and take her upstairs and put her down for a nap, Dalila. I'll be fine here."

Dalila quickly leaves the room with the child.

I glance over at Wolk, ready to share with him the amazement I am feeling, and discover that he has transitioned into his man form, which he does not usually do unless I request it. Furthermore, the man seems more overwhelmed than I feel.

What is going on?

"Her Guardian knows, Gregor. There was no way to keep hiding you once you touched her."

Chapter 27

Revelation

Ayola's

My beloved stares at the man Gregor once her mother lays her on the floor, as she always does whenever he visits the plantation. I know there is something unusual about him, and apparently she senses it as well. I have never been able to read his thoughts, or those of his Guardian. They are occluded, concealed, inaccessible. It is unexplained and troublesome, but has not seemed dangerous to Ayola, and I have grown accustomed to it.

I have never understood what it is about him that draws her eye. She can see me, but she cannot see other Guardians. Her perception of humans is normal. Other than his hidden thoughts, Gregor does not seem very different from other people. He is a quiet young man, thin, with pale skin, dark hair, and somewhat intense dark eyes in a chiseled face. I suppose humans would consider him attractive, but this is not something that Ayola is old enough to recognize. He does seem interested in Ayola, which in itself is not terribly unusual. Most humans are drawn to her, finding her appealing due to her happy nature and intelligent gaze.

When she begins making a deliberate effort to reach him, using her new rolling skills, I am charmed but not too perplexed. As she grows, it is natural for her to find ways to achieve her goals. She doesn't know how to crawl yet, but has lately learned that rolling is a good way to bring herself to something she would like to inspect more closely. Since she often watches Gregor, presumably she wants to get a better look.

But then, when he reaches down to protect her from injuring herself by crashing into the table leg, and his hand makes contact with her little head, everything becomes clear.

There is a blinding flash of light, an explosion of warmth, as the auras of the two merge. And at last I see what is now impossible to hide.

He is a Seer too.

That is what she has been sensing.

I am overwrought at the unexpected revelation. My emotional response to this development completely seizes control of me. I am paralyzed with shock.

How could I have missed this?

At once I see his Guardian's manifestation transform from that of a wolf, into that of a man. And, to add to the overwhelming and bizarre developments still flooding my being with emotion and confusion, the man image looks directly at me, and speaks.

Speaks, to me. Speaks to another Guardian.

Guardians do not speak to each other. Why would we? We always know everything any other Guardians nearby know. With this one exception. I have never imagined another Guardian speaking to me, holding a conversation resembling that of humans.

But the Guardian speaks.

"Excuse me," the man says, *"I was concealing my Seer from you. Obviously this is no longer possible. I am sorry for the confusion."*

All I can do is stare speechlessly at the Guardian, at the form of the man.

As her mother carries my beloved upstairs, and I of course move along with them, I maintain contact with the Seer and his Guardian. Being in a different area of the house makes no difference to my ability to see and hear what is happening elsewhere.

I can do nothing but wait to see what the Guardian will say next.

Gregor's

"Are you quite well, Mr. Slavson?" Margaret asks. She sees him staring after Dalila as the servant leaves the room with the little Seer, and notices that my beloved seems shaken.

It rouses him, redirects his attention to the room around him. "Yes," he replies, "yes, of course. I was just concerned that the baby was all right. I tried to prevent her from hitting her head, but it sounded like she was crying." He tries to direct the conversation away from his own behavior, which he does not wish to appear strange to the others.

Marguerite smiles. "How good of you to be concerned, Mr. Slavson. The baby is quite well, you do not need to trouble yourself."

He nods, and is relieved when the conversation moves on without him, leaving him to question me in peace.

"What just happened?" he asks me silently.

"When you touched the little Seer, it created a burst of illumination. The souls of Seers are especially powerful, and when they make contact, there is a rush of energy which is visible to their Guardians."

"That didn't used to happen with Yosh," he objects.

"Yes, it did, but I never needed to mention it to you. It did not influence your interaction with him in any way. But even if you could not see the visible effect of the contact, you felt it."

"I did," he admits. "I know she did too. It felt ... wonderful. I had forgotten how wonderful. It's been so long since I was with my old friend."

He surreptitiously looks to the side, to view me standing in my man form, while he pretends to concentrate on the discussion the others are having. "Why did you change forms?"

"As you know, I have been disguising you, as always, so that our thoughts are hidden from other Guardians. This was effective with the Seer's Guardian until you made physical contact with her. The Guardian is connected to her soul, as I am to yours. When the souls met, the blast of energy this created was far too powerful for me to hide. The other humans' Guardians did not sense it, but Ayola's Guardian immediately recognized that you are also a Seer."

"It was inevitable," he thinks to me, resigned to this development. "I should have realized there was no way to keep me a secret from her Guardian. What now?"

"The Guardian was entirely overwhelmed with the realization of your nature. I transformed into my man form, thinking it might assist with the further shock of my initiating conversation. Guardians do not speak to each other. I have never spoken directly to a Guardian other than Yosh's before. I will attempt to explain to the Guardian your purpose."

"Isn't that obvious, since my secret's out?"

"No, as soon as your contact with Ayola ceased, my concealment of your aura resumed. The Guardian knows of you, but still cannot sense either of our thoughts. This is why I must converse directly."

He considers. He wishes to maintain our habitual anonymity, but recognizes it will be a barrier to communication with Ayola's Guardian. Now that the Guardian knows the secret, he wishes to be more open. "Can you make an exception for Ayola's Guardian? Just let that one hear our thoughts?"

I change my image to reflect a facial expression of bemusement. *"I do not know, beloved. I have not attempted this previously. I can try. First I must have a conversation with her*

Guardian, who is waiting with some perplexity to hear from me. Since our thoughts are still hidden, our current conversation has continued to be private."

"Well, carry on, then," he tells me. "Keep me updated about how they are both doing."

Stephen

I feel the life behind me dwindling in significance compared to the life which lies before me. My upbringing, my education, my medical practice, all seem to fade as I face my upcoming position as a husband and plantation owner. Truthfully, when I first considered courting Margaret, the fact of her family's prosperity did cross my mind, and I imagined that securing an engagement with her would bolster my financial plans.

However, that was reduced to unimportance once I realized how deep my feelings for her had rapidly become. By the time I proposed marriage, all I was thinking about was how desperately I loved her, how much I wanted her to love me back. The bliss of hearing her accept me was utterly transcendent.

Now that more time has passed, and I grow acclimated to the idea that we are truly going to be married, my original consideration of financial security has come again to my attention. The love Margaret and I share only grows with each visit. But I am also being made to understand the practical ramifications of this union.

Her father has already informed me of the overwhelming gift he intends to settle on her at our marriage, the generous plantation lands near Natchez. He is making every effort to instruct me in the workings of a plantation, and during each visit to Ellis Cliffs he carves aside time to educate me on proper management techniques.

I am deeply grateful to him, for not only granting me his daughter's hand, but also ensuring that I will be able to properly support her and our future family.

Dalila

I have no idea why Ayola suddenly seems fussy. She has never fussed before. I have never heard any sounds other than happy ones come from her mouth. But she is whining unhappily as I carry her out of the room and up the stairs. I was watching as she rolled over and Mister Slavson kindly reached down to shield her head from the table leg. I know she isn't hurt. I worry that perhaps she is getting sick.

When we get to our sleeping place, I sit down and offer her my breast, hoping to comfort her and get her to settle down for a nap. Soon she is nursing, eating as enthusiastically as always. If she is becoming ill, it isn't affecting her appetite.

Soon enough, she drifts into sleep, and I lay her in the little box that Samson and Richard helped me make. The young master was so kind to think of it, when he overheard me mention to Miss Margaret my concern about Ayola rolling away in the night. So I can feel secure to leave her here, knowing she will stay inside while I am not here to watch. I know it won't keep her contained for long, because soon she will be sitting and crawling and a box will be nothing to her. But for now it is enough. I go back downstairs to wait on my mistress.

Dalila's

My beloved puts the little Seer down for her nap, perplexed by the baby's unusual discontent. Both Ayola and her Guardian seem strangely unsettled, and I cannot understand why. After the baby's brief interaction with one of the guests, both she and her Guardian became agitated.

The guest is unusual, with oddly hidden thoughts. I have never before encountered a human whose thoughts are not accessible. Neither are those of his Guardian. It is very peculiar.

But, it does not seem to be anything that can affect my own beloved, so I do not spend time accessing the thoughts of the baby's Guardian to try to untangle the mystery. My priority, as always, must be the well-being of my own beloved, my Dalila. So I whisper to her, trying to provide comfort and support and love.

"Worry not about your baby's health, my darling, I have never seen a healthier human child. All is well."

All is not entirely well, of course. Dalila knows that tonight she must dread the sound of Abraham's feet on the stairs as he climbs them in the dark, wondering whether he will again summon her to his study. Her helplessness tears at me. It is agony to experience her violation, to be unable to protect her or assist in any tangible way. All I can do, all any Guardian can do, is try to bring some vague sense of solace, whispering words which are never heard, but that sometimes might generate a feeling of peace in troubled times. I will be ready again tonight.

Chapter 28

Explanation

Ayola's

As the other Seer's Guardian presumably explains to him what has occurred, I watch Dalila feed my beloved and lay her down for a nap. Little Ayola was uncharacteristically whimpering after being parted from the other Seer, and I have only a slight understanding of why.

I sense from my beloved that at the moment she and the man Gregor made physical contact, when their souls touched and flared as one, she experienced a blissful sensation unlike any other. She felt a warmth from him, a light, which corresponded to the brilliant flash created as their auras burned together. The moment she was deprived of the new sensation by being lifted away by her mother, she longed for it to return.

She wanted to go back to the other Seer. She senses that they are the same, that they belong with each other.

I am still overwhelmed at the presence of two Seers together. I have never heard of this occurring before. A Seer is an incredibly rare creature, and it seems so unlikely for two of them to meet each other as to be actually impossible.

Yet, somehow, it has occurred.

Gregor's Guardian soon finishes their conversation and again addresses me directly. *"I apologize for the delay. My Seer had questions which I needed to answer."*

I direct a sense of understanding to the Guardian, and realize I am going to have to join this conversation, actually attempt to communicate directly with another of my kind. It feels very strange, but I make the effort. *"Thank you,"* I say to the Guardian, then am at a loss to know what else to say.

"Gregor calls me Wolk," he tells me, *"I would be very pleased if you would do the same."*

A Guardian with a name? This situation grows more and more bizarre. *"Yes, Wolk."* I hesitate. *"I ... have no name."*

"Of course. I expect at some point your Seer will give you one, when she is old enough to begin communicating with words."

I agree. It had not occurred to me until now that this might occur, but as Gregor has named his Guardian, it does seem logical. Humans assign names to all sorts of creatures, and I suppose I should expect to receive one from Ayola someday.

I take the initiative in the conversation, and sense Wolk's slight surprise that I am able to do so. I believe I am learning quickly. *"How is it that I did not recognize Gregor as a Seer until he touched Ayola?"*

"It is because I deliberately conceal his aura, and our thoughts, from other Guardians. He long ago determined that it would be best for him to try to remain anonymous. Recognizing a Seer might cause consternation for other Guardians, which might in turn inadvertently cause their humans to feel unease. Gregor lives his life among the other humans as best he can, and attempts not to seem too extraordinary."

I had not thought of this, but it is in line with my concerns about keeping Ayola safe by not creating an image which would cause her to unduly stare at me. Her position in society is precarious, and I have already decided it would be best to try to help her blend in with the other humans, lest they fear her and try to do her harm. I understand this further desire to prevent Guardians from being unsettled enough by the presence of a Seer that they might transmit negative emotions to their Guarded.

Wolk follows along with my line of thinking, nodding affirmation. *"It seems the best way to keep him safe,"* he explains. He pauses, then goes on, *"Gregor has asked me if there is a way for me to drop the veil, just for you, so that only you, as the Guardian of the other Seer, can know our thoughts. He believes, as do I, that it would be best for you to be included in our plans and discussions regarding Ayola."*

They have plans regarding Ayola?

"Yes, of course," Wolk explains. *"Gregor wishes to watch over her, help protect her as she grows. After she is grown we cannot know what she will choose to do, but while she is a child she is vulnerable and Gregor wants to help her."*

I am moved by powerful emotions at this. To know that another Seer, and his Guardian, are also motivated by a desire to protect my beloved is an incredible discovery. *"Thank you,"* I tell him, *"my thanks to both of you."*

"I appreciate your thanks, but it is almost as though this is involuntary. Gregor feels compelled to do this. He could not choose a different course even if he wished to. He feels that he and the child are bound to each other by their shared secret."

I think I can understand that. Even Ayola, just an infant, has sensed this about Gregor as well, constantly staring at him even before I knew what he was, and today longing to return to him after their brief contact. She knows they belong together as well.

"There is no way to know how this will develop over time. But Gregor at the very least wishes to be a mentor to Ayola, as once an older Seer spent time with him, teaching him."

He knew another Seer? This grows ever more astonishing.

"Yes, once, long ago, he met another Seer who was even older than Gregor is."

Surely that cannot have been terribly long ago. Gregor does not seem very advanced in age, surely not more than two or three decades old.

Wolk regards me, apparently trying to decide how to proceed. *"It was the Guardian of the other Seer who taught me how to conceal Gregor and myself from other Guardians. If you will indulge me, I am going to attempt to find a way to undo the glamour which I have cast over us, so that you are able to perceive us as you would other humans and Guardians. Once you can share our thoughts you will understand everything. I must do this carefully, because Gregor wishes to continue being anonymous to all others. Please give me a moment."*

I wait, watching, as Wolk appears to concentrate intently on his thoughts, the thoughts which remain inaccessible to me. Ayola slumbers peacefully in her little box, while her mother is downstairs assisting with the serving of refreshments to her mistress and the guests.

After a few minutes pass, Wolk speaks to me again. *"I believe I can do this. Please focus on us, and I will attempt to bring you into the glamour that I share with Gregor."*

I am not sure what to do, but I concentrate on the presence of Gregor, of his soul, of his Guardian. In a few seconds I sense it happening, I feel the lifting of the veil that had concealed them from me. I am more overwhelmed than ever.

It rushes over me, the explanation, the knowledge, the awareness of their existence. Their terribly long existence. The joy, the pain, the everlasting companionship they have shared. I never would have imagined how long Gregor has walked this earth. I had no idea that Seers could live for so long. It has been centuries. It is unfathomable.

Even as I am stunned by this new information, my hope soars for Ayola. Will this be her fate as well? To live an incredibly long time, to have me by her side, loving her, indefinitely?

Wolk nods sympathetically. He knows how incredible this information is, how impossible to process quickly.

And it appears to have worked. I can see, now that I have access to the thoughts of Wolk and his Guarded, that I am the only other one who knows their truth. None of the other Guardians have any idea about what is happening, other than simply sensing that Gregor is somehow peculiar. None of them pay any particular attention to Gregor and his Guardian despite their perplexing obscurity.

"Yes," Wolk says, *"that is exactly how Gregor wants it to be. How it must be, to remain safe. I will teach you to do it for yourself and Ayola as well, as the other Seer's Guardian once taught me."*

Gregor's

"Ayola's Guardian is now inside the veil of concealment, my dearest," I tell him. *"It is working well. The Guardian understands everything, and is pleased to know your plan to watch over the child."* I need to explain this to him, because he did not perceive my conversation with the child's Guardian. As when I had discussions with Yosh's Guardian so long ago, my Seer did not hear what I was saying. It seems a Seer only hears their Guardian's comments when directed specifically to them.

Gregor is currently walking along the river with the other gentlemen, discussing plans to build a dock with Abraham Ellis. Without breaking stride or pausing his conversation, he acknowledges to me that he understands, and is pleased to hear it. We both feel it is a positive development to have Ayola's Guardian joining together in our efforts.

As the afternoon wears on, I continue my conversation with the other Guardian, beginning to share the concealment technique. All of the Guardians in this family obviously already know of Ayola's status as a Seer, and will notice when her thoughts become inaccessible, but this will presumably not interfere with her safety. It seems best to begin shielding her from others as soon as possible.

The glamour taught to me long ago by the other Seer's Guardian involves the use of the power normally used for communication with our Guarded. I have learned how to cast it over my beloved and myself, in such a way that our thoughts are disguised. We are visible, but our thoughts and silent conversations with each other are unknowable.

Ayola's Guardian practices the technique, and is soon able to cast it over the little Seer. I sense as the other Guardians become perplexed about no longer being able to detect the

Seer's thoughts. However, as I had anticipated, they are not alarmed. Other Guardians are so focused on their own Guarded that anything not directly involving their well-being might be noted, but then the Guardian redirects their attention where it belongs.

As the Guardian of a Seer, I have found my focus broadening and expanding over the years. My attention is directed not only at my own beloved, but at the entire surrounding area. A Guardian is able to detect the thoughts of any human within a distance of about two miles. This is of extreme use to Gregor. I continuously and intensively monitor the activities of all humans around him. This would not be necessary for the Guardian of an ordinary human, who would be unable to share any relevant information with their Guarded. But I am in constant communication with Gregor. He knows I will immediately notify him if there is any activity which might concern him. This has protected him well throughout the years. There are many scrapes which have been avoided because Gregor could anticipate the actions of all other humans around him.

I will assist Ayola's Guardian with this, as well as all other aspects of Guarding a Seer. I realize that, in addition to Gregor's role as the mentor to the child, I will be a mentor to her Guardian.

The Guardian and I spend the afternoon perfecting our joint shield. Because we are each deliberately excluding the other from the concealment, we are essentially creating and sharing one large shield, casting a joint glamour over both of the Seers together. We four are all together in what is essentially a protective screen, sharing a shelter from the rest of the world.

It is a new experience for me, to be in communication with another of my kind. It has been centuries of isolation, of knowing that other Guardians see me but cannot know me. I have not truly felt lonely, of course, because a Guardian is always together with their beloved. And furthermore, Gregor communicates with me constantly. We have genuinely become friends, the companions of many years.

But it feels very nice to be sharing my thoughts with another Guardian. It has been such a long time since I have been able to do so.

Gregor is pleased that before the visit ends, Ayola has awakened, and he is able to see her again, although she is again being held by her mother and he has no further opportunity to touch her. The child looks at him with clear longing in her eyes. Her Guardian whispers to her that she will see Gregor again soon, tries to bring her comfort.

Then, as we are leaving, her Guardian turns to me, and wishes me farewell. *"Thank you, Wolk, for everything you have taught me. I will continue with the concealment of my beloved. I look forward to your next visit."*

"Farewell," I respond, as Gregor and his friends climb back onto the carriage after making their own farewells.

This was not how either of us expected this visit to turn out, but I am very glad that it did. Having a new member in our group is a welcome development.

Gregor

Stephen chatters exuberantly with me and Thomas, as I drive the carriage back to Natchez. I am pleased to participate in his conversation, predominantly about Margaret, of course, but also about the plans Stephen and Abraham are making for the plantation at Homochitto which will be their home after they are married. The wedding will not be for some nine or ten months, and by that time they hope to have the Homochitto plantation nearly ready for production. There is much work to do.

The steamboat project will factor into their plans, with the expected arrival of the boat sometime next year. Stephen and Abraham have become quite enthusiastic about the prospect of shipping their crops once a regular river route is established.

Everything is falling into place, including my mentorship of the little Seer. I still tingle with the memory of the few seconds that I touched her tiny head. I feel fatherly towards her, protective, loving. I am pleased that her Guardian knows about this. Wolk has described their conversation to me, and the way her Guardian is now able to hear our thoughts. This is a good thing. It is more of a relief than I had anticipated to have her Guardian aware of me, and actively communicating with Wolk.

Wolk is back to his wolf form, loping along beside the carriage, keeping pace with the horse. He doesn't have to, of course. I know he is not a physical wolf. He needn't run alongside. He could float in the air, or be anywhere nearby. But he always tries to form his appearance in a way to seem natural to me. He is always focused on whatever he thinks would be best for me.

Exactly like I want to focus on whatever is best for Ayola.

The late afternoon is growing chilly as we proceed northwards on our route home. The year is nearly over, the hot summer months behind us. The deciduous trees are losing their leaves. The road is still fine, though, winter not having set in enough to cause any traveling problems. It reminds me of the question of when to travel to Pittsburgh to view the steamboat construction.

We are approaching Natchez when I realize that Wolk is puzzled by something. This has been a day full of perplexing developments, but his demeanor seems increasingly bemused.

"What is it?" I think to him, listening to Stephen speculate about what Margaret is thinking about him.

"Something very unusual has occurred, my dear."

I laugh internally. Only one unusual thing? It seems to me that everything about this day was unusual. I certainly can't laugh out loud, Stephen would think I am laughing at him. But Wolk knows. "Well? What is it?"

"I have maintained my ability to hear Ayola's Guardian throughout this journey. I have never been able to hear from such a distance before."

"Really? You are still hearing her Guardian?" I know his limit for such things is about two miles. I constantly rely on this, knowing that he is always listening to learn whether there is anything happening nearby I should know about. We are nearly fifteen miles away from Ayola now.

"Yes. Just as clearly as if we had never left Ellis Cliffs."

"Can her Guardian hear you?"

"Yes. We have maintained communication throughout this journey."

"Well, how?"

"I do not know. It must be the result of our sharing the same shield, the four of us together within the concealment which keeps out all others. It is a very unexpected consequence."

Unexpected, indeed. This day has been full of many unforeseen events.

I think about how this might benefit Ayola. For surely it must. Everything I do now is to benefit her.

I am trying to picture what has happened with the Guardians sharing the same shield. It reminds me ... "Is this what happened with Yosh?" I ask him, a slight flare of hope striking as it occurs to me to wonder whether Wolk would ever be able to hear Yosh's Guardian from a distance.

"No. The shield was different then. Yosh's Guardian is the one who taught me how to create my own shield, just for you. There were two separate shields, one for Yosh and one for you. Yosh's shield remained intact, not allowing even me to penetrate it. I never actually heard the thoughts of Yosh or his Guardian. I was only able to communicate with

his Guardian by directly speaking. Today, rather than that, Ayola's Guardian and I have formed a joint shield, and are sharing thoughts within it."

Wolk falls silent again. As we approach Natchez, I know we are both considering everything that has happened today, and how it might influence us moving forward.

Chapter 29

Journey

February 25, 1811
Natchez
Rosy

"Do you really have to go?" I ask him, lying naked in bed together, the dawn breaking after our long night of passion. Gregor usually lets me sleep much later than this after we have been together, which has been more and more frequently. Most weeks he has come to see me two, even three times. Even more lately. I think he's been here almost every night for the past two weeks.

Every time he is here, we are utterly lost, usually for hours, in the ecstasy he has taught me how to share. We always are thoroughly exhausted afterwards, and sleep like the dead. But this morning he is already awake, almost as though he never slept at all.

"I'm afraid so," he says, nuzzling against my neck. "I still have a few minutes, though. Can you stand just a little more?"

I smile and clutch him to me. I can always stand more, with him. He embraces me again, pulling me underneath him and showering me with kisses. I feel him moving beneath the covers, positioning me just right.

I gasp.

Even though I know he is in a hurry, he doesn't act rushed. He never does. He caresses me just so, in exactly the right way to make sure that I experience as much delight as he does. We achieve our fulfillment together.

We cannot fall asleep this time, though. I know he is leaving on his journey as soon as the sun comes up. He has told me all about the steamboat project, and how he must travel all the way to Pittsburgh to observe the assembly of the boat. I cannot fathom how far away Pittsburgh must be, but he has told me that it will take weeks and weeks to get there. He expects to be gone at least two or three months.

I know how lonely I will be without him. I will be busy, though. Madam will certainly fill my time. I have been much less available to other customers since Gregor takes up so many of my nights. The other girls have told me this makes the other men more interested in me, thinking there must be something special about me that makes Gregor want me all the time. They all know I'm the only girl he comes to.

I know there isn't anything special about me. It's only Gregor. He is the one who is special.

In the funny way he has of guessing what I'm thinking, he says, "You are very special, sweet Rosalind. You have no idea how much you have done for me. I almost wish that I could keep you to myself."

I laugh. "Small chance of that if you are going to be gone for months." He sighs and sits up. I rub his lean, muscled back, telling him, "I'll miss you. I will be waiting for you."

We use the cool bathwater still in the tub to clean up. He usually orders a bath once a week, and he also wanted it for this last time before he departs. Just washing each other is pleasurable with him, even without getting back to the more intimate business.

But too soon, we are finished, I help him dress, and it is time for him to go.

I feel tears brush my lashes as I bid him farewell. He kisses them away. "Stay safe," I beg him, "stay healthy."

Stay, I think to myself forlornly.

"I guarantee I will be fine," he tells me with a sad little smile. "I will be back before you know it. I'll want to see you again right away, you know. Be ready." He grins as he warns me, and tries to make me laugh by waggling his eyebrows up and down. I know that after three months he will have a lot of pent up energy to expend.

I am looking forward to it already, as I watch from the window while he climbs the hill back up to Natchez.

Gregor

Rosalind is such a tonic for me. I have been trying to drink as much of that tonic as I can, in the weeks leading up to my journey. I have no plans to attempt to locate such companionship while I am away, so I know my usual problem with insomnia will no doubt recur after a couple of weeks of traveling. But I do not intend to dally at all while on this trek. I must hope that my time with her will sustain me while I am away.

Even knowing that Wolk is now able to maintain contact with Ayola's Guardian, it makes me terribly uneasy to leave the area for so long. He believes this contact will continue even as the distance grows between us. Truthfully, it is the only thing which has allowed me to find the resolve to go. At least he will be able to monitor the little Seer, and I will be comforted to know that she is safe. If there is a problem, Wolk will be able to tell me, and I will cut the journey short and return to Natchez as quickly as possible.

But at this point, everything remains fine with her. She has continued to grow, in both size and abilities. I have visited every week or two with Stephen, and have even contrived ways to briefly touch her a few more times. Whenever it happens, I know she is also feeling a profound connection with me, the unique sensation which I believe only exists when Seers touch.

I can tell her mind is developing, and her thoughts are becoming clearer as she grows. She is six months old now. She has already begun crawling, and even forming some basic words, although it is so early that the humans around her do not recognize most of her sounds as intentional speech. "Ma Ma," she can say to her mother, and a slightly different version of the same sound is used to refer to Margaret, who is the other human with whom she spends most of her time. She also has a sound she uses for me, not a name exactly, but a sort of whooshing noise she makes by humming and blowing out with her adorable lips pursed as though she is trying to whistle. I am not sure why exactly she has settled on this as my appellation, but I believe it is meant to be similar to the sensation she gets when we touch, the rush of feeling that swoops over us both. None of the other humans realize it is me she wants when she makes her little whistle.

I stop by my boarding house room to retrieve my packs, one with a few supplies for the journey, and another full of the river maps and diagrams I have been preparing for Robert.

I glance around the small chamber which has been my home for six months, before departing for the stables to get the horse I have purchased for the journey. He's a large American Quarter horse, with a rich, deep brown color. When I met with the Choctaw horse trader from the nearby tribe, he claimed that the horse is also part Mustang. I don't doubt it - he's a very swift runner. I've named him Issoba, which is the Choctaw word for horse. He and I get along very well, and I'll try to keep him with me for the whole journey rather than changing horses along the way.

To my surprise, Samuel is waiting there to see me off, with the sun not quite peeking over the horizon.

"Samuel!" I greet him. "You needn't have risen so early just to say farewell."

He smiles and claps me on the back. "I wanted to, my boy, to see you off, and wish you the best on our venture. You are representing all of Natchez now, you know."

I am touched by the gesture. "Thank you, Samuel, that means a lot to me. I will try to do Natchez proud."

He grins and hands me a basket. "I had my cook make up a batch of her special cornbread for you. This should keep you from going hungry for the first day at least."

The bread is still warm. "How very kind of you. Please thank your cook for me." This is an unexpected treat. I have not packed many provisions, since I don't mind being hungry for a few days at a time. But this smells delicious. I tear off a chunk to eat in the saddle, and carefully store the rest away in one of my packs.

He stands with me as I load the packs into the saddle bags, and prepare to mount the horse. He looks dubiously at me. "Are you sure you want to just ride a horse? Wouldn't you be much more comfortable in your carriage?"

"I think this will be better. Winter is ending, but the roads are probably still going to be muddy and rough in places. I don't want to risk getting the carriage wheels stuck in the mud. I don't mind riding horseback."

He sighs. "Well, at least you have the list I made for you of all the best stops along the Trace. Some of those places are better than others for a night's sleep. Mind the Kaintucks, don't run into any bandits. Keep your eyes open."

I nod, step up into the stirrup and swing myself onto the saddle. Issoba patiently accepts my weight. "Thank you, Samuel, for all your help and advice. I am sure I will be perfectly fine. I'll write to you once I arrive in Pittsburgh."

He nods, pats the horse's neck, and steps back. I wheel around with the reins and ride off at a trot, the sun just cresting the hill and starting to shine upon my face.

Gregor's

He has no need of Samuel's advice, of course. Not only will I make sure to guide him away from any people intent on mischief, but he intends not to stop at all until the horse needs rest. He will not seek lodging along the road. He understands that it takes most people some three weeks or more just to reach Nashville on the Natchez Trace, but he anticipates making the journey in about half the usual time. He will ride through the night, getting a good distance off the road before dismounting to rest the horse. He will simply lay on the ground while waiting for Issoba to be ready to continue. He will change horses if he needs to, but would prefer this steed, who is strong, tireless, and sensitive to Gregor's wishes. The only provisions he intends to obtain at the stops along the road will be fodder for the horse. For himself, centuries of experience with traveling has taught him enough about edible plants to find a bite to eat here and there along the road. He won't need much.

From Nashville he will take other roads and eventually come to Pittsburgh. The journey is some thousand miles, but as he intends to ride for most of each day and night, he hopes to complete the entire trip within a month or less. With about two weeks in Pittsburgh to talk to Robert Fulton and see the boat under construction, and a return journey of another four weeks or so, he optimistically hopes to return in less than three months. I have cautioned him that it is impossible the excursion will proceed without any mishaps, so he must anticipate delays, but he is determined to keep the journey as brief as possible.

The types of difficulties people experience on journeys such as this one will present little hardship for him. He has brought some food, but he can go without for nearly as long as he can go without sleep. Water he will find along the way, the streams being full after the winter of precipitation. Even the cold nights will have little effect on him, as another aspect of his unusual physical makeup is easy endurance of temperature extremes. The only true worry he has is simply the length of time he will have to be away from Ayola.

Her Guardian has assured me that I will be kept updated regularly, even if there is no actual news to report, simply to keep Gregor's mind at ease about his charge.

It has been a few months since I began communicating regularly with Ayola's Guardian. I wonder how I endured so long without. The glamour concealing my thoughts has for centuries cut me off from any meaningful contact with other Guardians. My relationship with Gregor is, of course, all-consuming, and literally the reason for my existence. However, communing with one of my own kind again is a palliative treat. It soothes me, entertains me, stimulates me, to have conversations with a being who can understand me better than even my beloved human ever can.

The baby's Guardian, although still in an amorphous state with no shape, has assumed a female voice, very like the voice of Ayola's mother. Guardians have no gender, of course, we have no actual physical bodies which would require such a designation. Gender is inapplicable to noncorporeal beings such as ourselves. But I have found myself inclined to view her as female, as she does for this incarnation. If she were to create a form, it would be that of a woman. I generally think of myself as male, as Gregor views me in this way and it is how I normally manifest. The image that a Guardian creates is a way to feel bonded to their human, and having a sense of gender identity can also assist in this bond. The identity might change in the next incarnation. It is utterly fluid, depending entirely on the circumstances of the individual human lifetime. Guardians have no permanent gender preference.

I enjoy conversing with Ayola's Guardian, as Gregor daydreams in the saddle. I must be attentive to the road, though, to best assist my beloved. The journey will be long and risky. Even though I am speaking with Ayola's Guardian, I am also diligently tracking all of Gregor's surroundings. He has been thoroughly warned by his friends in Natchez against the dangers which could present themselves along this road. I will make sure he has plenty of advance notice of any hazards that he cannot avoid.

Chapter 30

Friend

March 5, 1811

Natchez

Stephen

Abraham has decided to help me get the first crop of cotton planted at Homochitto this spring, so that soon after Margaret and I are married and move to the house there, we will already have a crop nearly ready for harvesting. In this way our financial security will be assured.

Their whole family has come to Natchez, so that we can all visit the land and make plans for the planting. Abraham will be providing some slaves for this task, but has recommended that I also acquire my own, to make sure the fields are well tended once the seeds are in. I will need to hire an overseer as well. My future father-in-law is sponsoring all of this, and I have assured him that I will be able to reimburse him once the first crop is sold.

He has been such a good friend to me, even though I am starting to fear that he is working too hard, both managing his own plantations and helping me with mine. Sometimes I have noticed that he seems somewhat overwhelmed with the duties thrust upon him, and will have occasional bouts of temper or forgetfulness. When this occurs I suggest that we have done enough for the day. I am a doctor too, and cannot overlook the signs that Abraham's duties are wearing on him.

It's too bad the steamboat route won't be ready yet for this year's harvest. We'll have to send it all down to New Orleans by flatboat to the port there for sale and shipping. It's how Abraham has always done it, but we are both already eager to try a better method. Many of the region's planters have heard of Gregor's project, and if the steamboat ever truly materializes, there will be many customers seeking to utilize the new mode of transportation.

Gregor has been gone for about a week now. We don't expect any word back from him for quite some time. He promised to write to Uncle Samuel as soon as he arrives in Pittsburgh. Hopefully he isn't running into any trouble on the road. We are all relying on the success of his mission.

I'm afraid that the shifting of my focus to the Homochitto plantation has caused me to neglect my medical practice to some extent. There are a few other doctors in Natchez, but there are more patients than can be serviced between all of the medical offices in town. I feel bad about not carrying my full share of the burden of the region's medical needs, but I must focus on building the life Margaret deserves. The plantation is the way. It must be my priority.

Natchez Trace
Gregor's

"The horse is tiring, my dear, it is time to leave the road and find a place for him to rest."

I am able to monitor the animal for him, but Gregor is sensitive to the needs of the horse and would have been stopping soon anyway. However, he follows my advice at once, knowing that I can sense the thoughts of beasts as well as those of humans.

I have tried to describe to him how they differ, but it is difficult to explain. As only human minds have developed the ability to capture the matter of which Guardians are made, only humans possess the souls which we Guardians exist to Guard. Because of this, animal minds do not have the same spark of creativity, or the brilliance of a human. This does not mean they are not intelligent, however. Animals have their own emotions, their own instincts, their own memories, their own awareness.

Domesticated animals like horses develop strong preferences and relationships, and this horse quickly bonded with Gregor. In the creature's own way, he considers Gregor a friend. Most creatures are drawn to him, more so than to other humans. I believe they are attracted to the brilliance of the Seer's soul. Gregor's control over the beast, and any other animals he encounters, exceeds that of other humans. It is not exactly as though Issoba can sense Gregor's thoughts, but he is incredibly responsive to the directions given to him by his rider, able to detect more than what is being conveyed through the bridle. The horse is quite content, even eager, to perform whatever task Gregor wishes.

It is past midnight, the gibbous moon casting sufficient light for the horse to be able to continue along the path through the nighttime hours. Gregor slows, pats Issoba's neck, and pulls the reins to turn the horse to the side, climbing a slight embankment off the edge of the road. After getting through a stand of trees, and coming to a slightly sheltered area in an overhang on a nearby rocky hill, he dismounts. There is some late winter grass in the small pasture where the horse can graze, and a spring of clear water trickling out of the rocks. The road is nearby but not visible from this vantage point. It is an ideal location to rest for a few hours. Gregor intends to remain in this place until dawn, at which time the horse should be sufficiently rested to proceed.

He removes the saddle and bridle, leaving only a simple rope about Issoba's neck, attached to a tree, to secure him for the night. The saddle blanket he places on the ground in the shelter of the overhang, and sits upon it. He will not attempt to sleep. It has been slightly over a week since he said farewell to Rosalind. It appears that his plan to build up a reserve of rest by visiting her quite frequently for several weeks, sleeping together with her after their activities, was successful. At this point he is not at all fatigued, other than physically spent from a long day in the saddle. He hopes he will be able to make it at least to Nashville without feeling the need for sleep.

He leans back against the rock behind the spot where he has laid the blanket, chewing upon a small piece of jerky from his pack. "How's Ayola?" he asks, watching Issoba bend his head down to nibble the grass. Even in the dim light of the moon, his Seer's eyes see the scene with perfect clarity.

"Her Guardian reports that today she crawled to a chair, and managed to lift herself up, standing at the edge by holding on to the seat."

He smiles, picturing the baby practicing this new skill. "I wonder how long before she is walking?"

"It is reasonable to assume that she will walk early, as she has also been early in crawling and beginning to speak."

"Has Stephen gone down to Ellis Cliffs to visit again?"

"No. Rather, the Ellis family has traveled to Natchez, because they intend to visit the Homochitto grounds and make plans both for planting the first crop, and preparing the house to be ready for the new couple to live in after their wedding."

"Well, rats. That's terrible timing. I would have liked to be there when Ayola visited Natchez."

"She and Dalila have remained at Ellis Cliffs. The family only brought two servants, and Dalila was not one of them."

"Ah." He lapses into silence, gazing at the horse, immersed in his thoughts. He spends a great deal of this inactive period remembering the times he has spent in Rosalind's company. He misses her. He does not intend to fall in love with her, he has felt too much pain in the past to slip into that trap again. But he is very fond of her, considers her a good friend, enjoys her company, admires her sweet and uncomplicated nature, and desires the intense intimacy which she quickly adapted to under his tutelage. His primary reason for wanting this journey to end quickly is of course to return to where he can better guard Ayola. But he also is eager to be again with the plump little prostitute who has brought him so much pleasure.

Ellis Cliffs
Ayola's

It is surprising to me how easy it was to adapt to the bizarre situation. Two Seers, together, with their two Guardians conversing. Preposterous. But after the first day or so of utter astonishment, talking to Wolk has become entirely natural.

One of the unexpected surprises which occurred was realizing that we can continue speaking to each other no matter how far apart we are. Neither of us has ever before been able to sense other Guardians or their humans more than a few miles distant, but sharing the same concealment shield appears to tie us together in some way.

Even as I sense Gregor and Wolk growing more and more distant while they journey, I am pleased to be able to easily converse with my new friend.

For friend he is. Guardians don't even speak to each other, much less become friends, but we have done exactly that. We have endless topics of conversation at our disposal. I am interested in comparing notes of our past experiences. My current incarnation is only months old, but Wolk has been Gregor's Guardian for hundreds of years, and has many interesting tales to relate. Much of what he tells me contains information which will be useful to Ayola as she grows. I am learning in ways I could never have imagined. I hope I will be a better resource to her with the knowledge I am gaining.

For instance, assuming that she and Gregor are as similar as they appear, her life will presumably be of indefinite duration. Wolk has described to me the astonishing good health, and accelerated healing abilities, that his Guarded enjoys. They knew one other

Seer, centuries ago, who also shared this ability. Both Gregor and the other Seer recovered from wounds which would have been fatal for a mortal. There is something about the physical makeup of a Seer which interacts with the matter which comprises Guardians, and this alters their abilities, makes them more durable than other humans.

Some of the unexpected hardships which Gregor endured might be avoided by Ayola due to the forewarning I am receiving. For instance, as Gregor became an adult it was confusing and even terrifying to begin to recognize the physical differences which differentiated him from other humans. The first time he should have died from an injury, and instead quickly recovered, led to him being shunned by all who knew him. His impossible recovery was seen not as a welcome miracle, but as threatening magic. He had to flee and start a new life elsewhere, which was an intensely painful and traumatizing experience for him. Then, when he realized he was not aging after his first few decades, he had to adjust to the grim reality that he would never be able to simply settle down in one place to lead an ordinary life. He would never be normal. Ayola will be spared the shock of these discoveries, as I already know and will be able to guide her once she grows somewhat older.

Are Seers literally immortal? It is unclear. They do not suffer illness, but they can be injured. There must be some injuries which even their healing abilities would not be able to overcome. They do have physical needs, especially in childhood. Ayola requires food and sleep as much as any other human infant. But Gregor's need of these things apparently diminished greatly as he approached adulthood.

Wolk has described to me his struggles with finding the ability to sleep when needed, and the method he has found which best assists him in resting. A Seer's sexual functioning, therefore, appears intact. Indeed if Gregor is representative, it is quite robust. Not reproduction, though, as far as Wolk knows. Neither Gregor nor his other friend had ever reproduced. It is impossible to know if this is a gender specific trait, or whether it will be the case for Ayola.

There is so much that I do not yet know about my beloved. But it fills me with joy to consider the long years ahead of us, the eternity that I will have to learn.

In the meantime, she is a happy and healthy six-month-old child. Although small for her age, possibly still due to her premature birth, she is advanced in her abilities. She already crawls quite easily, causing her mother and the other servants, even the members of the family, to have to be constantly chasing after her to make sure that she is not injured during her enthusiastic explorations of her surroundings. Her endearing personality draws them all to her, makes all humans committed to ensuring her well-being. I am pleased to report this to Wolk, so Gregor knows that she is being well tended. She will be perfectly safe while he is gone.

She misses him, though, when he is not here. It has only been a few days since last she saw him, and she often stares around the room as though hoping to see him appear. "Woosh, woosh," she whistles as she searches for him, causing the other humans to chuckle. They don't know what she means, but of course it is simply adorable, and further endears her to them.

Dalila

It is strange, and welcome, this time of relative peace. It makes no difference to the field hands whether the family is here or in town, the overseer drives them just the same regardless. But for the house slaves, the absence of the family transforms our lives. We are not at leisure, though, as Hester has been left by the Missus with an extensive list of tasks to complete before they return. We are kept busy polishing, dusting, scrubbing, beating carpets, and other duties that are more difficult to perform while also waiting on the family. But it is a happier place, less fearful, with only the servants in the home.

Especially for me. What a relief it is to sleep without the anxiety of knowing that at any moment the Master can summon me to his study. Once he started again, it became even more frequent than when I was a field hand. He passes by my sleeping mat every time he climbs the stairs to move into his chambers, and it is the rare night he simply ignores me.

Even more horrifyingly, he has started asking me questions while I am with him. I wish to endure the ordeal in silence, but he seems to expect me to affirm his actions, tell him that I admire and appreciate what he is doing. "You like this, don't you," he will demand while his hands roam over me, grabbing and pinching. What can I say? "Yes, sir," of course, is the only acceptable response.

I constantly worry that Ayola will leave our sleeping area while I am not there to monitor her, that she will crawl away and get hurt. But strangely, even though during the day she is nearly impossible to contain while she explores everything in sight, at night she remains on our sleeping mat. Often when I return, disheveled and sickened, she is awake and simply appearing to wait quietly for me. When I lay on the mat, if I have not picked her up, she will clamber over to me and cuddle up. It always comforts me. It is not lost on me that my infant is the one trying to care for her mother.

She is the only reason I do not try to run away, to escape the terrible attentions I endure night after night. I am only glad that she is still breastfeeding enough to stop my courses from coming. As much as I love her, I do not wish to have the Master get another baby on me.

So for the few days the family is away, leaving the servants behind, the constant dread has lifted and I experience the first peace I have known since I came to this terrible land.

If it weren't for the Master, I might be able to resign myself to this position, as Miss Margaret is a kind young woman. I do find myself caring for her and enjoying her delight in planning for her upcoming wedding. She is fond of me, I believe, and she obviously adores Ayola. If only the Master would forget about me.

Chapter 31

Brigands

March 14, 1811
Natchez Trace
Gregor

We are making decent time on our journey. I hope that another day of traveling will get us into Nashville, where the Natchez Trace technically ends. I am led to understand that the roads north from there are more well-traveled, less rustic, more orderly.

I have not had any insurmountable difficulties on the Trace. Issoba is strong and patient, carrying me willingly across the varied terrain. He has managed admirably crossing numerous streams, often with me on his back. When they seem particularly deep or difficult I swim or wade alongside him. Only once have I needed to pay passage for a ferry to cross the Tennessee River, where a Chickasaw man runs one of the Inns used by travelers.

Wolk tells me when any other people are approaching. The Trace is used by travelers going both north and south. I have been passed by the postal workers with their sacks of mail, galloping along in both directions. Northbound traffic is much higher since it includes the masses of boatmen returning to their home ports after their flatboats are dismantled in Natchez or New Orleans. There are also a fair number of people, usually in groups, coming towards me from the north. Wolk summarizes their intentions for me long before they are in sight. If they are simply travelers, either returning home or heading south to visit or conduct business, I stay on the road and greet them amiably as we pass. If they are ruffians, searching for any opportunities to pick pockets or otherwise create mischief, I leave the road and travel parallel, out of sight, until the miscreants have moved on.

Once or twice I have passed by unfortunate travelers being victimized by such brigands, but I do not stop. I continue past silently on my hidden path. I learned long ago that I can not intervene every time I see other people in need of assistance. There are far too many victims in the world to try to save them all. I spent many years in the past delving into the role of rescuer, and eventually determined that it is like trying to bail out a boat with a large hole in the bottom. In the end, it doesn't make any difference, except that it is exhausting and disheartening.

I cinch the saddle tighter to Issoba, check the packs, and swing up onto his back. Day is breaking but the sky is full of thick clouds, so it is unclear whether we will be able to enjoy any sunshine today. It's not unlikely that I'll spend at least some portion of the day being soaked by rain, alas.

A few hours into our day, as we are passing by one of the inns which service travelers along the Trace, Wolk tells me, *"My dear, about two miles ahead, directly to the east of the road, there is a group of three men lying in wait, hoping to find some easy targets for robbery."*

"All right then," I reply, and direct Issoba to veer left off the road, planning to follow it at some distance along the west side. I'll get past the brigands before returning to the Trace.

Soon, Wolk adds, *"Two gentlemen are approaching from the north, riding horses and chatting with each other. They will soon fall into the trap."* He often updates me on such things, even if he knows I am not planning to become involved, because not only do I want to be informed of everything relevant around me, but because traveling is boring business and at least it is interesting to hear what others are doing.

I'm surprised when Wolk waits another moment, then continues, *"My dearest, I have information about the gentlemen that might interest you. They are related to friends of yours."*

"What? Really? Who are they?"

"They are brothers to your friends Stephen and Samuel. Stephen's brother is also named Samuel. The other gentleman is his uncle, Henry Postlethwaite. They are traveling together to visit their brothers in Natchez."

Oh! Well, so much for my plan not to become involved. I'm obviously not going to let the brothers of my friends fall prey to robbery or worse. Not only would I not wish for people I have befriended to have family suffer hardship, but by intervening I will further my efforts to be accepted into Natchez society. I wish to secure my position in the community as a respected and well-liked citizen, which will create more options for me later as the little Seer grows. I don't know what she will need, but I want to have the ability to provide anything. Always, what I do is for Ayola.

So, I spur my horse to a faster trot, wanting to intercept before the gentlemen come to harm. I plan to continue off the road until I am upon them in an effort to advance unnoticed. The rain I have been anticipating all morning suddenly starts to fall in blinding sheets, providing some cover to my approach. Issoba stalwartly continues speeding forward through the brush, and I guide him back onto the Trace to prevent injury from rushing across uneven terrain.

I have encountered situations like this countless times before, and Wolk knows exactly the information I will need. As we approach he tells me the names and backgrounds of the ruffians. I will start by appealing to them as though I know them, which is often enough to defuse any situation without violence. They are all Kaintucks, the boatmen who journey down the river then walk back up the Trace. Wolk tells me that I have spoken to the captain who employs two of them, during my conversations on the docks, and that they have seen me there, so are familiar with me. One of them is a stranger to me, who is new to this work. He is a much more villainous character who only took a job as a boatman in a desperate attempt to evade arrest in a town to the north. Getting on a flatboat heading south was his fortuitous getaway.

The unfolding robbery tableau comes into view as I round the curve at a gallop, the sound of the pouring rain covering the pounding of Issoba's hooves. One of the ruffians is lying on the muddy ground, where Wolk tells me he is feigning injury to trick the gentlemen into stopping to render him assistance. Just as they rein in their horses and prepare to help him, the other two brigands dash in from the side of the road to grab the bridles fastened to the horses' heads, thereby controlling the animals and leaving the mounted gentlemen with no easy way to escape the situation. The villain on the ground, a burly, bearded fellow, rises to threaten the gentlemen with harm unless they relinquish their valuables. It is a common ploy of highwaymen.

My plan is also to deceive. It is my common ploy.

None of them see me until Issoba brings me directly into their midst. I know it must seem to them that I suddenly materialize out of nowhere, but it is really only because it is raining so hard, while they are all distracted, that they do not notice me before I arrive. I charge up at a gallop and pull back on the reins so hard that Issoba rears back as he comes to a sudden halt. His hooves flash in the air over the head of the thief who had feigned injury. He is the one who is a stranger to me. He briefly cowers back from Issoba's hooves, and I ignore him to focus on the other two.

"David?" I bellow, making sure to yell loudly enough that there is no mistaking my words over the rain. "Ben? What are you fellows doing here?"

Their mouths fall open, as they squint up at me from the side of the other two horses, still grasping the reins to prevent their riders from escaping. The gentlemen are utterly alarmed and confused, having no idea what is happening and whether I present a new threat.

The third fellow, Mason, recovers enough to begin to approach, as though he will grab the bridle of my horse as well. Wolk warns me, but I already know what he plans. I jerk the reins, causing Issoba to spin into him, which catches Mason off guard and knocks him to the muddy ground. It buys me a couple more seconds.

"Remember me?" I ask the first two. "I'm Gregor, your Captain's friend. He's introduced us a couple of times." It is a bald lie, of course, I have never been introduced to these men.

"It is working. They don't remember being introduced to you, obviously, but do recognize you from the docks. They grow uneasy, fearing that word of their thievery will reach their captain and deprive them of their livelihood."

Mason is clambering to his feet. When I glance his way I'm briefly distracted by the sight of a tooth protruding strangely from his mouth. I wonder if ugly people are more inclined to a life of crime.

Wolk ignores my irrelevant speculation and provides me with information I actually need. *"Mason is armed with a pistol, however he realizes the rain would interfere with the flintlock mechanism. Instead he considers the use of the knife he has tucked into the outside edge of his right boot."*

I know this means I have a few extra seconds before I have to deal with Mason.

I frown down at David and Ben, the Kaintucks holding the gentlemen's reins.

"The gentlemen are at a loss to know what to do, but unless this ends quickly they will intervene which will complicate the situation."

"Does Captain Price know what you are doing?" I ask the Kaintucks. "You aren't trying to harm these gentlemen, are you? I will be seeing him in a few days, I would hate to have to give a poor report of you to him."

This works. They release the horses and both back up. David lifts his hands, and says, "No, of course not. We ain't trying to harm nobody. Just was trying to help out with this hurt fellow here." He gestures over to Mason.

"He knows it is a lame excuse."

"Of course, I understand. How good of you to help." I want to make sure they think they have succeeded in preventing negative news from making its way back to their employer.

"Mason is furious. He plans to use his knife."

Before he gets the chance to do it, I surprise him by leaping sideways off my saddle, straight onto him, thumping him down into the mud for the third time in five minutes. The wind is knocked out of him, and as he lies stunned and breathless I quickly reach down and relieve him of the knife in his boot.

I rise and hold the knife up, not quite threateningly, walking towards David and Ben. "You wished to help the hurt fellow there." I gesture with the knife towards Mason, still gasping for air on the ground. "Now's your chance." They back away further.

"They will take a few minutes to regroup and form a new plan. The situation is under control for now."

I thrust the knife into my own boot, then quickly remount Issoba. I wheel back around to face the two other mounted men, rain streaming down their startled faces. "Gentlemen, may I escort you to shelter? There is a small inn a mile or two down the road, where we can wait out the storm."

They are too surprised to do anything else but follow.

Chapter 32

Brothers

Gregor's

Gregor masterfully manages the situation. I enjoy the show. He enjoys putting it on, knowing that the brothers of his friends watch with amazement. When he leaps onto the brigand from the horse, he is utterly heedless of any injury to himself, because he knows that whatever happens will heal quickly. He relies as always on his ability to recover immediately from almost any injury. He does wrench his shoulder in the fall, but only feels a throbbing for a few minutes while leading the other men south down the Trace to the inn. He doesn't mind the delay, since this effort will contribute to his greater purpose.

The rain is tapering off by the time the men arrive at the inn, but they are happy to get under a roof to try to dry off.

The appellation "inn" is perhaps too generous for this structure. It contains only one small room into which the men crowd after tying their horses to posts on the porch outside, under a rugged slanting cover which partially shields the animals from the rain. Although primitive, the shack does have a roof, a fire burning in the fireplace, a couple of rough tables with benches where the men can sit, and a staff consisting of a somewhat sullen married couple. They are a white man and his native Choctaw wife, the sort of couple who tend to live on the fringes of society, their union not being accepted socially.

Gregor and the two men enter, stamping their feet and shaking the rain off their heads, before sitting down. Gregor led them to the inn at a very fast pace, in order to prevent the brigands from following on foot, and they therefore have not yet spoken to each other.

Gregor turns to the men with a ready smile. "I am Gregor Slavson," he says, extending his hand to shake. "Sorry to burst in on you like that, but it did seem like you could use a bit of help."

They shake his hand and make their own introductions. Of course, I have already told Gregor who they are, but he feigns surprise very convincingly. "Wait," he says, "your names are Samuel Duncan and Henry Postlethwaite? What a funny coincidence! I have friends in Natchez with those same last names. You can't possibly be related, can you?"

The younger man exclaims, "I'll bet we are! Do you mean my brother Stephen?"

"The doctor, yes?" Gregor replies with a wide grin. "He's one of the first people I met when I came into town." He makes a show of staring at Samuel Duncan more closely. "Hold on a minute. I see it now! You are the very image of your brother!"

Samuel laughs. "I'm only younger than Stephen by a year and a half. Growing up, people always used to think we were twins."

Gregor nods. "I'm sure of it. I don't know how I will tell you apart." We share internal amusement. We both know I would never allow him to mistake one brother for the other.

The other gentleman adds, "My brother is Samuel. A different Samuel, of course. It's a family name."

Gregor shakes both of their hands again. "Well met, then! Both of your brothers are my dear friends, and I am so pleased to have come across you today."

They fall to conversation, enjoying the rough provisions which are the only fare offered at the inn, a flat bread the innkeeper's wife cooks on hot stones in the fireplace. Gregor is pleased to describe his mission, explaining the steamboat concept to a new group. Henry and Samuel share that they have decided to come to Natchez to not only visit their brothers, but quite possibly to join them in living there.

"I'd like to help Samuel out with his mercantile. The other Samuel," Henry clarifies. "I know since he opened the bank a couple of years ago he hasn't had much time for the store, and he has written me that he would appreciate having someone come along to give him a hand."

Gregor nods again. "Natchez can use all the merchants it can get. The town is growing, and I am certain that once steamboat traffic is established, there will be profit to be had for all. You'll do well in the mercantile."

Samuel is accustomed to the confusion with the name he holds in common with his other uncle. "I'm considering whether to stay as well," he remarks. "I've followed in Stephen's footsteps, studying medicine at Dickinson College, same as him. I haven't established a practice anywhere yet. Our mother wants me to settle near her and our sisters in Pennsylvania, but first I wanted to see for myself what Stephen is up to."

Gregor smiles at him, and shakes his head. "Well, it isn't my place to share any private news of your brother, but I must say that he is making very welcome changes in his personal situation soon, and will no doubt be delighted to welcome you to Natchez."

Samuel tries to wheedle more information out of him, but Gregor is firm that he should allow Stephen to share his good news with his brother himself.

"Darling, the three brigands have parted company with each other. David and Ben have decided to leave Mason behind and proceed northwards along the Trace to their destination. They had been convinced by him to participate in their first robbery, and considering how disastrously it ended thanks to your intervention, they want nothing more to do with him. Mason is proceeding back south towards Natchez, and will be coming to this inn shortly."

"Gentlemen," Gregor says, standing up, "I think we should go check on the horses, and feed them the corn that fellow over there was so kind as to sell us."

Henry and Samuel look at each other and shrug, somewhat surprised at the abrupt turn in conversation, but follow Gregor back out the door. While Gregor is facing away from the road, holding some dried corn up to Issoba's mouth and patting his side, Mason begins approaching from the north along the Trace. When I whisper that Mason is close enough and intends to come into the inn, Gregor turns around and faces him. "This inn is full," Gregor tells him coldly. "Move on to the next one."

Mason's jaw tightens under his bushy beard, and he glowers at my beloved, who is flanked by the two other men. He is outnumbered, and there is still a moderate rain falling which would prevent the use of his flintlock. His knife has been confiscated by Gregor. He quickly realizes that he cannot win any confrontation here, and with his face darkening in fury he turns without a word and continues stalking southward.

Henry

This new fellow Gregor is full of surprises. "Do you know him?" I ask in astonishment, as he waves off the brigand who nearly robbed us.

He continues feeding and rubbing his horse. "Not at all," he replies in his unusual accent. "I just wouldn't want to share the inn with his type."

"What about the other two?" I ask.

"Oh, I imagine they are really decent fellows. I'd be willing to bet they were only doing what that one told them to," he says, indicating the bandit we can still see stomping down the path in the rain. "I see they aren't together any more. I wouldn't be surprised if this fellow was abandoned and has to make his way alone now."

Samuel and I glance at each other, then again at the brigand who nearly robbed us.

Gregor watches after him for a moment. "You two should be careful on the road. He's not the only outlaw you might encounter. I'd advise you to keep a weapon at hand as you ride, just in case you are set upon again."

Samuel nods, impressed with our new friend. "That's good advice," he agrees. "And I'll make sure to be more observant."

"Also," Gregor adds, "don't be so trusting. Any more injured fellows you come across, I'd suggest you leave them be. It's a pretty common trick around here."

I wonder how he is such an expert. He seems quite young, no older than my nephews. Where did he get this kind of experience? "That was a pretty good trick yourself, jumping off your horse right onto him."

"Oh," he replies, waving his hand self-deprecatingly, "that was nothing more than a lucky accident. I actually got my foot tangled in the stirrup trying to dismount, and fell off. It wasn't planned, just a bit of clumsy happenstance."

Samuel guffaws. "I'm glad it worked out the way it did!"

That's not at all how it seemed to me. From my vantage point it appeared that he had deliberately flung himself on top of the ruffian, but if he wants to claim it was only clumsiness, it would be boorish of me to doubt him. It was all to our benefit.

Once the brigand has disappeared down the road, and we are finished tending to our horses, we go back inside the inn. It seems too late to continue on the road, and furthermore I'd not like to follow too closely behind the man who has already tried once to rob us. I ask the fellow who runs the place, "Can we lodge here tonight? Do you have any beds available?"

He dourly indicates a corner where some dirty straw is scattered over the wooden floor planks. "You can spread your blankets there," he responds. I sigh. I miss civilization.

We all head back to the horses, to retrieve our packs and extract the bedding we will need for the night. To my surprise, Gregor gets out not a blanket, but a piece of paper. He holds it out to me.

"Here is a list your brother Samuel made for me, of the inns along the Trace he recommends. I won't need it any more since I'm nearly to Nashville, but you can take it to guide you down to Natchez." I look down at the paper and, sure enough, I recognize my brother's tidy penmanship. For a piece of paper that has presumably been used during weeks of travel, it is surprisingly clean and unrumpled.

This is a touching and unexpected gift. As I accept it, Gregor grins, "It'll be like the other Samuel is traveling with you as well." He prepares to mount his horse.

"Aren't you staying here tonight?" Samuel asks him. This Samuel.

"Nah," Gregor says, hoisting himself up into the saddle. "It's only a few more miles to Nashville. I want to get there tonight. My greetings to your brothers, gentlemen!"

We can do nothing more than stare as he quickly departs and trots back up the road, disappearing like the apparition he seemed to be when he suddenly came to our rescue.

I meet Samuel's eyes, and we share a moment of amazement. This is an event which will grow in the telling, I am sure. I can hardly wait to get to Natchez and regale our brothers with tales of their friend's heroics.

Samuel is laughing, probably thinking the same thing, as we carry our packs back inside.

I stare at the piece of paper in my hand. If it wasn't for this tangible token of our experience, I'll bet that I would grow to wonder if I imagined the whole thing.

Mason

Goddamned foreigner. I see his prissy face before my eyes as I continue down the long road. His arrogant eyes, his fine clothes, his strange accent. What did he say his name was? Gregor?

Well, Gregor, you have ruined everything. I finally get those other blokes to go along with me, try to get a little profit from our trip up the Trace, and this Gregor comes along and wrecks it all. Those dandies were easy marks, I could tell they were seconds away from handing over their wallets, without even having to pull my pistol out. Then this idiot comes crashing into us with his horse practically braining me, and scares David and Ben away with his threats to tell their boss about them.

Their boss, of all things! How could such a ridiculous concern frighten them off? If they'd stuck with me they needn't have returned to their tiresome boat jobs. A fellow could make a decent living here on the Trace, coming across all the gullible folk roaming around.

But without my new partners, I'm just going to head back down to Natchez. I didn't really want to head north again anyway, where I might run into the authorities who are probably still searching for me. Under-the-Hill seems a likely place to find some profitable pursuits. Forget this idea of walking all the way across the country to find another boat to float back down on. Natchez will have something for me.

It's getting colder as I walk. How much further is the next goddamned inn? It has kept up with raining, but not enough to wash off all the mud. That's Gregor's fault too. I am ready to explode with rage when I think about the humiliation of having been knocked back down into the mud by him. Twice. Not to mention the fact that he stole my knife. I'm muddy, wet, tired, cold, hungry, and livid.

I hear that foreigner's words in my ears, in time to my steps squelching down the muddy road. "This inn is full." I clench my fists and carry on.

Gregor

It is very late by the time I finally get into Nashville. I can't be bothered to find real lodgings, but I do want to tend to Issoba. He's had a long day, running in the rain. So I seek out the public stables, make arrangements for a stall, and lead him in. I curry and brush him myself, pick out the mud from each of his hooves, inspect him all over to make sure he is sound, give him the fodder they keep here.

When he is settled in, I take off my outer layers of clothing, draping it over the walls of the stall to try to dry it out. Then I lay down on the straw behind him in the stall. It's more soft and warm here in the stable than the ground where I have spent my last several nights, and I am perfectly comfortable. Wolk's wolf form curls up on the hay next to Issoba.

I almost feel like I could sleep. It's been a couple of weeks. I close my eyes, and to the sound of Issoba's breathing, I let my mind drift. I am not asleep, but I am in a restful state, thinking about today's events.

"How's Ayola?"

"Very well. She spent a great part of the day practicing her new skill of standing along the side of chairs or sofas. She is also enjoying her new diet which Dalila has introduced to her, some soft vegetables and gruel."

"Has the Ellis family returned to Ellis Cliffs yet?"

"Not yet. Ayola's Guardian believes they should return in the next two or three days."

"I wonder how Stephen is doing with them up at Homochitto?"

He has no information about that, of course. He can only hear Ayola's Guardian, so his information is limited to the area surrounding the baby.

I start picturing the scene that will unfold when Samuel and Henry make it into Natchez. I can well imagine the way they will gossip about me.

Wolk huffs in amusement. *"It was fortuitous, running into your friends' brothers."*

"Yes. Another coincidence, I suppose. Although I am starting to think that nothing is really a coincidence." It will never stop seeming incredible that I happened to run across Ayola. My encounter with her, with all the folks from Natchez, with my new friends from the road, all seem to be leading to something. I just don't know what yet.

I feel my thoughts grow foggy and my breathing slow. I think I might actually sleep.

Chapter 33

Family

March 16, 1811
Homochitto
Margaret

We are leaving the Homochitto house tomorrow. It has been a busy two weeks, the men making arrangements for the planting, and Mama and I trying to put the house in order. Even my siblings have participated. Richard has been accompanying Papa and Stephen around the grounds, and Nancy has been making herself surprisingly useful with the house.

There are hardly any furnishings yet. Our biggest task has been making lists of items we will need to order from manufacturers up north, which will all have to be shipped down the river by flatboat. Papa had the house built some years ago, and I believe that he and Mama stayed in it for only a brief time before moving to the mansion at Ellis Cliffs. The house here is nowhere near as grand as home, but it will do for a newly married couple.

It makes me smile to think of it. Stephen and I as a newly married couple. We will live here as a family. We will sleep here, together. A blush comes to my cheeks when I remember the things Mama has told me about what Stephen will expect on our wedding night. She told me not to be afraid, but I cannot imagine being afraid of Stephen. I am eager to please him, and although such an act seems like it must be uncomfortable and awkward, if he wants it, I know I will want it too. And it will lead to babies. I love the idea of Stephen and I raising our babies here in this house.

"Margaret," Mama says, sharply. I come back to reality, realizing that she has said my name more than once.

"Oh, yes, Mama?"

She shakes her head and gives a little laugh. "Dreaming about your fiancé again, were you? Even when you aren't together, I can't get you to focus on anything else!"

Nancy laughs.

"Oh, listen you," I tell my sister, "just you wait until it's your turn. You won't be any different."

She doesn't object as I would have expected. She just smiles somewhat mysteriously and shrugs. Mama glances at her with an expression of speculation.

Nancy couldn't possibly already have a beau, could she? But suddenly it comes clear. It's Thomas Butler. I know it is. She's too young, only fourteen, but thinking back on Stephen's visits, I realize that Thomas and Nancy always come together, talking and laughing. I haven't been paying that much attention, obviously I am always distracted by my wonderful Doctor Duncan, but it seems clear to me now what has been happening.

Mama and I lock eyes for a moment. I see that she is already aware of this. She nods, but doesn't comment. We three seem to have come to an unspoken understanding of what lies in Nancy's future.

But that isn't for some time. For now, we will focus on my future. We return to our plans for the arrangements we are making for my household. The household I will manage as Mrs. Stephen Duncan.

April 5, 1811

Natchez

Henry

It's long past dark by the time we finally reach the end of the Trace, after a grueling three weeks along the rough road. The rumors I had heard of it were well-founded. We had only primitive lodgings along the way even with the help of my brother's list, the terrain was difficult for much of it, and more than once we were accosted by miscreants. After the first episode, though, we were more on our guard, following the advice given to us by that unusual fellow Gregor. Despite the ordeal, we have arrived in my brother's town relatively unscathed. And at least the weather eventually cleared.

We would normally have stopped for the night long before now, but we both felt we were so close to the end of our journey that we wanted to keep going until we reached Natchez. Finally, we are here in the town I have read so much about in my brother's letters. I'm not sure exactly where his house is located. But in his written descriptions of the area he has mentioned a gentlemen's club in a tavern called American Eagle near the center of the town, so we look for any sign of that. I am hopeful it will be open, and provide us with food and either lodging for the night or advice about where we might bed down.

We find some stables where we can leave our horses, and tell the night groom there to give them everything they need, and we will come back for them in the morning. We ask him where the club is, and he gives us directions. It is not far, and it feels good to stretch my legs after so long in the saddle.

The streets are deserted, only a light or two shining inside buildings. It must be even later than we realized. The club appears to have at least some activity inside, as we can see light glowing through the windows of the brick building as we approach.

Samuel enters first, poking his head inside the door to see if there are many people inside. "Well?" I ask, trying to see around him while he is blocking the entrance.

There is a beat of silence, and I am about to push him aside when he gasps. "Stephen!"

He leaves me in the doorway, and I follow in time to see him quickly approaching his brother, who appears to be alone in the club, standing with his mouth gaping open as he watches Samuel approach him.

Stephen

"Are you real?" I gasp in amazement. "Is that actually you, Samuel?"

I cannot believe what my eyes are showing me. It is an apparition of my brother, who I have not seen for years, coming in the door of the club. Am I hallucinating?

Apparently not. He grins and strides over to me, while I stand frozen with my chin nearly dragging on the floor. He grabs me in a bear hug, and after a second I realize that this is actually happening. I hug him back, hard.

"Why are you here? What are you doing? How did you get here?" The questions tumble out of me in a rush when we finally let go of each other.

He laughs, keeping his arm around my shoulders. I don't want to let go of him either. We were as close as twins growing up. I have missed him more than anybody else in our family.

He points over to the door, where I finally focus on the other man standing there grinning at us.

"Uncle Henry!"

He comes over as well, for another round of hugging.

I start laughing like an idiot. "I can't believe you're both here! You have to tell me everything!"

They look at each other, and I suddenly realize they both appear quite shabby and exhausted. "Come here, sit down!" I lead them over to one of the tables with comfortable armchairs around it.

They sit with contented sighs. "Ah. Civilization at last," my uncle says, practically moaning. "We've been on horseback for weeks."

"More like months," Samuel says. "Say, Stephen, do they have any food around this club? I'm starving!"

I automatically glance over towards the door leading to the detached kitchen building which is across a small courtyard, but immediately realize it is pointless. The staff has already gone, I'm the last person here. I help manage the club, and since the other managers had to take over for me while I was gone to Homochitto with the Ellis family for a couple of weeks, I've been closing up every night for a few days.

I look back over to my family. They are such a sight for sore eyes. "Yes, of course. I'm afraid the cook already left, but I'm sure I can find something for you. Wait here, relax, I'll be right back. Then I insist on hearing your tale!"

I'm sure it will be a good one.

I cross the courtyard and open the door to the little kitchen with the key, and am able to rummage around locating some stores of food. I'm not much of a cook, but I can wield a knife at least. I am a surgeon after all. I soon have a passable meal prepared of cold sliced meats. Presumably they won't be too choosy after what was probably a rough journey.

As they help themselves to the heaping tray of bread and meat I put on the table before them, they begin to tell their tale. They both had reasons to want to visit Natchez, and impulsively decided one day while they were talking with each other in Pennsylvania to travel together. Their tales of the road are riveting, but when they get to the part about Gregor I have to stop them.

"Wait! No, really, you ran into Gregor? What a mad happenstance!"

Samuel gets a huge grin on his face. "Wait until we tell you what he did! We were just about to get robbed by highwaymen, and he literally appeared out of nowhere during a thunderstorm, his horse rearing and scaring one of them away. Then he convinced two of the robbers to give up, and when the third one looked like he might want to fight, Gregor fell down off of his horse and landed right on top of the fellow! He left him lying there in the mud and showed us the way to the closest inn."

I am sure my mouth is hanging open while he finishes this tale.

"Is he always like this?" Samuel asks, taking another generous bite of cold roast. "Dashing heroism and all that?"

"Gregor?" I laugh. "No! He is the quietest, mildest fellow ever! He spends all of his time dreaming about boats and drawing maps! Are you sure we are talking about the same person?"

Our uncle reaches into his pocket, and pulls out a bedraggled piece of paper. "He gave us this. He said Samuel wrote it out for him. The other Samuel."

I take the paper, bemused, and look at it. Well, that answers the question of whether we are talking about the same Gregor. "I helped Samuel put this list together!" I tell them, fully amazed.

"By the way," Samuel goes on. This Samuel. "Gregor said you were making a positive change in your life, but refused to give me any details. What was he talking about?"

My face must reflect my joy. "I am getting married!" I tell him.

Henry and Samuel both whoop with delight, and demand all the details. I am quite happy to oblige.

It is very late by the time we are done talking and they have finished all the food. It must be long past midnight, far too late to get rooms at the boarding house or knock on Uncle Samuel's door. "Come with me," I tell them. "My friend Thomas is out of town with the militia for the night, so I have two beds you can use tonight. I'll take the couch in the other room."

They are happy to accept, and I have to laugh when we get back to my rooms and I hear Henry groaning with ecstasy as he sinks into Thomas's bed. "I've missed beds!" he moans, making Samuel and I laugh even harder.

"Me too," says Samuel, "but my goodness Uncle, you sound positively indecent in your delight!"

I'd be tempted to make them stay up even later, laughing and talking, but I know they must be exhausted. I leave them in the bedroom to sleep, and go to take my rest on the sofa in the other room.

Chapter 34

Revenge

April 8, 1811
Mason

I finally make my way back down the bloody Trace to Natchez. I peek into the King's Tavern, the first building in Natchez at the end of the Trace, thinking I can get a drink here. But I don't like the looks of this place. Too many dandies in here. For all I know some of them are folks I relieved of their wallets in the past couple of weeks, who'd recognize me and be ready for a confrontation now that they are among their friends. I'd be more comfortable down Under-the-Hill with the Kaintucks. So I carry on, just a little further, skirting past the dandy town and heading down the hill to the area along the docks. It's late at night and most of the upper town is deserted, but Under-the-Hill is lively and loud.

I have money in my pocket. Even without those fellows who deserted me up north, I was able to scare up some wallets from gullible travelers along the road. Especially once it stopped raining and I was able to use my pistol to better effect. I'll have to find a way to acquire another knife.

In the meantime, I need strong drink. I head into the Kentucky Tavern at the foot of Silver Street, crowded with fellows carousing and drinking and gambling. I see a couple of people I know from last time I was here.

"Whiskey," I order at the bar. While I'm waiting for the barkeep to pour my drink, another fellow calls my name from across the room.

"Mason? What are you doing back here so soon?"

I turn around, and see Stu with a couple of other fellows playing cards. I take my whiskey and head over to their table. I settle into a chair, take a deep draught of the whiskey, then say, "I decided to come back. I didn't want to walk all the way up to another port. I'm sure I can find something here to fill my time."

Stu shrugs. "Deal you in?"

"Sure," I tell him. I'll gamble with the money I stole. What else is it for?

After a few lucky hands I'm feeling even more flush with money. Stu and the other fellows decide to pack it in. They are heading to their beds, but I don't have anywhere for the night. "Hey," I ask Stu, "which whorehouse is your favorite around here?"

He grins. "I figured you'd be wanting that next. Try Madam Beverly's. She's got some comely wenches there. There's one who all the fellows have been trying, since that foreigner took off up the Trace. He used to keep her to himself, so everyone wanted to see what the fuss was all about."

"What foreigner?"

"Some odd fellow named Gregor. He spent half his time down here chatting with all the boat captains, and the other half in the whorehouse with Rosy."

I hear a sudden rushing in my ears. All the rage comes flooding back. I spent the last few weeks walking all the way back to Natchez on account of Gregor, furious with him every step of the way. The memory of the casual way he bested me has been eating at me. My anger at him is the thing that kept me going through the journey. I have vowed to get my revenge on him, imagined a thousand ways to make him pay for what he did to me.

This sounds like an excellent place to start.

Rosy

I can scarcely catch my breath between the customers. As soon as one man leaves, I rush into our dressing room to freshen up while Madam collects her money. Then she sends me straight back up the stairs with whoever the next man is. It's been this way for over a month.

I can't really say that I mind it too much, though. If I can't have Gregor, who I have admitted to myself has won my heart, then at least I can stay occupied in his absence. I'd rather be busy than brooding over how much I miss him.

The way he taught me to enjoy relations with a man stays with me, even though nobody else has come even remotely close to making me feel the same. But at least I can remember it, try to picture Gregor, while I am under some other man. It's a hard task, usually, trying to trick myself into believing that some heavy, hairy, smelly man grunting at me is the man I love. But it is the only way to make it seem tolerable, and keep a smile on my face no matter who I am with.

I'm glad tomorrow will be my day off. Staying this busy comes with consequences, including being quite sore after I have entertained several men. Madam knows that she must allow the girls to rest and recover, to get ready for another round. For her, I think, it is simply that she is taking care of the merchandise. But I'm happy she cares at least that much. I am looking forward to just lounging on my cot for most of the day, although I know it will lead to daydreams that will make me miss Gregor. I know I still have another month or two to wait until he comes back Under-the-Hill. I wonder how he is faring on his journey. I pray that he is well.

When I have finished rinsing off and applying powder and straightening my corset, I run the brush over my hair one last time, take a deep breath, and walk back out into the parlor, forming my lips into a smile for whoever might be there waiting for me.

Madam summons me over immediately. "Rosy, take this gentleman upstairs with you, please. Use the red room." The red room is the smallest, cheapest one. She wants to make sure that the amount she is paid corresponds to the services being provided.

I turn to him with a smile. "Good evening, sugar," I greet him, taking his arm. "Will you come along with me?"

Rather than smiling back, as they almost all do, he has a startling glower on his bearded face, almost as though he is angry at me. I am slightly taken aback. I hesitate, and glance over at Madam, but she shoos me with her hand, telling me to get on with it. So I smile all the more and lead him up the stairs.

When we get into the room, he immediately turns and pushes me with no warning at all, so violently that I lose my balance and crash down onto the bed. I am so shocked I can't even react. Before I have the chance to try to sit back up, he has crossed to the bed, is kneeling on it next to me, and has grabbed my hair in his fist. I have no idea what to do or say, but I feel a panic growing inside me.

"Sir, please," I try to start, but he shakes me and I stop. His hand is hurting me, pulling my hair.

"Do you know Gregor?" he demands.

What? Why on earth does he need to know that? I don't know what the answer he wants is, so I am just honest with him. "Yes, sir," I say, breathlessly, wincing.

That is all the conversation I get out of him for the evening, except that once when I cry out in pain, he says, "Hush or it will go worse for you." I'm too afraid of him to call for help. If I just let him take what he wants, I think, it will be over soon and he will go away. I can get through this.

It takes much longer than I would have expected. It's like he wants to thoroughly hurt me, inside and out. I focus with everything I have on simply enduring, surviving. By the time he is done with me, after he has abruptly left the room with me lying on the floor next to the bed, I am a shaking mess. My head hurts from where he pulled my hair. My throat hurts from where he squeezed it while he forcefully took me. My lip hurts where I bit it trying to stay quiet. It hurts between my legs where he pummeled me mercilessly. There is an ache somewhere deep inside, too. I have sore spots all along my middle and thighs, even my face, where he violently pounded and pinched. I even have a couple of bite marks. I know that tomorrow I will be black and blue.

I give myself some time to try to get my crying under control before I creep back down the stairs. I've seen other girls come out of the rooms upstairs like this before, but this is the first time it has happened to me. I know better than to complain to Madam Beverly. As long as nothing is broken, she would shrug and tell me this is what I should expect, and any night that goes by without some bruises is a lucky night. I've heard her say it so many times to the other girls. It's just a part of the business.

I'm glad that by the time he is done with me there aren't any other customers waiting. I crawl into my cot, still shaking, and feel the pillow grow wet from the tears I can't stop while I fall asleep.

Chapter 35

Shipyard

April 10, 1811
Pittsburgh
Gregor

Finally, Pittsburgh. It took longer than I had hoped. Wolk was right. It was overly optimistic to think I could get here in four weeks. It has been over six weeks, with various delays including weather, and one period of two or three days I had to stop and wait when Issoba developed a limp. Wolk assured me there was nothing broken that wouldn't mend if I would just stay in one place for a few days. I am very attached to Issoba so I was willing to wait it out, rather than trading him for a different horse.

And, at last, here I am. I arrived late in the night, and waited for morning in the stables with Issoba. I have boarded him there for now, and at first light I began my exploration of the area on foot. I have not been in this city before now, somehow missing it during my previous travels in this new country.

The Monongahela and Allegheny rivers flowing through the area are large and impressive, merging together near the ruins of Fort Pitt to form the even broader Ohio, which eventually feeds into the mighty Mississippi. This link to the Mississippi River is the reason Pittsburgh can serve as the location to construct the steamboat which will eventually power its way down to New Orleans.

It is not the only shipping project underway along the rivers. As I wander through the area, the level of industry in shipbuilding is breathtaking. At the foot of an area known as Boyd's Hill, on the banks of the Monongahela where a little stream called Suke's Run flows into the river, is an extensive system of shipyards. Other shipyards build barges, schooners, and sailing ships meant for the Atlantic trade, but the yard I am interested in is where the steamboat is being built.

The New Orleans, it will be christened when it is done, optimistically named for its eventual home port. Robert has written of his preliminary plan, once the success of the voyage down the Mississippi is established, to use it for a regular packet route between Natchez and New Orleans. We believe it will not be long before more steamboats are built, for regular traffic along the entire course of the river, not just the southernmost portion.

The construction is being supervised by Nicholas Roosevelt, the same person who Robert engaged to explore the Mississippi in 1809 by flatboat. I look forward to meeting him, questioning him about the process. It seems that Roosevelt had to bring a force of mechanics with him to Pittsburgh from Newark where he had been building smaller steam engines for transit in that area. Much of the engine itself is being constructed in New York and will have to be transported over land for installation here. But the bulk of the steamboat will be constructed here on the banks of the Monongahela River. An adjacent foundry will be used for much of the iron work. The timber is being obtained from nearby forests and brought to the neighboring sawmill.

I settle down on a patch of grass behind some small houses on a bluff overlooking the shipyard, where I have a good view of the activity below. It is still early in the morning, and the workers appear to be just starting their tasks for the day. I see a load of timber delivered on a raft from the river, and watch it being unloaded while other workers perform tasks that I try to discern. Wolk is providing me with information about each aspect of the production below. I am thoroughly absorbed in surveying the scene before me, when I hear the giggling sound of a young child behind me.

I turn to see a young woman, about the same age as Stephen Duncan's fiancée Margaret, laughing together with a toddler she is holding by both hands, guiding the child who takes unsteady steps in the grass. Although this young lady is the same age as Margaret, there the resemblance ends. Rather than Margaret's porcelain doll coloring, this lady has the most astonishing bright red hair, with matching ruby lips and high color in her freckled cheeks. The child has red hair to match her mother's.

They are accompanied by an enormous dark, shaggy dog, a Newfoundland by the looks of it, who rushes past them and comes bounding over to me. I greet him happily, introducing myself by holding the back of my hand to his nose for a sniff. Then he thrusts his entire enormous body onto my lap, rolling us both over onto the ground, as he pants and wags his tail almost violently. I laugh and wrestle him, patting him wherever I can reach as he starts lapping his tongue all over my face. "Tiger!" I hear the young lady exclaim. "Stop trying to eat the gentleman!"

I look up from the friendly assault of her pet. I am surprised to see the unusual garb the young lady has adopted. Rather than the customary long skirt that all other ladies wear in this era, she has on some kind of breeches, with boots, a loose jacket, and her hair in a long braid underneath a cap. I can't stop myself from staring, not in horror, but in admiration for a lady who clearly does not feel bound by societal conventions.

I shush the dog and rise from the grass. He remains at my feet. "Good morning," I greet her, wishing to know such an unusual person better. Considering her appearance, I feel she will not shrink from a forward greeting by a strange man.

I am right. "Hello there," she responds, and follows along as the toddler's wobbly steps bring them closer to me. "Sorry about Tiger attacking you. Enjoying the view of the shipyard?"

"Why, yes, I am. I am very interested in what they are building down there," I tell her.

"I'm glad to hear it," she says, then lets go of the child with one hand so she can extend it to me to shake, as though she is a man, not a young woman. "Lydia Roosevelt. That's my husband's shipyard."

"Indeed!" I shake her hand, feeling quite amazed at her charismatic presence. I detect a slight British accent when she speaks. I also notice, now that she is closer, her eyes are a vibrant color of emerald. "I am very pleased to meet you, Mrs. Roosevelt. My name is Gregor Slavson, I am..."

She interrupts me. "Mr. Slavson! We have been expecting you! Please, follow me, I will take you right to Nicholas." She bends down to scoop up her daughter, and resting the child on her hip, leads me down a path to the shipyard.

Wolk walks alongside Tiger, making an impressive pair of animals, although nobody else is any the wiser that Tiger is not the only dog in our midst. My Guardian is clearly enjoying my amazement at this development. Lydia Roosevelt appears to be quite a force to be reckoned with.

Nicholas

The load of timber appears fine, the white pine which is the only feasible wood available nearby for my purpose, but we'll still need much more for the planking. I supervise the workers poling the raft with the wood up to the dock. I still haven't gotten any logs sufficient for the two masts that the ship will need. It will run on steam, yes, but I plan to have sails as well, so there is no question of the boat always having a means of propulsion.

"Nick!" I hear my wife calling and I swing around to greet her. I wasn't expecting her yet this morning. I see her coming down from our house up on the bluff overlooking the shipyard. A man I don't recognize is with her, our big dog Tiger walking at his heels. I leave the men to unload the timber and walk up the path to join her. She is holding our little fireball Rosetta.

"Hello, darling," I greet her, reaching down to kiss her cheek and then that of our daughter.

"Nick, this is Gregor Slavson," she tells me enthusiastically, "arrived at last from Natchez!"

The fellow extends his hand to shake. "I am pleased to meet you, Mr. Roosevelt," he says in an accent I can't quite identify. Some sort of Eastern European, I think. He seems much younger than I would have expected, considering the letters Robert Fulton has shown me, and the substantial funds he has contributed to our cause.

The strangest part of it is not that Fulton has a friend who offered to be an investor, but rather that this particular investor's only condition which came with the money was that his name is to be left entirely out of any documentation regarding the project. He insists on total anonymity in the documents recording our achievements, and says he trusts Fulton to fairly send him his share of any profits. He's not wrong about Fulton - I know he will be exceedingly scrupulous in making sure that Slavson gets the proper amount coming to him. But this level of trust is rare, and interesting. We are perplexed but pleased to accept the funding under these terms.

"And you! I have been very eager to meet our mysterious benefactor! This project would not have been so far along without your investment."

Lydia hangs back, holding Rosetta, letting me take the lead in the discussion with Slavson. She knows nearly as much about the construction plans and schedule as I do, and would certainly be able to guide our investor around the site. She finds it easier to converse than I do, her natural exuberance and intelligence making her a delightful conversationalist. But she tries to be sensitive to the feelings of people when we first meet them, trying not to be too overwhelming. She knows many people would be taken aback at such a young woman being as integral to the project as she is.

Although, I think, wryly looking at her trousers, she will only take this cultural sensitivity so far. When we started our first voyage down the Mississippi River two years ago, and she quickly got tired of her skirts getting wet and weighing her down, she impulsively grabbed a pair of my breeches and put them on. She has declared this is the only reasonable garment to wear most of the time, that skirts are entirely impractical around boats and shipyards.

And I learned long ago that Lydia is not to be contradicted. She is a force of nature, like a hurricane, or an earthquake, and one must simply bow to her will.

It is lucky for me that her will is nearly infallible. Her breathtaking beauty is exceeded only by her genius, with her daring close behind. When she settled on me, the much older friend of her father, as the object of her romantic interest when she was only thirteen years old, it was the luckiest day of my life. She has not only earned my eternal love and devotion, but her participation is the secret behind the success of the entire steamship endeavor. She has an amazing ability to untangle any problem. Given enough information, I suspect there is nothing she wouldn't be able to figure out. She is like the flaming torch which lights the path and guides our feet.

As I invite Slavson to come on a tour of the shipyard, I glance sideways at him to see his reaction when Lydia comes right along with us, holding our toddler. Usually a woman, having made the necessary introduction, would retreat back into the home with the child. Not Lydia. I am relieved to see that the young man seems not at all scandalized by my wife's unusual appearance and behavior. If anything, he seems impressed and even amused. This is a positive thing. If he was the sort of man who would not welcome the participation of a woman in what is generally seen as a man's domain, he would come to be very uneasy with our project.

Gregor's

As Nicholas guides my beloved around the shipyard, explaining the progress of the steamboat construction, Gregor asks me to provide details about the remarkable couple he has met. Lydia is less than half the age of her husband, which although unusual is not unheard of. But Gregor can see there is much more that is unusual about her than her comparative youth. Among other things, it is obvious her older husband holds her in high regard, totally aside from her beauty.

I search the memories of the couple and their Guardians to obtain the information he requires. As always, my thoughts are hidden and the Guardians are not aware that I am rummaging around in theirs.

"Lydia was born in England. When her mother died, her father came to this country, leaving his two children with family until he remarried. He sent for the children when Lydia was nine years old."

Gregor attends to the interesting tour being conducted by both Nicholas and Lydia, but also is listening to the history I am relating. My beloved has had centuries to perfect the ability to essentially carry on two separate conversations at one time, both listening to me while also interacting with other humans.

"When Lydia arrived, her father had become a well-known architect in Washington, D.C.. Nicholas was his business partner and best friend, which is how the couple met. At that time Nicholas was thirty-four years old. By the time Lydia was thirteen years old, they were engaged."

Gregor wonders if this is a case of predatory behavior on the part of Nicholas, a natural assumption considering the difference in ages. *"It does not appear to be so. In fact, it seems Nicholas agreed with her father that she was far too young to be engaged to a man more than twice her age. However, as you have surmised, Lydia is a remarkable person, with an advanced intellect and a very forceful personality. It was Lydia who insisted that her father consent to the engagement. They were eventually married a bit over two years ago. She was seventeen years of age, and he was forty-two."*

Gregor considers the length of time which has passed, and silently inquires, "Robert wrote to me that they both took the flatboat trip to explore the Mississippi River? How is that possible? This child appears to be the right age that Lydia's pregnancy would have overlapped with the journey. Was Robert mistaken? Or perhaps it was a different couple?"

"No, Robert was correct. Lydia insisted on accompanying her husband along the flatboat journey in 1809, despite her pregnancy."

"I'll bet that raised some eyebrows."

"Indeed so. Mrs. Roosevelt, however, as you have observed, is not overly concerned with the opinions of others about her behavior."

Gregor silently chuckles, showing no sign of this to the Roosevelts as they continue their tour. They are currently discussing the construction of the keel for the ship. Gregor participates fully, asking questions of them even as he is asking questions of me.

"Lydia is the person who designed a flatboat for their Mississippi River journey, which included living quarters for the couple. Nicholas had the boat constructed to her specifications. When they reached New Orleans, they took a ship back to New York, through the Gulf

of Mexico and back up north along the Atlantic Coast. Lydia's child was born in New York, almost immediately upon their arrival."

Gregor glances at the young woman and her baby, wondering at her hardiness and sense of adventure. He has no further questions for me at the moment, so I lapse into silence as he learns everything he can about the shipyard from the Roosevelts. I walk alongside, in the wolf form that Gregor most prefers, accompanied by the Roosevelts' large pet dog, hounds together.

It amuses even me.

Chapter 36

Appraisal

April 12, 1811
Natchez
Mason

It was worth every penny, all the money that I had. Knowing that I had bested that smug foreigner, made his woman pay for what he had done, was the most satisfaction I have ever gotten at a whorehouse.

I want to go back, get that exhilarating feeling of vengeance again, but it cleaned me out. I don't even have enough money left for a bed. I'm camping out at the edge of the docks. I slept outside all the way up and down the Trace, so this is nothing to me.

I could go back up the Trace, take advantage of the easy pickings there, scare up a few more wallets. But, I feel tied to this place now. Under-the-Hill has a wealth of resources for a fellow like me. I can even apply for work at the docks, just to fill my belly. And, after a few days, I'm sure I will have saved up enough for another go-round at Beverly's.

I'm hard just thinking about it.

Rosy

The bruises have faded, but not the memories. I fear his return. I never even learned his name, but I know he is still Under-the-Hill, because I have seen him through the window, working along the docks, moving cargo.

I try not to dwell on it, but it is difficult. Now that the pain is over, I find myself more confused than ever about what happened. Why was he so savage? After I admitted that I knew Gregor, he became both aroused and enraged. He took me in fury, and in silence. He was obviously punishing me for something, but I never got an explanation for why.

Madam Beverly has not been happy with me. My smiles for the customers have come only reluctantly, and she has even had a couple of complaints that my services were not satisfactory. This never happened before that terrible night.

Strange how the different men can affect me so strongly. After my time with Gregor, I was enthused about my work, and the customers lined up to spend time with me. After that other man, I am hesitant and fearful. Customers are no longer going out of their way to request my services.

Madam has lectured me that unless I fix my attitude, she will demote me to a kitchen worker, where I know I will be worked like a slave with almost no food or rest, not even a place to sleep at night other than a bare spot on the kitchen floor.

I am resolved to do better, try to find satisfaction in my work again. Madam inspects me as I enter the parlor, making sure I have on my costume and my smile.

My smile fades, though, as soon as I see the first customer come through the door. It is him. He has returned, as I feared, as I knew was inevitable. I try to fade into the back of the room, hoping he selects one of the other girls.

But, "Rosy," is all he says to Madam, while he hands her his payment. She beckons me forward, with a stern expression warning me to cooperate without complaint. I begin to tremble as he silently walks me up the stairs to the red room.

I try to smile at him when we enter, hoping that he is in a better mood this time. At least he is not as abrupt as he was the first time. I do not find myself flung onto the bed in the first moment, which I take as a good sign. He stands at the door, staring at me. It is not the furious glower of last time. Again, another good sign. He seems almost perplexed.

I am encouraged enough to try to take the initiative. "What can I do for you, sugar?" I ask him.

"Stay still," he orders brusquely, and continues glaring at me. I do not dare even say "Yes, sir." I simply remain silent, and stand perfectly still before him, casting my eyes to the floor.

I wait while he inspects me, for surely that is what he is doing. I don't know what he expects to find. It takes several minutes, during which I wish I could stop my trembling, knowing he must be able to see it, since he is scrutinizing me so intently. But it grows even worse, as my anxiety climbs in this silence, this suspense. I clasp my shaking hands together. I don't know what is coming, but I know I fear it.

After a couple of minutes, he begins to slowly circle me, his eyes still locked to my form. He stands behind me for so long, totally silent, that I want to turn around to see what he is doing, but I'm scared to move a muscle. All I can do is wait tensely, feeling utterly vulnerable with him behind me, not knowing what is about to happen.

Finally, he finishes his circle, coming back to face me. I cannot read the expression under his heavy beard.

At last he speaks. "So," he says with a tone of disbelief. "What is it about you?"

"Pardon me, sir?" I ask, feeling like he wants me to speak now.

"You aren't particularly beautiful," he says. My cheeks blaze. I know it.

"You have curves," he continues, apparently intending to undertake a humiliating appraisal of my physique. I stare at the floor, wishing to sink into it. "But," he goes on, "I've seen better. Your tits are too small, your hips are too large. You have more meat on you than I prefer."

I am becoming increasingly mortified.

"Your hair and eyes are a boring brown. Your face is only average." He circles around me again. "I just don't see it," he appears to conclude.

When he is silent, I feel he must be waiting for a response. "I am sorry, sir," I whisper.

"What?" he barks. "Speak up."

I clear my throat and try again. "I'm sorry, sir," I repeat. I don't know what else to say to excuse my shortcomings.

"What does he see in you?" he asks.

I dare to raise my eyes to his, questioningly. What is he talking about?

"Gregor," he clarifies, and I involuntarily shudder when I realize that he is still angry about my knowing Gregor. "What does he see in you?"

Tears spring into my eyes, but I know he expects a response. All I can do is be truthful. "I don't know, sir."

Without warning, his hand flies out and strikes me across the face. I am already seeing stars before I even land on the floor. It takes a moment for my vision to clear, and I look up at him from the floor, cowering before his feet, not daring to rise.

"Don't lie to me," he snarls. "You know. What has he told you?"

"I'm sorry, I don't know," I cry, not able to stop the tears that have started flowing down my cheeks.

He kicks me, his boot making painful contact with my hip, where I know I will be adding it to a catalog of bruises tomorrow. Again, I just have to survive this. I need to endure. I have to find a way.

"Stop lying, or you will regret it," he says, not loudly, but with an ominous quiet. He doesn't even appear very angry. He just seems intense, like he is determined to find out what it is that Gregor sees in me.

I don't know what to tell him, so I just start babbling. "Maybe he liked that I didn't know very much before I met him, so he could teach me things?"

A terrifying light comes into his eyes. "He taught you things?"

It was a mistake to say it, I know it now, but it is too late to take it back. I try to shake my head. He leans over, grabs a huge fistful of my hair, and drags me up to my knees. I look up at him fearfully.

"What things?" he demands. "Show me."

I remember a heavenly time when Gregor asked me to show him. That seems so long ago, and so different from the hell I find myself in now. I swallow down a sob, and nod my head at the man before me, moving against his fist in my hair, to tell him that I will do whatever he says. I will show him. All of the beautiful, pleasurable things that I enjoyed with Gregor, I am going to have to surrender to this beast. It is how I will survive this.

I give him a shaky smile from my knees in front of him, hoping that he is ignoring my tears, my tremors. With his hand still clenched painfully in my hair, I reach up with trembling hands to unfasten his trousers.

Mason

I finally have succeeded in robbing him. I couldn't do it on the Trace, but I am doing it now. I am stealing the little secrets he shared with his whore, making her do to me all of the things that he taught her to do to him.

Her appearance is unremarkable, but I can see the appeal in training a woman in the exact best way to please a man. I don't know whether it is merely her technique that is so pleasurable, or the knowledge that I am taking something from him. But I quickly orgasm, overcome with the sensations she has created in me.

When I open my eyes, I see the relief in hers. She thinks I am finished. I smack her again, and she falls back to the floor. I am nowhere near finished.

Chapter 37

Fitting

April 25, 1811
Ellis Cliffs
Marguerite

The plans are all falling into place. With the wedding coming up in about five months, Margaret is maturing, and assuming control over the preparations. I am relieved she is taking charge, now that I have nudged her in the right direction.

I find myself increasingly fatigued, but I have not mentioned this to anybody yet. My maid can tell, I know, but other than diligently tending to me, there isn't anything she can do. I suspect there isn't anything to be done. I don't wish to ask a physician to examine me, because not only is our physician my daughter's fiancé, but I suspect the answer will either be that I must rest more, or there is nothing which can help.

I simply try to conserve my energy when I can, take a rest in the afternoon every day, and ignore my fatigue when necessary. I can relax after the wedding in September.

I am less able to accomplish all of the tasks of running the plantation. There are certain things I am ignoring. Well, not ignoring, as the lady of the household I cannot ignore anything. I should say that I am prioritizing things differently. The top priority is establishing Margaret's household and planning for her nuptials. The well-being of my other children is another priority.

But other than the immediate family concerns, I have been forced to become less diligent. For instance, I am relying more on the overseer and Hester to supervise the slaves.

I am also paying less attention to Abraham's activities on the plantation, and, I suspect, in the house itself. I refuse to speculate about what he is doing with Margaret's maid. It grieves me, not because I am jealous, certainly, but because it is so unseemly for a gentleman of his position in society to stoop to this level. He thinks I don't know, but of course I do. Every day I see Dalila grow more subdued and unhappy. I worry this will interfere with her duties. But after the wedding, Margaret will take her away to live at Homochitto, and it will no longer be a problem.

The passage of the next five months of time will bring relief on so many levels. I simply need to find the energy to get through them.

I'm pleased that Margaret has made the arrangements for the creation of her bridal trousseau. She has a scheduled time this week to travel to the dressmaker in Natchez for another fitting, and Nancy and I are planning to accompany her. Our gowns for the wedding are also being prepared and we will be fitted as well. I am sure that the journey will be tiring, but I need to come along, to offer my guidance to my daughter.

To see her settled is my fondest wish. I will do whatever it takes to make sure it is so. My own concerns, my personal issues, can wait.

Dalila

The moment Ayola opens her eyes, she greets me with "Woosh, woosh?" It is so funny. She has been doing this for months now. I still don't know what she means by it. It isn't my name, she calls me Mama. She calls Margaret something closer to Mar-Mar. She has names for Richard, for Nancy, for Missus, for Hester, for Samson. But what is Woosh? I don't know if I'll ever figure it out.

At eight months old, I think it is early for her to develop a vocabulary, but she seems to be. She has other words, not only names. And I think she's already trying to walk. She has been strolling along the edge of rooms, holding on to furniture and scuttling sideways on her tiny little legs. It's only a matter of time before she launches herself off into the middle of the room. Again, it seems very early for walking, but maybe it will be more helpful if she can follow me around while I work, rather than still trying to carry her with me.

Today Miss Margaret will be traveling to Natchez to have another fitting for the clothing being prepared for her wedding. She must have a whole trousseau, all manner of new things to wear once she is married. It is amazing to me still to observe how people live in this land, in this house. Imagine needing dozens of garments.

I try not to think about my queasy stomach as I change Ayola and prepare to tend to Miss Margaret. My courses have never started again since I first was pregnant with Ayola, and I thought that meant I wouldn't be getting another baby. But since the Master has been using me so often, I am afraid it might have happened somehow. I feel the way I did at the beginning with Ayola. The idea of bringing another child into this world, another child whose father will see it as nothing but another slave, another child I will have to find a way to somehow take care of while not neglecting my duties, is misery itself. I still am not sure, but I will know soon enough.

It is one of the many things I have to force myself not to dwell on while I serve Miss Margaret. She likes me, and I like her, and as long as she is pleased with me I am sure she will bring me with her after she is married. That is how I can get away from the Master's abuse. It is the only salvation I am likely to ever find in this land.

Natchez

Stephen

I think I'm going to convince my brother to stay. Samuel's arrival in Natchez right now is so incredibly fortuitous. He's looking for a place to settle down, and I need help with my medical practice. He has finished at Dickinson College with his medical studies, but hasn't apprenticed yet. I want to take him on here, then have him take over in a few months so I can focus on Homochitto after the wedding.

Thomas has obligingly relinquished his bed to Samuel. My friend sleeps on the sofa in the other room when he is here. Thomas has been spending more nights away, mostly with the militia, but sometimes in relation to some business dealings he has down in Louisiana, some fifty miles further south even than Ellis Cliffs. There is apparently some land available for purchase that I cannot dissuade him from. I fear he will soon be moving away from Natchez.

However, it does have the benefit of making way for my brother to stay in our rooms. Our uncle Henry, of course, has gone to stay with Samuel. His brother. The other Samuel.

Samuel, my Samuel, is quite willing to accompany me each day as I see patients, but he has not yet committed to remaining in Natchez. I am trying to make the practice seem as interesting and profitable as possible, in the effort to entice him to remain and become a doctor here in town.

Today we are getting an early start, because I hope to be finished with our medical duties by noon. Margaret and her mother and sister are coming to town today for another dress fitting, and as always I am eager to see her. It is a particular treat to get a visit from my fiancée without having to travel all the way down to Ellis Cliffs.

Our uncle Samuel has offered to host us and the Ellis ladies for a luncheon today at his home in Natchez.

We've seen our last patient, and I'm showing Samuel, my Samuel, how to take the notes on the charts that I keep. This isn't something which Dickinson teaches their medical students, it is just a trick I learned at my apprenticeship, but I find it to be very helpful.

I'm dictating to Samuel. "What were your thoughts about Mr. Reed's palsy?" I ask him, referring to our final patient. He tells me what he observed, and I instruct him to write it in the chart, adding a couple of notes of my own.

"Are we finished?" he asks, setting the palsy notes aside.

"Yes, let's go upstairs to clean up, then we can head over to our uncle's house."

In a few minutes we descend the stairs behind the building, and go back out onto the street. I see as we are passing that Thomas's office is empty. He must have already closed up, to go to Uncle Samuel's house. I know he was looking forward to seeing Nancy again as well. It's almost unseemly how much attention he pays to the young girl, but her parents don't seem to object to it.

When we arrive, we are shown into the handsome parlor by Uncle Samuel's doorman. We are apparently the final guests to appear. Margaret immediately rises to greet me, with a beatific smile, and extends her hand for me to kiss. Only five more months until I will have the freedom to do far more than kiss her hand. I can hardly wait.

I see that her maid has come with her, presumably to help with the dress fittings, and is standing in the back of the room holding her baby.

I turn to my brother Samuel. I am beaming with pride to introduce him to my lovely intended bride. "Margaret, my dear, may I present my brother Samuel Duncan? He has traveled here from Pennsylvania, and I am hoping to entice him to remain in Natchez and join my medical practice."

She turns her gentle smile upon him. "So pleased to meet you, Mr. Duncan. Or is it Doctor Duncan also?"

Samuel grins. The other Samuel chuckles. "Doctor Duncan now, madam, I have finished my studies."

She gives a little laugh. "I must say, you and your brother are so alike that I would think you were twins if Stephen had not told me otherwise. Imagine! Two identical Doctor Duncans in Natchez!"

I see Thomas sitting together with Margaret's sister at the back of the room, and he guffaws. Samuel and I grew up with Thomas in Pennsylvania, and spent all of our days teasing and rollicking with each other. Having our trio back together has put us all right back into our old habits, laughing and joking nearly constantly. Thomas remarks jovially, "I think one Doctor Duncan is quite sufficient! Good thing Stephen will be moving to Homochitto soon."

I laugh at the remark, but quickly calm myself. I must do my duty to my future mother-in-law as well. I drag Samuel over to the armchair where she is sitting near our Aunt Ann. The Postlethwaite children are playing at their feet. "Mrs. Ellis," I say, "please allow me to introduce my brother Samuel Duncan."

She does not rise, but she offers him her hand. "Welcome to Natchez, Doctor Duncan."

Our aunt adds, laughing, "Just what we need, another Samuel in town."

Henry, standing at the mantle at the back of the room near Thomas and Nancy, chimes in. "Well, Samuel, you apparently are either a duplicate of your brother, or a namesake of your uncle. It remains to be seen whether you are actually a person all on your own!"

My brother laughs good-naturedly along with everyone else. He has been hearing some variation on this his entire life.

Chapter 38

Tale

Ayola's

My beloved stares longingly at the two children playing on the floor at the women's feet, but does not fuss when her own mother holds her rather than allowing her to join them. Dalila realizes it would be seen as presumptuous to have her child play with the Postlethwaite children. Ayola is very young still, only eight months old, and normally I would not expect a baby of this age to have much understanding or patience in such circumstances.

However, Ayola is exceptional. Her perception far exceeds that of any other children her age. She is developing a vocabulary, and already understands a great deal of the spoken language she hears around her. Along with this, she has begun listening to my whispers with a great deal more comprehension and acceptance as she develops.

"You must be patient my darling, and simply stay with your mother. Be still and quiet. It is what is best."

She does not understand why it is important for her to remain quiet and accepting of her position, but she does it. She trusts my advice, even if she does not comprehend the reasoning behind my suggestions.

And she senses her mother's feelings. She always has. It is what keeps her still on their sleeping mat in the night when her mother is forced to leave her side. She does what she senses her mother needs her to do. So rather than whining or trying to escape Dalila's arms to play with the other children, she waits sadly.

It is an astonishing display of self-sacrifice for a child of this age.

However, her patience is soon rewarded. When a servant announces that the luncheon is ready, and the guests are being guided into the dining room, the nursemaid for the Postlethwaite children comes to bring them to the nursery. Ann turns to Margaret and offers, "If you would like to have your maid wait on you in the dining room, she can send her baby to the nursery with my children." Margaret turns to Dalila with the question in her eyes, and Ann adds kindly, "I couldn't help but notice that her little girl seemed like she wants to play."

"How thoughtful of you to notice, Mrs. Postlethwaite," Margaret responds happily. "I'm sure Ayola would love to play with the other children. She hasn't had the chance before. My brother is the youngest other child she has seen, and he's practically a young man."

It makes Dalila anxious to relinquish her daughter, as always, but Ayola's glee in being taken with the other children comforts her mother. The nursemaid carries the baby William, and another servant carries Ayola, while the Postlethwaite's daughter Matilda walks alongside.

Ayola is fully cognizant of what is occurring. When the servants enter the nursery with the children, and set the babies down on the floor together, Ayola smiles broadly at the little girl and boy. There are toys along the floor, including wooden blocks, simple dolls, a rocking horse. Ayola has never seen such things before.

The children are not yet old enough to comprehend the racial and societal divide between them. William and Matilda don't understand that Ayola is a slave. Soon, Matilda will begin to internalize the views of the area and time, and might then object to being expected to interact with a slave child. But that has not yet developed. So, the children are happy to play together.

Matilda, at four years old, sees Ayola as a baby the same age as her little brother. However, Ayola soon demonstrates that her abilities are far more advanced than little William's. She picks up one of the little dolls, hands it to Matilda with a smile, and asks, "Mama?"

"Yes!" Matilda says excitedly. "I am the doll's Mama!"

Before long, the girls are playing happily with each other, Ayola imitating all of Matilda's actions and words, while the servants watch indulgently and William sucks on a block.

I observe my beloved as she spends her first afternoon playing with other children, reveling in her delight.

My attention is diverted when I hear the name of the other Seer mentioned in the conversation downstairs. I begin listening more closely to what is being said, knowing that Wolk will certainly wish to learn of this.

The elder Samuel is saying, "Henry told me that Gregor encountered you along the Trace, Samuel. I can't believe the tall tale he told me, though, you must tell me what really happened!"

The younger Samuel grins. "I'm sure he told you exactly right, Uncle. We were a few miles south of Nashville when we came across a man lying on the ground, calling out for help. It looked like he had slipped in the rain - it was really pouring - and injured himself. So of course we were about to get off our horses to help him, and two other fellows suddenly leapt out of some shrubs they were hiding in and grabbed our bridles. The first fellow jumped up and demanded our money or our lives!"

Henry laughs. "Oh, come on nephew, don't exaggerate. I believe he only said hand over our wallets and we won't be hurt."

"Well," Samuel says, "it doesn't really matter what he actually said, because he didn't get our money or our lives. Just then, another man suddenly burst into our midst, from absolutely nowhere, on a huge brown horse rearing back over the thief standing in front of us. That fellow ducked away from the horse, and the man on it started talking to the two who were holding our horses' heads like he knew them. He called them by name, and told them they'd better not be up to any mischief or he'd tell their captain on them."

"Ah, they were Kaintucks, then," the elder Samuel notes. "I figured as much."

"I suppose so," the younger Samuel agrees. "At any rate, it worked, and the two let go of our horses and tried to tell him they didn't mean any harm. The third man started moving forward, and Gregor - we know now it was Gregor - jumped right on him!"

Henry adds, "Don't forget the part about Gregor knocking him down before that, too."

"Oh, right! When he first got there, when the other man came up like he would grab Gregor's bridle too, Gregor spun his horse around and knocked him down. Then, when he got up and started to come back, Gregor jumped right down on top of him. It knocked the wind out of him, so Gregor swiped his knife and left him there in the mud. Then he sprang back onto his horse and told us to follow him down the road to an inn!"

The audience is riveted, and the tale is told with many other interruptions, corrections, additions and exclamations of amazement. I am enjoying the story just as much as any of the humans, looking forward to relaying the entire thing to Wolk. I know it will amuse Gregor to hear what was said of him.

Henry carries on with the tale. "We got into the inn, just a little shack really, and when we introduced ourselves Gregor told us he knew folks in Natchez with the same last names, and that is when we figured out the connection. We had a meal, well, some Indian flat bread which was all the inn had to offer, and chatted for a while before he left to continue north."

Samuel now reminds him, "Don't forget about him telling that same fellow to get lost again!"

"Oh yes," Henry says, "when we were outside tending the horses the Kaintuck Gregor had jumped on tried to make his way into our inn, and Gregor said, 'This inn is full. Move on to the next one.'" He perfectly imitates Gregor's accent to much acclaim by all. Most of the audience have met and spoken extensively with Gregor.

The younger Samuel concludes, "He handed us the list of inns that Uncle Samuel had given him, then mounted his horse and headed north. It was like he was vanishing back into the ether from which he had materialized. He seemed more phantom than person!"

Thomas has been laughing throughout the performance. "What a jolly tale! You'd never know that Gregor has such skills. All he ever does is make plans about steamboats."

"Although," Stephen adds thoughtfully, "the first night we met him he did clean us out very thoroughly playing poker. He seems to be a man of many hidden talents."

The conversation moves on to the steamboat enterprise Gregor is engaged in. I listen attentively, anticipating the enjoyment the Seer and his Guardian will feel when I relate to them everything that was said.

Chapter 39

Conversation

Pittsburgh
Nicholas

Slavson has been in Pittsburgh for a couple of weeks, and we have established a comfortable pattern. He meets me shortly after dawn at the shipyard, coming from the boarding house where he has taken lodgings. We offered to let him stay in our home with us, but he declined, saying that he keeps odd hours and would not want to make any noise which might disturb our child. Lydia generally joins us in the shipyard at noon, bringing a basket of food packed by our cook to share for lunch. She usually stays for the afternoon, while Rosetta is napping in the nursery with the nursemaid, to go over the correspondence and ledgers.

Our newest partner comes every day to the shipyard to talk, but more than that, he comes to help. Unlike any other investor I have ever known, he wants more than anything else to roll up his sleeves and actually participate in what we are doing. He has helped unload timber, cut planks in the sawmill, stoked coal in the furnace, coiled rope, even examined our account books and made some helpful suggestions. Today he is assisting in the foundry, helping to pour molten iron into molds to create the fittings which will be used in mounting the engine.

He cheerfully works alongside all of the men, both the whites and the free blacks. He had asked me the first day he was here if any of the black men were slaves. I explained that there are few slaves left in Pennsylvania, and that the men I hire are all free. This seemed to please him.

We have been spending the days working on whatever tasks are most urgent, then returning home as the sun is setting, where Fulton joins us for supper. He is also visiting, from New York, a fortuitous coincidence to have three of the four partners on our project together. The fourth, Livingstone, remains in New York.

Slavson has assured us that if any additional funding is required, we can contact the bank in Pittsburgh where he had his New York agent transfer the necessary capital.

Tonight will be Fulton's last night in Pittsburgh. Tomorrow he begins his return journey to New York. As our maid Abigail serves her specialty for dessert, apple pie with cinnamon, Fulton asks Slavson, "Gregor, are you sure you don't want to have me draft up some documents with our understanding?"

Lydia looks up from spooning small pieces of baked apple into Rosetta's mouth.

Slavson shakes his head. "No, Robert, please don't bother. I trust you. You've always been very diligent in sending along any profits. I don't need to be a formal part of this."

"You certainly are an important part, though," I remark. "Not just the money. You've done the work of five men over the past two weeks. Are you sure I can't convince you to stay here in Pittsburgh until the New Orleans is ready to launch?"

He smiles around a mouthful of pie. "This is delicious, by the way," he tells Abigail who is still standing in the back of the room. She smiles her thanks. He looks back over to me. "No, you'll need me in Natchez to get ready for the boat to arrive. I need to get the whole community excited for the steamboat. The more publicity the better, you know. By the time it reaches us, everyone in the region will be dying to use a steamboat for travel and cargo." He reaches down to pat Tiger, who refuses to be anywhere except at Slavson's feet whenever he is around.

Fulton nods, and I reluctantly concede. I surely have appreciated Slavson's help, and hate to see him go. But I know he is planning to depart in another day or two as well. I look over at Lydia, who is smiling at me, knowing just what I'm thinking. She raises her eyebrows at me, clearly reminding me that she'll be here. The two of us can complete the project, together.

Gregor

Robert takes his leave, amid many goodbyes and fare thee wells. I have been happy to be able to spend time with my old friend. I was not certain our time in Pittsburgh would overlap. I enjoyed our reunion. He teased me a little about how boyish I still appear after so many years, but I was able to wave it off with comments about how youthful looks are a family trait. I believe this is the last time I will be able to meet with him, because with the passage of a few more years my unchanging appearance will cease being funny, and instead be baffling or even alarming. I am always very careful to avoid the attention or suspicion this would cause.

I linger after he has departed, continuing the conversation with Nicholas and Lydia. I greatly appreciate this time with the Roosevelts. They are welcoming, friendly, interesting, and very competent in their management of the shipbuilding. It is unusual to see a husband and wife team up in such a complex enterprise. I have seen plenty of married couples work together, of course, on farms, at inns, many places. But this venture is such an innovative and complicated project. The two of them together perfectly complement each other as they pursue it. It is marvelous to behold.

And a little sad, for me, to think that such a loving partnership has always been denied to me. Long ago when I was still young I had a wife, and when she died I found another. But after she was gone, taking with her most of the pieces of my shattered heart, I forced myself to stop searching for love in that way. The pain was too intense to ever want to repeat, as would inevitably happen.

After Lydia has been out of the room for a few minutes to settle their child into bed, she returns to silence in the parlor where Nicholas and I are sitting. Both Tiger and Wolk are with us as well, of course. Tiger is curled against me, and I am absentmindedly petting him. We are all lost in our own thoughts.

She sits next to her husband, then remarks, "Gregor, you look sad. Why?"

Lydia is both perceptive and blunt. I do not believe she ever refrains from asking a question, regardless of how it might be received. I have realized that she is on a lifelong quest to understand as much as possible. So, I just answer her honestly.

"Oh, I was thinking about how much I admire you and Nicholas, for how well you work together, and how much you love each other."

"And this makes you sad?" she asks.

I give a small smile. "Not everyone has been as lucky in love as the two of you."

Nicholas reaches his arm around her and pulls her to him. We have grown comfortable enough in each other's company that he does not worry I would find this public display of affection to be indecorous. Indeed not. It is charming.

"I am the lucky one here," he says.

She settles down against him. "Well, Nick, I didn't leave you much choice."

I want to hear their rendition of the tale that Wolk has told me of their relationship. I take advantage of this opening. "How did you two meet, anyway?"

Nicholas grins. "I'll bet you've been thinking that I am a dirty old man who preys on young girls, haven't you?"

I direct my answer to her. "Begging your pardon, Madam, but I have gotten to know you well enough that it seems very unlikely you would be preyed upon. I'm more inclined to believe you got exactly what you wanted."

She says with a twinkle in her green eyes, "You would be correct." She looks to her husband, silently encouraging him to tell the tale.

He obliges, as I sense he would oblige her in anything. "Lydia's father, Benjamin Latrobe, and I were friends and business partners, long before I ever met her. He had moved to this country from England after Lydia's mother died, and she and her brother stayed with relatives while he got himself established here." Lydia rests against his chest, her trousered legs curled under her on the couch. She is playing with the fingers of one of his hands, listening as he relates this story. She shows no emotion at the mention of the death of her mother.

"She was very young when her mother died," Wolk tells me in explanation, *"she has few memories of her."*

"By the time Benjamin sent for his two children after he remarried," Nicholas continues, "Lydia was nine years old. I will never forget the first time I saw her. I had gone to visit Benjamin at his home to go over some paperwork. Lydia was sitting with him in his library, a fiery little girl with shocking red hair." Lydia smiles with the memory. "She was reading some huge tome, far too advanced for a girl of her age, and asking her father questions about the contents. As soon as I interrupted them, she began firing questions at me. Who was I? What was I doing there? Did I know the answers to the questions raised by her book?"

I smile, listening to his fond recitation.

"Even then," Nicholas continues, gazing down adoringly at the little redhead curled against him, "she was overwhelming." He looks up at me wryly. "You might have noticed."

I laugh and shake my head, remaining silent, holding my hands up in surrender. I'm not falling into that trap. Lydia laughs too.

"Every time I went to visit Benjamin, Lydia was there, full of questions and opinions. She was no less brilliant as a child than she is now. I watched her grow, with amazement, into a person who might be the most intelligent I have ever encountered." He pauses, rubs his hand along her shoulder, and kisses the top of her head as it rests against him. He seems slightly sad.

"Nicholas is thinking that if a man had Lydia's mind and characteristics, that man would rule the world. He recognizes it is Lydia's gender which keeps her from advancing further in society."

It's almost like Lydia can hear what Wolk is telling me, about what her husband is thinking. Perhaps they have discussed this in the past. "If I had been a man, Nick, I might have gone further in life, but I would not have ended up with you. That is the most important thing to me."

He huffs in amusement, or perhaps amazement. "I have never understood why you think so, but I am very glad you do." He returns to his narration. "By the time she was thirteen, she announced her intention of marrying me. I do not think either her father or myself believed this to be anything other than a childish fancy, but, well...." He stops talking and waves his hand over her form, indicating that I can see for myself how that turned out.

I chuckle, and ask her, "How did you manage to persuade your father?"

"Oh," she says airily, "I could always convince my father I was right about anything. It took a few years, though, he wouldn't let me get married until I was seventeen. It seemed a very long engagement. And Nicholas absolutely refused to touch me at all until we were married. It was extremely frustrating." They look at each other, fondly, sharing private memories. I do not ask Wolk to share them with me.

I ask a question which is probably too personal, but I am moved by their story and can't help comparing their situation to mine. "How do you cope with the opinions of other people? I am sure that you have gotten a great deal of criticism, not only because of your age difference, but because of your other unusual choices. The flatboat journey, for instance. Does it bother you?"

Nicholas meets my eyes, then smiles at her. "It doesn't matter, as long as she is with me."

Lydia gazes at me quite seriously. "You can't let that kind of thing bother you, Gregor. How can criticism be more important than your own happiness?"

"She is sensing that you are asking about more than her situation. She doesn't know your own story, but she feels your questions are triggered by loneliness."

Loneliness. Loneliness? I am alone, true, it is natural to me now. Except for Wolk, of course. But the last few months have been filled with more relationships than I have indulged in for many years. Despite all the friends I have made, the connections I have formed, seeing the Roosevelts' love makes me realize what is lacking. My friendships can never provide me with the joy and fulfillment which practically beams out from Nicholas and Lydia. But that is not what I have set out to find. All of my efforts in Natchez have been because of Ayola. I have settled down and established friendships, deliberately to build a life which I can use to her benefit as she grows.

"Not Rosalind. Your relationship with her is separate from your other efforts."

I realize Wolk is right. Is it Rosalind? Is that why I am feeling lonely? Because I am missing her? It is true I think of her often, especially during the forced inactivity of the nighttime hours. How attached have I gotten?

I see Lydia watching me, waiting for me to answer her question about my happiness.

"I ... don't know how to achieve happiness," I tell her candidly. I suddenly feel terribly forlorn, and yes, lonely. Lydia is right.

"Who is she?" Lydia asks, quietly.

I stare at her, startled.

"The woman who you are missing? Is there something holding you back? Some criticism you are afraid of?"

I actually feel my mouth falling open. How is this girl, who I have known for only two weeks, able to discern so clearly something about myself that I have not even realized?

Nicholas says, with both compassion and humor, "Gregor, she can figure anything out. I've told you that. You might as well just tell her. Her advice is the best I've ever gotten, on any matter."

I stammer, very uncharacteristically, "It's not... I can't...." My dalliance with a prostitute is not a proper topic of conversation for mixed company. "I shouldn't talk about it."

Lydia chuckles. "Gregor. You're worried about scandalizing me? Me? Have you seen me? Out with it! I am sure there isn't anything about it which will cause me to faint."

Nicholas grins and nods, agreeing with her.

Wolk even nods in his wolf form. He thinks it will be good for me to talk openly with other humans.

I shake my head. Fine. I blurt it out. "I am very fond of a lady who works in a brothel." How can Lydia possibly make me feel young and inexperienced? And how can she seem so wise? Turning to a person who is practically a child for advice feels very backwards, but somehow comforting.

"And you miss her?" she asks.

I sigh. "Yes, I suppose I do." I submit to this experience, and just let the story flow out. "I met her the first night I arrived in Natchez. I went to her brothel for a bed and bath, and she was assigned to me by the madam." I check their expressions, to make sure that there is no sign of outrage.

"They are fine, my dear, carry on."

"I've been going back to visit her more and more frequently over the last several months. She brings me ... comfort. And a sense of peace. More so than I have had in a long time."

Lydia regards me, knowing there is more to it. "But?" she prompts.

I sigh again. This interrogation is hard, but I sense it will lead me to a better under-standing of what I should be doing. "But I am trying to find a way to respectably establish myself in the Natchez community, and I probably shouldn't be frequenting a brothel."

"So it is the criticism you are worried about. Worried enough to let it stop you from being happy?"

"Well, apparently not, since I keep going back to see her."

She shakes her head. "Give it some more thought, Gregor. I don't think just going to see her is what you need to achieve happiness."

We hear the baby stir and begin crying in the other room. Lydia rises, gives me a soft smile, and bids me good night.

I am left to stare at Nicholas. He shrugs. "Take her advice, Gregor, give it some thought. You'll sort it out. I don't think anyone else can ever be as happy as I am with Lydia, but if you have any chance to come close, you should take it. I've gotten a lot of chiding about basically marrying a child, but every time I see her looking at me, I realize it is worth any amount of condemnation."

I nod, lift Tiger's head off of my lap where he had laid it, and stand. "Good night, then, Nicholas. I'll see you tomorrow."

I give Tiger a hearty pat, then head off into the night with Wolk at my side and my head full of questions. What do I want, anyway? I can't have the kind of happiness Lydia is talking about. Can I have something close?

Chapter 40

Conclusions

Lydia

After I change Rosetta and get her settled back down, I spend some time patting her back to make sure she goes to sleep again. It is an excellent time to consider the facts before me. Gregor is extremely unusual. Nicholas sees only a part of it. I intend to parse the situation in my own particular way.

Like with everything else, I am fairly certain other people do not perceive things as clearly as I do. The reality of the situation lines itself up neatly for my inspection. The way I analyze facts is very different from how other people do it, but it's how I puzzle things out.

I picture each fact as though it is written on a page and tacked up on the wall. The wall in my mind grows thick with notes, facts about our newest acquaintance.

Fact: Gregor appears to be only slightly older than I am.

Fact: His appearance is deceiving. I have heard Robert Fulton talk about him, and know it has been over a decade since they met and Gregor began investing in Robert's various enterprises. If Gregor is really my age, that would have made him only a child at the time. Obviously impossible. Furthermore, Robert has teased him about this, jovially wondering about how Gregor manages to remain so youthful.

Conclusion: Gregor is older than he looks. At least ten years older. Assuming he was an adult when he met Robert, Gregor must at least be in his thirties.

Fact: Gregor has a large fortune, which he has generously applied to the steamboat project.

Fact: Gregor has refused to have his name associated with the project.

Fact: He says that he trusts Robert to send him a fair share of any profits, without having any sort of written contract.

Conclusion: Gregor is not investing in this project for the purpose of profit. He is too casual about it, too generous, too unconcerned. If it is not profit, what is his motivation? There are two apparent choices. The first choice is that his motivation is simply his interest in the process of building a new type of ship to bring to his community. The second choice is that he has an unknown motivation which he is not sharing.

I believe both of these choices are true. He obviously is interested in the project. He has demonstrated this by eagerly taking part in so many shipyard tasks. But I am sure there is some further hidden purpose to his participation. I do not have enough information to uncover it. Yet.

Fact: Gregor has displayed an astonishing variety of skills. He has taken part in most of the aspects of production in the shipyard, immediately learning how to perform each task as though he had done it before. In the sawmill and foundry he was able to work very quickly and efficiently at specialized and complicated tasks. He even spent one long evening with me going over our ledgers, immediately understanding what I have done with the figures, and making some very welcome suggestions about how I might more efficiently organize the financial records.

Conclusion: I believe this must make Gregor either the most extreme genius who ever lived, or even older than my initial estimate. Although he is clearly intelligent, I don't believe he is more so than myself. It must be that he is older. In order to have gained expertise in so many different areas, he had to have spent sufficient time with each one. I believe setting his age in his thirties is probably too low. But if he is Nick's age, why doesn't he look it? He doesn't have Nick's graying hair, or any lines in his face. His age appears closer to mine. There is definitely something unexplained about the disparity between his apparent age and his apparent wealth of experience.

Fact: Our dog Tiger immediately became completely devoted to Gregor. Although he is a friendly dog, he has never before been so enchanted by another person. I do not know what to conclude from this, other than that Tiger also senses something unusual about Gregor.

Fact: Gregor is lonely. He is a kind man, considerate of the feelings of others, always taking care to thank the servants or be friendly to the men working in the shipyard. Even Rosetta has enjoyed his attention. But it makes him sad to see the love which Nick and I share. Something is holding him back from trying to achieve it, either with his prostitute friend or with somebody else.

Conclusion: He is afraid. The question he asked made it sound like he is afraid of condemnation from other people. But I conclude that his fear is even deeper. He is afraid of something else.

Well, love is scary. It gives another person power over your heart. It makes you vulnerable, leaves you open to pain or grief or betrayal.

But the rewards of love are worth the risk. I wonder if Gregor will come to realize it.

Rosetta is quiet and still, sleeping soundly now. I picture the pages on my imaginary wall fluttering down, binding themselves into a book, and lining up on one of the many shelves in my mind where I store my thoughts.

I rejoin Nick. He has retired to our bed, but he is not asleep yet. He is waiting for me. I climb in under the covers with him, and he wraps his arms around me, gives me a gentle kiss, then lays his hand on my stomach.

"How are you both feeling, my darling?" he asks me.

For answer, I lean up over him, and let my hair fan around us as I kiss him deeply. The morning sickness has ended, I am feeling quite well, and have not yet started to show the pregnancy. Nick is the only other person who knows. "We have to take advantage of every chance we can now," I tell him, "before we have two children. And before the New Orleans is ready to sail."

He is breathing heavily, affected as always by my kisses. He rolls me over, his passion suddenly flaring and seizing control of him. Of us both.

I submit to him with delight. This is the only time I can get my mind to focus on just one thing. On him. On us.

Lydia's

It is always fascinating to observe as my beloved addresses herself to a puzzle. Her observations about the unusual man Gregor are both astute and interesting. I am pleased to take advantage of her thought processes to try to untangle something inexplicable even to me.

Gregor and his Guardian are the only pair I have encountered whose thoughts I cannot understand. It is quite perplexing. I look forward to knowing whether Lydia will be able to discover more about the mysterious man.

For now, I quietly observe while she enjoys relations with her husband. As she noted, these are the only times she is able to focus on one activity, without being distracted by other thoughts. Due to her extraordinary brilliance, her focus is intense and absolute, much to the pleasure of both her husband and herself.

Their love and joy with each other are a delight to behold.

Gregor's

He does not return to the boarding house where he has taken a room. He feels no need of sleep. Pittsburgh is a large enough town that he feels comfortable walking through the streets during the night, as he could not do in the smaller Natchez where it might be observed and questioned. Here, there are many people and much activity at every hour, so a man walking alone attracts no particular notice.

I, of course, monitor his surroundings so I can alert him just in case any criminals are nearby who might accost him.

Tonight, though, is peaceful and he does not encounter any other people. It is a pleasant spring night, cool but clear. The trees and plants are in bloom, the fragrance of young flowers filling the air along with the aroma of the river. He appreciates the smells of nature, and ignores the stench which comes along with human habitation. He walks up and down the streets, and along the banks of the rivers. His conversation with the Roosevelts left him deeply contemplative.

"I think when I get back to Natchez I should find a home for myself, rather than returning to the boarding house," he thinks to me.

"I agree. As it is your intent to remain in the area, it would be preferable and more acceptable to establish a permanent residence."

He sighs. It is easier to rent a room in a boarding house than it is to manage a home. "I suppose I'll have to get a staff." He knows that he will regret the loss of privacy this will entail, particularly as his sleeping habits are so peculiar. Servants in the home will notice that he hardly ever sleeps.

"Indeed, a staff will be needed. You will not want to spend time on maintenance and cleaning." He is also aware that a gentleman of his standing would be considered very peculiar if he undertook the managment of his own residence without servants. He tries to minimize the perception of his unusual characteristics whenever possible. He will bow to the cultural requirements of the era. Within limits.

"I won't buy a slave."

I am very familiar with his objections to the system of slavery which exists in this society. It is deeply offensive to him. He was born in an era when peasants were treated nearly as slaves, but they were considered free people. The slaves in many parts of this country are often treated as chattel, as though the owners do not even recognize their shared humanity. He considers this disgusting.

"You will be able to hire the help you need from among the townsfolk." Natchez is the home to a number of servants for hire, including some free black persons.

"Maybe when I get back I will stay at Madam Beverly's with Rosalind for a couple of nights until I can find a house to let."

I nod my wolf head, walking alongside him through the night. His thoughts linger on Rosalind again, considering the words of Lydia. He wonders if it is her advice that he should spend more time with Rosalind. He could continue frequenting the brothel, but with a home of his own this might generate more gossip than it had while he was merely boarding. The admonishment of the Roosevelts to be less concerned with the opinions of others seems unattainable, as his goal of being respectable for Ayola's benefit must take priority. He does not know how to untangle the problem.

There is not much he can do towards the effort of settling his housing situation until he returns to Natchez.

"Well," he thinks, reverting to his usual nighttime topic, "how is Ayola?"

"Ayola had a very enjoyable day," I tell him.

He looks down at me with interest. "Oh?"

"Today her mother accompanied her mistress to the dressmaker in Natchez, and Samuel Postlethwaite hosted the Ellis ladies for lunch, together with your friends Stephen, Thomas, and your new acquaintances Samuel and Henry."

He pictures the group convening at the Postlethwaite home. It occurs to him that the banker might be of help in locating a suitable residence when he returns to Natchez.

I go on with my description of the day's events. *"Mrs. Postlethwaite offered to let Ayola join her children in the nursery during lunch. Margaret agreed so Dalila could help serve the meal. Ayola spent a very agreeable afternoon playing with children her age for the first time."*

He is delighted to hear that his little charge had an enjoyable day. "How old are the other children?"

"Matilda is four years old, and William is slightly younger than Ayola." He nods, remembering the night that Samuel announced the birth of his son. I continue, *"Ayola*

was more interested in playing with Matilda, though, because her abilities are far more advanced than those of another baby her age. She and Matilda played with dolls, and Ayola practiced her growing vocabulary, repeating everything Matilda said."

It makes him both happy and sad. It is wonderful to hear that Ayola is flourishing, but it grieves him to know how much of her development he is missing while he is away.

I continue the tale related by Ayola's Guardian, knowing that the story of the conversation during lunch will entertain him.

"While Ayola was playing, the adults were in the dining room gossiping about you."

"Ha!" he actually laughs out loud, then continues silently, "What were they saying?"

"Henry Posthlethwaite and Samuel Duncan were enthusiastically relating the circumstances of your meeting. They both joined in, correcting each other, and even imitating your words, much to the amazement and entertainment of the whole group. This led to some speculation about what other hidden talents you might possess."

He chuckles while I provide the details of the conversation, shaking his head as he picks his way along a narrow path near the bank of the Allegheny river. He sees the path clearly despite the darkness of the night around him. He has come quite a distance from the Roosevelts' house near the Monongahela river, looping around the edge of the confluence where the Ohio river starts, and walking back up the Allegheny.

"After they finished gossiping about you personally, they moved on to discussing your endeavor to bring a steamboat to the area."

"Good, that's what I want them all thinking about. Although it is hilarious to imagine them gossiping about me. Tell Ayola's Guardian thank you for being my spy. This is quite gratifying."

He eventually stops walking before he gets too far away, and begins making his way back. He thinks about Ayola growing up in his absence, and realizes it is likely she will be fully walking and talking before much longer. He does not wish to miss anything else. "I think it is about time for me to start back home." He stops again. "Home. Yes, I guess Natchez is home now."

"Yes, my dear, yes it is. When will you depart?"

He resumes walking. "The day after tomorrow, I think. I'll tell Nicholas and Lydia in the morning."

Chapter 41

Goodbye

April 26, 1811

Pittsburgh

Lydia

I already have a feeling that Gregor is going to say goodbye today, so I am not surprised when I arrive at the shipyard, our lunch packed in the basket, to find him discussing this with Nick. My husband greets me with a kiss as always, then says, "Bad news, my dear, our friend here has decided to abandon us and return to Mississippi."

"Well," I say to Gregor, pulling the food from the basket and arranging it between them on the bench where they are sitting, "we knew you wouldn't stay forever. I'm glad you were here for a while. You've been very helpful."

Gregor takes a slice of the fresh bread baked by our maid Abigail this morning. "You've been very helpful too, Lydia. I'm going to take your advice, and give some thought to my situation. Maybe I will find a way to achieve some happiness." He chuckles and looks over at Nick. "Not on your level, of course. But perhaps something more ordinary."

Ordinary? That hardly describes Gregor.

I tell him, "You know that I realize there is more to you than meets the eye, right?"

He grins. "I could say the same of you."

Nicholas laughs at us both.

"Just keep in mind," I tell Gregor, "it doesn't matter how unusual you are. Everyone deserves happiness. If you can find a way to make it happen, take the chance. Don't be bothered by the opinions of others. And don't be afraid to take risks." I take Nick's hand. "A little love is worth a lot of risk, wouldn't you agree, my love?" He lifts my hand to his lips, kissing it gently.

Gregor nods, thoughtfully. "I will keep that in mind. All of it."

Gregor's

As he tells them goodbye while the sun is going down, declining their offer to dine at their home one last time, he says that he intends to leave at first light. He regretfully bids farewell to Tiger, the huge hound who has become so devoted to him, and climbs the hill up from the river, heading to his boarding house.

Once he arrives, though, he simply packs his bags and immediately departs for the stables. He has no intention of waiting until morning.

He is happy to see Issoba. The feeling is mutual. He has visited once or twice in the past two weeks, but has otherwise left the horse at the stables to rest. Walking around the town on foot has been perfectly suitable for his needs. Issoba is fully rested and ready for another journey.

We are on the way south before the sun has fully set. Gregor has a long night ahead. He leaves the stable on Issoba's back at a fast trot, both horse and rider excited to be returning to the road.

It took him six weeks to travel from Natchez to Pittsburgh, but he hopes the return journey will be briefer. Now that it is spring, the weather is warmer and much more accommodating. The roads should be in better condition than they were at the end of winter when he departed Natchez. With any luck, he thinks, he will be back home at around the end of May.

Ellis Cliffs
Margaret

"My goodness, Mama, you look half asleep." We are having an unusually quiet day at home. Our correspondence ordering furniture and supplies for the Homochitto house has already been sent, and we are just waiting to be notified when the goods arrive in Natchez. Our dress fittings are complete. It is not yet time to start planning menus and other details for the actual day of the wedding. Nancy and I are sitting in the parlor together with Mama, holding our needlework, while Richard is upstairs completing his morning lessons.

Mama widens her eyes and shakes her head. "I'm not asleep, my dear," she tries to claim, but I know what I saw.

"Are you getting ill, Mama?" Nancy asks. "Maybe something is going around. Dalila has looked half asleep since we got back from Homochitto."

It's true, my maid has seemed unusually tired lately, although it hasn't interfered with her duties at all. It is clearly exhausting chasing around after Ayola, who can crawl so fast that it seems she would win in a horse race. I look at the baby, who is cruising around the room, holding every surface she can reach while she sidesteps all along the edge of the ornamental rug. It seems clear that she will be walking soon, probably by the time she is only ten months old. Mama says it is very early to walk, but she has heard of some babies doing it. Dalila must just be tired from having to mind her little miss all day, between her duties waiting on me.

"Of course not," Mama tells Nancy. "I am still slightly fatigued from our trip to Natchez."

Nancy looks at her dubiously, then meets my eyes. We've been back for over a week. Surely she has gotten enough rest by now.

But, clearly Mama is not going to talk about it. She changes the subject. "Margaret, I was thinking about your dishes for Homochitto. I'm not sure we ordered enough china. Would you like to go through our pantry and decide if you will need anything else?"

I shake my head. "We won't be entertaining for quite a spell, Mama, I am sure the dishes we ordered will be perfectly adequate." She gives me the look I know means she is not satisfied. "But, of course, I would be happy to go over our dishes here, if you will do it with me, Mama." I should try to spend as much time with her as I can, obtaining the benefit of her wisdom and experience, before I get married and move away in another four months.

She smiles, but rather than getting up, she says, "Very well. We will do that in a little while." Her eyes close again. I look at Nancy, who just shrugs.

Dalila

I stand at the back of the room while they talk, keeping my eye on Ayola to make sure she isn't being disruptive, and waiting to see if Margaret might need anything. I hear Nancy speculate that perhaps Missus and I have the same illness, the same reason why we both seem tired.

I am certain we do not.

I know why I am tired. It is exactly what I feared. Master has got another baby on me. Apparently my hope that as long as I kept breastfeeding one baby, another would not come along, was misplaced. Maybe it happened because Ayola is eating other food now too, so she isn't nursing as much. Because here I am, already feeling the morning sickness subside, already starting to feel a slight thickening in my waist. I have not felt the baby moving yet, but I know it is in there, sucking away all of my energy and hope. I haven't got any idea how I will continue on after it is born. By that time, though, Margaret will have gotten married, and with any luck I will have moved with her to Homochitto. If I can get away from the Master, I think I might be able to find a way to tend two babies.

By then, Ayola will be walking, so I won't need to carry her. I will start training her to follow along after me as soon as I can. Even as accommodating as Miss Margaret is, I know that if it becomes troublesome to have Ayola around, some other arrangement will have to be made. Either I'll have to leave her alone all day, or even worse, she could be sold off to somebody else and I would never see her again.

My only comfort is in knowing that if it happens the same way it did last time, as soon as the Master sees my body growing with the pregnancy, he will lose interest in me, and leave me alone.

Chapter 42

Apparition

May 8, 1811
Gregor

A couple of weeks on the road, and the travel is going as smoothly as it can, but for some reason I am finding the time to be dragging. I don't know why I can't settle into my usual travel mode. Why can't I simply relax in the saddle, meditate, enjoy the scenery, like usual?

I feel impatient. My mind is full of the conversations I had in Pittsburgh, and also of what I anticipate occurring when I arrive in Natchez. It is a tangle in my head, the thoughts rolling around randomly, never coming to any conclusion, never solving any problems.

Wolk tries to entertain me, distract me, but I feel peevish with his efforts and he eventually goes silent. We continue traveling long after sunset.

After hours have gone by, he finally speaks. *"Issoba needs rest."* This is unusually terse for him. I suppose I've been so grouchy that he doesn't want to aggravate me. I send him a wordless apology, and the wolf simply regards me and nods. I know he understands.

I find a good spot to stop for the night, off the road, and after I tend Issoba I slouch down on the ground cover next to him. I sigh heavily. Wolk lays on the ground near me. My head is buzzing as I stare at the dark sky. Clouds drift past, intermittently obscuring the constellations overhead. The stars do not bring me any peace.

After a couple of hours have gone by, Wolk hesitantly suggests, *"Perhaps if you were to try to sleep?"*

Ugh. I know he's right. I genuinely can't remember the last time I slept. I do remember the last time I had any good, restorative sleep. It was in Natchez, with Rosalind, the night before I left. Months ago. I suppose that's why my thoughts are zooming around hyperactively in my head, and I have been so cranky and restless. Fine. I'll try.

Another hour goes by, tossing and turning. Will this night never end? I know that Issoba needs another few hours of rest before we move on. I finally give up and stand, and start pacing back and forth. Issoba looks over at me and nickers.

If only I was in Natchez already, with Rosalind. I am starting to think I'll never sleep again until I have been with her, until she has worn me out with her sweet understanding and enthusiasm. I try to picture her in my mind, but I'm too tired and agitated.

"Wolk?" I ask him. He has stopped making suggestions, knowing that it won't do any good.

"Yes, my dear?"

"Can you show me Rosalind?"

I'm sure he thinks it's a bad idea, since I won't be able to do anything but look, but he's willing to do anything to help me find some rest. *"Of course, beloved, please give me a few moments."*

I know that when Wolk makes a new form, it takes him a little while to think about how to create it. I don't know exactly how it works. But his usual form, the wolf, is incredibly realistic, and he can switch to it in a second. The same with his man form. If it is new, it takes some time.

I watch his wolf form dissolve into a cloud, which then slowly starts coalescing into a new configuration. Gradually, I see the outline of Rosalind's pleasant shape. Her long hair, her round limbs. After a few minutes have gone by, she stands before me, tangible enough that it could really be her, except for the shining glow Wolk always emits.

And that crafty wolf has dressed her not in the corset and petticoat she wears for customers, not even in her bare skin I have seen so often. No, she stands there wearing the long-sleeved, high-necked white nightgown I saw her in only once, the night I woke her up to come with me. The nightgown that made her seem so real, so comforting, so womanly.

He speaks in her voice. *"Gregor."* He smiles her smile, soft and gentle.

"Please, sit here," I invite her, settling back on the blanket where I had been trying to sleep. She sits, tucking her bare feet under the nightgown as she joins me on the blanket. Her nearness arouses me, painfully so.

I just look at her, while she gazes back at me. I could almost believe she is really here.

But of course she's not. I can't touch this apparition. I could speak to her, I know Wolk would imitate her precisely, but I can't have the comfort I truly need.

I suddenly jump back up, off the blanket, away from her. It is torment, the worst torture, seeing her, being so near her, but not being able to touch her. This was a bad idea.

"Wolf!" I beg, and Wolk instantly transforms back into the wolf, lying on the blanket.

No, this isn't helping either. "No, man, please."

And there before me is my oldest friend, the man, in his peasant garb, sitting cross-legged on the blanket, looking up at me.

I slump back down onto it.

I have to deal with the aftereffects of the arousal her image created in me. The man politely looks aside while I grasp myself and quickly find the relief that I need. Afterwards, when I have caught my breath, Wolk kindly asks, *"Do you feel any better?"*

"Better isn't exactly the word for it. But it was necessary."

We are silent for a few minutes, then I ask, "Why the nightgown?"

"It was the garment that pleased you the most when you saw her wear it."

"I suppose that's true." I give it some thought. "I wonder why, though?"

"I suspect it is because a woman in a garment like that seems less like a prostitute. More like a woman in her own home."

Hm. Yes. A woman in her home.

Seeing her like that felt like being at home.

I will be getting a home, as quickly as I can when I get back to Natchez. But of course, there will be no woman in the home for me. It will never be possible.

"Why?"

"What? You know why. I don't ever want to have to lose someone else like that."

"My darling, you will always lose everyone, no matter which home they reside in. I grieve for this truth, but you know it is so."

"Yes, obviously, and that is exactly why I can't have any of them live in my home. It would hurt too much when they die. I can't let myself care about them so much."

"But you already care about Rosalind. Lydia saw that."

"Not like that." Not like I loved my last wife, the woman who I still grieve for, even after all this time. I will never not miss her.

"Must you love so fiercely in order to find the happiness which Lydia encouraged? Can you not accept a lesser comfort? It doesn't have to be all or nothing, does it?"

I stare at the man, then lay back down on the blanket, gazing again at the stars. All or nothing. That is what I've been doing, isn't it. Not being able to have the love I once shared, the type of love I see in the Roosevelts, does not mean that I can't have something. I obviously know this, I have been frequenting brothels for most of my life. I can take that comfort. But I have refused to let it go any farther. I have been so settled into this pattern it has not occurred to me that I can change it.

"Why shouldn't you?" He is responding to my unspoken thoughts, as he often does.

To protect myself, obviously.

"Has this protected you from your frustrated desire to see Rosalind?"

Well, no. Also, I have to admit, I feel more for Rosalind than for any other prostitute. I wonder why that is.

"Perhaps you have finally gotten lonely enough, and tired enough of keeping yourself apart from others, that your heart took matters into its own hands, so to speak."

Wretched heart. "I don't love her, though."

"No, not like you loved your wife. But all love needn't be identical."

"Are you trying to talk me into admitting to Rosalind that I love her? How would it help anything? It would just make her feel worse, to have to be with the other men whenever I'm not there."

"Why would she have to do that?" The man seems determined to lead me somewhere in this conversation.

"Well, I'm not going to be at the brothel all the time."

The man actually rolls his eyes at me. I lift my head up in surprise. *"Gregor. The brothel is not her natural habitat. She is capable of leaving it, if she had somewhere else to go."*

"What? Are you suggesting she come to live with me? How, as my mistress? My own personal prostitute? That wouldn't be very conducive to establishing myself as a respectable citizen."

"My dear, what would Lydia say?"

"Um, she'd say I should take risks in order to ensure my happiness. But I don't see how having a prostitute in my house would be any better than in the brothel."

"Is she really only a prostitute to you still?"

Oh. Suddenly I see what he is getting at. At least he isn't actually using the words "you idiot" although he would certainly be justified in doing so. I am being so stubborn about keeping my perception of Rosalind that it is blinding me to the obvious solution. She does not seem like a prostitute. I think about the vision of her in the nightgown. She is a woman, who I am very fond of, who brings me great comfort, and who is a sweet companion. If I simply take the idea of "prostitute" out of the equation, I see what she could be.

"*Yes, you could marry her,*" Wolk says, as though relieved I have finally realized it.

"Other people would know where she came from."

"*Remember Lydia's advice. Don't worry about what other people think.*"

"It wouldn't be fair to her. I don't love her the way I think a man should love his wife. I can never be honest with her about who I really am. I can't give her children. I am a very strange person" - Wolk laughs at this - "and she might grow weary of me. She might not be accepted in society. And, eventually, I will lose her."

"*Honestly, Gregor, are any of these insurmountable obstacles? Frankly, none of these are problems that regular humans don't deal with every day. No married couple is free of such worries. Don't let your fear stop you.*"

"Are you calling me a coward?"

"*If the shoe fits.*"

The man lays back against the blanket and crosses his arms, smirking while I gape in shock at the insult. Wolk is normally far more diplomatic with me than this.

"*I merely want to help you see, beloved, and to make a decision that will make you happy. Lydia is right. You are lonely, and the solution is within your grasp. Yes, it will be temporary, but everything in life is temporary.*"

It is starting to sound like my concerns are ridiculous. Wolk's uncharacteristic bluntness is bringing me clarity I have not had before.

He nods. "*Furthermore, it will actually help in your efforts to establish yourself as a respectable citizen. What can be more respectable than a gentleman buying a home for his new bride, who can then manage his household for him?*"

Oh. That would certainly solve another of my problems.

"Still, I'm not sure it would be fair to Rosalind."

"*Don't you think she should be the judge of that?*"

"Fine. But it has to be her choice."

I start thinking about what to say to her, how to ask her. I realize that my thoughts aren't in such a tangle now, and I feel calmer. I close my eyes, suddenly feeling a drowsy peacefulness steal over me. Perhaps I can rest, after all.

Chapter 43

Done

May 30, 1811
Ellis Cliffs
Abraham

I've realized that the slave has gone and gotten herself pregnant again. I suppose I should have expected it, having her so often for the past few months. But it is very vexing. The first time I noticed her rounding belly I ignored it, but I can't overlook it any longer. It kills my desire.

So I'm done with her. For now.

Just as well. The weather is getting warm again, too hot and humid for wanting something which would make me feel even sweatier. When I come in from a long, hot day with the overseer, supervising the crop, or making plans for my future son-in-law's plantation, the only thing I want now is a cool drink and to have a slave waving a fan over me. I suppose I'm getting old.

Marguerite seems to feel the same. She is unusually quiet these days. At least with me. I know all she can think about is our daughter's upcoming wedding, so I suppose that is how she is using up all her energy and conversation.

It's fair. I am spending a great deal of energy getting ready for it as well, for Margaret and Stephen to have their plantation waiting for them as soon as they get married, with crops already growing. I go up there at least once a week, meeting with Stephen to go out and inspect the land. It's exhausting, but I want to see my daughter set up properly. Stephen has obtained the hands he needs to maintain the crops until harvest time, which will happen right around the time of their wedding. I suppose a real honeymoon will have to wait - he'll need to get busy right away with the harvest. Margaret has told me that they only plan to go to New Orleans for a couple of weeks after the wedding, then straight to Homochitto to establish their household.

It is late, the candles burning low again in my study. I close my books, and walk across the house to the stairs. As I pass by Dalila on her sleeping mat, I see her eyes watching me, then closing in relief as I continue on. I shake my head in annoyance at the bitch.

Natchez
Samuel Duncan

"Well, I wrote to our mother to tell her I'm staying," I inform my brother as we break our fast with some plain bread before going downstairs to his medical office. "I'll post the letter before we start working."

His eyes light up, and a huge smile comes to his face. "I'm so thrilled! I wasn't sure I'd be able to convince you to stay!" His expression grows more serious. "Thank you so much, Samuel. I can't tell you how much this means to me. It is such a load off my mind to know you will be taking over the practice."

"I know, I know," I grin at him. "I'm your hero. Now you can flit off to your new plantation with your bride to become a wealthy planter and pay no more mind to the citizens of Natchez." I duck as he takes a half-hearted swing at me.

Thomas is still laying on the sofa across the small room. He lifts the blanket off his face, and looks over at where we are sitting on our plain wooden chairs a short distance away from him. "Congratulations," he says, apparently to both of us, then covers his head again. He got in late last night, another militia excursion keeping him out until all hours.

Reminded that somebody is still trying to sleep in the room, we continue with hushed voices.

"What made you decide to stay?" Stephen asks me.

"I'm not sure it is any one thing. But it seems like Natchez has more opportunity. Everything is so much more settled up in Pennsylvania. It feels stodgy. This town feels like it is still new and growing. It's much more exciting. I like it here."

I'm not telling him one of the main reasons, the secret I keep, the shame that I hold. Mother would soon be searching for a bride for me were I to return home, and that is the last thing I want. I have never told any of my family, but I cannot imagine being with any woman in such a way, ever. I've known it since I was small and realized women do not draw my eyes the way they do for Stephen, for most men.

The three of us grew up together in Pennsylvania, and when Stephen and Thomas expressed longing for the assorted females of our acquaintance while we were teenagers, I would nod and agree, all the while baffled about how they could feel that way. They were a little older than I was, so I thought perhaps I would grow into it, but it never happened. The feelings they expressed towards the girls in town were evoked in me only when I beheld certain men.

I do not know how my life will unfold, or whether I can ever have the kind of happiness Stephen has found with Margaret. I don't know if there is such happiness in store for someone like me. I doubt it.

So, I will make do with what I can. I know I can be a good doctor to the people of this town, and make a living here. I admire the way my brother has established a medical practice in Natchez, and I appreciate what he has taught me already. There's a lot of knowledge that you don't learn in school, which only work and experience can teach. By the time Stephen moves to Homochitto in a few months, I think I'll be ready to take over here.

In the meantime, I have an idea. I feel the need for entertainment. "Do you have to work at the club tonight?" I ask Stephen.

"No, but I was planning to go for supper."

"Instead, would you like to go down Under-the-Hill with me? Play some cards?"

He shrugs. "Sure."

The blanket on the sofa gets tossed aside long enough for Thomas to interject, "I'm in," before he disappears beneath it again.

Stephen and I look at each other and burst into laughter.

"Shhhhh," the blanket scolds us.

Mason

It has become an addiction, an obsession. I work for the daily rate at the docks, using only enough money to have a meal or two, and save the rest. I sleep outside. After a few days, it's enough to return to Beverly's place.

I don't even need to say anything when I walk in the door. She knows, and summons Rosy over for me. Once she told me Rosy was busy with another customer, and invited me to try someone else, but I just turned on my heel and left. When I returned the next day, Rosy was waiting.

I don't need to say anything to her, either. After several sessions, she knows what I want, and gets busy right away. She is eager to please me. I try to pretend it is because she likes me more than Gregor, that she wants me more than him, but I can't lie to myself. She is just afraid of me, trying not to get hurt too bad.

I don't usually have to hurt her now to make her do what I want. Much. But it's part of the pleasure for me, seeing her pain, so I only hold back enough not to get blacklisted by Beverly. The madam warned me a couple of weeks ago, I suppose after Rosy complained about something, that if I cause any permanent damage, she will see to it I will not be admitted to any brothel in the area.

I can't have that, so I try to be careful. I don't think Beverly cares if there are bruises, so I make do with them. There are so many creative ways to inflict pain without the kind of damage which would get me in trouble with the madam. And as long as I can have Gregor's whore on her knees, frantically trying to please me, terrified of me, trying not to cry out in pain, it is enough. I don't care how plain she is. Knowing I am taking something of Gregor's is the best thrill of my life.

Not tonight though, sadly. I don't have enough saved up yet to return to Beverly's, since I was just there last night, having a particularly satisfying bout of pain and pleasure.

But a man needs sustenance. So after I am paid for my day's labor I head to the Kentucky Tavern for a drink and some of their cheap food. Stu is there, and a couple of other blokes. I'm sitting with them while they play cards, but I am resisting joining them. I'd like to win some money, but I will not risk losing the money I do have, now that I've got a goal. My money is for the whorehouse. So they've gotten me to agree to deal the cards for them as long as I'm sitting here.

The tavern is crowded and loud, but suddenly in the midst of the background noise I catch somebody saying an unwelcome name. "Gregor," I hear. I do not turn around, or stop dealing the cards, but I strain my ears to catch the conversation. It appears to be coming from the table directly behind me.

"I don't know," I hear one man say. "I would have thought he'd be back by now. It's been nearly four months."

"Well," another voice adds, "Uncle Samuel got the letter Gregor sent from Pittsburgh a few weeks ago. We know he made it that far."

A third voice chimes in, "I expect him back any day now. Who knows, maybe he's about to walk right in the door of this tavern."

Two of them start laughing. "That's how we met him, you know. He cleaned our clocks playing poker. Right here at this table, as a matter of fact!"

The other one says, "My meeting with Gregor was even more impressive - when he rescued me and Henry from those robbers on the Trace!"

More guffawing.

Goddammit. He has to be talking about the time I met Gregor too. One of those dandies is sitting right behind me. I doubt he'd recognize me, but I make sure to keep my face turned away.

I've lost my interest in cards. Especially for a game I'm not even playing.

I finish my drink in one swallow, stand and nod to Stu, and leave the tavern silently, carefully keeping my face hidden from the men at the table behind me.

I angrily sink down onto the rough bedding I have tucked into a little cavity in the bushes at the end of the docks, some salvaged burlap sacks from a dismantled flatboat. I have to make a new plan. That goddamned foreigner will not stop haunting my steps. He's coming back to Natchez? Any day now? I suspect he would remember my face. And furthermore, I'm sure he'll expect to pick right up again with his whore. She'll complain about me, no doubt.

As much as I would relish the opportunity to fight him, as much as I want to kill him, I am not willing to risk it. It is possible his actions on the Trace were not merely a fluke, and he wouldn't lose in a fight with me. I can't risk that. Furthermore, even if I do manage to kill him, if it is public, the militia might come for me, and eventually my past history will come back to haunt me as well. I'm still wanted in a couple of other places.

I have no desire to hang on account of the bastard.

Besides, I've already had my revenge on his whore. I will have to be satisfied with that. Who knows, maybe someday in the future I'll run into him unawares somewhere else, and finally get the chance to do him in.

But for now, I believe it is time to move on. I'm done here.

Every day flatboats from the north arrive at the docks Under-the-Hill, I help unload them, then usually load them back up with crops or other goods from around here to finish the journey to New Orleans. It will be easy to find one of the boats heading south tomorrow, and offer my services for hire to the captain for the trip. I'll figure out what to do next after I get to New Orleans. It is another town full of opportunity.

I'll miss having my way with his whore, though.

Chapter 44

Home

June 3, 1811
Gregor

This has seemed like such a long journey. Obviously I've had far longer. In fact there have been periods of years at a time that I have traveled constantly. But this was the first time I have been so eager to return home. I can hardly wait to get back into Natchez, see Rosalind, then find a way to visit Ayola.

First, though, I have some business to take care of.

Issoba and I have continued through the night, finally making our way through the fields surrounding Natchez as dawn is breaking, the river behind the town looking like a ribbon reflecting the pearly light as we approach.

I take him to the stables, lead him into a stall, and take off the saddle and bridle myself even though the groom is standing by. When I am finished, I reach my hands up to the horse's face, pulling his big head down so I can press my forehead to his. "Thank you," I whisper to him. He was the best companion for my journey, sturdy and dependable and tranquil. We understood each other perfectly during our travels. He snorts lightly through his nostrils, and moves his head to rub against me. I think he knows we are home.

Wolk watches silently as I commune with the horse.

Before I depart, I give the groom instructions to carefully tend to Issoba. I want him to be pampered. He deserves a reward for all of his hard work.

I shift my focus to my next step. Since I gave up my boarding house room when I left Natchez, and the club isn't open yet, there isn't anywhere to go to change or freshen up. I want to get straight to work, and start the day by speaking with Samuel. The elder Samuel.

"Where is he?" I ask Wolk as we leave the stables.

"Samuel is at home, but will be departing soon to go to the bank."

Perfect. I'll meet him there.

Samuel Postlethwaite

I can scarcely believe the sight that meets my eyes as I turn down Main Street to approach the bank first thing in the morning, ready to unlock the doors and start the business of the day. There, leaning against the building next to the front door, is none other than Gregor Slavson.

"My stars!" I exclaim as I approach, and he kicks off the wall to stand upright and greet me. "Welcome, welcome! Welcome home!"

I seize his hand for a hearty shake. He looks exactly the same as ever, not even tired from his journey, just his clothing a little travel worn, and a few days' growth of beard.

"Thank you, Samuel," he says with a broad smile. "It is very good to be back."

I use the key from my ring to unlock the front door of the bank, and usher him inside.

I invite him to sit in the chair in front of my desk. "You must tell me everything, son," I say as I move around to my own seat.

"I spent two weeks in Pittsburgh where the steamboat is being constructed, and I am very encouraged by the progress," he tells me, full of enthusiasm. "I met the Roosevelts, the couple who you had seen when they journeyed to Natchez two years ago. They are in charge of the construction, and I am extremely confident in their ability to finish it quickly. I expect their journey to start soon, and for the steamboat to be here before the end of the year. By next year it will be taking regular trips back and forth between here and New Orleans."

"What splendid news! And what of your journey?" I am eagerly waiting to hear his version of his meeting on the Trace with my brother and nephew.

"The traveling was smooth enough. Easier returning, since the season has turned and the weather and roads were finer." I keep watching him expectantly. "Oh yes!" he adds, obviously suddenly remembering. "I also ran into your brother! I gave him the list of inns you had prepared for me."

I clap my hands together with glee. "I know! He and Samuel have told us all about it! Your heroic rescue from the highwaymen! You have become quite the legend with the tales of your exploits."

He laughs and waves it away. "Oh goodness, that sort of thing always gets exaggerated. I'm glad to hear they made it into town all right. Are they still here?"

"As a matter of fact, they are both settling in Natchez. And both very welcome. Henry is working at my mercantile, being extremely useful. And my namesake is taking over Stephen's medical practice, so we won't be losing a town doctor when he gets married and moves to his new plantation."

"That is all excellent news. I am very much looking forward to reuniting with everybody." He pauses. "In the meantime, though, may I ask your assistance yet again?"

"Of course, my boy, of course! I am entirely at your disposal. What may I help you with?"

He smiles his thanks. "I've decided I need to establish a real home, now that I will be living here permanently. I don't think it would be suitable to go back to the boarding house. Do you happen to know of any houses in Natchez up for lease?"

"I certainly do! There are several, and also a handful of homes available to purchase if that is your preference."

He nods. "I appreciate it. I'd like to obtain one as soon as possible. Today, preferably."

"You really don't waste time, do you, my boy? Well, let's get started then." I am happy to clear my calendar and focus on Gregor's housing needs instead. "We'll have you set up with a household in no time."

"Thank you. Also," he goes on, "I've brought some additional funds to deposit. I figured as long as I was in Pittsburgh I should make a withdrawal from the bank there, save the trouble of sending a messenger to transfer more money later."

He draws a thick envelope from his coat pocket and lays it on my desk. I quickly open it and leaf through the banknotes within. This is far more money than he has already deposited here, and the earlier amounts were substantial enough. I cannot imagine how he felt confident enough to travel alone, unguarded, with so much money in his possession. He could buy ten houses if he wanted. Is there no limit to this boy's wealth?

"Excellent," is all I tell him, not wanting to appear overly impressed. "We'll get this sorted straight away." He looks to the side then smiles, like he can see right through me.

Gregor

If Wolk wasn't able to communicate with Ayola's Guardian, I probably would have gone first to Ellis Cliffs to check on her. But I know she is fine, so I have had the leisure to take care of my transactions.

It has been a very productive day. Samuel insisted on driving his buggy to take me all around Natchez himself to view the various available properties. We certainly could have walked but I suppose this saved a little time. It did not really matter much to me which house I chose, as long as it was one I could take possession of immediately. This limited the selection somewhat, but there were a handful which were vacant and ready to change hands. Samuel made sure it was possible, wanting to accommodate me in anything I wish, especially considering the funds his bank is holding for me now. This is one of the privileges of wealth that I actually do appreciate.

Samuel did have a few suggestions about what I should be looking for. He advised me to obtain a house large enough to have quarters for at least one or two servants, as well as sufficient room for entertaining downstairs, and some bedrooms upstairs. Fine. I basically let him pick the house for me, larger than I would have chosen for myself, and a purchase rather than a lease. But it was available, he had previously been personally authorized by the owner as the fiduciary allowed to conduct the transaction, he was able to transfer the funds between the proper accounts, and the keys were in my hand by late afternoon. We will still need to sign paperwork, but the transaction is essentially complete.

The house seems quite fine and grand, uncomfortably so. It feels like far too much for me. I can be content in a boarding house room, or even on the ground outdoors, for crying out loud. I know I'm the one who decided to obtain a residence to assist in my respectability, but this seems like such a huge transition for me.

"You made the right decision, beloved. Just accept it. You will grow to appreciate this home."

I suppose. I gaze around, after Samuel tells me to enjoy and then takes his leave. My favorite part of the property is a large yard behind the house, overlooking the river from atop the bluff. I spend a bit of time enjoying the view south towards the Natchez town center, and gazing across the river, with the sun approaching the western horizon, before heading back inside.

There are some basic furnishings, enough for the household to operate. The bedrooms have beds. The parlor has a sofa and a couple of side tables. There is a table with a few chairs set up in the dining room. Most of the windows have shutters or lace curtains. The roof appears intact. There is a convenient cast iron water pump in the garden. There are candlesticks enough, and chamber pots, some blankets, even a few dishes in the kitchen.

The walls are bare, though, the woodwork on display throughout the home. The floors are also bare, wooden planks which want covering with rugs.

It feels overwhelming.

"You know that you might be able to arrange a very agreeable partner to help you establish this household."

Wolk is right. What am I waiting for? I leave the house, my house, tuck the key into my pocket, and walk along the bluff across town to the path down the hill. Wolk helps guide me to make sure I avoid running into any of my friends. Not yet. Now that I have taken care of the essential business, there is only one person I want to see tonight. I'm sure by tomorrow Samuel will have told everybody in town I'm here. I'll leave that for a new day.

And now, Rosalind.

As I eagerly stride down the path to Under-the-Hill, cheerfully anticipating a joyful reunion, Wolk seems suddenly troubled.

"What is it?" I ask, worried.

"My dearest, before you see her, you should be aware that Rosalind has suffered in your absence."

I have reached Madam Beverly's door, and I am too eager to wait to hear what else Wolk has to say before I turn the knob. As I enter the brothel, I silently ask him, "Because she has missed me so much?"

"More than that," he begins, just as I sight her across the room.

Her sweet face, her round cheeks, her long brown hair, her bare shoulders, all the marvelous parts of her which I have been longing to see, here before me at last. Really before me, not the phantom image Wolk projected for me on the road. She is really here.

A moment after I see her, she glances over and meets my eyes, and an expression of utter shock crosses her face. Before I can go to her, though, lift her from her seat, Wolk goes on, brutally, rapidly, trying to transmit the information I need to know before I do anything else.

"She has been abused repeatedly by Mason, the brigand you encountered on the Trace before Nashville. He discovered that she was your preferred companion, and has been victimizing her as a means of revenge against you."

Chapter 45

Broken

Rosy's

I am as shocked as she is when my beloved sees Gregor come in through the door of the brothel. As always, his thoughts and presence are hidden from me, or I would have at least known he was again in town and tried to whisper words of comfort to her.

The last few months have been anguish. What horror to helplessly watch Gregor's nemesis abuse her, repeatedly, deliberately, maliciously. My beloved has suffered in body and in spirit. And in soul. Her beautiful, sweet soul has dwindled sadly, diminished by the constant fear and pain inflicted upon her.

When I observed the miscreant board a flatboat the other day and head south, I tried to transmit to her a sense that at least he is gone, at least she is safe, but of course she did not hear me. She has lapsed into a dull state of constant dread. The last few times Mason arrived at the brothel, it barely triggered a sense of fear in her. Rather, she has begun to expect it as the inevitable horror of her reality.

She has not forgotten Gregor, nor stopped loving him. However, she has lost hope. She stopped looking for his return weeks ago. She has come to believe that her lot in life is simply to experience pain at the hands of Mason and other men, and try to cling to the memory of her time with Gregor as something sweet but now lost, which happened to her long ago. She has been broken. And I feel broken along with her.

I wish I could sense Gregor's thoughts. I saw in Mason's mind, so many times, Gregor's face and words being the motivation behind his abuse of Rosalind. He was obsessed with retribution against Gregor, using my beloved as the proxy for his revenge. I have often wondered how Gregor would react if he knew about this, and whether he had any idea of what Mason was capable of when he confronted him on the road months ago. I wish to know, now that I see him, but still cannot hear him.

However, I believe I see it on his face. He cannot hide his expression from me, no matter how hidden are his thoughts. His joyous smile at seeing Rosy sitting quietly on the far side of the parlor immediately shifts to an expression of horror and remorse. It is unclear why, though. I know all he can see is what is visible here, Rosy in her corset and short petticoat, waiting for customers. Her bruises are barely noticeable, because Mason has become quite adept at inflicting injury in such a way that it is not easy to see on her face or other exposed areas of her body. Why, then, does Gregor suddenly seem so aghast?

Rosy

Is it...? It can't be. He has gone, he has been replaced by the beast who I serve now. I used to mainly serve Gregor, but now my usual customer is the beast. He never has told me his name. I know I must expect for him to come, every couple of days, and force me to please him, with my body, with my service, but most of all with my pain. I have resigned myself to this.

Gregor is but a dream from my past. I cannot believe what my eyes are showing me is real.

And, this is confirmed when I see not the gentle and happy expression I remember from the man I grew to love, but what appears to be revulsion as he looks at me.

I tear my eyes away from him and stare at the floor. Of course he is repulsed by me. Assuming he is really here, and I'm not hallucinating. Sometimes I think I have done so in the last few months, trying to escape my reality when it became particularly unbearable.

The beast has made it clear how inadequate I am, how plain, how unworthy. I have come to understand that it is true. I deserve nothing more than the pain he inflicts. A man such as Gregor would never be able to love me as I loved him. Either he is not really here, or he will leave, or he will choose another. He is not here for me.

But then on the floor where my eyes are focused, are a man's shoes, standing right before me. Startled, I look up, and there is Gregor. His eyes are filled not with revulsion, but with compassion. Slowly, he kneels next to the chair where I am sitting. He does not touch me, almost as though he is afraid to. Or more likely he does not wish to sully himself.

But then, "Rosalind," he says, my name once again spoken in his beautiful voice, with the accent I have dreamed of, "would you be willing to come upstairs with me?"

Tears spring to my eyes. I cannot speak, but I can nod.

Gregor's

He has never been so appalled. The awareness of the abuse she suffered is made a thousand times worse by the knowledge that it only happened because of him. If he had not encountered Mason on the road, if he had not enjoyed defeating him during their insignificant little battle, this never would have happened. Mason would not have come here, would not have found Rosalind, would not have been torturing her for months. Gregor blames himself entirely, and does not know if Rosalind can ever forgive him. He will certainly never forgive himself.

However, he does want to punish the beast who did this to her. "Where is he now?" he asks me silently, grimly, as he tersely orders the best room and a bath from the Madam before approaching Rosalind.

"I have been searching the area, and can not detect him anywhere nearby."

"Find him. Somebody in this town knows where he is."

I immediately begin searching the minds of all who are in the vicinity. He is right. I will find the brigand.

In the meantime, I am also monitoring Rosalind. She is damaged. She literally cannot believe her eyes when she sees Gregor. Then, when she sees the horror in his expression as I explain to him what has been happening, she assumes it means he is disgusted with her, not at what has been done to her. I am relaying to him everything which might assist him in handling this situation.

He kneels before her, tenderly asking if she will come upstairs with him. His plans have changed utterly. He had considered asking her immediately to leave the brothel with him, but now he realizes that he must prioritize her needs. The situation with his house and proposal and everything else will have to wait. She is injured, both in body and in mind, and he must see what he can do to heal her, to help her. He must take her someplace familiar, not try to further shock her with exposure to his new house tonight.

As she silently rises and accompanies him upstairs, not believing it is really happening, I have news. *"Darling, some of the dock workers observed Mason take a job on a flatboat heading south to New Orleans two or three days ago. He has not returned to Natchez."*

"Good," he thinks to me. "I will deal with him later."

When they enter the room, he makes it his first priority to reassure her. He leads her to the settee, and sitting close to her, tells her, "Rosalind, I am sorry I was gone for so long. I will not leave you alone again. You are safe now."

She looks at him, confused. She does not know he has any idea what was happening in his absence. This entire scene seems very unreal to her still. She doubts the truth of his return. He lifts his hand to her face, planning to brush her hair back from her cheek, and is dismayed when she flinches.

It is her little action in flinching away from him which makes him realize, more than anything I have told him, how serious is this situation. Tears spring to his eyes, to match those in hers.

They are interrupted by the staff beginning to arrive with buckets of hot water, and pouring it into the large metal tub. He decides to simply sit quietly, next to her, not touching her, until the tub has been filled. This will give her a few minutes to acclimate to his presence once again. And give him time to try to contrive the best way to approach the conversation. He knew this was going to be a difficult discussion, but before he arrived he had no idea how challenging it would really be.

Gregor

I have to force myself not to start weeping. My sweet Rosalind, who means more to me than I was able to admit to myself before now, has been hurt by actions which I set into motion. It feels like I did this to her.

She sits quietly beside me, looking down at her clasped hands which are resting in her lap. When I left her months ago, she was lively, eager, loving. Today she seems so broken, like a sad shadow of her former self. She seems less like herself than the apparition which Wolk created on the journey.

Now that I am closer to her, I see the fading bruises along her throat, the imprints of his fingers. I see dark circles around her eyes, and I cannot tell whether they are caused only by fatigue, or by the impact of his hand. As my eyes roam further, I see purple marks along the edges of her corset, where obviously more severe bruising hides underneath. I am sickened.

I wish I could heal her. But I don't have that ability. I never did. Not like my friend Yosh, the other Seer, who spent his entire existence focused on healing, and was often able to alleviate the suffering of other humans with his touch. I wish more than ever that he was here.

Apparently there is something about a Seer's touch which impacts other humans. Yosh was the expert. I don't really understand it, and have never spent enough time exploring it to be able to use it to any effect. It has been decades since I even tried such a thing.

I have tried to imitate Yosh occasionally over the years, laying my hands on a person in need. Although Wolk sometimes told me it was helping to bring emotional relief to another person, I never was able to detect any genuinely tangible benefit, no physical healing. Not like Yosh.

"Her primary injuries are far deeper than bruising, beloved. It is the intangible harm she suffered which troubles her the most. The fear, the horror, the depression have transformed her psyche, and her soul."

"I don't know what to do," I think to him in despair.

"You will do what she needs. You were just considering using the Seer's touch, which you have not attempted in a very long time. It would be worth a try. But at any rate, simply being gentle and patient with her, as you always are, will act as a salve to her wounded spirit."

I am frustrated with myself. Why haven't I spent more time trying to experiment with the touch that Yosh used so successfully? Why have I been so selfishly focused on my own desires? I could have been perfecting the technique instead of drifting around the world, staring into the sky and feeling sorry for myself. And my selfishness has led to this tragedy, the destruction of this young woman.

"It is not too late to try now. I will help you. I will provide you with every detail about anything which seems to result from your touch."

I feel my heart pounding. She sits perfectly still and continues gazing down, passively, brokenly. I wonder why she can't even seem to look up at me. *"She is behaving as Mason instructed, afraid to do anything other than simply wait for him to begin the abuse."*

"Stop!" I shriek at him in my mind. I have never been sick, have never felt the urge to vomit before, but I think it must feel like this. "Nothing else about that monster. I just want to focus on what I can do for her going forward."

The wolf lowers his head. The servants are nearly finished filling the bath. I tell Wolk, "Man." I want the support of the fatherly figure who helps me in understanding. He transforms instantly, standing silently with his hands clasped before him, waiting and watching.

When the door closes behind the last servant, I think to Wolk, "Tell me everything."

Then I reach, very slowly, over to her clasped hands, and gently take one of them in my own.

Chapter 46

Touch

Rosy

I do not dare to look at him. A part of me tries to remind myself this is not the beast, and Gregor has never hurt me, but that was so long ago. My memory of him seems dim. Not so my memory of the beast, of all the times daring to lift my eyes to him without permission earned me another beating. I finally learned not to do it. Ever.

All I can do is wait, wait like I waited for the beast, wait for the pain to begin. Because I cannot remember the pleasure any more. I only experience two sensations now: pain and not yet pain. Pleasure ceased to exist for me long ago.

I know my thoughts are tangled up, overlaying the reality of the beast with the faded memories of Gregor, but I cannot seem to separate the two. I have spent more time with the both of them than any other men. The beast constantly mentions Gregor, and this makes them seem so intertwined that they have merged together in my mind.

I suppose if I was to dare to look up, I would find the beast there. I am just imagining it is Gregor, and of course it is really only the other man waiting for me to make a mistake so he can land another blow.

So I wait.

Finally, after a long time, while I am only dimly aware that the bath is being prepared, we are alone.

What man am I with? I am confused, and afraid.

I do not dare to check.

Then, as I stare at my hands, I see his hand reach over, and take hold of mine. I tense up, waiting for the agony to start.

But instead of pain, it is something so different.

It is a warmth, suffusing my hand then quickly spreading throughout my whole body, like being wrapped in a soft blanket on a cold night. It is ... pleasurable, yes, that, but not the kind of pleasure I vaguely remember from my time with Gregor before. It is strange, yet it feels so comforting. I have never felt anything like this before, not even when I was with Gregor.

It is enough to break me out of my trance, my fear, my apprehension, and lift my eyes despite my training, to see who is really sitting here.

And it actually is him. It is Gregor. I was not imagining it.

The warmth continues to flow through me, just from the feeling of his hand holding mine. He allows me to look into his eyes, which are filled with so much care and concern and sympathy.

I am struck dumb, staring at him, feeling his hand, simply existing in this moment of warmth and comfort.

Gregor's

"Your touch indeed has an effect, my dear. She feels a warmth, and a lifting of the fog of fear which has clouded her mind. She hadn't even been convinced it was really you, but now she realizes that you truly have returned. And her soul seems to shine more brightly. It had become very dim, very suppressed with the suffering she has endured."

He listens intently to my words, continuing to hold her hand while gazing into her eyes, making no other moves.

"This warmth," he asks me silently, "is it something she felt before when I touched her?"

"Not in this way."

"Why is it different now?"

"I do not know, but I think it must be either because she is in need of healing, or because you are concentrating on doing it. Possibly both reasons." He wants me to continue, he wants to hear every possible analysis of what is happening. He is intently focused, so I am as well.

I resume my description of her reactions. *"It is plainly helping her feel better, and making her mind clearer. Her emotions are starting to stabilize. Her fear is diminishing, being replaced with a calm she has not felt in some time."*

He waits, as patient with her as I always am with him, and watches as her face relaxes, and I update him about her shifting emotions. Finally, after several minutes have gone by, she speaks, for the first time.

"Gregor," she whispers.

He is filled with elation. He does not allow it to alter his path. "Rosalind," he replies. He waits a moment, but when she remains silent, he continues. "I am truly glad to be back here with you, after so long. I have missed you, so very much."

She watches him, feeling his comforting touch as he continues making contact with her. "I..." she starts, finding it difficult to speak. "I missed you too."

He nods, and sensing that she would accept more, he lifts his other hand and slowly, delicately, caresses her face. She does not flinch, which causes his heart to leap. Rather, she closes her eyes, and leans her cheek into his hand.

"The additional contact adds to the impact of your touch. Her tension is ebbing even further. She begins to feel that she actually is enjoying being touched, for the first time since ... in a long time." He told me to stop talking about Mason, so I adjust what I had been planning to say.

"So," he speculates silently to me, "the more touch the better?"

"Quite possibly."

"Only one way to find out," he thinks to me.

With exquisite care, the hand he is holding to her face brushes lower, caressing her jawline, tracing softly across the bruises on her throat, moving to rest at her shoulder. She tenses slightly, opening her eyes, again making eye contact with him.

"She had been afraid to meet your eyes before, but as you see her fear has diminished."

Encouraged, he lowers his head, ever so slowly, and places a soft kiss against her cheek. She again allows it without flinching. He keeps his lips against her skin, moving along in a tender path to her mouth, where he gently, sweetly, kisses her again.

There are now three points of contact, her hand, her shoulder, and her lips. The Seer's touch creates a healing energy which flows out from each point, flowing through her entire being, touching her soul, bringing healing to her spirit, her mind, her psyche.

"Your efforts grow ever more successful. Each point of contact is bringing her a sense of healing."

Her emotions begin to overflow. The love she feels for him, which she had suppressed and hidden in terror, begins to make its way to the surface of her mind. Tears come to her eyes, tears of emotion, of relief, of affection.

He suddenly realizes she is crying when he feels the moisture flowing down her cheeks. He leans back from her lips, looking into her eyes, then kisses away the tears.

"You're going to be all right," he murmurs to her. "I am going to take care of you. You will never be hurt again."

Rosy's

I cannot understand what is happening. It is delightful to watch her restored under his touch. But how?

I have been watching with grief over the past few months as she withered under the abuse of the miscreant who has been torturing her. As her psyche suffered the harm no less than her body suffered the pain, her soul sustained corresponding damage. Her soul has always been a lovely thing, reflecting her placid nature, gently glowing and thriving in its own quiet way. But it has been mutilated and lessened, barely recognizable. I feared that she would never recover.

But, the moment this man Gregor touches her, I see a feeble glimmer of her soul's former light. I have never seen such a thing before, never known a human touch could reach a soul. I have watched her experience delight under his touch many times before he left Natchez, but it did not have this effect. Even while she was in the throes of passion, her soul had maintained its gentle glimmer.

But today, it shines, with the merest touch of his hand. What is happening?

Gregor's Guardian has unaccountably transformed, shedding the image of the wolf and becoming the image of a man. The man stands nearby, focused intently, silently, on his Guarded. I hear no whispers, can detect no thoughts.

I watch in astonishment as Gregor increases his contact with her body, and her soul reacts in unison. Not only her soul, I see. Her mind appears to be coming clearer, fear losing its grip over her senses, a slight sense of calm penetrating the ongoing anxiety she has been locked in for months.

It is utterly baffling.

I can do nothing but stare.

Well, I can do the one thing that I always do. I can whisper to her. *"Yes, my beloved, enjoy the touch of this gentle man, this man who has never harmed you, this man who clearly wishes you well. You are safe, my dearest, you can feel secure, you can try to find enjoyment once again."*

Gregor

It is working. Wolk tells me everything, but even without his descriptions I am able to tell. It is like she is thawing, slowly coming back to life after being frozen in a block of ice. She has been in the lowest, darkest, coldest depths of Hell, and she is reaching up to join me in the light.

I am taking my time, willing to do nothing all night but hold her hand if it seems to be what will best help her. But when I begin kissing her, hesitantly, I sense she would be willing to go further. As I said to Wolk, I believe the more contact, the better. Now that I have confirmed for myself she is helped by my touch, I want to touch her everywhere, as much as I can. I consider how to proceed without alarming her. The last thing in the world I want is to cause her more anxiety or fear.

Much to my surprise and delight, she provides me with the opening to move forward. After I tell her I will take care of her, her eyes happen to shift and light upon the bathtub sitting across the room.

"Oh!" she says, with the first glimmer of her natural character showing itself, "your bath must be getting cold!"

I laugh and impulsively wrap my arm around her in a gentle embrace. This action does not alarm her, and I feel I can go further. "Would you be willing to take a bath with me?" She hesitates, and I say, trying to find a light way to encourage her, "I've been on the road for weeks, I know I surely need one. I must smell worse than my horse."

It makes her smile, softly, the most wonderful sight I have seen all night. I had not truly hoped to achieve a smile considering how apprehensive she was when I first arrived.

But then, her smile vanishes, and she nervously reaches up to touch her throat, starts to say something, then lapses into silence.

"She has remembered that her body holds extensive bruising, which you have not yet seen. She is embarrassed to have you behold this, worried you will be repulsed."

I pause, considering what to say. "Rosalind," I tell her, deciding to be as honest as I can, "I heard when I got back into town that you had been abused by another man while I was gone. I can promise you it will never happen again. And I assure you it doesn't matter to me whether you have any marks upon you as a result. It wasn't your fault, and it will not diminish your beauty. I will adore every inch of you, as much as I always have."

She gazes up at me, her brow furrowed, obviously still worried.

"It is not only her embarrassment. She no longer believes her body can be seen as beautiful by you or anyone else. She spent the last several months being told frequently by the other man that she is inadequate. She also fears his return, and that he will punish her when he learns you have been here." I told Wolk not to mention Mason, but there was no way to avoid this. I need to know it too.

"You should also know he is gone," I try to soothe her. "He has left Natchez. He will never bother you again."

It is too early to tell her that I plan to take her away from this place altogether. I could never leave her here after what has happened to her on my account. I will eventually get around to my proposal, but even if she rejects me, I am not leaving her here. I will establish her anywhere she wants to go, if she doesn't want to be with me. But this is all too much, too early. I must take this one step at a time. And the night is still young.

Chapter 47

Healing

Rosy

It is sweet of him to try to reassure me, but he's wrong. I cannot stay safe, not when Gregor isn't here. The beast will return, I know he will, and the pain will return with him. But I can at least try to enjoy this night with Gregor. The mysterious warmth his hands are bringing to me is spreading, my mind is clearing, my fear is diminishing. Whatever happens after tonight, I will wait to face it then. For now, I will simply accept this. If it is a dream, I hope not to wake up yet.

He is waiting for my answer about the bath. I want to do it, I want to try to enjoy the pleasures he had taught me before I was forced by the beast's demands to sully their memory. But I know my body is hideous. My entire torso is livid with purple bruises, bite marks, scars, stripe marks. My breasts were the particular recipients of this treatment, and are barely recognizable. It has been three days since the last visit from my tormentor, so the bruising has diminished somewhat, but it is still painfully present. I wish there was some way to proceed without Gregor noticing this. I don't want to witness his horror when he sees my body.

While I am hesitating, not knowing what to say, how to proceed, he tells me, "Just one moment." He lets go of me, and I suffer a brief burst of cold and fear, as soon as his hands leave me. The warmth dies, the anxiety returns. But he is away from me for less than a minute, and I soon see what he is doing. He is moving about the room, blowing out every candle, extinguishing every lamp. The sun set much earlier, and only the dimmest light of late twilight is coming in through the window. He returns to me, puts his arm around me again, takes my hand in his, and the warmth resumes.

The darkness is a great comfort. I don't know what he knew, and he doesn't mention why he did it. He has never darkened the room before while we were together. He has told me he enjoys seeing me while we are bathing or indulging in other activities. Just as the beast likes to watch my suffering, Gregor has enjoyed watching my pleasure. But now, tonight, he has found exactly the way to make me comfortable enough to move forward.

"What about that bath?" he whispers into my ear, nuzzling his nose along my jawline.

I nod my head, knowing it doesn't matter if it is too dark to see, because he is touching me so closely that he will feel it. Slowly, as though he is afraid of alarming me, he begins to unlace the back of my corset. Each movement is deliberate and slow, and I realize he is giving me time to stop him if I wanted. However, I do not want him to stop. I can hardly believe it, but I am growing eager for this night to progress. I thought I had lost my ability to feel desire, but Gregor has rekindled it in me.

When he finishes unlacing the corset and slowly lifts it from my body, I feel the relief that comes from having the garment no longer pressing upon all of my bruises. It makes my desire grow even further.

I hear Gregor draw in a sharp breath, as though he is shocked. However, I know it is too dark for him to see me clearly, so it must be that his own desire is growing as well. He tenderly reaches up to me and caresses my body, bringing his wonderful warmth to the tangle of pain which has been left upon me. It is amazing how much better it feels. I reach over to him and begin to help him with his own clothing.

Gregor

As soon as Wolk tells me she is hesitating for fear I would see her bruising, the solution is obvious. It matters not to me whether the candles are lit. But she doesn't know I can see in the dark. Darkening the room gives her the confidence she needs to proceed. Wolk tells me that she feels a growing desire, and I begin to feel passion to match. I'd almost forgotten about the plans I had made before I arrived. I have been so focused on her needs that my own are insignificant.

I can't stop myself from gasping when I lift the corset from her body and see the ghastly damage which has been inflicted on her. It is horrifying. But I don't want her to realize I have seen her, exactly the thing she wanted to avoid. So I cover my lapse by moving my hands over her body, as gently as I possibly can, because I know the bruises must be causing her pain. I must be as delicate as possible. I want to remind her of pleasure, not bring her more pain.

When she begins helping me remove my clothing, hope surges in me. I believe this is going to work. I believe I can help her recover herself, heal from the damage, move on from the pain. Wolk agrees, telling me that every moment she is feeling better.

"In fact, my dear, the warmth she feels from your hands is bringing actual physical comfort to her when you touch any particularly painful areas."

Is that possible? Yosh might have been able to physically heal, but I never imagined I would. "Do you mean it is actually healing her?" I silently ask, while proceeding with the preparations Rosalind and I are making before our bath.

"It is unclear. She feels better. I do not have enough information yet to know whether it is because the physical wounds are healing, or if it is simply that your presence is so comforting. I will continue observing closely."

I will also continue what I am doing. Hope is surging within me. As well as desire.

Rosy

With the thoughtful way he is allowing the darkness to conceal me, I am able to relax and try to enjoy him. There is barely a glimmer of light in the room, but once my eyes have adjusted I can see at least well enough to know where he is and what he is doing.

Once our garments are discarded, we enter the tub together, using the maneuver we have practiced many times, he reclining in the tub, lifting his legs back out, and me balancing across him. The water has cooled somewhat, but is still warm enough to be comfortable. Once I lower myself against him, feeling his skin pressing against mine, I am flooded with the same warmth I had felt from his hands. The sensation it causes while within the cooling water is distinctly pleasurable. My injured flesh is somehow hurting less all the time, even though his hands move across the areas made sensitive by bruising.

He washes me in a leisurely way, and I do the same for him. We shift around in the tub as needed to accommodate our bathing, comfortable with each other, practiced in this activity. I haven't forgotten.

I had thought before I might be dreaming, but it strangely feels instead like I have awakened from a dream. This time with him begins to feel more like my reality than the horror of the last few months. It is like I have come home after a long journey. I think he must feel the same, because he has actually just come home after a long journey.

I hear a low chuckle. He kisses me softly on the neck from behind, as my back rests against his chest in the bath, while he gently lifts water in his hand to stream down my breasts. "I feel like I am home, when I am with you, Rosalind," he says, and I realize that I had almost forgotten the way he always used to guess what I was thinking.

I twist around to where he was kissing my neck, trying to catch the kiss on my lips. This seems to encourage him, excite him. I am growing excited as well. The fear and pain seem like the memory now, and Gregor the only real thing in my world.

Gregor's

"She is ready," I whisper.

His attempt to use his touch for healing has been remarkably successful. Her fear has nearly gone, she is not noticing the painful remnants of her abuse, and she feels desire for Gregor to continue, to move beyond bathing and caressing.

Careful to maintain contact with her, wanting his touch to continue its work, he lifts her from the bath, setting her on the wooden chair next to the tub. This is rewarded with a sharp intake of breath from Rosalind, who clearly remembers what he intends to do next. He reaches over for a towel from the pile nearby, and drapes it over her shoulders to make sure she does not get cold.

Then, kneeling back down in the tub, he wraps his arms around her hips, and begins to recreate their first time together, the time that he introduced her to this particular pleasure.

I revert to my wolf form and settle across the room. I do not need to whisper any further words to him. He does not need my guidance right now. He is being guided by his instincts and her responsiveness.

Rosy's

The damage of months is being undone in hours. The unexplained warmth that she feels from his touch is somehow healing her spirit, and even to some extent her body. Most of all, though, it is her soul which is benefitting, expanding, glowing more brightly than it had since Gregor left months ago.

By the time she is sitting on the chair in front of the bath, she is so restored to herself that she is not feeling any trepidation. It is only desire. Once he begins his ministrations while she sits before him, the glow of her soul only expands with her passion.

Then, later, when he enters her, I am astonished to see that the warmth from his touch, now reaching her both inside and out, flares to a new high, reaching the last vestiges of the damage which had been inflicted on her body and soul. Her rehabilitation appears to be complete. The fading bruises are the only remnants from the abuse she had suffered. Now, she feels only ecstasy.

I do not understand Gregor, I do not know who he truly is, but I am incredibly grateful to him for what he has done for my beloved.

Chapter 48

Proposal

June 4, 1811
Rosy

I awaken warm, strangely comfortable and happy, not with a start like I have been doing lately. The first thing I feel are his arms, still wrapped around me from behind, holding me to his chest.

It is real. It really happened. I had lost hope, resigned myself to my damnation, to my eternity of torment, but instead he brought me salvation.

He begins gently caressing my arm, as though he was waiting for me to wake up before moving. "Good morning, Rosalind," he murmurs into my hair where I feel his face nuzzling against me.

"Gregor," I whisper, still shocked that I am here with him once again.

"How do you feel?" he asks me.

What a strange question. I haven't heard such a caring remark since he left to go on his journey. I am not used to such consideration.

I hear him chuckle behind me, feel his breath rustle my hair. "You must get used to it, Rosalind. I will always want to make sure that you are well."

I am distracted from the first question he asked. I roll over, rotating within his arms, to face him. I look up into his dark eyes. "How do you do that? How do you always guess what I'm thinking?" I ask him.

His lips quirk in a half-smile. "Context?" he asks. But then he grows serious. "There are some things I will never be able to explain to you, Rosalind. I hope you can find it in your heart to accept this about me."

I feel like I can accept anything about him.

He smiles softly. "So, how are you feeling?"

I consider it. "I don't think I have felt this well in a long time."

"Good." He pauses, as though trying to think of a way to tell me something, then changing his mind. "Are you hungry? I am. I can order us some breakfast."

I nod, realizing that I am famished. When was the last time I felt so hungry? I've actually been feeling a little queasy lately. "Are you staying long enough to eat?"

He looks seriously at me. "I am staying long enough to eat, and to talk to you. I would like to ask you a question."

Oh. I don't know whether that should make me nervous.

"Don't be nervous," he says, doing his strange trick again. "Can you wait here for me? I'll be right back."

He extracts himself from the bed, slowly untangling himself from me. He pauses and looks at me for a moment, a question I don't understand in his eyes, then smiles and caresses my cheek before rising. I watch while he dresses himself in his trousers and shirt, enough to be presentable for going downstairs to order food.

I would normally get up to help him dress, but I am glad for the opportunity to wait under the covers until he leaves the room. I still don't want him to see all the bruises. I don't want to ruin his good mood.

As soon as the door closes behind him, I leap from the bed, intending to be fully dressed before he returns so he cannot see my body in the light of day. However, as I glance down at myself while briefly using the cooled bathwater before putting my costume back on, I am very surprised to see that the bruises have faded quite a bit. My skin still bears the traces of them, and the scars, but the purple marks have become substantially less pronounced.

That's a relief. Surprising, too. Maybe I have lost track of how much time went by. I know I have been feeling very foggy and confused lately.

Not this morning. I feel a striking clarity of mind to go along with my appetite. I'm very glad to be feeling so much better for Gregor, and I hope my responses to whatever he has to say to me this morning are pleasing to him as well.

I try not to think about what happens after he leaves, and the beast returns. For now, I will simply enjoy having Gregor with me again, as I had dreamed for so long.

When he comes back into the room, I had feared he might object to my being dressed already, but he does not mention it. Instead, he invites me to the settee to sit with him while we wait for breakfast to arrive.

Gregor

Wolk keeps me informed, as always. *"She waited for you to leave the room, then jumped up to quickly get dressed, still wanting to hide her injuries from your eyes. She was surprised to see that the bruises have faded substantially."*

"So did it actually work?"

"Apparently. The improvement in her bruising is clearly accelerated. The most significant improvement is in her soul, and her psyche. Her mind is clear, she feels restored to herself. It appears she is in a receptive state, and she will be able to consider your proposal without the fear or confusion which has now ended."

"Well, now's my chance, then." I feel my heart start pounding as I climb the stairs and enter the door. I have grown convinced that her companionship is what I need, but I feel what I am asking her to do is unfair to her. This can never be a conventional relationship. I can never be a normal man, a normal husband. At least she has been fully healed before I thrust this decision on her, so her mind will be clear and she can understand what I am offering. I feel terribly nervous that she will reject my proposal as the selfish request that it is.

"It will be her choice," Wolk reminds me, *"as you have said."*

I can tell she worries that I won't like to find her dressed when I return to the room, but I refrain from comment. Whatever makes her comfortable is fine with me.

I decide it would be best to wait until after she has had breakfast before broaching the topic of our future together. So, I begin simply telling her the tale of my journey, of the construction of the steamboat. She listens with polite interest. I do not inflict on her the story of my meeting with Mason. After we have finished our buckwheat cakes that are brought to the room, I decide it is time.

I try to think about how to begin. I am not a great orator or poet, do not really know how to phrase my request in a way which will best appeal to her. So, I decide to just proceed with honesty. I take her hand in mine as she sits beside me on the little sofa, and look into her clear brown eyes.

"I have a request, Rosalind, something I would like to ask you to do for me. Something that will help me enormously."

"Anything," she whispers, her face utterly open and accepting.

"She wonders if there is some new sexual activity you would like to try with her before you depart."

Of course that is what she must think. When have I ever proposed anything else?

I think I must try to explain myself. "While I was gone, Rosalind, I began to realize how much I was missing your company. I thought of you often."

She smiles softly. "I thought of you too. All the time." It gives me courage to go on.

"I didn't realize how much I missed you until I was talking to the wife of the man who is building the steamboat. Her name is Lydia. I think you would like her."

She nods, accepting my story, willing to listen to whatever I want to say.

"She told me I looked lonely. I realized that I was. I was lonely for you."

I see emotion cross her face, a strange mixture of sadness and hope.

"She has not allowed herself to believe you truly care for her, as she cares for you. She has yearned for you, but did not believe that you could return this feeling."

I use the information Wolk provides, as always, but it feels somewhat unfair to have access to her thoughts in this way, during such a crucial moment. I should not use this power over her. However I can't stop myself from talking, from using what Wolk just told me to guide my words. "The more I thought about it, the more I realized I was longing to be with you."

This brings color to her cheeks, and moisture to her eyes. Wolk doesn't say anything. I continue, "I know now that I want to be with you, not only today. Not sometimes. Not just to visit you here. I want you to come with me, stay with me."

Rosalind looks even more emotional. She is surprised, but confused. She doesn't say anything in response, apparently not knowing what to say. I am not sure my message is coming across properly.

Wolk all but rolls his eyes. *"Don't forget the most important part, Gregor."*

Oh, right. I reach over to take her other hand in mine as well.

"Kneel!" Wolk reminds me, thank goodness. I clearly am terrible at this.

I slip off the settee and rest on one knee in front of her. "Rosalind, will you agree to be my wife? Will you come with me, marry me, live with me?"

Her mouth falls open, as tears start to slip down her cheeks.

Wolk starts to talk, but I silently shush him. I want to hear this from her, the proper way. I don't want any agreement from her to be the result of undue manipulation.

To my dismay, she shakes her head.

I start blathering, trying to forestall her rejection. "I know you don't really know me very well, and I've already told you that I can never explain some things about myself to you. But if you will have me, I will always take care of you."

The tears are streaming down her face, but she remains silent. I can't stop babbling. "I have a house in Natchez now, so we will have a place to live."

I can tell that Wolk has things to tell me, but I don't want his input right now. If I am going to ruin this I should do it myself. And if I can salvage the situation, it should be without the unfair advantage I always use. This isn't like cheating at poker.

"I won't be able to give you children," I say, realizing I should be honest with her about that. She needs to know what she would be giving up.

This is the one thing that evokes a response. "Really?" she whispers through her tears. "How can you know that?"

Wolk is practically biting his lip.

"A doctor told me. I can't have children." I have been a doctor from time to time, and I know it to be true, so this isn't a complete lie.

Her tears turn into true sobs. The situation is unraveling fast. I clamber back off of my knees to the settee, and take her in my arms. I should have known better than to try to find a wife. Why can't I learn my lesson?

I have to comfort her, try to fix this. I tried so hard to heal her last night and now I am just causing more damage. Enough with my idiotic idea to propose. "I'm sorry, sweetheart, I understand that if you want children you won't have me. I will still find a way to take care of you, even if you won't marry me."

She shakes her head, sniffling. She tries to get control over her voice. "I would, but I can't. Especially if you know you can't have children."

All I can do is plaintively ask, "Why?"

She takes in a shaky breath. "Because I think I'm already pregnant."

Chapter 49

Please

Gregor's

I realize now that it was a miscalculation on my part to decide to withhold from him the information about her early pregnancy. Last night it would not have changed the way he wanted to proceed. This morning I would have shared it with him as soon as he thought of the topic of reproduction, but he has decided he does not want my input right now. I can understand his desire to accomplish this important task on his own.

It is both difficult and touching to watch him stumble his way through his proposal without my help. His longevity has given him many skills, but not the ability to smoothly navigate this delicate conversation with the woman he loves.

He does love her. Yes, the love is very different from that he felt so long ago, but it is certainly a kind of love. It is a deep affection, and a sense of comfort in her presence. He has been so protective of his heart over the centuries since he lost his second wife, he has never learned to recognize that love and happiness can take many forms.

I am pleased he is making this attempt. I watch silently, earnestly hoping that he is successful. I wish for him to find the happiness Lydia encouraged him to pursue.

Rosy

His eyes grow wide and he stares at me, obviously totally surprised. I have ruined everything. I haven't told him the main reason I can't agree, but now that I know he can't have children it is completely impossible. He would know my baby isn't his. If I hadn't just told him, he would have had to turn me out once he learned of my condition.

"You're... how... when...." He apparently has forgotten how to speak.

I move away from him, out of his arms, and wipe off the rest of my tears. I take a deep breath. I have to try to be practical. It was never going to work anyway. I know my place. I know that thinking Gregor would truly want me was nothing but a silly dream. When he actually asked me, I immediately knew it couldn't happen, before I even allowed myself to hope it was true.

"It isn't that astonishing, Gregor. It's an occupational hazard." I wish he wasn't so shocked.

I have never seen him so unsettled. He always seems so in control of everything, but right now he just looks young and confused. I have no idea what else to say to him.

We both lapse into silence for a few moments. He stares at me with wide eyes.

Finally, he says, his brow furrowed in confusion, "But, I don't understand...."

Does he not know how pregnancy happens? What can he possibly not understand? I stare at him, feeling more confused than he looks.

He goes on, "Wouldn't it be better for you, if you are expecting, to be settled? Wouldn't it be easier to have a baby someplace other than here?"

What? "Yes, of course, but it's not possible."

He stares at me like I have grown another head. I guess in a way I am. This thought would normally make me laugh, but there is nothing remotely funny about the situation. Gregor is speechless. Where is his ability to guess what I am thinking? He seems unusually dense at the moment.

"But why?" he bursts out. He looks utterly baffled.

"Well," I say, just as baffled as he is, "because you know you can't have children. You already know it isn't yours."

His mouth drops open, then closes, a look of dawning awareness on his face. "Wait. Are you saying you think the problem would be on my part? That I wouldn't want to be a father to your child?"

I gape at him. What can he possibly mean? Of course that is the exact problem.

He takes a deep breath, then lets it out. He takes my hands again, and says very earnestly, "Rosalind, I would be honored to have both you and your child, if you will accept me. I never thought I would have the chance to be a father. You could give me the greatest gift of my life by agreeing to marry me."

"But," I begin. He stops me.

"I would never treat the child as anything but my own. It would be my child. I do not think you understand how much it would mean to me."

Can he possibly mean this? Men don't want to raise children who are not their own. I know this for a fact. But, he lifts my fingers to his lips, and with imploring eyes, whispers, "Please?"

It makes my tears start to flow again.

Gregor

I feel wrung with emotion. I felt hope, then dismay, then astonishment, then more hope, and now I am back to dismay. Why is she crying?

Wolk lifts his head, but I hush him. I will not cheat in this moment.

All I can do is beg. "Please, Rosalind, please, tell me why you won't agree? Don't you want me? I had thought...." Maybe I was only imagining that her feelings matched mine. Even if she would reject me otherwise, I want to be able to help her with the child on the way. It would be a remarkable privilege.

Ayola enters my mind. How would this affect her? Would Rosalind's child come to know Ayola?

Obviously not, not if Rosalind won't accept my proposal.

I reach up with both hands and caress her face, wiping away her tears with my thumbs. I wait anxiously to hear what she has to say.

Finally, she whispers, "Yes, I do want you. But I can't leave here."

"What? Why?"

"I owe Beverly too much. I won't be finished paying her back for years."

Oh. This is some kind of financial issue? Well, good grief, that isn't a problem, but I suppose sweet Rosalind cannot know this.

"Can you explain this to me? Maybe I can help?"

Rosy

This is so bad for me. I have allowed myself to overlook the reality of my situation, and fall in love with a customer, and believe for a moment that I could have a life with him. Why am I such an idiot? Of course none of that is possible. My place is to be here, be abused, be Beverly's property. There is nothing Gregor or anyone else can do.

But I owe him an explanation. This sweet man, this man who has brought me so much pleasure, who has made me feel so much better, deserves that much. At least I can tell him why. So he can leave me in peace, leave me to my fate. Stop tempting me with dreams of what can never be.

"Do you remember what I told you the first night we met?" I ask him. "About my family?"

He thinks for a moment, and says, "I believe you told me that your family was from Kentucky, and you were the eldest child?"

I nod. It hurts to talk about it, but I will do this for him.

"When I was eight years old, my father died. I was their only child." I can't talk about how much I loved my father, how much that hurt. "My mother remarried within a year or two, and had three more children. My stepfather was a farmer, he only had a small plot of land, and our family was barely scraping by."

I don't share all the details of how my stepfather mistreated me, disliked me, resented me. He did not want to raise another man's child. This is how I learned that men are this way.

"There was a very bad winter, with a lot of flooding, and our crops failed. I was twelve years old. There was no way to feed all of the children."

His eyes are full of sympathy, as though he can see where this story is going. I suppose it is pretty obvious.

"My stepfather told my mother that I had to go. She didn't want to agree, but she had three babies, and I was nearly old enough to go into service. So she said goodbye to me, and let him take me into town to find a position. I don't think she realized what he intended."

I know he is watching me, but I can't meet his eyes. I stare at my hands while I continue, barely able to whisper. "He brought me to Madam Beverly. She worked in a brothel in Kentucky. He sold me to that brothel. I was too young yet to work there as anything but a scullery maid. A couple of years later the owner wanted to open a brothel here, and hired her to run it. She brought me here, and changed my position."

He waits, silently, as though thinking there must be more to the story. When I don't go on, he asks, "Why can't you leave? It has been years."

"She paid too much for me in the first place. Then, when I heard that my stepfather had died, Madam agreed to send more money to my mother, to help raise the other children." I sigh. I haven't seen them in six years, they must be so grown up now. "She sends more than I can earn for her. I owe her more and more all the time, but I can't stop because my mother needs the money. She has no other way to feed her children. I don't think I will ever be able to repay Beverly. I just have to keep trying."

Gregor

It is so easy to forget how normal humans can find themselves in such predicaments, over something as intangible as money. The situation she finds herself in seems so unsolvable to her. But I know I could fix it all in a trice.

I wait a minute to make sure she is finished with her story, while she stares sadly down at her hands.

"My sweet Rosalind, I believe I understand why you think you cannot leave here. But can you believe me if I tell you that I can help you?"

She glances up. "No. It is too much money."

She still doesn't understand. "How much?"

"I'm not sure exactly. Madam hasn't really told me all of it. I just know she sends all the money I make, and more, to my Mama."

I sigh, and wrap my arm around her. When she doesn't resist, I pull her against me. "May I ask you another question, then?"

She nods, leaning against my chest, not looking up at me. I reach around her with my other arm, enveloping her. "You have said that you can't marry me because you are expecting another man's child, and also because you owe a great deal of money to Beverly. Do I have it right?"

She nods again, and reaches up to wipe a tear which starts slipping out.

"Do you have any other objections to me? Is there some other reason you would not accept my proposal? Am I personally disagreeable in some way? Perhaps I am too ugly or smelly or annoying? Is there anything else that makes our marriage impossible?"

She looks up at me with surprise, and seeing the smile on my face, she realizes I am teasing and almost laughs. "No, Gregor, you are not disagreeable. I ..." she hesitates, as though not wanting to confess a terrible truth. But then she cannot stop herself from going on. "I love you." Her tears start to flow again, at the tragedy she perceives of having to reject the proposal even though she loves me.

"Darling," I murmur, kissing her cheek, "I love you too." It is true enough. "And I promise you the child is not a problem, and furthermore I will find a way to settle with

Beverly so she will let you go. I will even make sure your mother and siblings are cared for. I have enough resources that all of these things are possible."

She hiccups, and looks up at me, as though she cannot dare to hope.

I smile down at her. "Assuming I can solve all of these problems, THEN will you have me?"

She meets my eyes disbelievingly. "Well, yes, of course, but...." My heart surges. That is the answer I need.

"Shhhhh. I will fix everything. Just relax here for a moment, sweetheart, I am going to go talk to Beverly."

She stares at me with alarm, and shakes her head as though to warn me against danger.

"It will be fine, Rosalind, I know I will be able to make things right with her. You won't be in trouble. You will only be with me. All right?"

She nods worriedly.

"Wait here," I tell her.

Time to finally talk to Wolk.

Chapter 50

Arrangements

Gregor's

"Thank you for waiting," my beloved thinks to me as he leaves the room.

"Of course, my darling, it is always your right to converse without my intervention. I must say you handled the situation beautifully."

He rolls his eyes. "Eventually maybe, after I finally caught on to what Rosalind was saying." He pauses. "Does she believe me? Is she really willing to marry me?"

"She is not allowing herself to think you can truly resolve the situation with Beverly. She would be willing to marry you, but cannot believe it will really happen."

"I'll just have to show her. What is the financial situation with Beverly? Can I assume she is not being honest with Rosalind?"

"Not entirely. She is actually sending money to the family as Rosalind believes, but it is not more than her earnings. Especially since you arrived in Natchez, Beverly has profited from Rosalind's customers."

"Does Rosalind really owe money to Beverly any longer?"

"In Beverly's mind yes, but she does not have a careful accounting of the funds."

"Well, it doesn't matter. It can't be more than I can pay."

"Of course."

He makes his way into the parlor, where Beverly greets him with a practiced smile. "Mister Gregor, I hope you enjoyed your night?"

"Yes. May we speak privately?"

Beverly's smile falters.

"She worries that you are irate about the condition in which you found Rosy."

"Did she know about the abuse?"

"Yes. She warned Mason not to do any permanent damage, but tolerated the injuries he inflicted, as long as he paid the price she was charging him."

"Then I am irate," he frowns.

Beverly leads Gregor to a small back room, a cupboard off the kitchen, where she keeps her ledgers. There is barely enough space for the two of them to stand within the tiny area. She turns to him. "What can I do for you, Mister Gregor?"

"I would like for Rosy to leave this establishment with me."

"My apologies if she complained to you, Mister Gregor. Sometimes the girls try to induce a gentleman to feel sorry for them. I assure you that Rosy is perfectly happy here. She will not be going anywhere. I'm sorry she has tried to impose on you."

Gregor's face is stony. "You misunderstand. She did not impose on me. It is my decision, and I believe she is willing to come with me."

Beverly's lips tighten. "She is not free to do so."

"That is what she said. I am here to settle any account she might have with you."

Beverly frowns. "It is not that easy. She owes money, but there are other reasons she needs to remain here with me. I will certainly ensure she is available whenever you would like to visit, though, Mister Gregor."

"Please do not try to dismiss me. I will be taking Rosalind with me when I leave. If you believe there is an account which must be settled, tell me the amount and I will have it sent to you promptly."

"That is impossible."

"To her credit, she is keeping Rosalind's secret regarding the money being sent to her family, rather than revealing it to a customer."

He is not impressed with her discretion. He glowers at her. "I will be taking her with me, with or without your approval. If necessary I will purchase this entire brothel, and see to it that it has new management by morning."

"She does not believe you have the resources, or the knowledge, which would be necessary to accomplish such a thing." I know the information he needs to complete his bluff. It is like cheating at poker. *"The property owner is a man named George Kent, who owns a number of such establishments across the area, predominantly in New Orleans. He is currently staying in the Natchez area while looking for additional workers for his other brothels."*

When Beverly shows no sign of conceding, Gregor sighs, and tersely tells her, "I will make a fine profit off of this business once I acquire it from Mr. Kent. I know George will be pleased to accept my offer, when I see him tonight at the club in Natchez. I suggest you start making plans for your future employment since it will not be here."

He does not like to threaten people, but is perfectly willing to do it to achieve his ends. Furthermore, he would carry out this threat if it is the only way to free Rosalind from her situation.

Beverly says in a rush, "Now, Mister Gregor, no need for that. We can come to an arrangement, I am sure."

"She finally believes you. She is trying to think of a way to get as much money out of you as possible, calculating figures in her head. She is trying to determine whether claiming to be owed three hundred dollars would be outrageous."

"Is she owed it?"

"Possibly half. Again, her accounting has been very imprecise."

He regards her. "I believe five hundred dollars would more than settle Rosy's account with you?"

Her eyes gleam. "Not at all, but as I of course only wish to accommodate you, I am willing to accept it." Neither of them mentions again the threat of Gregor taking over the brothel.

"I am glad to hear it." He pulls the money from his pocket. "Here is..." he quickly counts it, "One hundred and twenty dollars. I can have the rest to you shortly. I will be returning to town briefly to make arrangements. I will be back with the funds soon, and once I have paid you I will take Rosalind away."

Beverly takes the money, both pleased and dismayed.

He asks me, "Who is Rosalind's closest friend here?"

"Either Samantha, or Genevive."

"Are Samantha and Genevive available?" he asks Beverly.

Her eyes widen. She does not know what he wants now. "Yes, they are in the parlor."

"I would like to hire their services for the next couple of hours. I will bring money for this as well."

She sighs, flustered. "Very well, come with me." She leads him back into the parlor, and summons the two other ladies, instructing them to accompany Mister Gregor back up the stairs. They look at each other, startled, wondering what could be wanted next.

"They wonder how many ladies you can possibly want to service you at one time."

He refrains from chuckling, and simply leads them back up the stairs to the room where Rosalind is waiting.

Rosy

I am anxiously waiting to see what is going to happen. I refuse to let myself hope for anything other than that I will not be in trouble with Madam Beverly after Gregor talks to her. I am sure she will be angry with me. I can only hope it will not lead to too much misery.

I start when I hear the door open.

He enters with a smile, and behind him, much to my astonishment, are my friends Sammie and Jenny. They look completely confused. So am I.

He comes over to me, and draws me into an embrace. He whispers to me, "She agreed, Rosalind, you are free. Will you still have me? Is your answer still yes?"

A sob bursts out from me. "Yes," I say, overwhelmed. My friends are staring, having no idea what is happening.

"Then," he says, still whispering, "I need to leave you for a little while, and go up to the town to make some arrangements. Then I will come back to get you, and you will leave here forever. I brought your friends here to keep you company while you are waiting. Is this all right with you?"

I can't even speak, so I just nod my head. He kisses me, quickly, clearly focusing on whatever he is planning to do next. "I will be back in an hour, no more than two. Wait here for me in this room." He smiles. "I'll let you explain to your friends what is happening."

Then he is gone again.

Samuel Postlethwaite

Gregor surprises me with another visit, entering my office looking quite wild.

"Samuel, I need your help," he says, before I even have the chance to greet him. "You are the only person in town who I know that can help me."

Alarmed, I get up from my desk, reach behind him to close the door, then turn to regard him. Is he in trouble with the law? What can the problem be? It can't be that he wants to undo yesterday's transaction, can it?

"Is something wrong with the house?" I ask worriedly.

"What? Oh, no, not at all, it's fine," he says, seeming strangely jittery. He does not sit down, but paces back and forth, too full of nervous energy to even stand in one place.

"Then what is it, my boy? Tell me!"

"I'm getting married," he says, his eyes wide and his brow furrowed, looking like a man who is terrified and overwhelmed and ecstatic.

I am not often rendered speechless, but this is one of those times. I know I am gaping like a fish.

My discomposure seems to settle him. He takes a breath, and lets out a short laugh. "I am sorry to shock you like that, Samuel. I am a little shocked myself."

"Let's sit down, shall we?" I ask him. "You can tell me all about it, and about how I can help."

He nods and sits in the chair, but by the time I have rounded the desk and taken my own seat, he has already surged to his feet. Clearly he cannot sit still. Well, I can. I stay in my seat.

"All right," I say, "let's start with the basics. Who is the lucky lady?"

"Her name is Rosalind," he says, pacing back and forth before my desk. He stops and looks straight at me. "I must impose upon you, and beg for your discretion as well as your assistance."

This is all very peculiar, but I simply say, "Go on."

He pauses before speaking further, and I say, "My discretion I can guarantee. You can trust me with whatever you need to say."

He exhales sharply, then says, "She works for Madam Beverly, Under-the-Hill."

Ah-ha! Now I see. I knew, of course, that he frequented a brothel, I had even heard the gossip about his favorite prostitute, by the name of Rosy. She apparently has managed to get her hooks into him.

"Son, are you sure you want this? You know those ladies will try anything to -"

He cuts me off. "Samuel, I appreciate your attempt to guide me in this, but please be assured this is absolutely what I want, I have not been pressured in any way, and in fact I am the one who had to convince her to have me. A large part of the reason I bought the house yesterday was that I planned to propose to her today."

I nod. "Very well, Gregor, I'll trust that you know what you are doing. So, how can I help?"

He seems relieved. "I know you can appreciate that this will provide plenty of fodder for gossips. I want to try to minimize it, and establish Rosalind as respectable within society as soon as I can. She is waiting for me at Beverly's, and I plan to fetch her in my carriage momentarily. I do not want her to have to walk through the streets from Under-the-Hill."

"Yes, that seems wise. And considerate."

"But, I can't take her straight to my house. Rosalind is no longer a prostitute, from the moment she leaves the brothel. I must treat her in a proper manner. She does not have any place to go while I am making arrangements for us to be married. So -"

This time I cut him off. "I see what you need. You want a place for her to stay for a few days until a wedding can be scheduled?"

He practically melts with relief. "Yes, that is exactly what I need."

"Well," I tell him, "my wife is an unusually tolerant woman. I believe Ann will be willing to let Rosy - Rosalind - come and stay in our home with us. Especially now that my brother has moved into a place of his own."

He seems deeply moved. "Samuel, I cannot tell you how much this means to me. I will be forever in your debt."

"I am glad to help, Gregor. You are an important part of our community now, so I am very pleased to know that you will be settling down and making a home with your new bride." This is all completely true. This young man has brought benefits to our city through his presence. He is already a major investor with the bank, and promises to generate revenue through his promotion of the steamboat project. I want to keep him here in Natchez, and if he is happily married and settled down with his new bride, it will be to the benefit of the entire town. Totally aside from where he might have met the woman.

"There is something else," he goes on, finally sitting down in the chair. "I need to make a withdrawal. I have some financial matters to attend to, including establishing an account at your mercantile. I will need to obtain a few items before I go to get Rosalind. Does your mercantile sell any cloaks, anything like that?"

Ah, of course he would have to see that his intended has more suitable garments than whatever she would otherwise be leaving the brothel in. "I understand. Yes, we have some cloaks, even a few dresses. Henry is there now, he can help you with whatever you need."

"One last thing," he says. "Do you know where we can get married?"

I smile. "I know just the place. I attend the Methodist Chapel on Locust Street. The minister there is very amiable and I am sure will be most accommodating in scheduling a service for you."

He nods, and slumps back into the chair, his eyes darting back and forth as though he is trying to think what else he might need to do. I feel for the boy. This is a momentous occasion, and he certainly is not going about it in the usual way. Which is perfectly in line with everything else he has ever done. Nothing he does is ever in the usual way, it seems.

"If that is everything, Gregor, why don't I get your withdrawal ready, while you go and have the stable hands prepare the carriage for you."

He looks up at me with relief. "Yes, yes, exactly perfect. Thank you." He moves to rush out.

"Wait!" I have to call him back. He skids to a halt and stares back at me. "How much did you want to withdraw?"

"Um, a thousand dollars should do it."

Oh my goodness! Well, it's fine, we still have all the notes he deposited yesterday. This won't even make a dent in it. "Very well, I'll take care of it."

He zooms out the door without another word.

Chapter 51

Content

Henry

It is a quiet morning in the mercantile, until the door opens and in comes the last person I would have expected.

"Gregor!" I exclaim. "Is that actually you?"

He grins. "Henry Postlethwaite! How good to see that you managed to navigate the rest of the Trace safely."

"Thanks to you, my friend. Welcome back to town! Everyone has been eagerly waiting to hear everything about your steamboat project. We had hoped to see you at the club for supper last night, after Samuel told us you had returned."

He ducks his head. "Well, I was otherwise engaged. Actually, that is exactly why I am here. I am literally engaged. I have been busy proposing to my intended bride."

"What? Well, congratulations, sir, what fabulous news!" I'm starting to think Gregor does nothing but spend his life bursting in and astonishing people.

"Thank you," he says, smiling. "I need to pick up a few things for my ... fiancée." I feel like this is the first time he has said the word, and it seems to bring joy to him.

"Of course, Gregor! Anything you need! What would you like?"

By the time he leaves, he has established a generous ongoing account with the store, and has parcels in his arms containing a dress I think should more or less fit properly based on his description, a cloak, and a few other items that I suggested when he explained his bride has essentially no possessions and will be staying with my brother for a few days until the wedding.

He didn't specifically explain why, but I certainly have my suspicions. I have heard all the gossip about his frequent nights with a particular prostitute Under-the-Hill before his trip to Pittsburgh. In fact, we were all laughing at the club last night about his absence obviously being caused by a burning need to visit the docks. Clearly, the lady he has proposed to must be coming from there. I hope he knows what he's doing.

But, considering how unconventional everything about him seems to be, this suits him. Furthermore, Natchez is a bit of a wild frontier town, even the more respectable area up here on the hill. The community here is far more accepting of eccentricity than the staid Pennsylvania area I came from. There are a lot of characters here, in this town which I have already grown to know and love. An odd foreigner with a slightly risqué wife sounds like a perfect addition to the population.

Rosy

I still find it hard to believe it is really going to happen. I have gone from yesterday's haze of pain and fear, to being engaged to the man I love. It can't be real. But here I sit with my friends, who squealed with delight when I told them that Gregor just proposed to me and is making arrangements to take me from Beverly's. They almost seem more excited about it than I am. They are chattering enthusiastically, wondering what I will do next, where I will live, what will happen. I am listening to them, in a daze, unable to adapt to what is apparently happening.

It doesn't seem like very long before the door opens, and my fears that he won't return seem suddenly ridiculous. Of course he has returned. He told me he would.

I only see his happy smile for a moment before he is kissing me. I hear Jenny and Sammie tittering at the side of the room. My anxiety melts away in his arms, and I give myself over to his kiss.

When he breaks away, he indicates some parcels he brought in and dropped by the door before reaching for me. "I brought you some things," he explains. He turns to my friends, "Ladies, can you please help Rosalind get ready to go?" They turn to each other with wide eyes and giggle, hearing my full name for the first time.

He gazes down at me. "There are some things here for you to wear." He bought me clothing? I am overwhelmed with gratitude and relief, since I had been worried about having to appear up in the town wearing my brothel costume. But before I can thank him, he goes on. "And you should pack any of your belongings which you would like to bring with you."

I shrug dismissively. "I don't really have anything."

He whispers into my ear. "Oh yes you do. I seem to recall that you have an extremely fetching nightgown which I would like to see again."

I burst out laughing. He grins, hands the parcels to my friends, and says, "All right, go on downstairs with these things to get ready. I'm going to settle up with Beverly. I'll be waiting for you in the parlor. Take as much time as you need."

Gregor

It doesn't take long to draw Beverly aside, and give her the rest of the amount I agreed to pay, with extra for the time of the two ladies who are helping Rosalind. I even add a little bonus to sweeten the deal.

This does not prevent Beverly from glaring at me sourly while we are sitting in the parlor waiting for Rosalind to emerge from the back room. It bothers me not at all. I wait, in apparent perfect serenity, surrounded by several other ladies who are whispering and gossiping about the events of today.

My mind, however, is anything but serene. Wolk is just laughing at me, enjoying my exuberant anxiety. I can hardly believe I am doing this. After spending centuries vowing not to become attached ever again, here I am getting myself into another marriage, and with a child on the way no less. All of my trepidation and timidity have vanished. I am eagerly looking forward to this. Pain and loss will come, as it always does, but I hope it is a long way down the road.

Rosalind's friends step out of the back room first, to make sure I am watching when she appears. I rise and face the door. When she steps out, I literally gasp, much to their obvious gratification.

Rosalind is wearing the dress, the cloak, a nervous smile, and an elegant upswept hairstyle. She looks for all the world like an entirely respectable young woman. And at the same time exactly like my sweet Rosalind.

Even Beverly seems impressed. While I stand frozen like a statue, overcome with the vision before me, Beverly moves over to Rosalind, and gives her a tender embrace.

"She does genuinely care for Rosalind, beloved. She is thinking about the fact that she has basically raised her since she was twelve years old."

"It didn't stop her from allowing Rosalind to be abused," I respond to him darkly. Beverly isn't the worst villain I have known, but I cannot excuse the suffering she permitted that miscreant to inflict on my intended.

Rosalind, however, gives a fond and tender farewell to her Madam and the other ladies of the brothel. She appears to hold no grudges regarding her abuse, and in fact has tears in her eyes as she parts from Beverly.

"In many ways," Wolk tells me, *"Beverly has been a mother to her."*

"Fine," I think back, "I can't forgive her but for Rosalind's sake I will accept her view of things. Besides, I do owe Beverly for introducing me to Rosalind in the first place. She's the one who selected her for me that first night." Wolk nods.

When Rosalind is finished with her farewells, I take the small bag holding her meager possessions. *"Yes,"* Wolk assures me, *"your favorite nightgown is in there."*

I offer her my arm, and she takes it, unaccustomed to this gesture, but adapting beautifully. "Come along, my dearest."

Rosy

It happened. This is real.

Is it?

I look up at him, grinning hugely at my side.

Yes, this is real.

When my foot leaves the brothel, for the first time in ... I don't even know how long it has been since I was outside ... I feel an enormous burden lift from my mind. I don't have to fear the beast ever again. I am free. I am not only free, I am with the man I love, the man I have dreamed about, the man who changed my life.

And now he is transforming it utterly. I have no idea what will happen next.

I feel my heart pounding.

There is a fine carriage right outside the door, with a horse standing in front, and I realize with shock that it is waiting for us. A groom is sitting on the seat up on top, holding the horse's reins.

Gregor helps me inside the carriage, and sits beside me on the seat, closing the door behind him. We are enclosed in this little space together, the groom waiting in front for us to settle in.

"Sweetheart," Gregor says to me, "would you like to go for a little ride first? So we can talk and I can explain some things to you?"

"Yes?" I cannot say what I want, because I really have no idea what is happening or what to expect.

He waits for a moment, then leans up to tell the driver, "Just go up the hill and take us for a ride on the outskirts of town. We want to take some time."

The driver nods cheerfully and guides the horse to the street leading up the hill. I have watched people walk up and down Silver Street for years, but I have never been on it before. I stare out the window. Gregor holds my hand comfortingly.

"Are you all right, Rosalind? I know this has been a very strange day for you."

I look over at him. "Yes?" I am still plain confused and don't know what to say or do.

He laughs softly, and leans over to kiss my cheek. "Let me just explain the plans I've made, all right?"

All I can do is nod.

He squeezes my fingers. "First, I bought a house yesterday, so we will have someplace to live after we get married."

I think he might have mentioned this earlier, but I wasn't concentrating on that. He bought a house? Just like that? I already feel my eyes growing wider.

"Yes, I was only staying at a boarding house before I left for Pittsburgh. Well, unless I was staying with you. So I needed a home. I hope you will like it."

I am watching him, adoring his handsome face, listening to him speak, and realizing that I trust him. I know whatever arrangements he has made will be just right.

He smiles, and again I get the sense he is guessing my thoughts.

"I can't take you to my house yet, though. Don't worry," he says, seeing my brow furrow, "you'll see it soon enough. But you are a respectable lady now." He waves his hand over my fancy dress and cloak. "We have to act like it. We'll have to get married first, and it will take a couple of days to arrange."

"But, where..." I begin.

"A good friend of mine has agreed to have you stay at his family's home. His name is Samuel Postlethwaite, and his wife's name is Ann. They have two young children, and plenty of room for you to be a guest. They will be very welcoming." He looks into my eyes, and adds, "Try not to be nervous. It is only temporary. Soon enough we will be in our home together."

I realize my free hand, the one he isn't holding, is twisting around the cloth from my fine cloak. Easy for him to say not to be nervous.

"Really, sweetheart, it is going to be fine and I believe you will enjoy your time there. Ann Postlethwaite is really a very kind woman, and I believe she will guide you through everything to get ready for the wedding. She'll help you buy anything you'll need. Including a dress."

"Another dress?" I have never had two dresses.

He smiles, knowing my thoughts again. "You'll have more than that, dearest. I'm afraid you're going to have to get used to it. I'm not sure you have noticed, but I have plenty of money, and I plan to use it to keep you comfortable and happy."

I can't stop a little giggle. I have noticed. But I had no idea how much, enough to rent this fine carriage and a house and buy dresses.

He looks to the side and smiles, then just pats my hand. "Do you have any questions?"

I shake my head. I wouldn't even know where to begin.

"Then let's enjoy this carriage ride for a few minutes, then we'll take you to the Postlethwaites'. All right?"

When I nod, he pulls me to his side, and we watch the passing scenery in silence. It is very peaceful, to listen to the clopping of the horse's hooves and watch the trees and fields, with Gregor's arm around me.

I believe this might be what it feels like to be content.

Chapter 52

Grateful

Samuel Postlethwaite

When the carriage pulls up in front of our house my wife and I are waiting. Ann, bless her, has readily accepted the idea that Gregor's intended bride needs to stay here for a few days until their wedding can be arranged. I haven't shared any of the details with her about where Gregor found his bride, because he asked me for my discretion. However, Ann obviously has guessed. She's an intelligent woman, and I have never been able to truly hide anything from her. I don't mind this, in fact I am grateful to have such a discerning and tolerant partner in life.

And she seems perfectly amenable to the idea. I believe she finds it to be a charming notion, that a gentleman would fall in love with a lady in a brothel, and elevate her to be his wife. She seems to be quite looking forward to this. She has had the servants prepare the best guest room for Gregor's intended, the chamber Henry had been using until he located a suitable residence of his own.

I told my wife that Gregor has instructed me to use whatever funds are necessary to outfit Rosalind as needed for the wedding, so Ann has already made an appointment for tomorrow at the dressmaker's shop. I believe she is eager to take the young lady under her wing.

Also, I know that Gregor's new house is fairly bare, and he has asked me to consult with Henry to send over any items from the mercantile which we believe would be necessary to establish a reasonable household for his bride. He seems remarkably cavalier about this process, as though he doesn't care at all what is in his home, except that it should be suitable for her. And he trusts my brother and I to make the arrangements.

As we will. It is easy to accommodate such a generous and friendly and interesting young man. He seems particularly in need of the guidance of older and more experienced fellows as he enters into this new phase of his life.

He has told me he hopes to be out of town tomorrow while we are making these arrangements, because he plans to ask Stephen Duncan to go to Ellis Cliffs with him to invite the Ellis family to attend the wedding. He only has a few close friends in the Natchez area, and includes Abraham Ellis with his wife and children in that group. He would like to have us all witness him commit to his new wife.

When the groom from the stables pulls the carriage to a halt in front of our house, Gregor leaps out, then reaches his hand in to help Rosalind. Ann actually lifts her clasped hands in front of her, a smile on her face, so eager is she to see the lady.

When Rosalind appears, she looks not at all like a woman from a brothel. She is wearing a respectable outfit, her hair arranged in a modest way. Her young face, though, is full of wonder and anxiety. She is obviously overwhelmed at what is happening. Ann immediately approaches.

"Hello, Rosalind," she says with her kindest smile, taking her off Gregor's hands, "I am Ann Postlethwaite. Welcome to our home." She wraps her arm around the young woman's shoulder.

She immediately ushers her inside, without a backward glance at us men standing beside the carriage.

I look over at Gregor with a grin. "And that, my boy, is how marriage works. Just let the wife handle everything, and everyone stays happy!"

I have to laugh at his expression of utter astonishment.

Gregor

After I get Rosalind settled at the Postlethwaite's house, with the enthusiastic and kind welcome of Ann Postlethwaite, I must continue with the arrangements I need to make. I know Rosalind will be fine here, and when I leave she already seems relaxed in Ann's company.

I have promised to return for supper this evening. It is a sign of how accommodating Samuel is being that he is willing to give up his evening at the gentlemen's club in order to make Rosalind welcome. My gratitude for Samuel and Ann is enormous. Wolk grins wolfishly up at me. I'm sure he is pleased to see me accepting so much help from my friends. Sometimes I know my solitary lifestyle is wearing for my Guardian. It looks like the lonely era of my life is ending, and for that we are both grateful.

I next go to the Methodist church which Samuel recommended, to talk to the minister about scheduling a wedding. One generous donation later, and we are set for a ceremony in three days.

Next, to talk to Stephen. I must see Ayola. All of these arrangements with Rosalind are needed, and welcome, and wonderful, but I am pining for a visit with my little Seer friend. And I wish to invite the Ellis family to come to Natchez in three days to attend my wedding. I have spent more time with them than most people in Natchez, and feel that I can count them as my friends.

I arrive at Stephen's office as he is finishing his work for the day. I wait outside until the last patient departs, then I walk in the door.

Stephen looks up to see who is coming in, as does his brother Samuel.

"Gregor!" they both exclaim at the same instant. I laugh and come in to shake both of their hands.

Of course the brothers must enjoy a rehashing of the adventure on the Trace, which has grown in significance far beyond the reality of the event. I hope people will soon forget about it, because it makes me cringe to know my actions that day led to so much pain for Rosalind.

Then, I get to share my news. Stephen is familiar with Rosy, I know, as is his friend Thomas, but he delicately declines to mention this fact. We spend a very enjoyable hour conversing about all of the developments in our lives since I was last in town.

"I don't have a large guest list for the wedding," I tell them. "You two Duncans, of course, and Thomas if he has returned from Louisiana by then, and the Postlethwaites. And I would like to invite the Ellis family, as they will be your relations shortly, and I feel they are my friends as well."

Stephen laughs. "I can't believe you are beating me to the altar, Gregor!" Then he turns to his brother. "Samuel, can you manage the office tomorrow? I can take Gregor down to Ellis Cliffs to issue the invitation personally."

This is exactly what I want.

Ann

She is just a delightful young thing. I will overlook what her profession has been.
It can't have been something she chose for herself. She must have been only a child
when she started. It wasn't her fault. I do not even mention it to her.

I am quite pleased to take her under my wing, now that Mr. Slavson has rescued
her from a life of iniquity.

She seems quite young and inexperienced, considering.... No. I am not considering that.

I start over.

She seems quite young and inexperienced. She obviously hasn't got the foggiest
idea how to prepare for her wedding, and I am happy to help her do it. I have tried
to explain everything to her as thoroughly as I can. I wonder how much her fiancé
even told her. It doesn't seem like very much. I believe he swept her off her feet and
left the details to the women.

As it always happens. Good thing women are excellent with details.

I think she is already acclimating. After what I feel has been a pleasant and
productive afternoon, getting to know each other and making wedding plans, we
are sitting in the parlor, waiting for the men to arrive for supper. Samuel had to
return to the bank, and Mr. Slavson assured us he would come back after running
some errands related to the wedding.

Rosalind is playing patiently with Matilda, entertaining her with dolls, while
William crawls around at our feet. Rosalind has already shown me that she is very
good with children. She will make a fine mother.

I am happy for Mr. Slavson. He has always seemed lonely to me, whenever he
came by before, even though he is always cordial and pleasant. I am gratified that
he found this sweet young woman.

The men arrive together. When Rosalind sees her fiancé enter the room, her eyes
light up, as do his. In a very courtly manner, he approaches her, bows, and kisses
her hand, all with a knowing smile on his face. Samuel and I know exactly what he
is doing, demonstrating that she is now a lady to be treated with respect.

Poor Rosalind seems surprised, presumably expecting a more demonstrative greeting. I see him lean in to whisper something to her, and her mouth forms a little "oh", then she nods her head. I'm grateful that he recognizes when he should be explaining things.

The nursemaid comes to retrieve the children, while the rest of us go into the dining room.

"Well, Gregor," Samuel says, "what arrangements have you made?"

Gregor directs his answer to Rosalind. Again, this is proper and I am pleased to see him treat her with such consideration. "We have a wedding ceremony scheduled for this Friday at the Methodist chapel, at ten in the morning. I hope this suits you?" he asks her.

She blushes and nods, her emotions on display in reaction to the news that an actual wedding date has been set. I am not sure she has really been able to believe this until now.

Gregor goes on. "Tomorrow I will be out of Natchez for a few hours. I am planning to go south to Ellis Cliffs with Stephen Duncan to invite his fiancée and her family to come and see us wed." He gazes into her eyes solicitously. "You'll be all right while I am gone, yes, sweetheart?"

I break in. "Of course she will, Mr. Slavson. She will be with me. She has an appointment at the dressmaker's in the morning, then we must go to several other shops to obtain the things she will need. That will probably take longer than your trip to Ellis Cliffs."

He grins, but still looks to Rosalind for her confirmation. She says to him, softly, "Yes, Gregor, I will be fine."

I notice a bit later during supper that he has taken her hand under the table, unobtrusively, but very sweetly.

Yes, this is a good match. I am very pleased for them both. I meet Samuel's eyes, and know he feels the same.

Chapter 53

Woosh

June 5, 1811
Ellis Cliffs
Margaret

Mama has not had much energy lately to plan for the wedding, and it is still a few months away, so we are having a quiet day at home. I have been working on some lace which will be added to my trousseau. Mama is resting her eyes. Nancy is slumped on the sofa, reading a book and chewing a lock of her hair she has stuck into her mouth in a most unladylike fashion. Dalila is attending me as always, her child playing at her feet.

When the doorman announces that Doctor Duncan has arrived, I look up from my needlework with surprise, as do Mama and Nancy. We were not expecting him today. As I rise, I am even more surprised when they join us in the parlor. He is accompanied by Mr. Slavson, who has been gone for some four months on his journey to Pittsburgh.

Stephen comes immediately to me and kisses my hand, as always.

Mama remains seated, but she says, as graciously as ever, "Welcome, Doctor Duncan, Mr. Slavson. How good to see you. Please be seated. I trust your journey went well, Mr. Slavson?"

"Yes," he begins, somewhat distractedly, his eyes straying to Ayola who as usual is standing along the side of a chair, balancing. She is so close to walking. When she hears him speak, she turns her head to look at him from across the room, her little eyes as wide as saucers.

I remember how he always used to be so taken with Dalila's child. "You can see how much the baby has grown, can't you, Mr. Slavson?"

"Indeed yes," he says, perched on the edge of his seat rather than making himself comfortable in his armchair.

Before anyone else can say another word, suddenly Ayola makes her funny little sound, which we have all heard quite often, but have never been able to figure out why she makes it. "Woosh! Woosh!" she says, apparently tremendously excited.

We all watch the adorable little creature as she turns around, and lifts her hand from the chair. She is standing without support on her tiny legs. Rather than plopping down on her bottom and then crawling, as she always has before when she lets go of her support, she launches herself across the room on her feet, her hands held up in the air for balance, and takes her first real, wobbly steps across the room. Straight towards Mr. Slavson. She looks so funny, wearing a little tunic Dalila made for her, tottering with her tiny little legs pell mell across the floor.

He watches this display with such astonishment and obvious delight it is as though he is seeing his own child take her first steps.

"Dalila!" I say to my maid. "Do you see that? She is walking!" I look over, and see Dalila glowing with pride at her little girl, but also alarm, obviously worried that Ayola may bother the gentleman.

However, before Dalila can take any action to prevent it, Ayola has made her way over to Mr. Slavson, toddling all the way across the ornamental rug, propelling herself forward in the funny top heavy way babies do while they are first learning to walk.

She quickly reaches him, and starts pounding her hands against his knees, saying, "Woosh! Woosh!" Then she lifts her hands up in the air, opening and closing her fingers, clearly requesting that he pick her up.

The smile on his face is gigantic.

He looks at Dalila, and says, "May I?"

Startled to be asked, she softly says, "Yes, sir."

So he leans down and lifts Ayola into his arms. When she makes it up onto his lap, she isn't content yet, for she then reaches up further, stretches her arms around his neck, and cuddles herself to him just as lovingly as I have seen her hug her mother. "Woosh! Woosh!" she continues saying.

Stephen bursts out laughing. "Well, Gregor, apparently your name is Woosh now!"

We all enjoy a hearty laugh.

Dalila

My little Ayola manages to enchant the entire room once again. I know how lucky I am, that my baby is indulged by these people who obviously find her to be adorable. Even the gentleman who is visiting seems happy with her intrusion and willing to hold her in his arms. She appears to have no desire to get back down to play, and is sitting happily in his lap, where he is allowing her to play with the lapels and buttons of his coat.

It could just as easily be that our owners would not want to be bothered, and might have even sold her by now. I am grateful to the Ellis family, despite everything.

I wonder how it will go with the next baby. I am not sure anybody else has noticed yet, except the Master. The last time he brought me to his study, when he put his hands on my stomach and felt the bulging roundness there, he lost all interest in me, quite immediately. He sent me back to my sleeping mat at once without going any further, and has not touched me since. I am glad of it.

I believe my garments are still sufficient to hide my belly from the other members of the family. It is possible that Missus is suspecting, because I have seen her eyeing me. And probably Hester. But nobody has said anything about it yet.

I have to just wait to see what happens. By the time Margaret gets married and leaves, I believe the pregnancy will be more than half finished. Hopefully by the time the baby comes I will be living with her and her Doctor Duncan at their new plantation.

I feel Mister Slavson's eyes on me, while Ayola plays in his lap, and I glance at him to see if he wants me to take her. But he is just gazing at me, with a kind expression, almost sympathetic, and he gives a little shake of his head to let me know I don't need to bother. He seems as happy as she is.

He is an odd fellow, and as intimidating to me as all the other white folk, but I'm glad she seems content. And I think we have finally figured out what she means when she says "Woosh."

Ayola's

It is such a delight to see Gregor and Wolk again. I have been in near constant contact with Wolk for the last few months, since they departed the Natchez area for Gregor's journey to Pittsburgh. But that is not as satisfying as actually being in the presence of the other Seer.

My beloved has missed him dearly. Wolk and I feel the separation in some ways has been harder for Ayola, because even though I have constantly assured her that Gregor is well, and will return soon, she is not really old enough to understand the passage of time and the ongoing absence of her mentor. At least Gregor was able to benefit from being kept updated constantly by Wolk about the details I have shared.

She is overjoyed with his return, crowing the name she has given him. Her little "Woosh" deeply puzzled the entire family until today. Now that they realize it is Gregor who she means, they are amused but do not give much thought to why she has been calling out for him for months. They do not believe the antics of a baby hold much significance.

But of course they do. Ayola has longed for the other Seer, has wanted to be together again with the person who is so similar to her. She has no concept of how unusual they are, but she has certainly never seen anyone else like him. Nor has anybody else, but she does not have the life experience to put this into context. As far as I know, Ayola and Gregor are unique among the humans of the world. Gregor has not encountered another Seer for centuries.

It is charming and delightful to watch her approach him, the baby taking charge of the situation at once. She has wanted him for months, and nothing is going to stop her from achieving her goal. Her first little steps would have been soon anyway, but this was the impetus to take them, to cross the room and reach him.

His delight in her is marvelous. I have heard from Wolk everything about how concerned he is with her, how much he has missed her, how reluctant he was to leave her behind. Now that he is back, as she sits upon his lap playing with everything she can reach, it is as though two pieces of a broken plate have been glued back together.

When she first touched him, Wolk and I reveled together in the blast of light the contact of the Seers created, the miracle hidden from every other human and Guardian in the room, our joint protective shield concealing the Seers.

The light continues to glow from their joint presence, slightly reduced after the initial flaring moment of contact. This is the longest time they have been able to remain with each other, and they each clearly feel a deep pleasure and fulfillment in the contact. It is perfectly understandable why Ayola wanted to be with him. There is no other sensation which feels as good to her as this merging of the Seers' souls. She enjoys the "Woosh" feeling for which she has named him, the rush of delight that fills her the moment they touch.

After the conversation in the room turns away from the amusement caused by the baby's antics, Mrs. Ellis remarks, "We had not known you planned to call on us today, Doctor Duncan. To what do we owe the pleasure?"

I already know, of course, why Gregor wanted to come, totally aside from his desire to see Ayola. He answers. "Mrs. Ellis, Doctor Duncan agreed to bring me here today so that I can issue an invitation."

The sisters look up with interest. "Oh?" Mrs. Ellis inquires.

He smiles, his hands occupied with Ayola's as she is currently grabbing and inspecting his fingers. "I would like to invite your family to attend my wedding."

This leads to some amazed gasping on the part of the young ladies. "Why, congratulations, Mr. Slavson, we had no idea that you were engaged," Mrs. Ellis says.

He grins. "Nobody did. It was extremely sudden. I proposed as soon as I returned to Natchez from my journey, having realized while I was gone how much I was missing my intended bride."

Mrs. Ellis nods wisely. "Sometimes absence can make the heart grow fonder," she notes. "Who is your bride-to-be?"

"Her name is Rosalind," he says, and by way of making some explanation, goes on, "her family is from Kentucky."

"We would be delighted to attend your wedding, of course," Mrs. Ellis tells him. "Thank you for the honor of the invitation. What will be the date of the ceremony?"

His lips press together in amusement. He knows that the expedited nature of his proposal and the speedy ceremony will be considered somewhat scandalous. "Friday."

Nancy bursts out laughing, and is quickly shushed by Margaret.

"Well," Mrs. Ellis smiles, unflustered, "no time like the present. We will be happy to come to Natchez for the wedding."

Mr. Ellis enters the room that moment, having finished his business in the fields, and asks, "Wedding?"

His wife turns to explain to him what has been planned.

Gregor

My heart is so full as I finally enter my house, to spend my second night within. Today's trip to Ellis Cliffs was incredibly delightful. I was able to sit with Ayola on my lap for over an hour, while the conversation proceeded around us, enjoying the warm and wonderful sensation which swept over us both the moment the baby reached me. It is comfort made tangible. It is the "Woosh" of warmth and relief she has named it, named me.

We even had a little conversation together. She is not yet ten months old, far too early for walking or talking. But Wolk told me I was like this too. Apparently Seer development is somewhat accelerated. She has a little vocabulary, and enjoyed practicing it with me, pointing around and naming things. "Mama," she told me, pointing at Dalila.

"Yes, sweetheart, she is your Mama," I whispered to her. I affirmed everything she pointed out and named around the room. She wanted to share with me the things in her world.

It was utterly enchanting, and made me love her more than ever. It is not only her status as another Seer which draws me in. She is a beautiful child, her dark hair starting to grow in loose curls all around her face, her caramel skin somehow the same exact shade as her eyes, a happy yet knowing expression on her small face. She is a delightful little person and I am more committed to her well-being than I have ever been. I am very pleased with the efforts I have made to establish myself here in this community so that I can continue to see her, and if necessary, help her.

Later, I had another enjoyable supper at the Postlethwaite home, listening to Rosalind recount the bewildering array of shops she and Ann visited, and items which they purchased. She can hardly believe the fuss being made over her, the funds being expended, the life that she finds herself thrust into. At one point I grinned and whispered to her, "This is only Natchez, my dear. It's a small town. Someday I will take you to New York or Paris and you can really see what society is like." She stared up at me, amazed.

I sigh, remembering it as I look around my empty home. I don't know if I will really take Rosalind to New York or Paris. I am committed to remaining in this area until Ayola is grown. Who knows what will happen in the next couple of decades. It is nothing to me, but it could be a whole lifetime for Rosalind, frail human that she is.

Like any other human, though, I can only live within the moment in which I find myself. And in this moment I plan to familiarize myself with this house I have purchased.

I move throughout the home, solitary but not lonely, impressed with the progress I see has been made by the Postlethwaite brothers. I asked them to send some things over from the mercantile, but they have done far more than that. They must have shopped all over Natchez, and employed a whole crew to set things up in the home. There are now a few rugs upon the wooden floors, more chairs in the parlor, more bedding upstairs. I see that the kitchen is more fully stocked with equipment and even some food staples, ready to be prepared. There is a substantial pile of firewood which had not been here when I first arrived. There is even a small bookshelf in the parlor, with a handful of books within. Wood for a fire has been laid in the fireplace there, and it occurs to me that I can simply enjoy this, relax in my own home with a book before a warm fire.

What a concept.

Wolk smiles at me with his wolfish grin. *"I told you that you would come to enjoy this home. It is happening already."*

I look at him wryly. "Man," I say. When he transforms, I gesture to the other armchair set in front of the fireplace. "Might as well join me."

He settles his image into the chair, while I light the fire. We sit quietly together, as I read a book, and the fire illuminates the room.

I look forward to Rosalind joining me here in two nights. Although, I do not anticipate that reading by the fireplace will be the primary activity of the evening.

Wolk chuckles as he stares into the fire.

Chapter 54

Secrets

June 6, 1811
Rosy

I can scarcely keep up with the flurry of activity that I have been engaging in. I spent the entire day yesterday in town with Ann, having my measurements taken at the dressmaker's, then visiting what seemed like a hundred shops, buying items I had never even heard of. Servants from her home followed along to carry the parcels which accumulated as we visited each store.

She assures me it is all necessary, and I needn't worry a bit about the expense. That is obviously impossible, but the prices and numbers are so foreign to me that I cannot truly understand the amounts at any rate. She has handled every transaction while I stand awkwardly by.

She has introduced me to many people, most of whose names I cannot recall. There were a few uncomfortable moments when a man would do a double-take, and I would know that he had been one of my customers at Madam Beverly's, but nothing was mentioned. I could feel my face burning each time.

I spent the day missing Gregor, and was quite relieved to see him when he arrived at the Postlethwaite's home for supper on the second night. Apparently the Ellis family, whoever they are, will be attending our wedding. He told a charming story about the baby of one of their servants taking her first steps straight towards him. It made me glad to hear him sounding so pleased about a baby, and gave me hope that he will be this way when my baby comes.

Today I am glad Gregor and I will be spending the day together. He arrives at the house after breakfast. As he escorts me outside, so we can walk to the church to meet with the minister about the ceremony, he huffs with relief.

"Finally, a moment to be alone with you!" he says, smiling down at me as I take his arm. I am so relieved to hear him say it. Being in this peculiar world has made me miss the simple times he and I were together at Madam Beverly's. This all feels so different and strange and even lonely without him.

"I feel the same way," I tell him. "I have been missing you."

He lifts my fingers to his lips for a kiss. "Are you enjoying your time with the Postlethwaites?"

"I truly am. They are so welcoming and kind. Especially Ann. I mean Mrs. Postlethwaite. They are taking very good care of me. The room I am staying in is fancier than the best room at Madam Beverly's."

He laughs, then pats my hand. "I am so glad." He pauses for a moment, then asks, "Are you worried about something?"

I shake my head. But of course he is guessing my thoughts again.

He chuckles. "I think I know what it might be. Is it all the shopping?"

"Well, yes, if you must know! How on earth can I possibly be expected to use all of the things Ann bought for me? And how on earth can you possibly be expected to pay for it? It seems very extreme, and ..."

He interrupts me. He stops walking for a moment, and turns to face me. "Rosalind, you know how I have told you that there are some things I cannot explain?"

I nod anxiously.

"Well," he goes on, "this is not one of them. Please understand that I have a ridiculous amount of money, and there is no possible way you can buy anything we cannot afford. Please don't worry at all about that."

It makes me laugh, to hear him say that he has a ridiculous amount of money. For it must be true, considering the ridiculous number of items it has purchased for me. He seems to hear me think that, and he laughs too.

"How do you have so much money?" I ask him.

"Hm," he says, and thinks for a moment. "That might be one of the things I can't really explain, after all. Mostly, I inherited it. And I have made some good investments." He looks at me worriedly. I think it bothers him that he is keeping secrets from me.

I don't say anything else, while I am thinking about this. He takes my arm and starts walking again. "Gregor," I say after a minute, and he watches me expectantly. "I understand about keeping secrets. Sometimes my customers - I mean my former customers - have told me things I know must be kept in confidence. I think sometimes

I was the secret they were keeping from someone else. But I do understand. Everybody has some things they cannot explain to everyone."

He stares at me, with an expression of confusion and hope. "What I mean to say," I tell him, "is it's all right if you do not explain everything to me. I know you have secrets. I trust you to tell me what is important."

He looks more moved by this than I could have expected. He stops walking again for a moment, and gazes into my eyes. "My god, Rosalind. You are so perfect for me. I am so grateful to you for accepting me." His eyes are full of love. All I can do is smile and blush. I am the one who is grateful.

Rosy's

The transformation in my beloved's life is astounding. From her position as an abused prostitute, she is suddenly made into a respectable young lady planning for her wedding. She adapts to her new circumstances with bemusement, but with her characteristic placidity. Her natural disposition is to be calm and accepting, especially now that she has been fully healed from her anguished state of only days ago.

I can only assume her sweet nature must be one of the things which appeals to Gregor about her. I realize I am going to have to get used to the frustration which comes from being unable to access his thoughts, as apparently he will be an integral part of the rest of this lifetime. I constantly reach for his thoughts and am always somehow rebuffed. I must make do with nothing more than his behavior to interpret his motivation.

From what I can determine from his words and actions, though, his commitment to Rosalind is sincere. His emotional reaction, to her promise to trust him even though she understands that he has secrets, is very telling. Yes, he is keeping secrets, and he knows she is aware of it, and is relieved to hear that she will accept this.

It is an odd basis for the formation of a relationship, but I am optimistic that this can be a happy one.

Rosy

We stroll for a while before we approach a little church, and walk up the steps of the building. It looks like it was built not too long ago. As we enter, a man greets us. "Welcome to Cokesbury Chapel," he says, "I am Pastor John Johnson."

It has been a very long time since I have been in a church, not since I was growing up in Kentucky, and it makes me a little nervous. The pastor seems kind, though, a young man not much older than Gregor, his skin a deep tan, and his dark hair brushing his collar. He welcomes us in, and asks us to sit down, in the front pew next to the plain altar. He sits on the wooden pew next to Gregor. I glance around, see the whitewashed walls, some candles, a cloth over the altar, and a wooden crucifix on the wall behind.

"I understand that you are recently engaged, and wish to be married tomorrow morning," he starts.

I nod, and Gregor says, "Yes, sir."

Pastor Johnson smiles and says something I don't understand, something like "Mazel Tov!"

Gregor gets a big smile on his face, and says something else I don't understand, that sounds like "Toda Raba."

The pastor lets out an amazed laugh. "You speak Hebrew, Mr. Slavson?"

Gregor smiles and shakes his head. "Only a little bit. I had a friend once who taught me some."

They spend a couple more minutes saying things I can't understand while I look back and forth between them in confusion. But soon Gregor takes my hand, and says, "Perhaps I can come back another time, Pastor Johnson, I would love to continue conversing with you. But for now we should make the arrangements while Rosalind is here."

"Oh, of course. My apologies, Madam, I was quite carried away to find somebody else who can speak Hebrew."

I can't stop a little giggle when I hear him address me as "Madam". Gregor looks to the side and grins.

"That's fine," I tell him. I can't help but like Pastor Johnson. He has a very open face and a friendly voice.

"We need to plan how your ceremony will go, how many guests will attend, if you need any special arrangements, that sort of thing," he says.

"There won't be many guests," Gregor tells him. "Only a few friends. Neither of us have any family nearby."

"Ah," he says, and I think that might seem odd to him. "Who will be standing up with you? And who will walk down the aisle with the bride?"

I look to Gregor with some alarm. I hadn't thought about any of this. He watches me while he gives the answer. "Mrs. Postlethwaite has said she will stand up with Rosalind. Is that all right, darling?"

I nod, relieved. Ann has started to feel like a genuine friend to me in the last two days.

Gregor goes on. "And Mr. Postlethwaite will walk you down the aisle."

The pastor nods. "And you, Mr. Slavson?"

"Doctor Stephen Duncan has agreed to stand up with me."

They continue talking, a few more details about tomorrow, and my mind drifts a little. I'm glad Ann will be here with me, but she'll be my only friend. My mother and little siblings are far away in Kentucky. My friends from Beverly's might as well be just as far away, even though they are right down the hill. It makes me feel a little lonely.

Gregor pauses in his conversation with Pastor Johnson to look at me, concern in his eyes, as though he is guessing what I am thinking again. He takes my hand and holds it for the rest of the conversation.

When we are finished, Gregor and the pastor say a few more things to each other in that strange language, then we go back out.

"Where to next?" I ask him.

"To meet some more people, but first, Rosalind, what is making you sad?"

He always knows.

"I guess I'm missing my friends. And my mother."

"I know the guest list is very one-sided. I'm sorry for that. There is no real way to bring your family here from Kentucky on such short notice. And I am not willing to postpone the wedding long enough to wait for them to arrive. It would take months."

"I know," I sigh. "I wouldn't want to wait either."

He looks at me closely, and asks, "Do you want me to figure out a way for your friends from Beverly's to come?"

I have to laugh a little. "Well, I don't think they would really fit in with your plans. I know you have a whole scheme to make me 'respectable'. I'm not sure that would help."

He gives me a crooked smile and then shrugs. "True, but the most important thing is making you happy." He thinks for a minute, but I can tell he can't invent any way for it to work either. "I tell you what. How about a compromise. Maybe in a couple of days, I can take the carriage down Under-the-Hill and fetch your friends Samantha and Genevive, and bring them up to our house for a visit?"

I suddenly feel quite emotional. Not only because of what a thoughtful suggestion it is, but because he referred to it quite easily as "our house".

"That would be so nice," I tell him, gratefully.

"It's settled then. Now, I have to introduce you to the Doctor Duncan Brothers!"

Chapter 55

Bridegroom

June 7, 1811

Gregor

How can I be a nervous bridegroom? I am centuries old, for god's sake, this sort of thing should be nothing to me. But here I am, pacing nervously back and forth in my bedroom, with my friends laughing at me and trying to make me stay still for two seconds so they can help me with my wedding attire. After I am finally and finely dressed, the Duncan brothers manage to make me sit briefly so Thomas can try to smooth my hair, before I can't stand it and leap up again.

Stephen laughingly says to Thomas, "Grab him!"

Thomas, who I am very pleased has returned to town in time to participate, jokingly pins my arms behind my back. Stephen picks up the gold wedding band, wrapped in silver paper, and tucks it into my waistcoat pocket.

"Do Not Lose This!" he commands me imperiously.

We all share a wonderful moment of laughter. Wolk is laughing as much as are the humans.

Then, taking a deep breath, I say, my voice full of audible emotion, "Thank you, all of you. It is marvelous to have found such good friends here."

"Well," Thomas says, grinning, "before we all start weeping, let's go to the church and get you married."

Gregor's

My beloved is full of joy and nerves on the day of his wedding. My manifestation is the man today, as Gregor decided a wolf in the church would seem too odd even for him. I will stand beside him, next to Stephen Duncan, with nobody the wiser except for my own Guarded.

When he and his groomsmen arrive at the chapel, Rosalind has already arrived, escorted by the Postlethwaite family. They await the ceremony within the minister's private office.

The Ellis family is seated in the chapel. Dalila was not required to accompany her mistress today, so Gregor knows he will not see Ayola, but he is content as he wishes to focus entirely on Rosalind. A handful of other members of the local community have arrived to witness the ceremony as well, such things being a welcome diversion in a small town such as this.

Thomas gives Gregor a last handshake, then joins Samuel Duncan and Henry Postlethwaite in the pews.

Gregor stands at the entrance to the church, trying not to be obviously jittery. Stephen whispers into his ear, "Buck up, there, it's time." Gregor smiles gratefully at his friend. They walk to the front of the little church, and stand before the pastor, waiting for the bride.

When she appears, Gregor's emotional intake of breath at her appearance is audible and endearing to the assembled group. The gown that Ann Postlethwaite managed to have the dressmaker create on short notice is quite lovely, a pale rose color. Gregor appreciates the homage this makes to his bride's name. Pale pink gloves reach above her elbows. A lovely garland of rosebuds is woven into a wreath and sits upon the crown of her head, with her long brown hair flowing loose down her back. Her round cheeks are covered with a blush which matches the rose of her gown. She is a vision of loveliness to his eyes.

Mrs. Postlethwaite walks down the aisle and takes her place before the altar, followed by her husband with Rosalind on his arm. Once he delivers her to Gregor's side, he sits back down next to the other men.

Rosalind is also full of nerves, which are settled as soon as she makes eye contact with Gregor. They smile at each other, then both find themselves much calmer as they turn to Pastor Johnson.

As he conducts the service from the Book of Common Prayer, I remain silent and smiling at the side of my beloved. It is moments such as these that bring such fulfillment to a Guardian, to see one's beloved engage in a joyful activity designed to honor love. It is no less moving to me than it is to any of the human witnesses.

Rosy

It passes in a blur, with only the strong and comforting presence of Gregor by my side giving me the courage to go through with it. Tears come to my eyes as Gregor reaches into his pocket, takes a gold band out of a little silver sheath of paper, and places it upon my finger.

I am somehow shocked when, at the end, Pastor Johnson introduces us as Mr. and Mrs. Slavson.

I am a whole new person. Gregor has transformed me.

Before we walk back down the aisle to greet and be congratulated by everyone who is watching, he leans down and whispers, "You are the same person you have always been, my wonderful Rosalind, the sweetest person I know." He manages to make me relax and smile with his little mind-reading trick.

Soon, our entire group has made its way back to the Postlethwaites' home for a celebratory reception. Gregor's friend Stephen introduces me to his fiancée Margaret Ellis. She seems very amiable, and she and her younger sister Nancy spend a great deal of time chatting with me as though there is nothing scandalous about me at all. I really do feel transformed.

The afternoon passes quickly, a happy time of conversation and laughter. By mid-afternoon, the Ellis family must take their leave, to make the return drive to Ellis Cliffs before it gets dark.

Once they have said their farewells, Gregor leans over and murmurs in my ear, "Can I take you home now too?"

I look up at him, and I can feel my eyes go wide. Is it time? "Yes, time to go to our home, my darling," he says.

My heart starts thumping strangely. It is not as though I am the normal sort of bride for whom the wedding night holds any mysteries. Still, I find myself oddly nervous and shy to think of being together with Gregor, not at Beverly's, but in our home, just the two of us, husband and wife.

Husband and wife. Oh my goodness.

He looks at me with a smile.

It takes some time to say our goodbyes as well, but finally, we get into the carriage, which I have learned actually belongs to Gregor, not one that he rented as I had thought. The driver takes us the extremely short distance to Gregor's house.

When we get out of the carriage in front of the door of his house, which he has shown me only from the outside as we have passed by in the last two days, I pause for a moment. "Is this really happening?" I ask him. It still seems a bit like a dream to me.

He grins, opens the door, then bends down to sweep my feet up off the ground, holding me in his arms. I shriek out a laugh. "What is this?" I ask.

"Tradition," he says. "I must carry my bride across the threshold for good luck."

He sets me down on the other side, and closes the door behind. I stare around us. I see the wooden walls of a parlor, with a rug on the floor, a sofa, some chairs, a couple of lamps on small tables, and a fireplace. It seems like this is a place that could be peaceful and relaxing, so different from Madam Beverly's parlor.

He wraps his arms around me and gives me a gentle kiss. "Welcome home," he whispers.

I feel unexpected tears begin to flow.

He sees this, and his face fills with concern. He touches my face, wipes away a tear. "What is it, Rosalind? Aren't you happy?"

I sniff and try to nod. It takes me a minute, before I can say, "Home."

"Ah," he says. He puts his arm around me. "Yes, Rosalind, home. Our home." He pulls me further into the parlor. "It feels strange to me too, darling, I haven't had a home in a long time." He gets a grin on his face. "Want to explore?"

It makes me smile. He seems so unhurried, like he has all the time in the world, like there is no hurry to get into bed. I have heard that bridegrooms always hasten to bed their brides, but Gregor is no ordinary man. He has never seemed rushed to me.

We move through the house, and every room I see makes me gasp in delight. It is smaller than the Postlethwaite's house but bigger than Madam Beverly's. It seems homey, comfortable.

"It's a little bare," he says, "but we'll fill it up with more things. Whatever you want. I'm afraid we don't have a wonderful bathtub like we've used before, but I plan to order one as soon as possible!" He waggles his eyebrows up and down suggestively, and it makes me laugh.

When we get upstairs, he shows me the rooms, and leads me into the largest one. "This is our bedroom," he says, looking down at me, his eyes suddenly seeming quite serious. "I have longed for you to be here with me." There is a large bed, with a quilted counterpane on it, and matching pillows.

The shyness unexpectedly returns, and I look down. I feel his fingers touch under my chin, and I lift my eyes to his. "I have something for you," he says, and holds up the little bag I brought from the brothel with my belongings.

"Oh!" I say, surprised. I had forgotten all about this.

"I haven't forgotten about it," he says, grinning. "Is there any way I could convince you to put on that wonderful nightgown for me?"

Chapter 56

Letter

July 1811
Pittsburgh, Pennsylvania
Lydia

Coming out of the house, I stretch out my back before continuing down the hill to the shipyard along the Monongahela river. Rosetta was fussier than usual while trying to get her settled down for her afternoon nap. I had to take over rocking her from the nursemaid, until she finally drifted off to sleep. She's a year and a half old now, an extremely active and willful toddler. I hope she isn't going to give up napping, because the afternoons are the only time I get to focus on working at the shipyard.

I observe the activity along the riverbank as I approach, holding the basket containing our lunch. Men are engaged with all the different aspects of the steamboat construction, as busy as ants moving over the area.

I see Nicholas on the other side of the yard, next to the growing structure of the steamboat. It is starting to take shape, seeming more real every day. The keel has been built, and the wooden planks steamed and bent to comprise the frame of the vessel. The steam engine itself has finally started to arrive, in pieces transported by wagon over the mountains from New York. It will be installed inside the hull before the deck can be built. Eventually, the two masts will be erected, made from the huge logs waiting nearby that were finally located in the nearby forests. The two paddle wheels, one for either side of the boat, are being constructed separately and will be added once the primary form of the vessel has been completed. Our plans are being realized, with our hard work and the funds of our investors.

Poor Nicholas is probably starving, since I am so late after lingering with our headstrong baby. I wonder if the one I'm carrying now will be any less stubborn. I guess I'll find out in a few months.

He looks up and sees me approaching with his lunch. He stops what he is doing at once to come over and greet me. "Hello darling," he says, taking the basket with one hand while reaching behind my head with the other. He brings my face closer for a kiss, then puts his arm around me, leading me to the bench where we normally eat lunch. "I'm very glad to see you." I look at him as we sit down, adoring his handsome face, with the creases around his eyes deepening as he smiles down at me, framed by his graying temples.

"I'll bet you are," I laugh, "you were probably wondering whether your lunch would ever arrive."

There's a twinkle in his eyes as he sets the basket on the bench between us. "I think I can guess the reason for the delay? A certain red-headed little girl?"

"Obviously. She will only take her nap if everything is exactly to her liking. She is very obstinate."

He guffaws. "I can't imagine where she got that from!"

"Well, 'Obstinate' is my middle name," I reply. "Here, eat this before you faint from hunger."

He laughs again.

We enjoy a pleasant few minutes together, sitting on the bench and chatting while we watch the workers go about their tasks along the edge of the river. Soon, he returns to his duties, and I move into the small office we keep at the shipyard, to attend to mine.

The books and ledgers are right where I left them yesterday, with a pile of recently received mail nearby which needs to be opened and answered. I start with the ledgers, entering the information about our expenditures for payroll and supplies, totaling up columns of figures, determining whether we will need to withdraw additional funding from our primary investor's account at the bank in Pittsburgh. I am using his accounting methods, which he demonstrated when he visited us a couple of months ago. Gregor made himself useful not just with his investment, but with his knowledge and even his manual labor. We both wished he could have stayed longer.

When I finish with the books, I turn to the stack of correspondence. I sort through the bills and invoices, and find letters from both Robert Fulton and Gregor Slavson. Eagerly, first I open Gregor's, wanting to hear how his journey home went, and how things are going in Natchez as he prepares the Mississippi town for the arrival of our steamboat. I see his careful and elegant script filling up the page. Before I read it, I glance out the door of the little office to see if Nicholas is nearby, because I know he will want to hear it as well. We both grew very fond of Gregor during the two weeks he was here. I'm glad to see my husband a short distance away.

"Nick!" I call out to him. He looks up, inquiringly. "We have a letter from Gregor. Want to hear it?"

He returns to me at once. We settle back down on our lunch bench together, in the shade our little office building casts over it in the afternoons. He watches me expectantly. I unfold the letter with a flourish, and begin to read aloud.

"'My Dearest Mr. and Mrs. Roosevelt,' he begins," I tell Nicholas with a grin, trying to imitate Gregor's unusual eastern European accent. He laughs and waves his hand over to the letter so that I will proceed. "'I write to inform you of my successful return to Natchez, after a journey of some five or six weeks. The weather was better returning than it had been on the road to Pittsburgh, and my horse Issoba and I were able to return home without any noteworthy incidents.'"

"So far, so good," Nicholas says when I pause.

I rattle the paper in my hand importantly. "To proceed: 'The most significant thing which occurred during my journey home was that I spent a great deal of time following your mutual advice, and thought deeply about your suggestion to find a way to best secure my own happiness.'"

"Ah-ha!" Nicholas says, delightedly. "Go on!"

"'I concluded that there was only one feasible way to do so, and therefore acting upon your advice, upon my return I at once proposed to the wonderful woman whom you had so astutely realized I was missing while I was in Pittsburgh.'"

"Ha!" Nicholas exclaims, leaning forward with anticipation. "And?"

"'I am delighted to share that Rosalind' - apparently her name is Rosalind - 'accepted my proposal after I undertook certain tasks to persuade her,' - I wonder what he means by that? - 'and we were married at the local Methodist chapel this Friday last.'"

Nicholas whoops with glee. "Already! Gregor certainly does not waste time, does he?"

I grin and continue. "'We are now a happily married couple, living at the home I have acquired for us in Natchez (see return address), and I am most grateful to the both of you for encouraging me to discover what I was too blind to see for myself.'"

Nicholas enthusiastically embraces me, somewhat crushing the letter still in my hand, and says, "Young love! What could be better!"

"There's more," I tell him once he finally releases me, and continue reading aloud. "'I did receive upon my return the two letters which you had written to me while I was traveling to Pittsburgh, but as we discussed the contents thereof while I was visiting you last month, I do not feel the need to respond to them directly. For now, I will continue working on our joint project from my end. I will shortly begin to undertake improvements to the docks here in order to accommodate the steamboat traffic. I eagerly anticipate hearing back from you, and receiving updates about how the construction is going. Do not hesitate to draw any funds necessary from my account. When you arrive in Natchez with the steamboat later this year, Rosalind and I would very much like to host you in our home for a meal, or for as many nights as you are able to stay.'"

I grin up at him before continuing. "The letter finishes with, 'My love to little Rosetta. I look forward to my Rosy meeting yours.'"

Chapter 57

Evening

August 5, 1811
Natchez
Gregor

The sweat is streaming into my eyes as I help the men unload the heartwood logs which have arrived on the river by flatboat from a longleaf pine forest to the north. The huge logs will form the pilings for the dock extension I have hired a crew to build Under-the-Hill.

I know it is unseemly for a gentleman to engage in manual labor like this, but the Natchez community seems to have grown to expect unconventional behavior from me. Behind me sits the brothel where I met my wife, although of course nobody mentions that anymore. At least not in my presence.

So, I am not letting the question of my respectability prevent me from participating in this task. I enjoy such work, even in the stifling and humid heat of this bright summer day. I have doffed my fine coat, and am laboring alongside the other men in my shirtsleeves and breeches, getting as thoroughly sweaty and filthy as they are.

Good thing that big metal bathtub which I ordered after my wedding has arrived.

When we get the logs shifted off the flatboat and stacked nearby, I call an end to the work for the day. Most of the men head into the nearest tavern, mopping off their faces and looking forward to a night of drinking and ribaldry.

I have better things to do with my evening.

I retrieve my coat but don't want to put it on over my sweaty shirt. I'm willing to risk the scandal of being seen in such informal attire walking through the respectable part of Natchez up on the hill over the docks. My Guardian will warn me to quickly don my coat if somebody fastidious enough to require it approaches.

The shining wolf walks beside me, invisible to everybody else, as content as I am with the way my life is currently unfolding.

I intend to stop by the post office to retrieve any mail on the way home, but Wolk tells me, *"Rosalind has already gone to the post office for the mail."*

Ah. Helpful Guardian, helpful wife. How can my life get any better?

Wolk laughs, his wolfish face grinning.

Rosy

The afternoon is wearing on, and I have asked the new servants, Moses and Nadine, to get a bath ready for Gregor. I know he will want one when he gets home from the docks. I'm sure he is down there working as hard as anybody else on his dock expansion project, rather than supervising from the side like any other gentleman would do.

It's one of the things I love about him. He is not afraid to get his hands dirty.

But he also loves his baths. It's another thing to love.

So Moses has been carrying buckets of water inside, from the pump we have in our garden. Nadine has water boiling in pots, so that the bathwater will already be warm and ready when Gregor gets home. Although honestly, it's such a hot, muggy day, he probably won't want the water too warm.

I have to suppress a laugh when he enters the back door from the garden to the kitchen, because I was seriously underestimating how very dirty he would be. My goodness, what a sight!

He laughs when he sees my expression, and says, "I know, I'm a disgrace!" Yet another thing to love, the way he often guesses exactly what I'm thinking. He shakes his head and chuckles, clearly guessing that as well.

He lays his coat over the back of a chair, and moves over to embrace me. He lifts his sweat-stained arms and comes within an inch of me, then backs off, laughing. "I'm just teasing, I wouldn't dream of inflicting myself on you in this state. I need a bath."

It makes me laugh along with him. More to love. "You know I would let you. I wouldn't mind."

We are so comfortable together. It always feels like this, with him, light and happy and pleasant. Sometimes I can hardly believe that this is my life now, so different from just a couple of months ago.

Nadine hears him say he needs a bath, and says, "Mister Gregor, I have your water boiling for your bath right now. It's all ready."

I think Nadine enjoys mothering both of us. It's been easier than I would have expected to grow accustomed to living in a household with servants to wait on me. Very soon after we were married, Gregor made it clear that he would never own slaves, but he did want to get some help around the house. I would have taken care of the cooking and cleaning, like my mother did, but he was very firm that we could hire people to do all of that. And honestly, my husband is so generous, and treats the servants so kindly, that they seem very happy to be working here. Nadine is an older white woman whose children have grown up and moved away, and Moses is one of the free black men living in town. They are both very helpful and kind. It has been nice to see them as friends to spend time with while Gregor is away from the house working Under-the-Hill.

Gregor smiles at Nadine, glad she has anticipated his need. "Wonderful!"

"Will that be all, sir?" she asks. She and Moses know that Gregor likes to be alone with me in the evenings, so they make sure to finish all of their work long before the sun has set. She already has supper nearly ready for us, a stew simmering in a pot on the cast iron stove alongside the water boiling for his bath. There is a fresh loaf of bread cooling on the rack next to a pie. I'll finish getting it all on the table later. Moses has done all of his tasks as well, tending the garden, splitting some firewood, carrying any heavy burdens around the house.

Gregor looks at me inquiringly, to see if I need anything else from the servants. When I shake my head, he says, "That's all for tonight, thank you."

Before Nadine goes, she indicates a washtub partially filled with water along the side of the kitchen, near the side room where we keep the bathtub. She says, before she walks out the door to join Moses who is waiting in the garden, "Sir, if you wouldn't mind leaving your clothes in the washtub, I will get to washing them in the morning." Considering the condition of his clothing, I fully understand her desire to have it soaking overnight.

He grins. "I promise. Thank you. We will see you tomorrow." We see them leave together, but know they will be going in separate directions, she to the small house she shares with her husband, and he to the boarding house where he rents a room.

When they are gone, Gregor says, "Ahhhh! Alone at last." He leans in to give me a kiss, but fastidiously keeps his hands away from me. I can tell he thinks he's too dirty to even touch me.

I'll fix that.

I close the distance between us, running my hands across his sweaty chest, starting at his shoulders and sweeping all the way down to the bottom of his cotton shirt. I begin drawing it slowly back up his body, trailing my fingers along his hot skin as I go. He sucks in a breath. When I get the hem to his shoulders, I tell him, "Up," and he obediently lifts his arms so I can pull the shirt over his head.

He is waiting for me, delight in his eyes, to see what I will do next. As always, he seems to be in no rush, simply happy to enjoy the moment he is living in. I boldly rake my eyes across his slender, muscular chest, then impulsively lean in to take a little lick, just under his collarbone. "Mmm! Salty!" I tell him.

"All right, now you've done it!" he laughs, finally giving up on his determination not to get me dirty. His hands are on me now, exactly as I wanted, and I clutch him to me as he kisses me again, running my fingers up and down his bare back. When he comes up for air, he says, "Now you're going to be joining me in my bath!"

I look down at my body. "I hate to tell you, but I think I'm getting too big for that."

His hands move around from my back to my front, cradling my swelling stomach where the baby is growing. "Nah," he says, pretending to carefully measure and evaluate my form, "we can still make it work."

It makes me giggle, remembering the first time he told me that, nearly a year ago at the brothel where we met. I didn't believe him, but he demonstrated it beautifully. He smiles at me, obviously knowing what I am remembering.

He lets go of me and moves into the little side room. It is probably meant to be a pantry for the kitchen, but we have been using it as the bathing chamber. It might be a somewhat less romantic location to have the tub than our bedroom, but it makes more sense to have the bath downstairs where it won't be such a chore to fill and empty it. We don't have a big enough crew to lug buckets up and down the stairs like Madam Beverly had.

He looks down into the bathtub, sees it is already partially filled with cool water, and is just waiting for the hot water from the stove. "Just give me a minute," he tells me, heading back into the kitchen.

"I'll help," I say, but he shakes his head.

"Nope. I'll do all the heavy lifting around here, Mama." I have to laugh. He has been very insistent on taking care of me, and making sure I am not doing anything that would strain me at all while I am carrying this baby. It's adorable, and unnecessary, but it seems to make him happy to pamper me. He looks at me and grins wryly, nodding his head. Yep, he's guessing my thoughts again.

Fine, then. I lean against the wall and let him do all the work, enjoying the view of his shirtless form lifting the heavy pots of water and pouring them into the bath.

When he's done, his happy expression transforms into something far more serious, and he approaches me with a gleam in his eye.

Yes, this is exactly what I wanted to do this evening.

Chapter 58

River

Gregor

I think I'll be able to sleep again tonight. It's almost miraculous, how much rest I'm able to get, now that Rosalind is with me every night. Her touch is magic for me, just the thing I need to get the sleep which usually eludes me. I used to go for weeks without, and end cranky and disoriented before I would finally collapse. But she is able to wear me out enough that sleep comes easily to me afterwards. Two months into our marriage and I feel better and more well-rested than I have in years. Decades. Maybe even longer.

But no sleeping quite yet tonight. After we are done with the bath, and the deep enjoyment of each other which usually comes along with it, Rosalind is sitting breathless in a wooden chair next to the bathtub. We've just been engaging in one of my very favorite activities. Hers too, by the looks of it. I gently untangle her hands from my hair, and kneel back up next to her to take her in my arms. It's time to take a little break for supper. I'm not actually very hungry, but I know she is, and I want to make sure to meet all of her needs. "I'll want more later, darling," I tell her, "but for now I am hungry." I wave my hand over her nude form, and add, "But, you know, for actual food this time."

She bursts out laughing. I reach over to the nearby shelf to pull out one of the cotton bath sheets and wrap her with it. Grabbing one of my own, we run giggling like children through the house and up the stairs to our bedroom, to find clean clothing to put on before supper. This is one of the reasons we have to send our servants home at night. We'd never be able to conduct such outrageous activities if there were other people here.

I suppose after her baby comes things might change. The baby. Our baby. Wolk has told me that Rosalind is finally acclimating to the idea that I intend for this baby to be my own, regardless of when or with whom it started. I never thought to have the privilege of raising a child, and I am deeply excited for this opportunity. I can't father children, so

I am nothing but grateful for whoever did the favor for me while she was still working at the brothel. Even if it was "the beast" as she called him. It doesn't matter. It will be our child.

"Sit down," she tells me as we come into the dining room. "I'll get the food. Nadine made stew."

Wolk settles his wolf form down on the floor near the table, looking as pleased with himself as I feel. He always reflects my emotions, and I feel such contentment right now that I could burst. While my wife moves about in the kitchen, I think about how this came about, how in Pittsburgh the Roosevelts made me see that I was stubbornly resisting what I needed to do. I had never intended to get married, even to develop a true relationship, because I was too much of a coward to face heartbreak again. Wolk made me realize on the journey back to Natchez that all of my objections, my fears, my hesitation, were nothing more than what ordinary humans overcome every day. My situation might be unusual, but my concerns are the same ones other people have. When I saw it from that perspective, it gave me the resolve to propose. And I am far happier for it than I had ever expected to be again.

Rosalind brings the delicious smelling stew and bread to the table. Before she sits down, she reaches over to the sideboard and picks up some papers, laying a little stack down before me. "I picked up your mail," she tells me.

"Thank you," I say, "for the mail, the food, the sex. For it all." I am perfectly sincere, but it makes her giggle anyway.

I leaf through the mail and am delighted to see a letter from Pittsburgh. "Ah!" I say. "Nicholas and Lydia Roosevelt have responded to my letter!" I have told her about them, and she is prepared to be as fond of them as I am when she finally meets them.

"When did you write to them?" she asks.

"A couple of days after our wedding." I grin at her, starting to open the letter, "After you finally let me get back out of bed."

She shrieks with laughter and throws the piece of bread in her hand at me. I swiftly snatch it out of the air and start munching on it while I scan the letter. "They send their congratulations on our marriage. As well they should. I am clearly the luckiest man alive."

She shakes her head and chuckles while she spoons some stew into her mouth. I continue reviewing the letter. "They've gotten most of the steam engine parts, they are framing the ship, everything is coming along. They hope to have it finished in a couple of months." I start slurping stew too. "I'd better get a move on with the dock!"

"Slow down, Gregor," she laughs at me. "You're not going back out there tonight. You have to finish what you started in the bathtub."

"Oh, I will. Believe me."

"I can't wait."

Gregor's

My beloved has little need of my commentary in his settled life right now, and I find myself quieter than usual. He enjoys loving his wife without my intervention, and I am diligent in remaining out of the way as much as possible.

Later, after Rosalind has drifted off to sleep in his arms, and he has even managed to doze for a short while, he awakens refreshed. It is barely past midnight, with dawn still hours away.

As he has started doing at such times, he very carefully and slowly slides away from her, trying to avoid dislodging any part of the bedding in an effort not to disturb her. He freezes when she takes a deep breath and shifts to one side.

"She is still asleep, darling," I tell him, speaking for the first time in hours.

He waits a few seconds to make sure, then finishes extricating himself from the bed, stealthily moving about the room to retrieve his clothing. Casting one last glance at his wife, admiring her beauty in the dark as she sleeps, he silently leaves the bedroom.

He dresses downstairs in his study, glancing at the map of Natchez which rests upon his desk. He has been drafting it during the nighttime hours, enjoying memorializing the area which has become his home. Before sitting down to continue the work, he decides to spend some time outside first, and slips out the back door into the garden. The moon has not yet risen, and a thick layer of summer clouds is obscuring the stars, leaving the night dark enough that it would be impossible for a normal human to see very much.

Gregor, though, does not need a great deal of light to see, and he is able to enjoy the view of the Mississippi River silently slipping by below the bluff at the edge of his garden. He can detect some faint lights along the other shore, speculating that they are perhaps lanterns or fires at the small settlement across the river. He does not ask me for details, so I remain silent.

He stands for several minutes at the edge of the bluff, enjoying the night air which has finally cooled after the very hot day. A few sounds drift up from the taverns Under-the-Hill, laughter, a shout, the crash of something dropping, evidence of the revelry which will continue into the night. He is glad to be up here, in the relative quiet of his own yard, his own home, his own wife sleeping within.

"I am very happy for you, my darling," I softly tell him. I love my Guarded so very much, and am deeply grateful that he has found a situation in life which brings him so much pleasure.

He can sense what I am feeling. "You can say 'I told you so,'" he jests.

I huff with amusement but do not comment otherwise.

"Man," he says, and at once I transform from a wolf into the man form which he feels comfortable with. He looks sideways at me, standing by his side, two men together on the bluff in the dark nighttime. The luminescence which I always exude does nothing to illuminate the surroundings. "I should have trusted that you would be right," he comments.

"You have always lived through the ebb and flow of joy and sorrow," I say, gazing across the water as he is. *"A time of peace and contentment was inevitable."*

"Little did I know how soon it was coming," he contemplates, "the day I arrived here on a flatboat."

"May it last a very long time, beloved."

He sighs, knowing that the future is as much a mystery to him as it is to other humans. He glances around the yard, his eyes falling on a wooden bench which Moses has built for the garden. Taking a seat, he relaxes under the dark sky, continuing to gaze west across the water.

After a time, he looks north, thinking of the Roosevelts and the steamboat they are building in Pittsburgh. "Think I'll have the dock and everything ready for them?" he asks.

"Yes, beloved, I believe you will. Your crew is already working on the project, and when the steamboat arrives, the new dock will be waiting."

He nods. "There's a lot left to do," he notes, then falls silent, contemplating the phases of the dock project, and more broadly all of the ways in which his life has become so full and busy and productive.

Not the least of which is, of course, the little Seer, at home with her mother at Ellis Cliffs, where they will reside for another month until the wedding of Stephen and Margaret takes place.

Gregor's eyes move up and down the river, to the north and then again to the south. "Strange to think how my life is centered by this waterway. I live in this rivertown. To the north is the source of the project which keeps me here, and to the south is Ayola, the reason that I stay."

My man form nods. *"True, beloved, it is interesting to contemplate how much your life has been transformed, and how happy you are now, in your home here on the river."*

END OF BOOK 1 OF THE SEER CHRONICLES

AUTHOR'S NOTE

February 2026

This was my first foray into writing historical fiction, and the process has been unbelievably enjoyable, compelling, and addictive. I have been utterly preoccupied with learning everything I can about the Natchez area in the early 1800's. I had never even heard of Natchez before February 2023 when I started the book, and did an online search to find somewhere for Ayola to be born. This immediately blossomed into a full time obsession.

My favorite part of the research I have conducted is a road trip which I took in October 2025. I was able to actually spend a week in Natchez, seeing the geography, absorbing the history, finding all the historical markers showing places which appear in my story. After having spent a couple of years obsessively researching the place, being there felt something like coming home.

A lot of what is in this story is based on real people and events. Natchez was an important town along the Mississippi River, and really was divided into two parts, the proper town up on the hill, and the rowdier Natchez Under-the-Hill where the flatboats and keelboats conducted their business, and the taverns and brothels serviced the boat workers. The Kentucky Tavern was one of them, and it was actually the historical Stephen Duncan who was told upon his arrival that it was a "damned rascally place". The flatboat workers really did have to walk back up the Natchez Trace after their boats were dismantled at the end of their journeys.

Most of the named families I have referenced really lived in the area. Anybody in the story with the last name of Ellis, Duncan, Butler, Postlethwaite, and Roosevelt were based on historical figures. I have their ages and important dates more or less correct. I took a lot of liberties with their personalities and appearance and actions. I particularly have to apologize to any descendants of Abraham Ellis, who may very well have been a perfectly nice person rather than the way I have depicted him.

Interesting note: Nicholas Roosevelt was the great uncle of President Theodore Roosevelt. It was quite a family. The background of Nicholas and Lydia, including the difference in their ages, is pretty accurate. The first Mississippi steamboat, the New Orleans, really was built in Pittsburgh in 1811 by Nicholas Roosevelt, in partnership with Fulton and Livingstone.

There was a brigand along the Trace named Samuel Mason. There were enough Samuels in the story already so I've just left his name at Mason. His dates are a little fudged - his reign of terror was taking place a few years before the dates in this book. There's more about him in the next book, River, which incorporates some of the historical details about Mason, and a lot of imaginary ones.

There are a few other pieces from actual Natchez history sprinkled through the books. I've tried to be accurate, but sometimes I shifted the facts around a little to suit the purposes of the story. For instance, the Methodist pastor John Johnson really did speak Hebrew, but I put him there just a little earlier than he would have arrived.

The map which is at the beginning of the book was created referencing historical maps, both before and after the era in which the story takes place. I couldn't find a Natchez map from around 1810/1811 for reference, so I did my best. As with all the manipulations of the historical record in this storyline, the fiction lies on top of the true history. Please excuse any errors.

I have absolutely loved sprinkling my fantasy story and characters among the people and history of the area, and I hope so much that you, my reader, enjoy it as much as I have.

Also by Julia Guroff

The Guardians Series:

This series is related to the Seer Chronicles. It is a modern day tale of a young Seer, Natalie, who with the help of her friends explores the nature of Guardians.

The first trilogy was published in 2025:

Guardian

Seer

Demon

The Seer Chronicles:

This series takes the tale of Guardians and Seers back in time, and tracks the story of the Seers Gregor and Ayola, beginning in 1810 along the Mississippi River.

Several more books are planned:

Watcher

River

Journey

Dream

Darkness

Daybreak